Now I lay me down to sleep,
I pray the Lord my soul to keep,
If I should die before I wake,
I pray the lord my soul to take.

To Nancy
with many blessings

Job 19:23-26

George Colton Publishing is pleased to announce two new titles
by the same author, soon to be released:

Merchants Above The Stars

Naked I Shall Return

IF I SHOULD DIE

by Keith Clemons

GEORGE COLTON
PUBLISHING

For information write:
George Colton Publishing, Inc.
PO Box 375, Orangeville,
ON. Canada   L9W 2Z7

Churches, schools, charities, and other not for profit organizations may acquire George Colton books by writing to the above attn: Ministerial Markets Department.

This book is a work of fiction. The characters, incidents, and dialogues are products of the author's imagination and are not to be construed as real. Any resemblance to actual events or persons, living or dead, is entirely coincidental.

National Library of Canada Cataloging in Publication

Clemons, Keith, 1949-
     If I should die / Keith Clemons.
ISBN 0-9731048-0-5
     I. Title.
PS3603.L44I3 2002   813'.6   C2002-902499-4

Printed and bound in Canada

First Edition

02 03 04 05 06 07 08 09 10 - 10 9 8 7 6 5 4 3 2 1

Acknowledgments

Writing is a lonely job. An author can bury himself in his work for months at a time without regard for family and friends. When his book hits the market, he's ready to hear the congratulations of his peers when, in fact, he should be giving, rather than receiving, praise. It is those closest to the author who, through their gifts of understanding and encouragement, are responsible for a book's success. With this in mind, I would be remiss if I did not take time to thank those who have helped me along the way.

First and foremost, I thank my God and Savior, the Lord Jesus Christ, of whom I can truthfully say: Without him, I can do nothing, but with him, all things are possible.

Second, I thank my loving wife, Kathryn, whose ongoing encouragement and unwavering support are a continuous source of inspiration.

I want to give credit to two men whose cultural insights have greatly influenced my writing: Dr. James Dobson, of Focus on the Family, and Charles Colson, of Prison Fellowship Ministries. May their words continue to provide a beacon to a world lost in a spiritual and moral fog.

God has also used men of wisdom to counsel and advise me on matters of publication. Among them are: Ron Hembree, author, and host of television's "Quick Study," Chuck Missler, author, speaker, and President of Koinonia House Ministries, Grant Jeffery, author, and President of Frontier Research Publications, and Mel Stevens, President of Teen Ranch, Canada.

I especially want to thank my friend and prayer partner, David Cairns, who has been diligent in bringing this work before the throne of God. Others too, labored with me in prayer, among them: Bill Bissell, Bill Murdoch, Bill Wallace, Erika Rodde and my pastor, friend, and dynamite radio and TV personality, Rod Hembree.

Two editors are deserving of my gratitude: Dave Lindstedt, who put me on the right track, and Marcia Laycock, who saw me across the finish line.

A special thanks also goes to Laurie Smith of AA Graphics for the many hours she put into the book's cover and layout.

And last, but certainly not least, are the many who read and critiqued the manuscript prior to its release: Brian Austin, Joyce Cairns, Ruth Dinsmore, Rita Lise, Barb McWilliams, Gary Murray, Jayne Self, Barbara and Lawrence Stuckey, David Thwaites, Oscar and Sandra Van Binsbergen, and Laura Vradenburg.

Thank you one and all!

ONE

The last time I saw Mom, I was three. I turn thirteen today. It will be just Dad and me again. We won't have a party. He'll buy a cake and I'll try to blow out the candles, and he'll laugh with a smile big enough to cover mom's absence, but I'll still miss her. Dad says we're a team, like two mules on a plow. He says we don't need anyone else. I can't tell my dad how I feel, so I just listen. I suppose he thinks I agree, but I don't. Truth is, I wish mom were here...

IT WAS A NIGHT to make strong men weak, and godless men fear. The wind shrieked through the trees, cracking dry limbs and driving loose chunks of bark into the ground. The rain had turned to ice, and then to snow, pelting the windshields of cars slip-sliding their way home. The faint of heart stayed behind, refusing to leave the pub. They stared at the world through blustery windows fringed with ice, and hid behind their vodka martinis, glad to be inside. "Have one for the road, just to keep warm," they said, but they tipped back one after the other. The sober and the courageous plowed on through, braving the messy night. Everyone thought they'd seen winter's last stand, but like the monster you can't seem to kill—*he was back!*

THE OLD MAN swept frost from his eyes. He shook his head to remove a matted layer of snow, but a clump caught his collar and trickled cold and wet down his back. *Burrrrrrrrr.* He reached around to pull the fabric away from his skin. Darkness had come too soon. He needed to be able to see. He tried tightening his lapels around his neck but after a few seconds his fingers froze. He let go. His thin windbreaker billowed out of control, flapping like a sail caught in a squall. "It's no use," he muttered, shoving his raw, useless hands back into his pockets. His toes felt numb but he had to keep moving. He hadn't figured on walking this far. They'd thought a bus would take him to the front door. No one anticipated the famous William Best living in a rural community.

The wind whipping across the lake stung his face. *Must be down near twenty degrees.* He put one foot forward, then the other, mechanically pushing his cold, wet tennis shoes along the icy pavement. No relief. He was caught in a swirling vortex, blinded by the white. *Sooooo c...c...cold!* He blew a breath of steamy air over his hands to try and thaw his fingers. Who would have thought he'd run into a blizzard this late in April? He should be back in his apartment drinking warm cocoa and watching television. *Nuts! Somebody has to do it.* They had to make someone listen. He tried again to pull his collar up against the cruel wind but his fingers were too stiff. He hadn't figured on Detroit being this *c...c...cold!*

BILL WAVED to his editor, his hand moseying up in the air to signal his leaving. He tucked his wool scarf snugly around his neck and buttoned his coat. Through the glass door he could see his taxi waiting at the curb, white smoke puffing from the exhaust against the bitter, driving snow. The meter was running. He scooped his hat off the rack, plopped it on his head, and turned the brim down, wishing it was a Stetson. The fedora kept his head warm, but did nothing for his image. He pushed the door open against the wind and stinging ice. A sudden gust ripped the door from his hand and slammed it closed behind him. The squall tore at his coat and scarf. He clamped his hat firmly to his head and trudged to the curb. The snow was already deep enough to drift over the tops of his shiny wingtips. He felt a sting as ice-water seeped around his ankles into his socks.

"Vely, vely bad night, no?" came the salutation from inside the cab. The driver turned and regarded his passenger over his shoulder. His beard was wrapped up over his head and tucked underneath his turban. "Whell do you go?"

Bill gave the driver his address and settled into the stifling warmth of the cab's interior. He was anxious to get home. *Tonight's the night,* he thought. *Only two more days and we're outta here.* He couldn't help thinking he should have saddled up years ago. You can't expect a beaver to make a home on a concrete dam. He glanced out the window letting the swirling snow stiffen his resolve. There'd be no turning back now. He eased into thoughts about his daughter's birthday—*cake and candles and the surprise of her life.* He couldn't wait to see the look on her face. *"Yes-sir-ee, Billy Bob, tonight's the night!"*

THE OLD MAN'S FEET slipped out from beneath him. His bones were too old and brittle to take such a fall. He picked himself up. His hand was too frozen to feel the gravel stuck to his palm. All around him bits of ice flailed his exposed skin. He was caught in a raging fury, the wind pummeled his face. He could no longer see the lights on the south shore—too much blinding white. He wanted to take a short cut across the frozen lake, but that was foolishness. He had to stick to the road. It might take longer, but at least the wind was partially blocked by the trees. On the lake he would be out in the open, unprotected. He'd freeze to death for sure. He had to keep moving, one foot after the other. His feet were completely numb, like they'd fallen asleep inside his tennis shoes—*tennis shoes???* He chided himself for grabbing a windbreaker—*no fool like an old fool. Just stick to the road, follow the shoreline. That's what the man said. You'll come to the house sooner or later, can't be more than a few miles.* He was determined to make it, even if it took all night.

THE DOWNTOWN CORE of neon and fluorescent towers slid by the glass in rippled patterns of swirling white. It was an awkward hour when workers scrambled for their cars, holding their coats in close, slipping on the ice. Bill could see their misery, but he no longer felt it. His refuge was warm, an envelope of protection against the chaos outside. The cab's interior was calm, a quiet broken only by the flapping of the windshield wipers and the static of the cab's two way radio. Bill tipped his hat forward and pushed back into the seat. He wondered how his daughter would react to her gift.

3

Big and bold as all outdoors, yet I can hold it in the palm of my hand, he mused. *The big surprise! I can't wait to see her face.* He'd promised before but the timing hadn't been right. *She won't be expecting it. That's the best part.* He wanted to rush in and whoop it out the minute he got through the door. He had to get a rope around his excitement. This had to be special. It was her thirteenth birthday. She was no longer a child, not that she ever really was, but now it was official. She was a teenager. He smiled inwardly, feeling his coat pocket to assure himself it was still there. His fingers tapped his lapel. He could hardly believe he'd done it. He wasn't big on radical change.

They were out of the city and almost home when Bill snapped out of his reverie. *Is the van ready?* He'd told the mechanic to leave it parked out front; he should see it as soon as they pulled in. He never did like taking cabs, he lived too far out of town, but the van needed a complete going over before the trip.

At a bend in the road the cab hit a patch of ice and began to slide. The windows were caked with snow but the wipers continued to *thump, thump, thump,* back and forth clearing the way. Suddenly, a figure loomed large in the headlights—a man, a swirl of cotton white hair, shielding his face with his hands. The cab swerved, sliding, bumping the man—*chhrumppp*—with its right rear fender as it spun to the left. The man's legs were in the air, then he was on his back. Bill twisted in his seat to see out the rear window. The cab continued spinning like a saucer until it butted the curb and came to an abrupt stop. Bill was out of the car in an instant, his feet losing traction as they met the ice. He fell to one knee, but he pushed himself up and kept going. His gloved hand brushed his wet pant leg as he limped toward the man lying in the street. He knelt down and attempted to cradle the man's snowy head in his hands. *Is he dead? How do you feel for a pulse?* The eyes opened for a moment, blue as winter, then closed. The man's hand came up, reaching inside his light nylon coat to withdraw an envelope. His lips were blue, and his teeth were chattering. "G...g...get...this tooootaaa..." but as Bill took the envelope the hand went limp and fell away. The wind died, and for a moment all was quiet. Bill leaned in to check the man's chest for a heartbeat but instead he heard a long throaty exhale, like wind whistling through a hollow pipe. The air in front of the man's mouth frosted in an eerie shroud of white. Bill stared at the document in his hand. Even in the dim streetlight he could make out the name. It was addressed to Mr. William Best. It was addressed to him.

TWO

BILL SQUELCHED an urge to rip the envelope open. *A letter—to me? What???* He shoved it into his pocket. He had to get help first. He patted down the sides of his coat looking for his cell phone. A silhouette loomed over his shoulder, the cab driver, obviously distressed. The cabbie turned away and began pacing the street, his hands holding the sides of his turban as he prayed for mercy, a white apparition with wings of snow.

Hey, calm down old buddy. No time to panic, Bill thought. A sudden attack of wind ripped his hat from his head and sent it spiraling down the street. He set his phone down and struggled to remove his overcoat so he could wrap it around the old man's shoulders. The body felt lifeless and heavy. He cradled the man in his arm to keep him warm. Then he brought his free hand up and bit the fingertips of his glove to pull it off. His exposed flesh stiffened like cardboard. He picked up the phone and tried awkwardly to punch the tiny buttons with his thumb. 911 would bring both police and an ambulance. His ear felt numb with the phone against it. Bill looked up to see the driver still moaning. The man was in shock. *Rrrrrringgggggg. Get a grip, son, use your radio, call for help.* Bill wiped falling snow from the injured man's face. No movement. *Is he dead? Sure looks dead. Rrrrrringgggggg.* The car had barely grazed the old man, not much more than a light tap. *What's he doing out in the middle of a storm? Rrrrrringggggg. Come on, somebody answer!* Bill tried to remember if they'd passed a stranded car but came up blank. Finally, a voice at the other end. He gave the 911 operator the information.

The driver was back peering over Bill's shoulder, "Does he live? Ohooo, this is vely bad. Merciful One, I beg you, let this man live!"

Bill looked up and shook his head. "I think he's gone, but I'm not a doctor. There's an ambulance on the way. Hey, look, take it easy, it wasn't your fault."

"Oh no, oh no, oh noooo!" The driver began pacing again.

BY THE TIME Bill arrived home he looked like he'd been through a car wash. His thick, sandy-brown hair was matted and heavy with moisture. No one had tried to identify the old man. Presumably that would be done at the hospital, or morgue, or wherever it was they took him. Maybe it was policy, or maybe it was just indifference—Bill didn't know, but to his way of thinking someone should have tried to establish the man's identity. The ambulance driver had been in a hurry, as though the dead man needed medical attention, and the officer seemed anxious to get out of the cold. Bill had recovered his coat, but he'd still shivered in the back of the police car while giving his account of what had happened. The officer had the heater going, but he'd kept his window cracked so he could smoke while filling out the report.

Bill peeled his wet gloves from red fingers. Then he stepped out of his damp shoes and slid them into the corner with a stroke of his foot. *Shouldn't leave a dead man without even knowing who he is.* He looked up to find himself staring into the anxious eyes of Mrs. Harper, his daughter's nurse. Bill apologized again for the inconvenience, though he had already called to explain why he would be late. Apparently it wasn't enough. Bill opened the door and held it, apologized to the nurse one more time, promised to have the walkway shoveled by morning, and cautioned her to be careful on the slippery roads. The woman squeezed by without comment. Bill shrugged and closed the door.

He turned to make his way down the hall patting his coat. He could feel his daughter's birthday card along with the other envelope. He rolled his lapel back to look at the pocket on the inside liner. Both were there. The envelope the old man had handed him was standing tall and narrow above the shorter, squarer card. *What kind of man puts on a windbreaker and sneakers to deliver a letter in the middle of a blizzard?* He wanted to drag it out and tear it open, but he was almost to his daughter's room and she deserved his full attention. He pushed his curiosity aside. It could wait. This was Angie's day.

"How ya doin' little partner?" Bill said, greeting his daughter as he entered her room. The environment was antiseptic and white, worthy of the cleanest hospital. It was a condition of Nurse Harper's employment that Angie's room be kept hard and sterile. "Soft things collect dust, and dust breeds germs," she frequently said. The only exception was the family cat, T.J. There was an inexplicable bond between T.J. and the little girl which Bill refused to undermine. Besides, there were therapists who actually believed pets provided a kind of unconditional love needed by shut-ins. It improved convalescence.

Angie lay prone on the bed. Chrome rails prevented her from wiggling off the mattress and falling to the floor. She tried to move inside the body that held her prisoner but was able to achieve only a writhing twist. Her arms flailed upward and a gurgling sound issued from her lips. "Daa...Da...aaaaa." Bill knew she was asking for a hug, but her arms never made it around his neck, and the words were muddled and obscure. Her eyes slowly blinked but a misshapen smile brightened her face. Her father leaned over and kissed her cheek. His damp hair mopped her forehead, disguising the moisture in his eye.

Angie's small, oval face was a petal of contentment. She was a gentle rose—but with a thorn. She had been born with cerebral palsy, a disabling disorder that manifest itself in erratic, involuntary movement. It destroyed her motor functions, crippling her ability to walk, and to communicate. She couldn't take a stroll through the park, or run with her friends, or even share a simple thought. She deserved better, and Bill was determined to see she got it. He wiped his cheek on his sleeve as he pulled away.

T.J., who had been vigilant in his watch at Angie's side, stretched his paws and raised his rear to yawn, flicking his tail before ambling over to have Bill scratch his head.

"Sorry, I'm late. Horrible weather out there," Bill said in answer to his daughter's unspoken question.

Angie's head lobbed side to side as she let out a groan. Bill ran his fingers over her forehead and let them comb through her honey-brown hair. Her hand lifted at the elbow and fell against his shoulder, the fingers bent like broken twigs, then dropped back to the bed. T.J. nudged his head up under the hand and Angie flexed her arm giving the cat a squeeze.

Bill looked around the room. He wanted to go out and fill the room with stuffed animals. This...this sterility wasn't right. The walls were empty, devoid of the girlish pictures that usually filled the living space of a twelve-year-old. There were no pink frilly things, no mirror and vanity, no collection of dolls. Things common to most pre-teens were not a part of Angie's life. Hers was a world of chrome contraptions. She spent her days strapped to a chrome hospital bed, one with a back that could crank up, and its own wheels so it could be moved around. If they were going out, she would be transferred to her chrome wheelchair so she could be rolled from one location to another. A world of chrome tubular frames with safety belts and wheels. What kind of life was that for a little girl? *Well, all that's going to change now, isn't it?* he thought. Looking around the room he promised himself he was going to buy his daughter every stuffed animal she ever wanted...well, within reason. His fingers did a tap-dance on the bed's chrome rail.

Angie's eyes continued to blink as she forced another twisted smile. Bill could understand how someone looking only at the extra work involved might think it wasn't worth it, but there was more to it than that. Every human being, regardless of their state, had the capacity to love—and love outweighed inconvenience. That's what he'd failed to make them understand.

Bill found himself gripping the rail, his knuckles turning white. He forced himself to relax as he began stroking his daughter's hair. "I know you've had your dinner, but I'm still hungry," he announced. "Here, you can watch TV while I go fix myself something to eat, okay?" He quit fondling Angie's curls and reached over to click on the set. Bill checked the electronic programming guide and selected a nature channel. Angie loved animals. The screen filled with birds in flight.

T.J., ever the fearsome cat, rolled over and eyed the flock, daring the creatures in the box to try an escape. Bill watched as the cat crept toward the set. They could have called him J.T. for, "Jungle Tiger," but it was "T.J." and it stood for, of all things, "Tomato Juice." And for good reason. When T.J. was just a kitten, Bill had bumped a jug of tomato juice with his elbow, knocking it off the kitchen counter. The plastic bottle had hit the floor and the lid had popped off, making a terrible mess. The cat had come to his rescue by volunteering to clean it up. He'd stood lapping up the juice until his paws turned red. Then he'd spent another half hour trying to lick his paws clean. The cat had had a passion for the vegetable drink ever since. So, for all the characteristics of a tiger he may have possessed, his name would forever be, "Tomato Juice."

"There you go," Bill said, adjusting the volume. "Just let me throw something in the microwave. I'll bring it back in here and tell you all about my day while I eat."

THE SUN ROLLED on the crest of the ocean like a deflated orange balloon. Laurie sat at a desk inside her small dusky apartment overlooking the Oregon coast. There was barely enough light to see. In front of her, a card lay open. She was a journalist, words should not be so hard to find, but she struggled to put what she felt on paper. She picked up her pen and tapped it against her fingers. Her daughter was two thousand miles away, and today it was her daughter's birthday. She felt the reproach again. Today. Not next week, not tomorrow, but today! She was late. She tried to comfort herself with the thought that at least she'd remembered. That hadn't always been the case. Many a year had passed without her sending anything. What was the point? How could she communicate with someone who couldn't communicate back? Angie probably wouldn't understand the meaning of the card, anyway.

Laurie buried her face in her hands feeling the cold pen against her cheek. Her fingers pulled her hair back taut as she took a deep breath and sat up straight again. It was a waste of time. But she'd bought the card. She had to do it, if not for Angie's sake, for her own. She had to attempt to make contact before they showed up unannounced at her door. She wasn't afraid of Bill; she was worried about explaining herself to Angie. Her daughter was innocent. She hadn't asked to be born. A child shouldn't have to pay for the mistakes of her parents.

She took the pen, held it in both hands for a moment, then put the tip to the card and wrote:

Dear Angie:

Well, it's your thirteenth birthday. You must be all grown up. A real lady. I guess I'll get to see for myself soon enough. Your dad says you'll be arriving around the first of the month. I'm looking forward to it. I hope you are too. We have a lot of catching up to do. In the meantime, I hope you have a very,

HAPPY BIRTHDAY!

Love, Mom.

P.S. Tell your father to give you a big hug and kiss from me.

Then she signed the card and slipped it, along with a photograph of herself, into the waiting envelope.

BILL WASN'T HUNGRY, he'd used hunger as a ruse to slip out of Angie's room so he could prepare her birthday surprise. He opened the drawer rattling silver as he searched for a knife. She would be expecting some kind of gift, but not this. *She is going to love her present,* he thought. He turned to grab the handle of the refrigerator, letting his fingers tap on the white metal as he opened the door. Her cake was on the rack. Bill slipped it out and placed it on the counter.

Chocolate frosting smudged his sleeve, reminding him that in his hurry to see his daughter he'd forgotten to remove his overcoat. He also noticed that down around his knee, about the same place he felt a dull but growing pain, his new wool slacks had sprouted a small, blood stained hole. So what? He didn't need dress slacks where he was going. He emptied his pockets and placed the birthday card on the counter. A second envelope came out with the first, which he also set aside. The second was an enigma because it had been delivered by a stiff old man dying on a snow-covered street. On any other night he would have ripped it open, but not tonight. He was already late. There was a young lady in there who needed her dad. He saw the old man, ice blue eyes, holding out the envelope, his body growing cold and stiff. Yes, an enigma, but it would have to wait. His daughter's birthday had to come first.

He opened the microwave, placed the cake on a dish and set the timer, one minute at low power, just enough to make it warm without melting the icing. The light in the microwave found life as the unit began to hum. Bill walked down the hall to hang his coat in the closet. It would need to be cleaned before he could sell it. He returned just in time to hear three beeps from the oven. He retrieved the plate and set it on the counter, the smell of warm cake filling the kitchen. In the cupboard he found a tube of icing which he used to squeeze, "Happy Birthday Angie," in bold pink letters across the cake's creamy surface. He found the candles and placed thirteen of them in a tight circle. She wouldn't be able to blow them all out, no matter how hard she tried, but the closer they were together, the easier it would be.

He lit the candles, the odor of smoke and wax mixing with the cake's sweet aroma. Then he picked up the card and his prize-winning desert, and headed back to Angie's room, singing Happy Birthday. His booming baritone voice bounced off the walls all the way down the hall.

Angie waited in anticipation. Her father always managed to build her birthday into a special event. She squealed as his large frame filled the door, her body writhing as he placed the cake on the tray by her bed.

"Here you go, birthday girl," he said, giving her the old Bill Best winning smile. "Bet you thought I forgot. Not a chance. No daughter of mine is going to say I forgot her birthday. Okay, let's get this party started. First, you have to make a wish and blow out the candles. Then we'll get down to the important stuff, like your present. Think you and I can eat this whole thing? Looks pretty good to me." He swiped a lick of frosting off the top and plopped it in his mouth. "Ummm, darn right. Hey now, don't look at me like that. I warned ya, I haven't eaten yet."

Bill leaned over to raise the back of Angie's bed. He began singing another round of "Happy Birthday" as he brought the cake to her lips. T.J., who was not fond of fire, dove off the bed leaving room for Bill to move in closer. "All right, take a big breath now. Let's blow 'em out. Atta girl." His daughter's cheeks inflated and then wheezed flat. When it became obvious she was out of breath, Bill leaned in to finish the job. "Yeah," he applauded. "That's my girl. I swear you get better at this every year." He took the cake away and set it on a stainless steel tray.

Bill picked up the envelope and flipped it over and over in his hand. "Now, before I give you your present, we have to read the card." Bill slid the blue and green card from the envelope and held it in front of Angie so she could see the picture. It was a watercolor of a little girl walking on a sandy beach at sunset holding her father's hand. Bill began reading the verse.

> *"Had I an ocean to give,*
> *Or mountain or plain,*
> *The world at my feet*
> *To honor your name,*
>
> *Yet would I ask*
> *Of you more than this,*
> *That you take all my love*
> *And give back but a kiss.*
>
> *Happy Birthday*

To the one I love more than the whole world.

Your Dad."

13

Bill turned to set the greeting card on Angie's tray so she could see it. He crossed his arms, still holding the envelope, letting his thick fingers tap on the paper while he worked up the words he needed to introduce her present. "I know you didn't ask for much this year, but today you became a teenager, and that's something special, so I decided you deserved something special for your birthday. I thought about it, and I thought, what could I give my daughter that she doesn't already have? I mean, you've already got the world's greatest dad." He puffed out his chest and made his thick thumb point at himself as he rolled back on his heels. "Uh huh, and of course you got old T.J., and this nice posh room, and that comfy bed, well, I figure there wasn't much I could do to top that. Then I saw this card and I realized I've already given you all my love, but what I haven't given you is an ocean. So I went out and bought you the whole ocean." Bill opened the envelope again and withdrew a photograph which he held in front of Angie. "So, what do you think?" The picture was of a yacht. It was a motor launch, fifty-four feet from bow to stern, with the words, "Handy Captain" stenciled beneath the rear gunwale in gold letters.

Angie's eyes widened, dancing with questions, so Bill launched into an explanation. "Okay, here's the story. Unbeknownst to you, a couple of months ago I was approached by a realtor who said he was interested in purchasing our house. Some young business executive was being asked by his company to relocate, and get this, his wife had been in a car accident and lost the use of her legs. They needed a house accessible by wheelchair. How do you like that? Well, the agent was asking around and he heard about our place, so he dropped by with his client to look it over. I guess they liked what they saw because they made me an offer. A darn nice one too. I wasn't about to turn it down, not when I figured it would give you and me an opportunity to do something we've always dreamed about."

From Bill's perspective, the offer couldn't have come at a better time. He hated working in Motor City. He hated the fumes, the honking horns and the constant press of people. That's why his house was secluded, set back on a half-acre wooded lot. It was a place of quiet refuge. But at the end of each month, with all the bills spread out on the dining room table, he would wonder how he was going to make it. They held their expenses to a minimum. It didn't take much to make them happy, a good book and a warm fire, or a pizza to eat while they watched TV. But sometimes it felt as though the pizzas were eating him.

The area in which he lived was typically reserved for six figure income, upwardly mobile types, which Bill was not. He could barely keep up payments on the mortgage. He wouldn't have been able to afford it at all, had he not received money from the sale of his mother's house after her passing. And still it was a stretch. He'd bought the property because it suited his purpose. He wanted Angie to be able to spend her summer days out on the deck in the warm, fresh air, enjoying the tranquil view of the lake, outside the reach of prying eyes and away from noise pollution, traffic and thick waves of smog. (He'd hoped also to provide impetus for Laurie to join them, a carrot to draw her east, the promise of a dream home, but she was still in the process of healing, so the purchase had failed in that regard.) Still, he needed it for himself and Angie. He had moved to Detroit to further his writing career, not to become an urban yuppie. He couldn't live in the asphalt jungle, if you could call that life; he just wasn't a city kind of guy. He was a country boy, a native of the great American Northwest...*give me blue jeans and a pickup truck and I'll sing you a lullaby by a campfire so sweet and starry skies in your eyes, my oh my.* All the New York suits with their Italian silk ties couldn't disguise his laid back attitude because city duds, no matter how custom-tailored they were, never fit. Clothes didn't make a man, a man was what he was in spite of the outfit he wore.

Trouble was, he was trapped. There was no way he could handle the physical, spiritual and emotional drain of living downtown, but he couldn't afford the shady acre estate in which he lived either. And if he was ever forced to sell, he knew he'd receive a depreciation in the value of the house. The purchasers would have to discount the amount it would cost them to remove all the ramps and rails and reinstall standard height sinks and toilets. Instead, the offer Bill received from the realtor included a premium, because all these amenities were in place. A rare opportunity.

Now the house was paying off in spades. He'd lived there a mere ten years, but his equity had practically doubled. The sale gave him not only enough to pay for the yacht, but it also enabled him to afford some necessary changes, like making the launch accessible by wheelchair. There was even money left over to put in the bank for a rainy day. Angie needed her mother. If Laurie was so all-fire determined to stay in the west, then it was out west they would go, by golly, all the way to the glorious Pacific. They would sit together on the deck of their yacht, with the hair on their arms tickled by a warm salty breeze and the dry crackle of sea gulls piercing the purple sky, while the sun lowered itself on the horizon like a plump pink grapefruit on blue ceramic tile. *Yes-sir-ee Bob!*

He had just received word that everything was ready. They would travel first class. The yacht boasted all the amenities, including four private bedrooms (they called them berths), one for himself and one for Angie, plus one for his office, and a spare. It had two baths, one with a shower, and a full kitchen. It even had sonar, radar and electronic mapping equipment, the works. He had given his notice. The van was sitting in the driveway with a full tank of gas. He'd been assured it was mechanically sound and able to make the long trip west. Friends at his church had agreed to sell his furniture, put ten percent into the offering, and send him the rest. He and Angie were scheduled to leave Saturday morning. They would drive across the northern states to their final destination in Seattle, where the boat was moored. Bill had used his computer to access weather forecasts along the route. Unlike Michigan, where the end of April had been cursed with violent snow, it appeared Washington was enjoying an early spring. They would cruise north through the gulf islands stopping at every port of call along the western seaboard of Canada, from Victoria to Desolation Cove. Second to spending more time with his daughter, he would begin working on the book he had always wanted to write.

Angie stiffened spasmodically and moaned. Bill took it for what it was, an expression of excitement. *The Grand Adventure. What more could a kid strapped to a bed ask for?*

BILL WAS CLEANING UP, thinking about how he no longer needed each chipped and scratched dish he slid between the blue, rubberized prongs of the dishwasher, when he finally noticed the other envelope still lying on the kitchen counter. He dried his hands, flipped the towel over the oven handle and rattled through the drawer for a knife to open the letter.

What's so important it had to be delivered on a night like this, at the cost of a man's life? He checked again to make certain he wasn't opening mail intended for someone else but, no, the letter was plainly addressed to him. The envelope yielded easily to the knife. He unfolded the two sheets of paper. The story was handwritten in block letters, adding to the mystery. In this modern age of computers, why wasn't it typed? There were a half dozen shaky signatures at the bottom of the second page suggesting they had been penned by elderly hands. Ahh, that explained it. He scanned quickly, picking up the gist.

"...at least two are dead...there could be more...they must be stopped...urgent...please hurry!"

Weird! It was a cry for help. They thought someone was trying to kill them. Someone who, they claimed, had already murdered two people—and had gotten away with it. *Just plain weird!*

THREE

The Grand Adventure. Yesss! We've talked about it forever. It's our dream, just the two of us, sailing off into the sunset...with Mom too of course. We both want Mom there—and T.J. I can see it in my mind, but I can't believe it's going to happen. The idea of taking a trip, and especially on a boat—wow! It makes my stomach flutter, but Dad must think I'm ready, so anchors away!

The best part is seeing Mom. She's still in Oregon working for the same newspaper Dad left when we moved here. Seattle's not that far from Portland. Maybe she'll let me stay with her awhile. I could learn so much. All I know about her comes from what she writes to Dad, and she only writes when she's upset about something he's said. I'm not usually mentioned, which kind of makes me feel like I don't exist. But I can't help it, she's my mother, and I love her, even when it hurts.

I can only imagine how my dad must feel. He loves her too. I can hear it in his voice, in the way he apologizes for her, and the way he comes to her defense. He won't say it, but I know I'm the reason they're not still together. He lost her—because of me!

THROUGHOUT THE MORNING, Bill sat at his desk digging for more information. *Somebody must know something!* The tip of his ear was beet red from the hours he'd spent on the phone. He'd called hospitals, ambulance services, the city morgue, and the police. The name of the man hit by the taxi was Ben Riggs, that much he'd learned, but little else. It was like prying a clam from its shell. The police weren't supposed to give out names until they'd notified the next of kin. Bill had a friend on the force: "Come on

Larry, I was involved in the accident, how about cutting a little slack?" It took some arm-twisting, but he'd finally uncovered everything the police knew, which wasn't much. Information gleaned from the man's Social Security card had led the police to discover that he'd come from an old folk's home in Oregon, the Emerald Valley Retirement Home, to be precise. They had not uncovered any reason for his being in Michigan.

Bill recognized the man's name. It was one of the signatures on the letter. According to the logo printed on the sheet of paper, the Emerald Valley Retirement Home was where the letter originated from. Bill was careful not to mention the note he'd been handed while kneeling on that dark, snow-driven street. There was no criminal investigation, he was not withholding evidence, it was simply a personal letter addressed to him. The writers had specifically asked him not to take their concerns to the police. They claimed they'd already been that route but were ignored. They were just old people. No one paid them any mind. A series of articles Bill had written, along with the fact that he frequently boasted about being an Oregonian, "corn-fed on the banks of the Columbia River," led them to believe he would have a sympathetic ear. They wanted him to investigate their claims for himself. Michigan Police had no jurisdiction in Oregon anyway, so Bill decided to honor their request.

But about his becoming involved, that was another matter. Unless he could get his hands on more information, and pretty darn quick, he would not be able to help. As of Saturday, he and his daughter would be off to see the world, or at least the northern U.S. No more dress suits and ties: denim and tennis shoes were the new dress code. He thumped his big fingers on the desk. He couldn't wait to leave the snow plows and sanders frozen to the road as he sailed off to white, cloud-castle islands of hideaway coves, yellow sunsets and tall rugged timber. That was the life! Of course he planned to take it slow, both for the sake of Angie and the special attention she required, and because he wanted to make the trip seem like a vacation. Point to point, he figured it would take about a week. They planned to stop along the way for quick tours of Mount Rushmore and Yellowstone, and any other place accessible by wheelchair.

19

There was one other possibility; he could have Laurie look into it. She was still in Oregon. Unfortunately, she, like the police, might be inclined to doubt the story. These were old people; sometimes old people could be strange. Would she take time to listen and give them the benefit of the doubt? Or would she see them as a bunch of old fuddy-duds and disregard what they had to say?

Another problem was the old folks seemed to embrace his conservative point of view. Over the years Bill had swung to the right. His head had been pointed in that direction anyway, particularly with respect to Angie. In justifying his actions, he'd inadvertently become a voice for the pro-life movement. Not so Laurie. When she'd been informed that her bout with German measles had damaged the fetus in her womb, she'd argued for an abortion. It was Bill who pressured her into saving the child, but it had destroyed their marriage. In order to defend her position, Laurie now championed a woman's right to self-determination. She stood firmly on the left. Bill had the impression the issue presented by these old folks was one of right to life. It could pose a problem. *Nonsense! A reporter has to be objective.* He should at least be able to count on Laurie for that. Besides, what other choice did he have? He couldn't get the facts he needed over the phone, and he was running out of time. Mr. Riggs must have been serious about all this—*dead serious!* He owed it to the old man to investigate to whatever degree he could.

He pulled his computer in so he could read the screen. It was a love/hate relationship. He loved the little notebook's portability, but his large fingers were constantly frustrated by its tiny keyboard, and his tired eyes frequently wished for a bigger screen. He used his mouse to find the file for his address book, and picked up the phone to dial. He looked at his watch, 11:00 A.M.; he had already wasted a whole morning on this thing. He needed to get some work done. He still had a column to write for the day's paper. It wasn't syndicated, so he could stick to local issues, but the story about the accident was now officially dead. He would have to think of something else. He also needed time to write a blockbuster for Friday's column. He was going to reveal his plan to go out on the road and report things from a mobile perspective. He needed a hook to keep his reader's interest...two rings...three...she should be there, it was only eight in the morning, west coast time.

Laurie scurried to pick up the phone. She'd just stepped out of the shower and had one towel wrapped around her body and another on her head. "Lo," she said. She pulled the towel tight under her arm, dripping water on the carpet.

"Hi Laurie, it's Bill." He waited, sensing by her impatient tone that he'd caught her at a bad time.

"Bill? To what do I owe the pleasure? Ah, oh...I get it. You're calling because you're upset about the article."

For a moment Bill didn't connect. Then he realized he hadn't yet read her most recent article. "No, actually I'm not," he said, "It's something else. I need a favor."

Laurie paused. "Then you'll have to call back, I can't talk right now, I have an interview in half an hour, and I'm running late."

Bill felt the cool distance. He spent half his time looking for reasons to call Laurie, and the other half thanking God he hadn't found any. "Okay," he said, "I just thought you might be interested in a hot tip for a story." He tossed the bait knowing she would take it. A good reporter would walk on hot coals for a lead. And Laurie was good.

"Oh, all right," she acquiesced. "But be quick about it. I'm late."

"Right. Okay, here's the gist of it. Last night a guy was killed trying to get a message to me. He died while handing me a letter. Long and short of it is, there's this group of elderly people in an old folks home just outside Portland, at a place called Emerald Valley. They claim at least two people have been murdered there in the past six months. They say they know who's responsible, but when they went to the police they were turned away. I guess the police thought they were having delusions—you know, like they're senile. They might be, for all I know, but six of them signed the letter and I'll be darned if I can figure out how six people could all be sharing the same delusion. That's about it, except they asked me to look into it, but I'm clear out here. I thought you might want to follow it up. It may be nothing, but you never know." Bill counted the seconds, one heartbeat, two...*come on Laurie.* When he reached five, she finally answered. "I have to run," she said. "Fax what you have to my office. And mark it personal. Gotta go. Bye." *Click.* Bill sat a few seconds longer with nothing but a dial tone ringing in his ear.

THE INTERVIEW had gone well. The candidate was a political upstart with crazy ideas about government overspending and the need for fiscal restraint. A Robin Hood in reverse who would steal from the poor and give to the rich so that the nation's economy could prosper and the rich could get even richer. She'd heard it all before: *a carbon copy of Bill's views,* she mused. *Speaking of which, where's that fax? It should be on my desk.* She had asked Bill to mark it confidential. If she was going to chase this thing, she didn't need other bloodhounds sniffing the trail. It should be right in front of her—but it wasn't. Her long fingers sifted through the mountain of paper. Nothing in her basket, which meant either her irresponsible ex got busy and failed to send it, or he'd used the wrong fax number and sent it to some other part of the planet. Just to be sure, she stuck her head out of her cubicle to ask the department secretary.

"Eleanor, I was expecting a fax. You didn't see it, did you?"

The woman continued typing.

"Elle, have you seen a fax addressed to me?" Laurie repeated.

It looked like the woman was trying to hide behind her monitor. Her gray dome of hair was barely visible, and Laurie could see nothing of her face. Her fingers stopped, but hovered over the keys as she mumbled something. It took a second for the words to register but it sounded like she said, "Baker's got it."

"Howard has taken a fax addressed to me?" Laurie intoned, holding her hand so her red fingernail pointed in at her sternum.

"I tried to stop him," Eleanor said, her head still bowed. She looked at the document she was typing and resumed clicking away on the keys. "He said to see him about it."

Laurie pursed her lips, her red lipstick forming a line of white at the pressure. *What the...?* She would get to the bottom of this, and pretty darn quick. She turned and stormed down the hall.

Laurie was, by all accounts, a good-looking woman, tall, sleek as a dancer, with healthy skin and a vitality that exuded strength. With her long blonde hair tied back in a perky ponytail as it was now, and those blazing blue, Barbie Doll eyes, some would wrongly assume she used her looks to get what she wanted. She knew better. Hard work and persistence, that's what it took—that, and not caving in under pressure. Controlling her emotions was the most difficult part. Journalism was an emotional business: people were hurt, people suffered, and people died, and all of it had to be written about without letting her feelings get in the way. She'd worked hard at dulling her emotions. She couldn't afford to show weakness, not if she wanted to be treated as an equal, let alone get ahead. And sometimes that meant confrontation. Baker had no business taking her fax. It should have been marked personal, and if it was, that's what it meant—personal!

She saw Mr. Baker's office, his name stenciled in gold letters on the glass of the partially closed door. She tapped once but didn't wait to be acknowledged. She'd had her run-ins with Howard before. He was a senior editor but she didn't report to him directly. Good thing. It would have been harder if she'd had to confront her own boss. But she was in the right; the fax was addressed to her. Howard must want one of his own people assigned to the story. She pushed her way into his office, huffing and puffing a full head of steam.

Howard looked up, eyes wide, startled by the intrusion. He removed his round wire-rimmed glasses, pulling a handkerchief from a vest pocket to wipe them clean. Then he leaned back while stretching his glasses back over his ears, and folded his hands across his lap. "Well, come on in," he said. "Don't bother knocking."

"Cut the bull, Howard, you have something that belongs to me, hand it over."

"Slow down, Laurie. Sit, take a load off."

"No thanks, I'll stand," she returned. "I want my fax. You had no right to take it."

"You're right," he said, "absolutely right. And I apologize. Here, you may have it back."

Howard leaned in to retrieve the article and held it out to Laurie.

Laurie had to step forward to take the document. She turned away, lifting the cover page to scan the original letter as she walked toward the door. It seemed pretty much the way Bill had described.

Then she paused. "I suppose you already have someone on this?" she asked.

"To the contrary. I don't have anyone assigned to it. I wouldn't touch it with a ten foot pole, and neither should you." Mr. Baker relaxed a little. "Look, the only reason I borrowed that," he said, pointing at the page in Laurie's hand, "was to warn you."

Laurie's face was flushed and she could feel a vein throbbing at the side of her neck. She folded her arms; the pressure from her fingers made white spots on her flesh. "I'm waiting," she said, her stance firm, her clear blue eyes boring holes in Howard's chest.

He pushed himself back from his desk. "We've already been there," he said, "and frankly, it's a joke. About a month ago those people went to the police with that list of accusations. Our man on the crime desk, Bob Matthews, happened to be there when they showed up. Their spokesman was a guy named Ben Riggs. I think if you check, you'll see his signature's there. He's the one behind all this. He gets everyone at the old folks home all worked up, gets them agreeing with him, and then makes charges. Naturally, the police have to check it out, so an investigation was launched. Bob was right on top of it. We thought we had a great scoop. I'm in here laying out space so we can run it as soon as it's written up. You can imagine our disappointment when we found out the old folks were wrong. There's a full-time doctor at the nursing home who recorded the two so called questionable deaths, and both turned out to be one hundred percent legit, documented and certified with no hanky-panky of any kind.

"But it didn't end there. I figured it was still a good story, maybe not front page, but good human interest stuff—you know, the plight of the elderly—so I told Bob to start reworking it. We were already shooting negs when I got a call from Mr. MacMillan telling me to kill the story. He'd just got off the phone with some muckety-muck at Emerald Valley, someone he knew from his country club, and the gist of it was, he didn't want me doing anything to embarrass his friend. So, that was it. When the owner of the paper says kill a story, I kill it, and my advice is that you do the same. Okay? And just so there's no misunderstanding, I'll be writing a memo to Jack letting him know we've had this conversation."

Laurie curled her lip. Jack Hardy was her Editor. She didn't need this. She looked down squinting at the paper she held clenched in her hand. The background babbling of keyboards was calling her to work. There were other stories to write. "Sure, no problem, didn't really have time to chase it anyway." She turned to leave but as she reached the door she stopped and spoke again. "Thanks, Howard. By the way, I like your tie." Then she hurried out, leaving Mr. Baker to wonder why she would comment on an obviously old and out of style tie, only to discover there was a rather large piece of his lunch stuck to it.

FOUR

S ATURDAY BILLOWED FORTH on the wings of the sun. The snow received by Michigan had moved into Canada, and the cold front was working itself out over Lake Ontario. Toronto residents grumbled at the weatherman and scurried to get their salters and sanders back on the road, vehicles they had hoped to have retired for the season.

Bill stepped onto the porch. He was a large man. He'd always been a little taller than most. Back in high school, the girls of his senior class did a parody of the song, "Big Bad John," changing a few of the words and inserting Bill's name wherever the name "John" appeared...*"Every morning in class you can see him arrive, he stands six-foot-two, and weighs one-eighty-five, kinda tall at the shoulder, and narrow at the hip, and everybody knows you don't give no lip, to Big Bill—dum, dida-dum, dida-dum, dida-dum—Big Bill!"* They kept it secret, of course; it was a cliquey girl thing they did whenever the shy football letterman passed them in the hall—a real giggle-fest. It wasn't until grad night that a trio from the Girl's Glee Club, decided to go public. After all, it was their last night. They wouldn't see him again. They climbed the stage and in front of everyone did a harmonized version of the song, "Big Bad Bill," to the hoots and jeers of the entire senior class. Bill thought he'd never live it down. But now, as he stood on the porch with boxes wedged under each arm and a suitcase dangling from each wrist, it was fair to say the image fit.

The sidewalks were clear, thanks to a firm back and a half-hour with a shovel, but drifts still languished along the wall, and the grass was quilted in green and white. Bill's Vibram-soled hiking boots

26

crunched the grit under his feet as he walked. Around him the air was bright and blue, and crisp as the snap of a cold apple. He juggled his load as he made his way out to the van. The motor churned, clearing puffs of white fog from its tailpipe. The engine was idling to generate heat. He wanted the inside warm for Angie. He set one of his suitcases down, reaching for the side door to give the handle a twist. The door slid open. *Thunk.* Both rear seats had been removed. There was only himself and Angie to think about. The garage was full of furniture waiting to be sold, including the rear seats, if anyone wanted them. He stared at the mountain of cardboard containers piled high and fitted into place like the three dimensional pieces of a block puzzle.

That's about it, he thought. He took the two boxes, balanced them on a stack behind the driver's seat, and placed the suitcases by the door where they would be accessible. He made sure to leave enough room for the wheelchair. It would be the last thing in, and the first thing out. The cargo squeezed into the back of the van filled most of the space. Bill was surprised at how much junk they had stowed, and they had packed light. Angie didn't own much, she didn't play with toys, didn't have a rusty bicycle with bent fenders to make room for, and her wardrobe was sparse, consisting mostly of nightgowns and undergarments. Dress and play clothes were worn only rarely. Bill himself had determined to leave behind anything he didn't absolutely need, with one exception; he had over a dozen cartons filled with books. Over the years, he had accumulated a collection of rare first editions, some of them classics, and contemporary books autographed by his favorite authors. He was not prepared to leave these behind. He had a rule: whatever didn't fit in the van, didn't belong on the boat, but that rule didn't apply to his books.

Angie waited in the house, strapped to her wheelchair. She struggled, twisting around so she could take one last look at the walls of a room she would never see again. She had grown up in this house; it was all she had ever known. A hollow feeling welled in her stomach. She wished she could make it go away, but she couldn't. And it bothered her, because she couldn't figure out why it was there in the first place. It wasn't like she was giving up a life of ease and comfort.

Her memories weren't of snapshots taken on a Sunday morning in a pretty yellow dress, or of a skinned knee received while skating down the sidewalk, or of her hair being plastered to the sides of her face as she climbed out of the pool. Mostly, she remembered long periods of insufferable discomfort, of tired bones, of aching muscles and watery eyes, of the long, drawn out recovery process that followed so many operations, and of the strict, impatient hands of Nurse Harper.

She should be anxious to leave it all behind, and in fact, until this very moment, she thought she was. But now her exuberance was being overshadowed by apprehension. They were heading off into the great unknown, and the unknown was filled with uncertainty. She shouldn't care, she told herself, it had to be better than this; it certainly couldn't be worse. She was ready for the grand adventure, excited by all it meant, but it was difficult leaving behind so many intimate things. She felt she was leaving a part of herself in the old familiar house to which she was now saying good-bye.

T.J. appeared from around the corner. His head flicked from side to side, his tail curling over his back. Something was up. The house was strangely empty; he could handle that, but his food and water bowls were missing. He paused to watch a fly skitter in front of his nose. He took a swipe at the invader but missed. He decided to find Angie's lap instead. Angie welcomed the distraction and snapped her head back so she could pay attention to the cat.

"Hey there, little partner," Bill said. He stood in the doorway, steam puffing from his mouth as his warm breath met the frosty air. "Everything's ready, you're all that's left." T.J. jumped off Angie's lap as her dad reached down to take her in his arms.

Angie moaned and stretched as Bill moved toward the door. "What's the matter girl?" He turned to see what was causing her concern. T.J. hopped into her vacant seat to absorb the residual warmth. "Oh, I see. Don't worry. I'll come back for T.J. Just let me take care of you first." He turned and ambled down the sidewalk to the waiting van.

As Bill stepped off the porch, the sun exploded into Angie's eyes causing her to squint. She wanted to see the house one last time, but it was too bright. Looking over her father's shoulder, all she could see was a thin silhouette. She tucked away the image. Even a poor memory was better than no memory at all. She continued to blink back the sun's brightness; the air around her face was cold. The door opened and she felt the warmth of the van's interior envelop her as her dad's hands tugged at the special harness, fastening her securely in her seat for the long ride.

THE CAB ROLLED into the looping driveway of the Emerald Valley Retirement Home. Mrs. Iversen opened her white patent purse, and took out a twenty, which she handed to the driver. "Keep the change," she said.

"Thank you ma'am," he replied. "Just stay put. I'll get that door for you," but before he could get his own door open, a man and a woman descended on Mrs. Iversen to offer their assistance. "Here, let me help you," said the man, extending his hand. "Watch your step now. There you go." The woman, whose close-cropped orange hair barely crept out from beneath her white nurse's cap, rolled a wheelchair up behind the elderly woman's knees and helped her settle into a comfortable position. The man stood erect in a dashing, double breasted, brown gabardine suit which shone in the light. He held a leather folder, which he now opened.

"Welcome to Emerald Valley, Mrs...ah...Iversen, or would you prefer I called you Ann?"

"Annie," Mrs. Iversen corrected him, "nobody calls me Ann, just Annie. Ann's too formal, you know. Except my niece. She always insists on calling me Ann. Of course to her it's Aunt Ann because Ann is what my sister, Claire, always called me. Claire's gone now you know, passed on three years ago. Nobody calls me Ann anymore, just Annie. Annie will do just fine." She looked up and smiled. "I don't need a wheelchair, you know, I can walk just fine, long as I have my cane, but it's nice of you to help."

The taxi driver pulled Annie's bag and cane from the trunk and set them on the ground. "There you go," he said. "Say the word and I'll be back next week to pick you up."

"Oh that would be nice."

"But it won't be necessary," interjected the man in the brown double-breasted suit. "By the end of the week, I'm sure Annie will have decided to stay with us permanently. Thank you for your help," he said, dismissing the cabbie.

The man picked up Annie's parcels and walked alongside, as the nurse began wheeling Annie toward two huge glass doors. Annie glanced around the grounds approvingly. What the ad had said certainly appeared to be true, it did look like a country club. The grass was manicured and golf course green, and flowers grew like rainbows in the gardens along the intersecting paving-stone paths. In the distance, acres of rolling green were bathed by sprinklers spraying a soft mist into the air, and guarding the estate were tall sentinels of pine, fir and blue spruce.

The building was covered in red cedar and exuded all the warmth and relaxation of a modern spa. Annie wondered if inside it would smell like a cedar chest, a fragrance she was particularly fond of. She was disappointed to find it didn't. At least the reception area was as bright and airy as the outdoors. Floor to ceiling windows ran the length of the east wall, letting the morning light flood in through louvered blinds. To Annie, it looked more like the lobby of a fine hotel than an old folk's home.

The "guests," which is what the man in the smooth brown suit had said the residents should be called, were milling about in small clusters. One woman, dressed entirely in red with hair the color of tin beneath a red feathered hat, put her hand up to whisper in the ear of the man standing beside her. The man wore a baseball cap with the words, "Gone Fishing," silk screened across the front. His face was unshaven and he wore a frumpy green T-shirt that covered his rounded belly. The shirt was tucked into his blue jeans around the middle, but the tail hung out loose at the back. And where you would expect to find shoes, he wore only slippers. They were a striking contrast: the woman in red feathered flamboyance, the pot-bellied man in blue-collar sloth. He inclined his ear, cupping it with his hand, trying with some difficulty to hear what the little bird-like woman was saying. A moment later he lifted his eyes. They were gray as river stones, and his eyebrows seemed to sprout from his forehead like weeds. He caught Annie staring at him, which made her look away. Annie surmised she'd become the topic of conversation. She counted five in the group, but didn't have time to draw a mental picture of the others.

Annie's chair turned. She saw she was being wheeled toward a room separate from the main lobby, where she was greeted by a person who looked to be in her early fifties, a walking copper tan with a smile as bright as new minted coin. The woman extended her hand to Annie and introduced herself as Barbara Marks. Like the others, Mrs. Marks wore a white, plastic name badge bearing the foil green Emerald Valley logo. Good idea, Annie thought, I hate remembering names. The badge also read "Hostess," but it didn't fool Annie. She could smell a salesperson a mile away. Mrs. Marks thanked the man in the brown suit, who had never bothered to introduce himself, but whose badge read, "Alfred Porter - Manager," and the orange-haired nurse, whose badge read, "Charlotte McKidry - Care Giver." They tilted their heads together and walked away talking in a hushed whisper. Mr. Porter was still holding Annie's suitcase. It made Annie nervous to think he might go through her personal things.

Mrs. Marks stood behind the wheelchair and wheeled Annie into her office. The room breathed organization. The deep red mahogany desk was shining in the window's light. Only one item dared to mar the desk's uncluttered surface, and that was a wood block that held two black pens and a brass business card holder. The cards were imprinted with the same logo as all the name badges. It was a green foil outline of three pine trees overlapping each other and the name, "Emerald Valley," spelled out in script. In front of the desk were two padded wing chairs tastefully covered in a textured mauve fabric. The carpet was dark rose with a lilac weave, and the walls were painted the color of warm sand. Two pictures hung ruler straight along one wall. Both were realistic paintings of purple, dusty rose, and white garden flowers. A large mahogany cabinet ran along the opposite wall. The cabinet doors were closed. Annie assumed they hid a large screen television for showing prospective "guests" the benefits of staying at Emerald Valley.

Mrs. Marks parked Annie in front of the desk between the two chairs. Her lavender and gold scarf waved from her neck like a flag as it bounced off her dark blue, two-piece suit. She had hair the color of polished brass and lipstick like purple wine, with fingernails to match. Annie suspected the hair was a dye job, though well concealed, because the woman's hands had telltale liver spots indicating she was much older than her facade of youthful hair would suggest. Barbara strolled around behind the smooth, graceful lines of her desk to take her seat.

"I would offer you a regular chair," the woman said, "but we'll just be a moment and I think you'll find it more comfortable to remain where you are so you won't have to get up again. As you know, you are here as our guest. There is no obligation on your part to purchase anything. Your apartment and all your meals are complimentary. It is our hope you will enjoy your visit so much you will decide to stay with us, but we'll go over all that later. Right now I need to give you a brief overview of our basic program so you'll have something to think about during your stay. Don't worry. I'm not going to give you a sales pitch. While you're here enjoying our hospitality, the accommodations will sell themselves. Our goal is to make sure your every need is taken care of. You're going to see how wonderfully relaxed life can be. We like to say it's a little piece of heaven right here on earth. Which, of course, makes it pretty hard to turn down, and that's why you need to be made aware of our various plans."

Mrs. Marks folded her hands on the desk in front of her and launched into a well-rehearsed sales monologue. "First, we have our pay as you stay, and outright purchase plans," she said. "To stay here, you can pay a monthly fee, much as you would pay rent or a house payment, only this is much better because it includes all your meals prepared to your liking by our qualified kitchen staff. It also includes any health care you require, other than long term hospitalization, and full use of our sports facility, exercise room and physical therapy center.

"You may also purchase a unit outright. An outright purchase includes access to all the amenities and services we offer. It is however, understood that you never actually own the unit. Title to the property remains with the corporation so that when you pass on, it can be resold.

32

"Our second program is what we call the equity exchange plan. This is for those who do not have the liquidity needed to pay a monthly fee, but do have a tangible, convertible asset. The person who wishes to stay on this plan assigns their asset to the home and, providing its estimated value is enough to cover the guest's expenses, stays for the one lump sum the asset brings. The plan is designed to be completely hassle free. The home takes care of all transactions. That way the guest doesn't have to deal with agents or the bank, and all the trouble of selling the asset, whether real estate, stocks and bonds or general items like boats, undeveloped land, jewelry and things like that. Of course, it is in our vested interest to see you get the maximum amount for your property. Anything over and above the amount required for living expenses is converted to cash and put in an interest-bearing account from which the guest may withdraw funds at any time to purchase a car, or take a pleasure cruise, or any other luxury they choose."

Annie squirmed in her seat wondering if she was expected to remember all this. She knew she wouldn't, but that didn't keep Mrs. Marks from marching on.

"And, of course, you may also use your equity to facilitate a lease. We will still convert your asset, but all of the money remains in your account, with the proviso that the corporation is given permission to withdraw your monthly lease payment. The only risk is that, should this money ever run out, you will be required to continue making your lease payments, or you will be asked to find other accommodations. Whereas, if the lump sum is turned over to the corporation, and the money is depleted, the corporation remains obligated to provide you with care for as long as you need it.

"That's about it. A variety of simple plans designed to accommodate all your needs. I won't take any more of your time. I know you're anxious to get settled in. We'll talk about the other benefits of staying here, after you've had a chance to make yourself comfortable. My door is always open. We want you to feel right at home, so if there's anything you need, please don't hesitate to ask. I am obligated, however, to stress the importance of your dropping by at least once during your stay. We ask you do this even if you decide not to join us, because your comments can help us correct deficiencies we might not be aware of. That's the only thing we ask.

"In the meantime, please avail yourself of all the facilities. There's a swimming pool, Jacuzzi, sauna, exercise room, tennis courts and a nine hole golf course, so you shouldn't be bored. Let me give you a brochure that lists all our benefits and has a full map of the grounds to help you find your way around." Barbara reached into her drawer to retrieve what Annie thought would be a single flyer, but it turned out to be a folder with several printed sheets and full color, glossy brochures. The cover showed a healthy, carefree, silver-haired couple enjoying obvious vitality and a robust zest for life. They were strolling hand in hand down an emerald green path like two lovebirds in the warm yellow haze of summer's dusk.

"Oh, I almost forgot, meals are served in the community dining hall throughout the day. Breakfast is served between eight and ten in the morning, twelve noon is lunch, and dinner is between six and seven in the evening, but you can call for a snack whenever you wish. You can also have your meal served in your room anytime you're not feeling well. Should you need assistance, you can reach someone twenty-four hours a day just by pressing a nearby call button. There's one conveniently located in every room of your apartment."

The woman stood and extended a hand across the desk signaling she was through. Annie leaned forward, taking three of the offered fingers and gave them a timorous squeeze.

"On behalf of the entire staff, I bid you a cordial welcome. I trust you will enjoy your stay." Mrs. Marks pushed a recessed button on the side of her desk. The door opened and the red-haired nurse immediately came to stand behind Mrs. Iversen's wheelchair. "This is Charlotte McKidry, head of our nursing staff," Barbara continued. "She will show you to your room." Annie recognized the woman. She wore a loose fitting white uniform, in typical hospital fashion. She felt the woman's hands grip the back of her chair as it spun around. "I've checked your room and everything's ready. You'll be staying in unit number twenty-two," she heard the woman say.

Annie's suitcase and cane were already inside the apartment awaiting her arrival. She did her best to excuse herself from the nurse.

She could see for herself that the accommodation consisted of four small rooms. There was a bedroom, a bath, a small living room, and a kitchen/dining area. The tiny kitchen had a coffee pot, a tea kettle, a little two-burner electric stove, and a miniature refrigerator for keeping things cold.

She was glad Mrs. McKidry didn't insist on showing her more. She had to get out of the wheelchair. She needed to stand and get the blood circulating in her legs. Alone for the first time, she took a deep breath, stood and walked to the bathroom to check herself in the mirror. It felt strange to see someone she didn't recognize staring back. *Is that really me?* Her face itched but she dared not touch the artful makeup job. She wondered if she'd be able to duplicate her disguise in the morning. More importantly, she wondered if she could make it through a full day without being discovered. *So far so good,* Laurie thought, *at least I'm in.*

FIVE

THE TEMPERATURE still hovered in the low forties, but the roadside patches of snow shrank around the edges and became fewer in number as the miles melted away. Bill saw the trees reaching to hug the sun in welcome of spring. It was probably his imagination, but he could swear he saw buds swelling on the tips of branches ready to burst into pennants of green.

After hundreds of miles of driving, he was getting punchy. He had stared at the asphalt so long his mind was turning to mush. The highway in front of him began to look like a never-ending strip of black tape. *They say the world's coming apart at the seams,* he mused, *but I know it's held together by electrical tape wrapped 'round and around from one pole to the other.* He smiled at the thought.

Bill was high on the freedom of the road. It was an elixir, a sugar-coated, adrenaline-pumping high that made him feel light-headed and giddy, carefree as a boy playing hooky from school. True, the decades define a man, but those same decades have a way of fencing a man in. Leaving it all behind was a form of emancipation. He'd been but a fledgling writer when he left Portland ten years earlier. His motivation for leaving had been twofold. He'd wanted to make a name for himself. He'd done that. But he'd failed in his second quest, because he'd also wanted to improve his marriage. He'd hoped a complete change of scenery, new places to see, and new faces to meet, would help Laurie mend.

It was not to be. The birth of Angie had produced a rift in the marriage that only seemed to widen over time. Try as she might, Laurie couldn't get past her guilt. Her German measles had damaged

36

the fetus. She'd had all the signs. She'd begun bleeding around the sixth month, and she'd had a foreboding excess of proteins in her urine. Her obstetrician had felt compelled to recommend an abortion. His position was clear: the odds were the baby would not be normal; the pregnancy should be terminated. But Laurie hadn't taken her doctor's advice. Instead she'd listened to her husband. Now her child was in pain, and it was her fault.

They tried to hold it together. Laurie became absorbed in her writing, while Bill managed his own career and did what he could to take care of Angie. But after three years it became clear it wasn't working. Then one day Bill learned of a job opening at a sister paper in Detroit. Submitting a resume seemed innocent enough. Frankly, he was surprised to be called for an interview, and was even more surprised to be hired. The offer was a good one, at a salary somewhat higher than a rookie typically earned. He was ready to move.

Already confused about where their marriage was going, Laurie was hesitant to agree. She had a career too. She wasn't anxious to throw it away. She needed time to think it through, to make sure it was the right decision. But Bill didn't have time. The newspaper needed an answer. "It will be good to get away. It's a chance to start over and build something new," he insisted. To avoid further conflict, Laurie suggested Bill and Angie go on ahead. She would stay behind and use the web to circulate her resume. She promised to join them as soon as they got settled—but it never happened. With Bill and Angie out of the way, her guilt began to dissipate, and her self-esteem to repair. Out of sight, out of mind. Without giving it any real thought, she found herself content to leave it that way. It seemed better for all concerned.

It might have been better for Laurie, but it wasn't for Bill. To him it was the final blow. At least he had Angie with him. She'd been there when he was at his lowest point, when he'd finally received word that Laurie wasn't coming—*ever!* When he felt alone and abandoned, and when all seemed lost, Angie, his deficient three-year-old daughter, his very own bundle of curls and smiles, was there to welcome him home. She needed him; he needed to be needed; they needed each other, ergo, their mutual dependence had been therapeutic.

Fortunately for Bill, about that same time he discovered an additional source of strength. He'd been brought up attending church; he thought of himself as a Christian, but because his faith was based more on religious dogma than personal experience, during his university days, he'd lapsed into agnosticism. His free-thinking professors had encouraged him to keep an open mind. "Question everything," they challenged. "Free your mind of preconceived notions; reject the status quo." By the time Laurie, the fiery blonde co-ed with a passion for liberal thought, entered his life, he'd become adept at vetting new ideas. It seemed only fair to explore the views of the other side, even when they cut across the grain of his conscience.

Bill's willingness to remain open soon became a matter of expediency. He knew there was a fundamental difference in the way he and Laurie viewed the world, but he chose to ignore it. Many years later he would acknowledge it was their differing world view, more than anything else, that drove them apart. They couldn't live in peaceful coexistence when virtually every subject was grist for debate. As he became reconciled to the idea that Laurie would not be joining him in Chicago, and faced with the job of raising Angie alone, he turned to the God of his youth for help. No longer infatuated with the opinions of men, he read the Bible to see what it had to say. It was a search that ultimately led him to reaffirm his Christianity.

Bill's renewed faith also brought wisdom, and wisdom, in turn, paved the road to success. He decided to write truth from a biblical perspective, whether anyone agreed with him or not. In the early days, his job at the paper had been tenuous. If he didn't satisfy his readers, he faced dismissal, but he'd refused to compromise.

Those were the days of testing. He'd written with conviction, though he couldn't tell whether his words were being rejected or received. The thought that he might, at any moment, be handed his walking papers, loomed tacitly in the background. As new talent, with no reputation to bank on, and a world not particularly in sync with the Bible's view of right and wrong, the odds were against him. But he'd beaten the odds. He'd fanned his passion into a flame of words, and let the heat be felt by his readers. He'd said what others felt, but were afraid to say. Over time, his common sense ideas found an audience. His readers seemed to like the way he called a spade—a spade! He became the voice of the politically incorrect. He established a following. Other papers sought him; he went syndicated; he became the common man's champion and grew to bigger than life proportions, but as he grew, he found the corral he'd built around himself shrinking in size. Now, after ten years, he'd busted loose. He'd kicked down the rails and was headed for home.

It was more than a reunion with his beloved west coast that pulled him on, or even the thin hope that the return would be welcomed by his wife. No, what kept his foot pressing the pedal was a commitment to doing what was right for his daughter. It was Angie who had seen him through those long empty hours when the night never seemed to end. And though it could be argued that, as a child, her level of understanding was nil, Angie had listened. This was payback. He had always given Angie his best, every possible treatment, every operation, every program designed to reduce pain, but it wasn't enough and he knew it. She needed more than the latest high-tech, chrome-railed, safety bed; she needed human contact; she needed human touch. It was something he, as a slave to the media, could not provide. Until he controlled the hours in the day, he would not be able to give Angie the attention she deserved. That's what had precipitated the move— that, and the timely offer on his house. The purchased boat, the loaded van, even the willingness to live on less, were proof of his commitment. As the miles droned away under the tires, Bill wrestled with his uncertainty. There were only two things he knew for sure: he knew the odds were against him, and he knew he loved the odds.

They'd traveled 350 miles west across highway 94 before he decided to call it a day. They were cruising across the core of downtown Milwaukee. He was looking for a place to stop. The unshaven sandpaper was itching his face, and his heel was burning from resting on the firewall. And though she'd slept most of the way, Angie looked as spent as old money. Besides, the billboards were driving him crazy. Bill had begun reading the giant street signs to help him stay alert, but now the information overload was grinding his brain into hamburger.

He pushed across city center looking for a place to stay. Each new exit looked less inviting than the one before. The barrage of speeding traffic and chemically washed brown air kept his foot pushing down on the gas pedal. He tapped his thumbs on the steering wheel. He couldn't keep it up forever, and be a responsible parent. It was time to find rest for his little girl.

Angie's eyes opened as she woke again, blinking. A blast of hot orange covered her face as she stared into the setting sun. Earlier, Bill had turned his visor down to shade his eyes. Now he attempted to do the same for his daughter, but without success. Angie sat too low for the visor to be of use. Bill reached down and found the piece of folded cardboard he kept on hand for solving this problem. He slid it over the visor to extend its length. He reacted to the horn screaming on his right, a sharp reminder to keep his eyes on his driving. T.J. was resting on the console between the two seats. Bill swerved but the sudden shift back to his own lane threw the cat to the floor. The cat bolted, causing Bill's feet to dance on the pedals. One moment T.J. was under Bill's foot, the next he was digging his claws into Bill's leg, tearing his way into Bill's lap, and up and over Bill's shoulder as he dove toward the back of the van.

Then it fell apart. Blinded by the cat while trying to pull his vehicle back to its own lane, Bill overcompensated. He looked up just in time to see they were headed toward the center divider. It was too late. He swerved as the van sideswiped the retaining wall and went into a slide. Instinctively, Bill jerked the wheel back to the right, buckling the tires beneath the van, which sent the weight of the vehicle over the top. The van collapsed as the grip of gravity pulled it down. Shards of chrome, splinters of glass, and pounding earth dusted the air as the sliding mass of metal careened toward the center lane. *Scrrreeeeeeeech!* Bill saw the window on Angie's side shatter and pop out.

He was caught in a time warp, the action taking place in slow motion. In that infinite crack of time that exists between two eternal seconds, Bill grabbed his daughter's hair and yanked her head up to keep her face from being scraped across the pavement. His ear rasped with the sound of grinding metal as the rear doors popped open and boxes were thrown across the highway coming apart as they rolled, spinning their contents into the street. Then it was over. Bill waited in the warp, listening for the sound of squealing rubber, anticipating the slam and crunch as the van crumbled like tinfoil under the weight of a second unstoppable car. But it didn't happen. His heart thumped, beating the air. Angie's eyes stared forward, then rolled upward to find her dad suspended above her, hanging by his seatbelt. A curl reached the corner of her mouth. She giggled in her distorted way letting Bill know she was all right. "Hey there little partner, that was some stunt, huh? How you doin', you okay?"

He didn't have to see the damage to know the van was finished. It was a miracle they hadn't been killed. He released his seatbelt and fell into Angie's lap, holding his hands out to protect her against his weight. Traffic was piling up. Bill covered his daughter's face and used the heel of his boot to kick out the shattered windshield, creating an escape. He pulled himself through the hole and reached back inside to recover Angie. She squeezed his heart as he held her to his cheek and kissed her hair. The pressure against his chest sent shockwaves through his body. The fall against the seatbelt had bruised a few ribs. *Better bruised than broken,* he thought. He raised his eyes and whispered thanks.

Cars were beginning to move slowly around both sides of the rubble avoiding the accident which had come to a stop in the center lane. Bill stood in the middle of the highway, his van demolished. His possessions were strewn across the blacktop, being thumped, bumped and run over. As he shivered in the descending cold, Bill caught a glimpse of T.J. ducking between the wheels of slow moving traffic. Then the rust-spotted cat disappeared into the tall grass along the road's edge, scrambling for shelter.

LAURIE POKED the floor with her cane, *thud, pull forward, pause...thud, pull forward, pause...thud.* She hunched over and leaned into each step. She hoped she wasn't overdoing it. It was hard getting into the part, looking, feeling and acting like something she wasn't. She wanted to kick those stiff podiatric shoes off her feet. She wanted to dance across the lobby. *That's just how they must feel,* she thought. She was trying to imitate those she saw sliding across the floor with slow painful steps, imprisoned in bodies of decay.

She eased herself into a thickly padded lobby chair, sinking low into its cushions with a sigh. She placed both hands atop her walking stick, which she held upright between her knees. As a reporter, she wanted to interview the small clusters of people she saw standing around the lobby. She wanted to introduce herself and start asking questions, but that would be too obvious. The secret to aging was patience. She had to become an old woman, isolated and withdrawn. She had to think old, speak old, and see old. Her mind must be clouded, she must appear to be trapped in cobwebs of the past. She closed her eyes, focusing on tired thoughts. If she appeared weary, perhaps she would seem less intimidating. She had to invite them in. She was the new kid on the block. The regular guests must be curious. They must wonder where she'd come from, what her name was, and why she was there. If she waited long enough, they would approach her, or so she hoped. She was pulled from her thoughts by a voice that brought to mind the sound of gravel being washed in a tin cup.

"Ah hurump, umph. Bad choice, little lady. These chairs are for visitors. Guests like us are supposed to sit in the folding chairs. They don't look like much, but they're padded."

Laurie looked up. A small man stood before her. He couldn't have been more than five feet tall, thin as a fence post, with close-cropped gray hair. His finely edged mustache bristled over the narrow pink slit of his mouth. His face looked as tan and brittle as sun bleached leather. Laurie couldn't tell if the cracks were scars, or the deep creases of age.

"Colonel Rosen, at your service." The man extended his hand.

Laurie lifted her fingers from her cane. She was hesitant. Her youthful hands were difficult to mask. She could duplicate liver spots, but bulging blue veins and crinkled skin were hard to imitate. The man didn't seem to notice.

"Mrs. Iversen," she responded in kind. "And what, may I ask, is wrong with this chair?"

"You're new here. I can always tell. Anyone who's been here more than a day knows these chairs are the enemy's trap. Once you're in, you can't get out. Try it. You'll see what I mean. They make these chairs with a built-in vacuum. They suck you in so you can't escape. Go ahead, try."

Laurie leaned on her staff and feigned that her arms were too weak to lift her body. She had fallen into a trap all right. There probably wasn't an old person alive, whether a guest or visiting, that would settle into a thickly padded chair so low to the ground. It explained why no one else had been sitting there.

"Allow me." The little man reached out and pulled Laurie from the chair. She was surprised by the strength of his small arms. She stood, rocking back and forth for a moment, feigning to be unsteady until she found the support of her cane. "There you go. Now be careful where you sit."

"Hello Jack. Who's your new friend?"

Laurie turned. They had been joined by a third person, a tall, thin woman with skin like burnished ebony.

The woman leaned in to introduce herself, extending a chocolate brown hand with red painted nails. "I'm Karleen Smith, but you can call me Karla. Everyone else does."

Laurie introduced herself again, holding eye contact to keep Karla from seeing her hands, only this time she introduced herself as Annie. Friendships should begin on a first name basis. She had been right. All she had to do was stay put and people would come to her. They had to be curious about the newcomer. She was off to a good start, meeting people so she could begin her inquiry. Unfortunately, she wasn't looking for a Smith, or a Rosen. She wanted to talk to the people who had signed the letter, and Smith and Rosen weren't on the list.

Karla broke into Laurie's thoughts, leaning in with her head tilted toward Laurie's ear as though sharing a confidence. "So tell me Annie, have you purchased a suite here at Emerald Valley?"

Laurie pulled back. She didn't want Karla's lips so close to her mask. The makeup itched; it might peel off. Laurie tapped the floor with her walking stick and started moving, *thud, pull forward, pause...thud.* Bill had said Ben Riggs was dead. That meant there were five people she still had to find, and rather quickly. The disguise wouldn't last forever. "No, not yet. I'm staying for a few days to see if I like it first," she said, answering the question.

The colonel moved into escort position. He took Laurie's arm, which made her wonder if her costume, like her makeup, might rub off. "Let me help you, ma'am. Pretty little thing like you shouldn't be left wandering alone," he said, ignoring the fact that Karla was right there, and the room was full of people. "Remember to always protect your flank. Sometimes the enemy's not easy to see."

Laurie blinked and turned but before she could ask Mr. Rosen what he meant, she felt Karla's warm breath again. She could smell the tart scent of the woman's overripe perfume. She was trapped between the colonel, who was restraining her arm on one side, and a pair of lips pinning her ear back on the other. She felt her disguise blowing up in her face. "Just go along," Karla whispered. "He overdoes his past. He likes to pretend he was some kind of war hero, just to impress the ladies, but he's harmless."

"What's that you said?" The little colonel turned and cupped his ear. "I heard that! I got my hearing aid turned up. You be careful what you say. I can hear everything. You can't keep secrets from me."

Laurie glanced around the room. She had to get away from these two. She wanted to meet the pair she had seen earlier, the potbellied man in the green T-shirt and the tiny woman in the red feathered hat. Something about the way they had stared at her, aroused her interest. And there had been five people in the group, which fit the profile.

At the edge of the lobby they came to a door marked "Community Center." Laurie turned to go inside. Her two escorts stayed with her, one on either side, refusing to break rank. The room was large and airy. One wall was made up entirely of floor to ceiling windows. Gray-haired seniors dotted the landscape, their bent bodies occupied with various activities, some reading, some talking, and some just sitting alone. It was as good a place to start as any. She scanned the room from side to side. The two she hoped to find weren't there. Still, it was a good gathering. She might as well try to learn what she could.

The oldest inmates were segregated and parked in wheelchairs along the inside wall. They were silent, bent over, and shivering in their shawls. Their faces were starched like peeled potatoes and their eyes were weepy with age. And all of them had hair that was tangled and white. Laurie figured they wouldn't be of much help. They were too far gone.

A cluster of people sat at a card table playing gin rummy. Laurie turned away. Cards weren't a good idea. Her sharp mind, and therefore better play, might reveal her younger age. And it might draw attention to her hands. Besides, getting involved in a card game could tie her up for hours. If none of the names at the table matched those on her list, she would be trapped. She needed the freedom to move around and meet as many people as possible.

That left the gang watching TV. A dozen folding chairs were positioned in a semicircle around the glowing tube. They seemed spellbound by the soap opera's plot. Laurie hated soaps, but there were at least seven people in the group. For the moment, they were her best prospects.

"I'm afraid I get tired when I'm on my feet too long," she said. "I was looking for a place to sit when the colonel found me. If you don't mind, I'd like to go over there. I think they're watching my favorite show."

"Oh my, yes, of course, we can do that." Karla began walking slowly in the direction of the group sitting around the television. "We can do most anything you want. It's such a lovely day, I was going to suggest a walk outside, but if you feel tired, TV is fine with me. We have lots of time for everything, except on days when people come to visit, then it seems there's never enough time. I expect you'll see what I mean soon enough. You have family around here, Annie?"

Laurie missed her cue. Her new name wasn't registering as fast as she'd like, but she recovered well. It wasn't like old people were quick to respond anyway. "Pardon? Sorry, my hearing isn't what it used to be. What did you say?"

"I asked if you had any family."

"No, no, just my niece. And I don't see much of her. She has a family of her own to raise. That's why I've been thinking about staying here. Karla, can you think of any reason why a person wouldn't want to live here?"

"Heavens no, honey, I love this place."

Laurie's pout was a natural reaction, but she could feel it cracking her makeup. She made a conscious effort to relax. She couldn't expect everyone to know about the murders.

She turned toward the colonel. He had wrapped a palm over his mouth and was chewing on a thought. "You can't be too careful," he mumbled through his fingers. "The enemy likes to grab you when you're not looking." Then he dropped Laurie's arm and walked away.

SIX

I'd seen accidents on TV, but I'd never been in one. My head was pounding so hard I thought it was going to burst. When you face death they say your life passes before your eyes, but that's not what happened. All I could think was: "I'm going to die without seeing Mom!"

It took awhile for me to realize the van had come to a stop and we were alive. When I looked up and saw my dad hanging there, I had to laugh. Then he took me in his arms and I felt his heart beating in his chest and I knew everything would be all right. But I couldn't look at the wreck. I had to keep my face buried in his shirt.

Good thing my dad's not a quitter. Remember "Rocky," that movie where a poor ghetto boxer gets a chance to fight the champ? Remember how at the end, Rocky's face is all bloody but he keeps going back for more? When I think of that movie, I think of Dad. To me, it seemed hopeless. We'd barely started our trip, and we'd already lost our car. Everything we owned was in the middle of the road. But my dad had his sights set on Washington. An accident might slow him down, but it wouldn't turn him around. So even before he said it, I knew we'd soon be on our way—I just didn't think we'd be leaving without my cat!

BILL ROLLED HIS SHOULDERS to loosen the knots. The pain in his chest smarted as he released a sigh. He knew it would feel even worse in the morning, after the bruise had time to settle. The room was okay, standard two beds, a dresser, television and a small bath—the kind of motel used by truckers and salesmen. The furniture was cheap laminate and the paneled walls were decorated with posters hung in chrome frames, but it was clean and the price was right. All they needed was a place to sleep. He pushed one of the beds against the wall for Angie. The taxi tooted its horn. Bill returned to retrieve his daughter. He paid the fare and lifted Angie from the seat, pulling her into his arms. He barely got the door closed when the cab lurched forward forcing him to step back to keep his foot from being run over. He tucked Angie's face into his shoulder and held it there to keep the dust and fumes out of her lungs.

What a day! Stranded on the outskirts of Milwaukee: the van demolished, their belongings impounded, and the cat missing. What else could go wrong? At least he'd had the presence of mind to grab his computer. Remarkably, it had suffered little damage. It had a few scrapes on the outside, but it didn't look broken. He wouldn't know for sure until he turned it on.

Bill carried Angie into the room and eased her into a sitting position against the bed's headboard. Her muscles were writhing, causing her to jerk and twitch. It was to be expected; her convulsions always increased with stress.

He sat down on the bed, the springs creaking under his weight. The room smelled like musty linen. He had already removed his coat. Now he unbuttoned the sleeves of his blue denim shirt and rolled the cuffs back on his forearms. He combed his fingers through his wavy, sand-colored hair and scratched his itching, stubbled jaw. Angie had every right to be agitated. Most normal adults couldn't survive a major accident without experiencing some kind of trauma. He had to do what he could to comfort her. "Hey there partner," he said, moving to sweep the hair out of her eyes. Angie's neck stiffened and her shoulders began to rotate. Bill placed a comforting hand on her collar. "You okay? I...huh...look, I'm sorry about what happened. I should have been more careful...I guess I was just tired, but that's no excuse." Bill began combing his daughter's hair with his fingers. "It was my fault. What can I say? Thanks to me, we're stuck here—at least for the moment. We'll have to buy us another vehicle, but I think we've had enough excitement for one day. Okay by you if we leave it till tomorrow? Of course, tomorrow's Sunday, a lot of places will be closed until noon. I hate to lose the time. This whole thing is going to throw us off schedule, but we have to find a church in the morning anyway. I figure you and I need to say a word of thanks. It's a miracle neither of us was hurt."

Bill squeezed Angie's shoulder to make sure he had her attention. He knew she understood. She was generally regarded as having an intelligence well above most children her age. That was the funny thing about cerebral palsy. It was a disorder that could affect both the mind and the body, or affect just one without affecting the other. It could impair the ability to think, while leaving the body pretty much in tact, or do the complete opposite and cripple the body, while leaving the mind unaffected. The latter had been the case with Angie. She couldn't articulate words, and she had only limited control of her muscles, but her capacity to comprehend ideas, process thoughts and learn, was uncanny. And her father, who believed a mind was a terrible thing to waste, read to her constantly, helping to increase her knowledge. She'd been through a battery of intelligence tests, and by blinking her eyes to communicate, had scored high on every one.

Bill waited until their eyes met. It was a meeting of blue on blue. It was the one trait he, Laurie, and their daughter, all shared in common, they all had deep blue eyes. But Angie couldn't hold his gaze. Her face went thrashing to the side, causing Bill to reach out with his hand to keep her head from bumping the wall. When the squirming stopped, he placed his hand on her collar again and gave her an encouraging squeeze. "Now, don't be worried about T.J. He's not hurt. I saw him running off across the field. I admit he looked pretty shook up, so he might be in hiding, but soon as you rest a bit, we'll rent us a car and go see if we can find him. How does that sound? I...ah...well, just don't get your hopes up. That's all I ask. That cat was mighty scared. He may have run off and got himself lost. He doesn't know his way around these parts. We have to face the fact that if he doesn't come when I call, we'll have to go on without him."

Angie began to squirm but Bill held her gently in place. "I'll get in touch with the animal shelter and let them know where we'll be in case he shows up later." Angie's head jerked back and her spine arched away from the bed. "Daaaa...goaaaaaa." Bill wiped the spittle from her lips and tried to decipher her muted response. She wanted to get up; that much he understood. It seemed she wanted to start looking

49

right now, but it wasn't a good idea. She needed her rest. Bill held her gently but firmly in place. "We will, darlin', we will, soon as you get some rest. Hey now, don't be sad. We'll do what we can, I promise." He used his thumb to wipe away the silver drop forming in the corner of Angie's eye. "You need to pray, so God can show us where to find T.J. Anyway, the sooner I get a shower and get changed, the sooner we can get a car and go looking. What do you say to that? Here, you can watch TV if you want." Bill knew he'd delivered a hard message. The odds were they wouldn't find T.J. He had to be honest about it. He wasn't surprised when Angie's gyrations continued unabated.

He gave her hand a light squeeze. "Everything's going to be all right. You'll see." He leaned over to kiss his daughter's cheek. Then he leaned back to click on the set, momentarily filling the room with a noisy hiss until the static gave way to a picture. An ad for the six o'clock news filled the screen. It gave Bill an idea. He reached to turn down the volume and pick up the phone. He was thinking like a journalist again. He called information for the number of the news channel. Then he dialed the station, introduced himself, and explained why he was calling. He nodded. He'd been right, the helicopter he'd seen hovering overhead was from the station. They had footage of the accident, and the snarl of traffic it caused, which they were scheduled to air at six. It didn't take much to convince them to tag on a sympathy plea. A little girl, the victim of cerebral palsy, had survived the accident but had lost her closest friend, her kitty, and was now pleading with the community for its return. It made a nice story. The other stations and even a few newspapers would pick it up the moment it broke. The world was full of Good Samaritans. Instructions were given that anyone seeing a calico cat prowling the scene of the accident should call the humane society, who would in turn contact Bill.

Listening to her father's conversation released some of Angie's tension, letting her tremors quiet down. Bill knew what she was going through; losing T.J. was traumatic. He felt the anxiety as though it was his own. She loved that cat. And he had defended her right to keep it. It was good therapy. Animals don't question a person's physical, emotional, or mental ability. But what was he supposed to do? If T.J. didn't come when he called, they'd have to leave him behind. They had to at least try to stay on schedule. If he showed up later, Bill would be notified. But if the animal never did turn up, he'd just have to buy his daughter another cat. It was a hard lesson to learn: sometimes you have to let go of the things you love. The accident had cost him some of his favorite books. He'd watched the pages being steam-rolled by traffic, *thump, bumpity, thump.* He loved those books as much as Angie loved her cat. Yer sir, there was no doubt about it, one of life's hardest lessons was learning how to give things up.

Bill stood. He needed a shower, but there was something he wanted to do first. He hadn't checked his e-mail for messages all day, a cardinal sin for a journalist. Angie appeared okay for the moment. She was distracted by the TV.

He unplugged the room phone and replaced it with the plastic connector from his modem. "I just want to see if my computer still works," he said over his shoulder to Angie. "Then I'm going to pop in the shower while you rest. If you want, I'll turn up the volume."

Bill gave the knob a twist, just in time to hear highlights of the news stories that would follow at the top of the hour. He looked at his watch. The program would start in five minutes. Angie always enjoyed current events, and she'd want to hear what they said about her cat. He found an outlet for his computer, plugged it in and flipped the switch. The little portable sprang to life, loading programs. *That's the ticket.* He clasped his hands together and felt the pinch of his University of Oregon class ring against his wedding band which, though he'd been separated ten years, he still refused to remove. He went straight to his e-mail and found four messages waiting. The first was from his policeman friend in Detroit, letting him know that Emerald Valley had been notified. Apparently the deceased man didn't have a family, so as far as his friend was concerned, Bill was free to publish the information he had recently acquired. The rest home was not able to explain Mr. Riggs disappearance, or why he had showed up in Michigan. They cited a policy stating that their responsibility ended the minute a guest left the premises. Guests of the home were free to come and go as they pleased. Mr. Riggs had not let the staff know he would be leaving, so unfortunately, they were unable to provide additional information.

Bill pondered the report for a moment. He had decided not to write about the death of Ben Riggs so the release was irrelevant. He was glad Milwaukee media hadn't felt the same way about his accident. He wondered if two mishaps so close together wasn't some kind of omen. Before leaving, he'd spent time in prayer with Pastor Jim, senior pastor of the church he attended in Detroit. Jim was more than his spiritual mentor. He was a friend. They'd been in perfect agreement. The unsolicited selling of his house, the exceptional offer it entailed, his desire to spend more time with his daughter, and his goal of reuniting Angie with her mother, all seemed to confirm the Lord was calling him back to the west coast. But now, after one day of travel, he was stranded in Milwaukee, and he had to wonder: had he misread the mind of God? He didn't know what else could happen but he'd heard that bad things come in threes. Of course, that was just superstition.

Two other messages were from people who had read his parting column. One was from a person who was glad he was leaving Michigan and hoped he would take all his intolerant, narrow-minded, right-wing opinions with him and stay as far away from Detroit as he could, the Pacific Ocean being deemed not far enough. The other was sorry to see him go and vowed to continue reading Bill's weekly syndicated column.

The last message was from Laurie.

Bill:

I'm following your lead. I spoke to my editor but he refused to let me cover the story. Like you said, they think the old people are crazy. But you know me, when they say no, that's when I go. As far as the paper is concerned, I'm out of town covering a forum on women's issues.

That presents problem number one. I can't go poking around Emerald Valley asking questions. If they discover I'm a reporter, word will get back to the paper and that will be the end of it. So I've gone undercover. I had a friend, Peter, who does makeup at KPDX, put together a disguise that makes me look old. You wouldn't believe how awful it is to stand in front of the mirror and realize this is the way I'll look in a few years, but that's another story. I'm registered at Emerald Valley as Annie Iversen. It's important you remember that, in case you have to call. Don't slip up and ask for Laurie Iversen. I know that's who I was when we met, but I decided to drop the "Laurie" and use my middle name, Ann, instead. And whatever you do, don't ask for Laurie Best. It's Annie Iversen. Please don't forget. I don't know how long I can keep up the ruse but I'll go as long as I can. I want to make it until I at least find out if there's a story here or not.

Which presents problem number two. I can't send my notes or drafts to my office. They'll end up on the server. I'm supposed to be password protected but you know how it is; the guys in our software group make a practice of cracking everybody's code. They read everything. I plan to send them false info about the fictitious story I'm supposed to be following. That should keep them off my trail. But I don't like having all my notes in just one place. I don't trust computers. I've lost whole files before. Or worse, the whole silly computer can go missing. Of course I doubt anyone here would steal a computer, they wouldn't know what to do with it, but I'd still feel safer with a backup.

That's where you come in. I plan to send you a copy of everything I write. In fact, I want you to consider running the story as a syndicated piece. I'm even willing to share the byline. After all, the old folks did approach you first. But what I'm really after, is readership. If there is a story here, it has all the makings of award winning journalism: the truth told but ignored, the police bungling the investigation, the media stymied. Should it turn out my peers botched an important scoop, I'll be forced to expose their negligence, which won't make me popular around the office.

I also want it understood that I'm not entertaining any preconceived notions. There may not be a story here. I've decided to take a pragmatic approach. For the moment, I'll give my old newspaper, and the authorities, the benefit of the doubt. If the police didn't uncover anything, there probably wasn't anything to uncover. This kind of thing can be risky. All the attendants have keys to the rooms and can walk in unannounced, so unless I see evidence of the alleged crime, and I mean pretty darn quick, I'm out of here. It goes without saying that old people can become easily confused and suspicious. They may think something is amiss, when actually it's not, but I promise to try and keep an open mind.

I haven't been out of my room yet. I just got checked in and decided to write before getting started. As soon as I sign off, I'm ready to roll. I need to begin meeting the other inmates ASAP. Let me know if you're in agreement, and wish me luck.

Laurie

For the first time in several hours Bill found a reason to smile. The lady had chutzpah. He could see her running around in her granny outfit, the proud Laurie Best humbled by age. He looked at his watch. It was almost six. It would be three, west coast time. Knowing her, she'd have a notebook full of information by now.

IF ONLY ONE WORD were used to describe Emerald Valley, that word would be, "efficient." The staff prided itself on perfect balance and, whenever put upon to indulge a cliché, boasted their facility ran like a finely wound clock. Beneath the surface, every activity had a support staff that kept the exercise running smoothly. The tour given to Laurie revealed only the superficial operation. She saw the apartments, the dining hall, and the gift shop. There was no need to see the laundry, the kitchen, or the administrative offices. These were areas where things were done to benefit the guests, but about which the guests knew little. All the guests needed to know was that when their towels got dirty, they were replaced, as if by magic. They never saw the chef or kitchen staff. For all they knew, food materialized out of thin air, like manna from heaven. Thus, they were encouraged to live their lives to the fullest without worry or concern.

It was also important to maintain harmony among the live-in population. If two guests found themselves at odds over an issue, such as what happened when Paula Gurz claimed that Abbie Holtzstedder was stealing her fresh-baked cookies and using them to win the heart of Charlie Jackson—a man both women claimed to love—or what happened when Walter Pierce refused to pay a poker debt to Norman Needlemeyer because he believed Norman had cheated, the aggravated parties were encouraged to let a staff administrator arbitrate, to see if an agreeable solution could be found. For a small fee, professional counseling could also be arranged.

If two or more neighbors were found to be incompatible, as the light-sleeping Mrs. Doorchester was with the snoring Hanif Yousef, who she claimed could be heard snorting through the walls, keeping her awake at night, they were separated and assigned new quarters. A stipulation in the contract signed by each guest assured that the cost of the move could be deducted from the resident's account.

Complaints against the facility itself were dealt with as soon as they were known. Guests were asked to state their grievance and suggest what management could do to correct the problem. This is why the five people Laurie had been looking for were now with Alfred Porter, the site manager, trying to explain what they knew about the recent disappearance of Ben Riggs.

Ruth Agatha Wheatly, the lady with the red feathered hat, spoke first. "I'm not sure what you want from us," she said. Her white-gloved hand floated through the air until it reached the red beret, pushing it up as though a hatpin had come loose. Once assured it was still attached, her spotless glove fell neatly back into her lap, but she kept her little dark eyes fixed confidently on her inquisitor. "I know I haven't seen Ben around, but when you think about it, people come and go all the time. There's nothing unusual about that." She was pleased that she'd been able to answer without telling a lie. *The Lord is my judge,* she thought. *But remember, he's your judge too, Mr. Porter. He's your judge too.*

Sitting on the credenza at the end of the room, Mr. Porter wore a glossy brown worsted wool suit that rolled smoothly in the light. His dark hair was combed back in waves; his olive eyes, under heavy dark eyebrows, were furrowed in skepticism. His lips pursed as he leaned over and removed a page from the file lying beside him. "All right, correct me if I'm wrong. You five, along with Mr. Riggs, signed a letter which you hand delivered to the chief of police in which you state, and I quote: 'there are strange things going on at Emerald Valley Retirement Home. Several recent deaths attributed to failing health and acute depression, have happened to people who, according to those who knew them, were of sound mind and body. It is our belief that these deaths were unnecessary and wrongful. We request an immediate investigation of Emerald Valley management and staff. If our suspicions are correct, our lives could be in danger. Please send help immediately!'" Alfred Porter slid the letter back into the file and laid it down beside him again. The room was climate-controlled but Ruth could see a line of dew-like perspiration hiding under his hairline. He looked back at his audience, letting his eyes sweep from right to left, pausing for a moment to probe each person individually. The group remained silent.

"That was written on March tenth," he continued, "a letter each of you signed. Now look. We have been most patient with you about this. I mean, be fair, what you accuse the management here of, is nothing less than murder. If we were of a mind, we could sue the whole lot of you for slander and defamation of character. We haven't done that have we? No, in spite of the fact that we always encourage our guests to come to us first with any concerns, a request which you ignored, and the fact that instead of coming to us you wrote this libelous letter, we've been fair, haven't we? We welcomed the police investigation. We assisted in every way we could. And we proved that nothing out of the ordinary took place. Yet in spite of the inconvenience and embarrassment caused by your accusations, we have continued to treat you as welcome guests. Have any of you been made to feel uncomfortable? Have any of you noticed any lack in the care we provide? I don't think so. I think we've gone out of our way to be patient and treat you as though none of this ever happened. Only now one of your group turns up in Michigan and the police want to know why he was there. He doesn't have family in Michigan, he never got letters or packages from anyone, and he hated to travel, so what was the point? I'm sure if Ben had a reason for flying off to Detroit, he would have told someone. You were his friends; you hung around together. He didn't leave word with any of our staff so I'm assuming he told one of you. Come on, help me out here. Cash, you must know something."

Cash Williams looked at his feet; his heart was doing flip-flops in his chest. He had been trying to remember how he got himself into this mess but was having trouble putting places and faces together. His legs were stretched out in front of him in a relaxed pose, but he was anything but relaxed. He crossed his feet, then crossed his arms, and then uncrossed his feet again while contemplating the question. He swallowed hard to clear the lump in his throat. He was too old to be playing cat and mouse. Long, slow seconds were passing and he couldn't seem to open his mouth. He didn't know if he could handle intense interrogation. He was glad there were others in the room. There was strength in numbers, at least for the moment. He wouldn't be the first to crack. "Don't know nothin' about it," he finally said, without looking up.

The manager didn't bother challenging the response. Instead he turned his attention to the man seated on his right. "Bonner?" he queried, arching his eyebrows.

Joe Bonner, whose baseball cap Laurie had noticed earlier, pulled a handkerchief from his hip pocket, blew his nose, and wiped the hollow sockets of his cloud-gray eyes. He pulled his T-shirt over his tummy and tilted back in the boardroom style chair. He and Ben had been friends. He'd just been informed that Ben had given his life for the cause. Joe would do the same, if he had to. "Ben didn't say a thing to me," he grunted, "but he was funny like that. I'll bet if you check your file there, you'll find a report that says he was mentally unbalanced, just like all of us are supposed to be. How do you want us to account for a man that, according to you, is crazy? And if we did, how are you going to trust what we say, since we're supposed to be crazy too?"

Alfred Porter took the shot without flinching. He seemed unfazed by Joe's reference to the notes the police had found which questioned the mental stability of the five individuals seated around the table. He flicked a piece of lint from the lapel of his slick, brown jacket. He appeared perfectly composed, but beneath the surface he was grinding his teeth. He turned to Louis Wiarton. "Louis, you and Ben were pretty close. He say anything to you?"

Louis squirmed, rolling his huge body against the cushion of his chair. It always scared him to sit in chairs like these, scared him to think that once in, he might not be able to get out. His expansive size could barely be squeezed between the hard plastic arms which pinched him like a clothespin.

It was obvious this was some kind of meeting room, but he had never been here before. He felt awkward, like a schoolboy called into the principal's office. He didn't know if he'd get the strap, detention, or the gas chamber; all he knew was the suspense was making him sweat. He could feel drops rolling freely down his chest. He would have to change his shirt, if he got out of here alive. His curly fop of orange hair mopped the brow of his forehead, keeping the moisture from falling into his eyes.

They wouldn't try to kill him, would they? He was only sixty. He wasn't there because he was old. He'd used his inheritance to buy a suite because he couldn't make it on his own. He didn't like being alone. People on the outside were strange, and threatening. He needed the kind of support Emerald Valley provided.

Besides, there was no proof they'd done anything wrong. Whenever he and his pals got together, whatever they said made sense, but when Mr. Porter defended the corporate position, that sounded good too. At least Mr. Porter was right about one thing, their letter should have caused Emerald Valley a load of embarrassment, but they hadn't retaliated. It appeared they had nothing to hide. Still, he wasn't about to betray his friends. "N-n-noo, d-d-didn't say n-n-nothin' to me." He tried to swallow, but suddenly he found he couldn't breathe. His face flushed red, and his jelly-roll stomach shuddered until he broke through the fear that was choking his windpipe. He gasped for air.

Mr. Porter shook his head. His jaw tightened. The back of his neck felt hot. He wiped the moisture from his lip and sucked in a slow breath, intending to calm himself. To the others, it seemed more like a sigh of resignation.

The last person to be questioned was Edith Woodhouse. She was the only other female in the group. She was brought in because she had, in her working life, been a legal secretary. It was assumed she had a grasp of legal matters, but in fact, she knew very little. Her job had been to take dictation, transcribe memos, arrange court dates, and organize case files. Typing reams of legal briefs was a mindless task which taught her nothing about the law itself. At best, she might be able to quote a bit of legalese, but not on a day like today. Today it was too cold to think. It was always too cold. She closed her sweater around her shoulders. *Cold!* "Could you turn up the heat? It's cold in here."

"Certainly Edith, in just a minute. I asked if you knew why Ben would fly off to Detroit?"

There was one thing she remembered from years in the legal profession: never confess to anything. She shook her head firmly. "No! Are you going to turn up the heat? A person could freeze to death in here."

ON THE OTHER SIDE of the wall, watching the interview through a pane of one-way glass, Mrs. Marks, hostess, a la salesperson, and Dr. Stuart VanEtter, the staff physician, monitored the session and recorded everything.

"Well, that makes it unanimous," Barbara said, her silk scarf struggling to hide the sagging skin around her neck. "None of them knows anything."

Dr. VanEtter bit his lip and folded his hands behind his back. It was difficult for him to watch people deteriorate. It pained him to see a person so far gone that they answered a specific question about a deceased friend with a comment about the room's temperature. The room was quite comfortable. It was climate controlled to a perfect seventy-two degrees. "I'm not so sure," he responded. "I think they probably know. They must. They're just confused, that's all. Their minds aren't thinking clearly."

Barbara finished writing and put down her tablet. "I guess it's a moot point. Al's having them moved. They can't get into trouble if they can't talk to each other."

ALFRED PORTER STOOD, scanned his folder one last time, and paced the length of the room. "All right, no one wants to say anything. I respect that. We can let it go for now. However, as a corporation we have to protect our interests. Your little group likes to huddle and circulate rumors which, though completely false, are nonetheless detrimental to the good name of Emerald Valley. We have decided that we can't allow this to continue. Our administrative staff has met to discuss the matter and the solution we've come up with is to separate you. As of right now, all your possessions are being moved into new apartments. All except yours, Edith, no one could move all that. The rest of you are being relocated to different parts of the campus, as far away from each other as we can possibly manage. You can protest if you want, but it won't do any good. The contract each of you signed clearly gives us this right. If you're paying monthly, and you decide you want to find somewhere else to live, that's fine, we'll let you out of your contract. If you paid in advance, you can still go, but we cannot refund your money. You are entitled to a lifetime of care and this you will receive as long as you remain with us. Should you desire to leave, we are absolved of any responsibility while you are away. Of course, you are welcome to return at any time. But remember that while you are here, you must abide by our rules and as of today, those rules include no communication among yourselves. You will find your telephones have been removed from your apartments. From now on you'll have to make your calls from the phone in the lobby. Our staff has been given a list of your names and will be monitoring your movements throughout the day. Anytime they see two or more of you together, they have been instructed to break up the group. Are there any questions?"

"You can't do that!"

"Sorry, but I'm afraid we can."

LAURIE WAS MAKING her way slowly back to her apartment, curious about all the activity. It seemed a number of tenants were relocating, moving either in or out of various suites. A door opened on her left and she turned, surprised to see several people exit, among them the frumpy man in the green T-shirt, and the little woman dressed in red—the very two she had been looking for. And there were five in total. They stopped and huddled, forming a tight circle. She quickly drew mental pictures of the three she didn't recognize. It was apparent something was amiss. They were talking in hushed whispers, while sneaking furtive glances over their shoulders.

Laurie tried moving closer to hear what was being said, but she was intercepted by four badge wearing Emerald Valley staffers, who took the members of the group by their arms and ushered them off in different directions. The woman Laurie hadn't seen before was left standing alone. She folded her arms looking cold and confused, before turning to wander off down the hall.

But the man in the green T-shirt and baseball cap, was being pulled in Laurie's direction. His escort took his arm and said: "Here Bonner, let me show you to your new quarters."

Bingo! Bonner is one of the names.

She'd been right; he was one of the people that signed the letter. Her reporter's instincts had been dead on. But something else was terribly wrong, and it had an impact on everything. Laurie felt her heartbeat accelerate. She felt like she was being pulled through a wormhole, from the realm of fiction, back to reality. It was a sure bet she'd found the right group, but what she observed challenged their credibility. "They killed him," the lady in the feathered hat said before she was captured. Her head was bobbing as she was led away but she turned to look back over her shoulder so she could say it again: "Don't let them do this. They followed poor Ben and killed him. We'll be next!" Was she blaming Emerald Valley for the death of Ben Riggs? Laurie knew otherwise. Ben had died under the wheels of a taxi hired by Bill, not as the victim of an assassination plot. Feeble minds were prone to paranoia. But paranoid minds couldn't be trusted. If this was the kind of thinking the accusations were based on, she was wasting her time.

So far she had made only two observations, and both were negative: first, none of the other tenants seemed upset about the rumored homicides, which seemed to indicate the problem didn't exist; and second, one of those who apparently believed people's lives were at stake, just jumped to the conclusion that Mr. Riggs had been murdered, when he hadn't. It didn't bode well. It was probably this kind of irrational behavior that caused the police to drop the investigation in the first place. Laurie had better things to do than chase a wild goose. It wasn't too late to back out. She'd only been there a few hours. No one knew where she was. She could leave and be back in her office tomorrow, none the wiser, no harm done.

She watched Bonner being led away, the hole formed by the sizing strap at the back of his baseball cap revealed a shiny spot on his bald head. His feet were doing the step, shuffle, step, with his slippers scuffing the carpet as he was pulled down the pale-green, fluorescent hall. Then his fingers did something peculiar, something so obvious and deliberate it was hard to ignore, yet Laurie knew if she acknowledged the action she risked being pulled back into the fiction from which she had just escaped.

SEVEN

Living in a body like mine is hard. My limbs have a mind of their own; they move when they want. On the inside I scream: "Stop it, stop it, stop it," but it doesn't do any good. I have to wait until it's over.

It happens mostly when I'm upset. That's why Dad works so hard at keeping things calm. His voice is cool and soothing, like crystal-clear water, and he has a surgeon's touch. But sometimes there's just no avoiding it. I couldn't stop thinking about my cat. T.J. was my friend. I knew we couldn't wait forever, but thoughts about losing my little Tomato Juice made it impossible for me to keep my arms from flailing. So for my own protection, Dad put a pillow in front of me before buckling me into the station wagon. That way my arms couldn't come flinging up and hit something, and maybe even cause another accident.

THE STATION WAGON, a 1984 four-door Country Squire with simulated wood panels, oxidized penny-brown paint, and rust-pitted chrome, was breezing down highway 90 West. Bill kept the pedal to the metal along the stitched line that joins the north-central states. He was avoiding radar, and making up lost time. The memory of Milwaukee was fading into the cloudy, wet distance as Bill put miles between their present and their past. They were ready to start over—for the second time. A church not far from their motel had boasted three morning services. Bill had made sure they attended the first at seven A.M., so they could get an early start. "God is open for business twenty-four hours a day, and appoints convenient times for all," he'd said, encouraging Angie from her sleep.

The car deal had been completed the night before. Bill went to the paper to find something to rent, and instead found something to buy. His needs were simple, and the station wagon seemed to satisfy the criteria: it had to be big enough to carry all their boxes, or what was left of them, and it had to be strong enough to make it out west. After that, they planned to live on the boat and wouldn't need a car. Bill had called and explained his predicament to the seller, who'd agreed to drive the vehicle over to the motel and give Bill a look under the hood. The man had seen their story on the news: "Say, are you the guy that had that accident where the little girl lost her cat? Why didn't you say so? Think nothing of it. Be right over. Glad to help out."

Dust, rust, and fender dents notwithstanding, the old grocery-getter was perfect. It wasn't quite as tall but it was a bit wider than the van, so everything fit. It could have been a covered wagon for all Bill cared, long as it got them where they were going. The tires were fair, the engine was pushing 100,000 miles, but it started with the first turn of the key. A thousand dollars cash (five-hundred dollar withdrawals from two different instant teller machines) put the pink slip in his hand. He'd wait till they were in Washington to register the vehicle, or he'd turn around and resell it, or failing that, drive it into the ocean in celebration of their new beginning. Why not? He could hardly purchase airfare for that amount, let alone ship all his goods. And he was sure to receive a few thousand from the insurance company to compensate him for the wrecked van. He might even come out ahead. He looked over at Angie. She looked miserable cinched in behind that awful pillow. So much had happened in the past twenty-four hours, she was bound to be tense. Sometimes you have to put a lamb in a pen for its own good.

The vehicle carried only two passengers. Bill and Angie were now catless. After dropping the car-seller at his house, they'd gone back to look for T.J., but it had been dark and the frost biting. Bill had paced back and forth, treading and up and down the road, calling through cupped hands. He had called till his knuckles turned blue, till the voice seeping through his clouded breath was pinched and raspy, until he'd determined the answer to his prayer was, "no," and still he'd called. And then he'd called some more. Angie had waited in the warm car with the engine running and the headlights boring holes in the night. For over an hour she'd continued to stare out the fogged window hoping for a glimpse of her lost friend, but the search had been futile. They'd gone back to their room, cold and weary and determined to try again after church the following morning.

They were passing the quiet miles alone in their thoughts. Bill had discovered the radio didn't work. A low drone of static poured from the speakers but no words or music. No problem, he needed time to think. He watched the sky darkening. The low rolling clouds looked pregnant and heavy, ready to deliver. He could see sporadic fireworks sparking on the somber curtain, and hear their rumble off in the distance. Better rain than snow—even cold rain. The air was hanging from the clouds in sheets of frost gray. They were in for one doozy of a storm.

Angie's thoughts were focused on T.J. The loss of her friend left her feeling like someone had punched a hole in her chest. She didn't blame her father. He'd done all he could. She didn't blame God either, though she couldn't understand why he'd let this happen. She'd sent up a dozen prayers, but to no avail. It seemed her supplication had fallen on deaf ears.

They'd tried twice to rescue the lost kitten, but failed both times. After paying to redeem their belongings, they'd gone back to spend another bleak hour searching the weeds along the road's shoulder. Bill had scuffed through bits of red tail-light plastic, crunched glass and strips of chrome. He'd found one of the van's hubcaps, a busted side mirror, and two of his missing books, but no cat. The fields along the highway were overgrown with dead straw, scrub weeds and brown thistles, which restricted visibility. Bill had paced, Bill had called, and Bill had prayed, but Bill had finally given up. No cat was to be found. "I tried, little partner, I truly did," he said as he slid across the wagon's bench seat. "I don't see much point in waiting any longer." But the look of despair on Angie's face made him promise to try again. He poured hot coffee from the thermos, warmed his hands around the cup, let the steam roll up around his nose as he took a sip, and slipped out reluctantly from behind the wheel to once more forage in the cold, misty muck. "Teeee-Jaayyyy, Teeee-Jaayyyy, come on little buddy, let's go." But the cat didn't come. He cupped his ear to listen for a telltale *meow* but heard only the raw *varrrrooooooom* and *whoooooooosh* of cars passing as they pelted him with tiny bits of gravel. When the coffee was gone, he climbed back in the car and drove away.

LAURIE POKED at her face trying to duplicate the contours and folds of old age but no matter how hard she tried the lines looked fake. Her makeup flaked; the bags under her eyes were peeling and the creases were smoothing out. And she kept getting smudges of brown on the gray hairs of her wig. She threw the compact down. Her clothes smelled of linseed oil. This was not going to work. She wouldn't last ten minutes out there.

Peter would have to help. She bit her lower lip, picked up the phone, and dialed. Peter was a friend, and a good one to have in circumstances such as these because Peter was also a studio make-up artist. The application of his skill had got her into the home, but another layer would be required before she could get out. She couldn't leave until her face was perfect. She didn't have a car, and she couldn't go hobbling down the road half done up, dragging her suitcase behind her with her sweater tied around her neck and her floor-length skirt sweeping the ground. If she couldn't leave with the story she had come for, it was important she keep her cover intact. She couldn't risk letting anyone know she'd been insubordinate. She had to keep up the masquerade. She had to convince Emerald Valley she was leaving because she'd decided their program didn't suit her needs. And that meant she had to make an appointment with Barbara Marks. Of course Mrs. Marks would try to counter her objections, but she would be ready with a long list of concerns (bad food, hard beds, rude personnel—she'd think of something) and have Peter ready and waiting to give her a ride so she could excuse herself quickly. But she couldn't do any of that until her makeup was perfect.

She eased herself onto the short sofa, using one of the padded arms as a pillow, kicking her feet up over the other. As she brought the phone to her ear she imagined what Colonel Rosen would say if he found her this way. She could hear his gruff little voice: "These chairs are for visitors, ma'am." There must be a rule against little old ladies sprawling on the couch, but she was a fake; she wasn't playing by the rules. Only she had to be careful to keep her greasy chin makeup from rubbing on her nightgown.

She caught Peter on his cell phone dodging traffic as he zipped down the freeway in his tiny Volkswagen Golf. He was running late, *bleep, bleep, bleeeeping* his horn at anyone who dared get in his way while trying to make it downtown to an on-site location. The crew had fallen behind in their shooting schedule, *again,* and the director had everyone working over the weekend, *again,* to catch up. Peter was frantic. They were waiting for makeup before they could start; the director was known for his temper, and for throwing those who angered him off the set. Peter couldn't bear such humiliation. The conversation was brief. He huffed and puffed through the rush and, while resigning himself to the unwelcome obligation, left just enough uncertainty to keep Laurie hanging. "Yes, yes, of course I'll do it, but I don't know how soon I can be there, earliest is two but it could be late as four. Things never seem to go right when you're shooting off the lot."

Laurie puckered her lips as she put down the phone. It was a less than perfect solution. She didn't like asking favors. She didn't like owing anyone, and especially not someone like Peter, but that was unfair. Besides, she already owed Peter, whether she liked it or not.

She looked up, realizing her chest was pounding. The room was becoming claustrophobic. She wanted to leave, but she was trapped. She would have to lay low until Peter found time to do her face. Last night she had decided to remove her mask so she could get a good night's sleep, but putting it back on hadn't been as easy as Peter made it look. She'd done her best, playing with the putty until her fingers were tired and brown. She might be able to fool someone with failing eyesight, but she'd never pass the inspection of those with 20/20 vision. All the more reason to make this her last day. She couldn't do her own makeup, and she didn't like calling on Peter. It was time to leave.

It was a shame, really; the story had the potential of being the kind of front page scoop every reporter dreamed of writing, but it hadn't panned out. She'd spent the entire evening interviewing as many residents as she could, but instead of sensing fear and paranoia, she'd found the group to be reasonably content, with the possible exception of the curmudgeons who complained about everything from the tasteless food to the smell of bleach in the bathrooms. She couldn't have been more clear. She'd alluded to, hinted at, implied, suggested and insinuated. She'd done everything but out and out ask if people seemed to be dying for no apparent reason. One steely-eyed woman had finally looked her in the eye and said: "We're all going to die sooner or later, dearie. That's what we're here for." She had come up with zip.

Even the letter had been a disappointment. She reached back over her head, her fingers exploring the lamp-table until they found the piece of paper. The letter was difficult to read. The words, which lacked any semblance of articulation, were swollen because apparently the ink had blotted up sweat while riding around in the man's hip pocket. She read it again, wishing there was more. It was possible the man in the green T-shirt—yes, okay, right, she should call him Bonner now that she knew his name—really believed his life was in danger. But it was also possible he was suffering from some kind of dementia.

She had watched Bonner's overly assertive escort dragging him down the hall by his arm, but before they disappeared, Bonner managed to hook a finger into his back pocket and jettison the envelope. Laurie had kept her distance. She'd waited until they were out of sight before retrieving the discarded letter. Then she'd retired to her own quarters to examine what the old man had so blatantly disposed of.

The envelope was standard letter-size, folded in half, scuffed and wrinkled, and had a faded Emerald Valley logo in the upper left corner. It was addressed, stamped and ready to be mailed. But it was the name on the envelope that made her want to rip it open; it was addressed to Mr. William Best, care of his Detroit office. She debated the legality for only a second. As far as she knew, the law against mail tampering applied only to letters that had been posted. These stamps had not been cancelled. And none of that mattered anyway because she realized she was still legally Bill's wife, ostensibly one flesh, and had a right to read his mail. She tore into the envelope and flicked the folded letter open, scanning the page, laboring through multiple misspellings, poor punctuation and bad grammar magnified by terrible penmanship, only to find the man had nothing to say. She was able to discern that the writer expected the letter to be found after his death and hoped that with postage already affixed, it would be mailed posthumously. Other than that, it merely requested that Mr. Best add his name to the list of deaths that needed looking into. What the letter did not do was offer any reason why Bill would want to look into Bonner's, or anyone else's, death in the first place. It did not explain who was doing what to whom, or why.

But at least it had helped her make up her mind, which was why she was now preparing to leave. If something criminal had happened to one of Bonner's friends, there would have been names, and dates, and places given. She needed the five W's and an H: the who, what, where, when, why and how of journalism. If Bonner didn't provide such details, she could only conclude they didn't exist. His letter didn't try to prove that things had somehow run amok because...well, because it would be hard to prove what was actually a figment of his imagination. She hated the thought, but it was becoming clear that Howard had been right. You can't write a story without something to base it on. The hearsay of a bunch of old folks, who for all she knew were senile, didn't cut it. They wouldn't be the first to wrongfully believe someone was out to get them.

It appeared Bill had sent her on a wild goose chase. Had it been anyone else, she would have asked more questions before accepting such and assignment. She didn't have time for following bad leads. That was the irony. She trusted Bill. They might not agree on much, but she knew he wouldn't say anything, unless he believed it to be the absolute truth. But this time he'd been wrong. She should have seen the flaw in his logic sooner. He'd said he couldn't understand how six people could all suffer from the same delusion, but he hadn't thought it through. It happened all the time. What about the disciples of Jim Jones, hundreds of them, who stood in line to sip the hemlock cup because they believed Messiah Jimmy was taking them to the promised land, or David Koresh and company who doused their homestead in gas because they thought it better to burn on the inside together than die on the outside alone, or the Manson maniacs who went on a killing spree to start a war between blacks and whites so they, as survivors, could rule the world, or the followers of Father John who thought boarding an alien spacecraft, cloaked in the tail of Hale-Bopp the comet, was to die for? She could name a half dozen cultic brotherhoods that had suffered mass delusions.

If Bonner, the little bird woman, and the rest of their gang, were being singled out for special treatment, it was to be expected. They were out of control. Who knew how many letters they'd written? They had written the chief of police, and they had written Bill, why not the mayor, or their congressman or their senator, why not the army, or the National Guard for that matter? They were convinced, at least in their own minds, that their lives were in danger. They had lots of time, and probably nothing better to do. They could write hundreds of letters.

You had to have sympathy for an organization with a problem like that. It was a no-win situation. If they simply ignored the group's accusations, more letters would be mailed. The retirement home would find itself under constant investigation from one branch of the government or another. But if they tried to squelch the rumors it would be regarded as an attempt to muzzle their accusers, which would tend to confirm the allegations.

No wonder they had been so adamant about preventing newspaper coverage. The suggestion that something was amiss could ruin their reputation. It didn't matter if, after the fact, the accusations proved false. Just the inference would be enough to keep people away. Laurie hadn't seen or heard a single thing that supported the claims made in the letter. She had no desire to hurt an innocent party, especially since her meddling could get her fired. It was a sacrifice she would gladly make for the right cause, but this little fiasco seemed all for naught.

She kicked her feet off the arm of the couch and spun around. She needed caffeine. In the cupboard she found five flavors of tea and three different blends of coffee: Colombian, Irish Cream and Swiss Mocha. Laurie chose the Irish Cream. She poured the blend into the filter and plopped it into the plastic drawer of the coffee maker. She found a water purifier on the tap, suggesting the water was purged of impurities. It was too bad they couldn't do the same with the minds of their guests. Unpolluted water did make great coffee. She might as well enjoy it; she had to be there all day. The coffee maker began to gurgle and spurt as the room filled with the aroma of her favorite morning brew.

She had to compliment the senior's home on its stock of amenities. Of course, they wanted her to feel especially welcome. It was all part of a sales strategy designed to demonstrate how well she would be taken care of. If she were the age she was pretending to be, she just might be persuaded. The tea cup, chattering lightly on its saucer, appeared to be fine bone china. Putting something so fragile into the hands of shaky residents showed a willingness to assume risk for the sake of making guests feel special. She could appreciate the gesture. She tried to admire the floral design and translucent quality of the delicate, hand painted porcelain. It was certain to please most of the little old ladies she knew but, as for herself, she would rather have had her own ceramic mug, the one that said: "A woman has to be twice as good as a man, to be thought half as good." Barring that, she would settle for a copy of the morning paper.

Her heart stopped. She glanced up. Someone was pounding on her door.

Laurie considered not answering, but then she remembered the staff had keys and would probably let themselves in if they thought she wasn't home. She'd done a so-so job on her makeup, not perfect but passable, as long as she kept her head down. At least her wig was on straight. If she came to the door in her robe, pretending to have just climbed out of bed, maybe they would leave her alone. Her robe was in the closet. She pulled it off its hanger, flung it around her shoulders, tied the belt, and stepped into the bathroom. Her chest was thumping excessively. She glanced at herself in the mirror. *Yuck! Keep your head bowed. Avoid eye contact.* The pounding grew louder. She scurried through the living room polishing her lines, but paused to look out the peephole before opening the door. It was the man in the baseball cap...*Bonner?* Standing in the hall right outside, bold as a front page headline, was the man she had looked for all day yesterday—the man who had drafted another letter to Bill claiming his life was in danger. But of course he looked in perfect health. He'd lived to see another day. *What does he want?*

"Yes, what is it?" Laurie asked, trying to keep a tremor in her voice while opening the door a crack. She was careful to keep her head back out of sight.

"Sorry to have to bother you. I uh, I was wondering if I could use your phone?"

Laurie edged the door open. Bonner stood there in the same "Gone Fishing" baseball cap, the same green T-shirt, and the same slippers. He could have been a photograph of himself taken the day before.

"May I?" he asked, lifting one hand to suggest he would like to enter. The hand was crisscrossed with bulging veins and dotted with white bone bumps. He teetered back and forth placing his weight on one foot then, the other. His pants were buckled under the roll of his stomach and looked like they might drop down around his ankles at any moment.

Laurie took a step back allowing him to enter. What did it matter if he saw through her disguise? He was one of those she had supposedly come to help, though now that she'd decided to abandon the cause she wasn't sure she wanted to hear his side of the story.

Mr. Bonner entered, and she closed the door behind him. Laurie stood back and waited; he had knocked on her door, not the other way around. He turned and faced her, his jaw pumping up and down like the pistons of an engine idling in neutral. It seemed the key to his mind had been turned, but he was having a hard time getting his words in gear. "I hate to ask," he finally said, "but I couldn't help noticing you yesterday. Maybe you saw me too. I was being showed to my room, just down the hall. I dropped something, I thought maybe you found it." He stood there waiting, ball in Laurie's court.

Well he hadn't come to use the phone, no surprise there, and he wasn't shy about asking for the letter, which it was obvious he had come for. She went to retrieve it from the couch. "You mean this?" She held the single page out, waving it like a limp handkerchief.

He shuffled his feet with the embarrassed look of a boy caught stealing cookies. "I, uh, I thank you. I mean for returning it, but it wasn't exactly addressed to you," he said referring to the fact that the letter had been opened.

Laurie pointed to an empty chair. "Sit down, Mr. Bonner. Please," she said, slipping into her natural voice.

He blinked once, slowly, his gray eyes staring out of their caves, two gray boulders set in place at the beginning of time. Laurie began to think he hadn't understood, but then he turned and shuffled across the room to find a seat.

Might as well get into it. "Actually, Mr. Bonner, in a roundabout way, it was addressed to me. Bill Best and I are partners," she announced, hoping she could avoid having to explain the marital connection. "He works in the east and I cover stories in the west. I assume you know your friend Ben is dead?" She looked for a sign of recognition. Bonner's mouth opened and then closed. He blinked as though thinking about what she had just revealed, but said nothing. Finally, after considering her words for what seemed like an eternity, he nodded, giving her the go-ahead to continue.

"Well, before he died, Mr. Riggs was able to get in touch with Bill. Your idea for a story got his attention and, because I was already out here, he asked me to look into it." Laurie saw the look of confusion on Bonner's face. "I'm not a guest, Mr. Bonner. I'm a reporter."

For a moment, the gray stones looked crushed, then Joe widened his gaze with an intensity that made his eyes bulge from their sockets. He started to get up, then sat back down. His jaw was pumping iron. "You aren't one of us?"

"No, I'm not."

The fixed stare continued, but the eyelids narrowed to squint. "But you'd be, what, 'bout my age, right?"

Now there was a compliment to Peter's masterful art, and to her own reproduction. While she was worried her disguise had become transparent, it was obvious Joe was having trouble seeing through it. "No, this is all a mask," she said, pointing a finger at her face.

Joe's head shook in disbelief; his baseball cap jutted side-to-side like a pitcher shaking off a signal. "Ya don't say?"

"I do say. It's all Hollywood makeup."

"We'll I'll be!"

"Look, Mr. Bonner, what's going on around here? I gather you have an axe to grind. You made some very serious accusations in the letter you wrote, but you failed to offer any proof. I've talked to a number of people, and it seems no one else knows about the problem. To be honest, I'm inclined to believe there's no story here. In fact, that's what I plan to tell Bill, unless you can convince me otherwise."

The old man waited, both hands extended on the arms of the chair, his knuckles camped over the padded ends like a dime-store copy of the Lincoln memorial. He crossed one slippered foot over his knee, continued to chew his cud and waited as though deciding whether or not he could trust the person to whom he was speaking. "You're asking me to tell you things that could put you in danger," he finally said.

Oh boy, Laurie thought, *here we go with the everybody's out to get me routine.* "I'll take that chance," she quipped.

Joe paused for another few seconds, contemplating heaven knew what. He finally opened his mouth, but even then he stalled a moment before starting to speak. "Did you know that when you buy a place here, you have to sign a legal document that says they can gas you if they want?"

Laurie didn't answer, mainly because it sounded so ridiculous, but also because she hadn't signed any documents. She had nothing upon which to base a rebuttal.

"It's true. You decide you want to stay here, get your lifetime's worth of care, you better have your lawyer read the agreement, because you could be signing your death warrant. Of course it's supposed to be your decision. You're supposed to be ready to die and all, and you're supposed to be sick, but it doesn't always work that way. I've lost a couple of friends already, good men too, but you'll never convince me they chose to die. They were killed, plain and simple. They was led like sheep to the slaughter.

"Anyway, that letter you got there wasn't supposed to be opened until after my death, which I thought was gonna be last night. I was thinking they were going to come and get me, but I guess they chickened out." Joe leaned in and dropped his voice to a conspiratorial whisper. "They can't take us all at once. Too many deaths would raise questions, especially if it's the same six, well now five of us, that opened this can o' worms in the first place."

"You say there's five of you left. That's because Ben's gone, isn't it? Let's talk about Ben for a minute. Bill told me how he thought Ben was killed, but how do you think it happened?"

Joe looked puzzled, then his jaw began to pump and his face brightened. "Aw, so you heard. You were there. Pay no attention to that. She was just spouting off. She didn't have time to think. They couldn't have known what Ben was up to. We made sure not to tell anyone. I smuggled him out in the middle of the night and put him on the plane myself, and I was back before anyone knew I was even gone. He wasn't followed, and neither was I. He just ran into some bad luck is all. But he was my friend, and he gave his life to get that message to Mr. Best. That should tell you something about the serious nature of what I'm saying."

Good for you. Laurie was relieved to find Joe didn't accept the little bird woman's account of what had happened to Ben. Maybe they weren't all crazy.

"I only hope the others are all right," Joe continued. "They may have taken someone last night, but I don't think so. If one of us disappears, the others will raise such a stink they'll have to investigate, and they can't afford that. Of course, by keeping us apart, someone could be taken and the others wouldn't know." He stopped to rub the bristles of his jaw. "That may be what they're thinking. I don't rightly know. But I do know it's a lot smarter on their part if they keep us alive, because as long as they can show we're alive and well, all our fuming about them being killers, makes us look like a bunch a silly old fools. Besides, as long as we're alive, they're making money off us. Not like Henry and Leonard. They won't get any more of my money, not if they do me in."

"Hold on, back it up a bit. Are you suggesting that the guests here are being killed for money?" *It would establish motive, but...naw, no way.* "I don't buy it. I'll concede the possibility that the wrongful deaths, and I'm not even saying there are any, but if there are, that the real crime might be malpractice, where a person is given the wrong prescription, or wrong treatment, or a wrong diagnosis, or something like that, but not murder."

Joe reared his head back and began to laugh. His hands still gripped the arms of the chair. His lips peeled back exposing brown teeth. He laughed so hard his eyes began to water. "Whooeeee, now there's a rib-tickler. It's the exact opposite of malpractice. They knew exactly what they were doing. They took Henry and Leonard and executed 'em is what they did. It's all about money."

Laurie tapped her pencil on the palm of her hand. "That's a very inflammatory accusation. You have proof to back it up, or is this just your opinion?"

"Proof? What kind of proof you want? You got my word on it? There isn't any other proof. These guys aren't stupid. They aren't going to leave evidence laying around that says they've been killing people. But you don't need a snake to bite ya, to know it's a snake..."

They were interrupted by a knock at the door. *Now who...?*

"Should I answer that?" Laurie asked, wondering if her makeup was still holding.

Joe's head nodded yes, but his eyes scanned the room as though looking for a place to hide.

Laurie opened the door looking down and away to avoid detection. "Excuse me. You must be Annie. I'm Dr. VanEtter. I'm looking for Joe Bonner, someone said they thought he might be here." The voice was soft spoken and kind, almost apologetic. The man wore an official looking white smock, and had his arms wrapped around a clipboard he held at his waist. His shoes were shined so bright, Laurie could see her bathrobe reflected in their mirrored surface. She took a step back to let the doctor enter.

"Ah there you are, Joe. Did you forget our ten o'clock appointment? Come along now, you know how hard it is to schedule these sessions. It's important you continue your therapy."

Joe struggled to remove himself from the chair. He didn't say anything as he stood and faced the doctor. His slippers began to scoot slowly across the carpet in the direction of the door. Laurie saw that his Adam's apple hung from his throat like a goat's bell and his cheeks stuck out like cuds of chewed grass. But it was the change in his demeanor she noticed most. Where a moment ago his face seemed flush and animated, the texture of his skin now held an ashen pallor, and the eyes that seconds before were cognizant and alert, now wore a creamy white shroud. You'd think it was the grim reaper calling, like his spirit was heeding the summons of the last trump. His body stumbled forward like it was being beckoned—by the angel of death!

EIGHT

My dad says I'm brave. He says it takes courage to put up with so much pain, but it's not really true. I hurt, and things don't work the way they should, but when you wake up to the same thing every day, you get used to it. It's more like a nuisance than anything else. People on the outside see you and they see pain, but on the inside, since you've lived with it all your life, you just deal with it. It's not like you ignore the pain, it's just that it becomes so familiar, you don't feel it anymore. It's not fair to say I'm brave just because I endure pain. The truth is, I get scared a lot, and this was one of those times.

I became nervous when those black clouds started rolling in. It seemed they were rushing in to bury us (so much for being brave). It wasn't the rain that bothered me, I can handle rain, it was the lightning and thunder. I could see it crashing to the ground, exploding, and feel the crack and boom as it shook the earth. And this wasn't rain, this was someone holding a fire-hose against the windshield of the car. I tried to stay calm. My seat belt and pillow were holding me in place, but I was afraid. All I could do was sit there and watch. I began to wonder how T.J. was doing. He didn't like getting wet. And, like I said, this wasn't a gentle rain, this was a flood, and it was making my limbs start to jumble.

THE RAIN pummeled the car in heavy torrents. One lone windshield wiper worked at pushing it away, but it was as futile as trying to sweep back Niagara Falls with a broom. Bill stared at the liquid wall, expecting to see an ark float by; surely this was the second visitation of Noah. Angie was blind. The windshield-wiper on her side didn't work, another malfunction the car's previous owner failed to mention, but Bill was not deterred. In spite of the fact that others were pulling over to the side to wait out the onslaught, in spite of the fact that he occasionally felt his car hydroplane through deep troughs of water, in spite of the fact that he'd heard the gas station radio announce a severe storm warning, Bill kept pushing on. He had to reduce his speed. It was slowing him down, but he was determined to make the eastern border of South Dakota by nightfall. The storm was traveling east. He was heading west. If nothing else he would eventually break through the other side, and the further he drove the sooner that would be. They would spend the night in Sioux Falls, come hell or high water. The latter seemed more likely.

The car's one wiper continued to beat a cadence like a drumstick tapping out a staccato rhythm on the tightly stretched skin of clouds, *waflap, waflap, waflap.* Bill pulled his shoulder harness away from his chest and felt instant relief. The strap had been resting on the spot where he'd been bruised during the accident and the throbbing was pounding his chest like a fist. He felt like he'd had the wind knocked out of him. He eased the constraining belt, letting it settle in its original place but felt an immediate swell of pressure again. It was too much. He reached over his shoulder, tugging the harness as he brought it around his head so it would sit behind his back, easing the tension. It wasn't optimum safety, but the lap belt was still in place, and the strain was off his chest. He felt like taking a deep breath but his lungs were too fragile. Slow and easy, that's how he had to breathe, slow and easy, one conscious breath at a time.

At least they were making progress. He could handle the minor inconveniences, like the passenger side windshield wiper not working, though it restricted his vision, and he could do without a radio, except for the missing weather reports. Did the weather pattern extend across the prairies, or was this an isolated storm? Were they under a two-hour thundershower, or swamped by a three-day deluge? He had little faith in weather forecasts anyway, they were seldom reliable, but considering the intensity of the rain it would have been nice to know if they'd posted a flood warning. *Please God, let us make Sioux Falls.*

The sky flashed, lights blinking on and off the way a camera's strobe shatters the darkness of a room. The forks stabbed the ground.

Sonic booms shook the electrified atmosphere and the water continued to pour as though from a bucket. A bitter storm. Giving credit where it was due, one thing Bill had to admit was that in spite of its obvious shortcomings, the old station wagon kept plowing forward. A constant wall of water sliced away from the wheels like a thin veil shooting from the tread of a water ski. Bill looked at his watch. It was getting late, and they still had at least a hundred miles to cover.

Plenty of time to ponder the ravages of the storm; he needed to get his mind around his column. It had to be written while they were on the road and the more he organized his thoughts ahead of time, the easier it would be.

He'd toyed with a number of topics but the one that kept coming back was the idea of writing about the plight of old people. If he used the right slant, addressing their fears and concerns (whether real or imagined), he could use it as a lead for the article he expected to receive from Laurie. The problem was, every time he started thinking about what to write, his mind made the crossover to Laurie and to how he would position his article around hers. And then to thoughts about Laurie herself. And then to whether or not there was any hope they might get back together. But then he would look at Angie and realize what he had realized a thousand times before: there was no hope.

He would do it all again if he had to: give up one for the sake of the other, give up a part of himself, his passion for Laurie, if, in so doing, it meant that another human being would have a chance to live. But such thoughts only added guilt to an already burdensome load of confusion. After ten years, he was still trying to come to grips with his failing. If he'd shown just the slightest bit of compassion, he might have saved the marriage. He should have listened. He might not have agreed with what she had to say, but that wasn't the point. The point was, she had concerns, valid concerns, at least from her perspective, and he'd ignored them. He'd called his wife cold-blooded and hard-hearted—his wife—the one he'd betrothed and wed, the love of his life until death do them part. Words said in frustration and anger had a way of cutting to the bone. He'd even accused her of favoring eugenics. Bill found himself grinding his teeth. He tried to relax his jaw.

He looked over at Angie. Her little body was prickled with tension. It would be a long night; she would have trouble getting to sleep. He wondered what was going on in her mind. Was he doing the right thing making her endure the pressure of this long trip? It seemed like a good idea at the time, but now? Another bolt blew across the sky lighting the night with fire...*the Second Coming?*...but it flashed and popped like a bulb with a broken filament, leaving the world in darkness again. A sign flew past the rain-streaked window with its letters out of focus. It appeared to say that Sioux Falls was another hundred and twenty-three miles. No use worrying about it, they couldn't turn back now.

"THERE YOU GO, good as new, or good as old, since that's what you want." Peter smiled, patted Laurie's hair and picked up a mirror so she could see the back of her head. "You didn't look so bad. A little touch-up here and there was all you needed. You'll be able to do it yourself next time. You were paying attention to the bump and tuck procedure weren't you?"

Laurie turned her head to the left and to the right inspecting Peter's work. Technique was everything. "Nope, didn't pay any attention at all. This is a work of art, Peter, but you're the artist, not me. I could never do this, but it doesn't matter, I've decided to hitch a ride with you when you leave. I don't need to learn how you do what you do; I just have to keep up appearances till I check out, and that will only take a few minutes."

"Seems a shame. I thought you were here for a big scoop, a real undercover assignment. I thought you wanted to nail some bad guys."

Laurie walked over and retrieved her sweater from the couch. "I did," she said, "but it's too risky and frankly, I don't see enough story here." She pushed her arms through the sleeves, straightened her cuffs, and buttoned the collar around her neck. "I mean, if I thought I could make myself look like this and could keep everyone fooled, I'd probably stay. But I have to face facts, the only ones I can dupe are the ones so old they're half blind, and they're not the ones I need to fool." She paused to flip the hair of her wig over her collar and fluff it around her ears. Now the hard part would begin, the grueling walk in bent-over slow motion. At least she could stand straight for another few moments. She went to the bathroom to check herself in the mirror. "I know it sounds fickle," she continued. "There's a part of me that says I shouldn't leave. I've just started making contacts." She leaned in toward the glass and tugged at the globe of fake hair, making sure it held firmly in place. Her words echoed off the bathroom wall, sounding hollow. "One gentleman, the man I told you about, the one with the baseball cap, he said he knows exactly what's going on but he doesn't have any proof. I don't know whether to believe him or not, but I do know I need some kind of proof to write the story. And I can't go digging up the evidence myself unless my costume is perfect and for that, I'd have to have you here so you could patch me up all the time. Since that doesn't make sense, my only recourse is to leave."

Peter raised his voice a notch so he could be heard. "I think you're selling yourself short," he said. "If I didn't know who you were when I walked in, I would have been fooled."

Laurie returned to the living room, fluffing the sides of her nylon gray hair. "Thanks Peter, but that's not how I saw it. Now be a good boy and make yourself at home until I get back. You know where the teapot is. Make yourself comfortable, listen to the radio or watch TV; I'll only be a few minutes."

"All right, but don't be long. I have a date tonight. I want to be home in time to fix something special. Oh, mind if I use your phone?"

Laurie supposed Peter was alluding to Tina, his latest heartthrob. It was hard keeping track. He went through lovers like water through a sieve. "Go ahead. Dial nine for a line out. See you in a few minutes." Then she slipped out the door looking to all the world like an eighty-year-old grandma with arthritic feet.

She leaned on her cane, making her way across the court, *thunk, pull forward, pause, thunk.* She kept an eye out for Bonner, but either he had turned invisible, or he had gone underground, or...??? She refused to even consider that possibility. No sense in becoming paranoid. He could be anywhere. Still, not seeing him made her feel uneasy. He was probably resting in his room, or playing a round of golf, though he didn't look like the type that played golf, but what does a golfer look like anyway? Maybe he was out taking a walk. Whatever? There was no reason to be concerned.

She saw two of the others. The little bird lady stood outside the dining hall with a tray in her hand. She was definitely one of those who signed the letter. Was she Mrs. Woodhouse or Mrs. Wheatly? She looked like a Woodhouse, but she also looked like a Wheatly. She could be either one. Didn't matter, whoever she was, she had made the mistake of assuming her friend Ben had been killed on purpose. Not a rational mind, best left alone. The other member of the team was the enormous, carrot-topped fellow. Until she learned his name, she decided to call him "Big Boy." Presumably, he was either Mr. Williams or Mr. Wiarton. Interesting, Woodhouse, Wheatly, Williams and Wiarton, their names all started with "W." Maybe having a name that began with W made you crazy. Maybe it was something in the Water. Nice theory, but it didn't account for Bonner and Riggs.

Big Boy sat on a folding chair, his massive size overflowing the seat. He seemed absorbed in the flat two-dimensional life of the television. The room buzzed and tittered with conversation. It seemed anyone who knew someone was talking to somebody. But Bird Lady and Big Boy weren't joining in. Laurie understood Joe to say they weren't allowed to talk to each other. Were they being isolated from the rest of the guests as well? No, the extreme elders, the ones confined to wheelchairs along the wall, they didn't talk to anyone. It was a self-imposed isolation, an isolation of choice. Bird Lady and Big Boy probably weren't in the mood for chitchat. That's what their faces said. They both wore the same peculiar look Bonner had on when he was escorted from her apartment. Where was Bonner anyway?

The door to the sales office was open. Laurie leaned in and saw Barbara seated behind her meticulous desk, her image duplicated on the polished surface. She was clad in a new outfit, this one a blazing polyester that shimmered like blue silk under the fluorescent lights. A white, mohair turtleneck covered the loose baggage under her chin.

Laurie tapped lightly on the doorframe, careful not to scrape the paint off her knuckles.

Barbara put down her pencil and waved Laurie inside, flicking her hands as though hailing a cab. "Annie, come in, come in, I've been expecting you."

Expecting me? "Could I see you for a moment?" Laurie asked. She put a frail tremor in her voice as she leaned on her cane and took a hesitant step forward.

"Of course, my door is always open to our guests. Please, sit down, make yourself comfortable. Can I get you anything, tea, coffee, what would you like?"

Laurie sat in the chair offered. "Nothing, thank you. I'm fine."

"Then, what can I do for you?"

Laurie faltered for a minute looking anxious. "I'm sorry, but I'm afraid I have bad news." She paused to clear her throat. It was hard putting on a fake voice, let alone sustaining it over a period of time. She coughed lightly, hoping the conversation would be short. "I've decided not to stay," she said. "I'll be making other arrangements. I just wanted to stop by and thank you for your hospitality."

Mrs. Marks leaned back collecting her thoughts. The chair squeaked as she extended a long, blue-clad arm over the desk so her lavender nails could tap on the mirror of wood. Her smile stretched into a taut line. "I can't say I'm surprised. Not after Dr. VanEtter told me he found Mr. Bonner in your room this morning," she said. Then she recovered her professional self-control and tilted forward, lacing her fingers together in a prayerful pose. The frost in her throat melted as she took on an air of best friend and confidant. "Annie, I wish I could have warned you about Mr. Bonner, but my hands were tied. You have to understand. We make it a policy not to talk about our guests behind their backs. In this case, however, I need to make an exception. Mr. Bonner isn't well, Annie. He suffers from acute depression. We've tried to help, but about all we can do is keep him sedated so he stays calm. Unfortunately, sometimes he refuses his medication and, well, frankly, he becomes irrational. We have to keep him under constant supervision which is why Dr. VanEtter came by your apartment to make sure he wasn't bothering you. I assure you it won't happen again. Is there any way I can convince you to change your mind? You've only been here one night. That can't be enough time to have experienced all the benefits we offer."

Depressed...irrational? Un-uh. How 'bout lucid? At least until doctor Faust, whatever his name was, came around. Something didn't add up. No doubt there was a file somewhere, complete with diagnosis and treatment, attesting to the fact that Joe suffered severe emotional problems. He was, after all, under the doctor's care, but something didn't feel right. She had always thrived on gut instinct; that's how good stories were written, and in this case her gut told her something was wrong.

"Annie?" Barbara tried to pull Laurie from her thoughts. "Annie, we strive to make all our guests feel secure and happy. I apologize for any problem Mr. Bonner may have caused, but I assure you, he's been taken care of. He won't trouble you again. That's a promise. Your visit got off on the wrong foot. How about we start over? Let us have the opportunity to make it right. I know you're going to like it here."

The twinkle in Barbara's eye could have melted ice. Her smile broadcast: *I'm your friend Annie, trust me.* But Laurie didn't. She wasn't the simple old fool she was pretending to be. She could see Barbara wore an even bigger mask than the one she wore herself. The whole scene, everything about it, from Barbara's glib analysis of Joe's mental health, right up to her promise that Joe had somehow been dealt with, festered in her gut. She was forced to admit it. She was running from a good story because she feared what might happen if she were caught. Engraved on a plaque over her desk hung the words: "There is nothing hidden, that shall not be revealed." It had been a graduation present from Bill and served to remind her of why she chose to become an investigative reporter. The emphasis was on, "investigative." Risk was part of the package.

"I'm sorry. I'm not sure I understand. I did let that man use my phone this morning. I think he wanted to call his friends, but they were having problems because he couldn't get through. He was about to leave when that nice Dr. VanEtter came by. Anyway, my leaving has nothing to do with that fellow. I just wasn't happy with the dinner they served last night. It had too much salt. I'm on a low salt diet, you see. Salt is like poison. I can't have food like that; the doctor says it'll kill me. No, I can't stay where they serve salty food."

Barbara smiled. "Well why didn't you say so? You have to tell us your dietary preferences. I don't recall seeing a salt restriction on your application. We cook our meals to comply with the needs of each individual. Some of our guests are diabetic and can't have sugar, some have to watch their cholesterol, others, like yourself, can't have salt. All you have to do is let us know; we do the rest. Tell you what, I'll go talk to the chef right now and see if we can get this straightened out. Please say you'll stay. Give us a chance and we'll prove we can please even the most finicky appetite. Will you do that for me?"

Laurie folded her hands in her lap and nodded demurely. She felt a wave of nervous anticipation wash over her, a rapid pulsating behind the eyes and throbbing around the temples. What was she getting herself into? She feared she would soon find out. Talk about sacrifice, she loved salt—*why, why, why,* had that excuse come to mind? The idea of eating bland, saltless food was a curse. And how would she ever convince Peter to come back in the morning to do her makeup?

LAURIE WAS making her way through the community center hoping to spot Joe. She needed to know he was okay. She paced each footstep leaning on her cane, *thunk, pull forward, pause, thunk,* which gave her time to observe the room and its surroundings, but bending over was putting a kink in her back. She wanted to stand erect, whirl the cane around her head and let it fly. She wanted to take off on a mad dash to her room, throw herself on her bed and await the judgement that would follow (old ladies can't run willy-nilly through a rest home without some kind of retribution), but she knew it would have to wait. Some other time perhaps, but not today.

Joe was nowhere to be seen, and Bird Lady had disappeared, probably into the dining hall to eat. Across the room she could see the orange dome of Big Boy still watching television. Bird Lady had accused Emerald Valley of killing Ben Riggs, she had to be one of those who signed the letter, but Big Boy? He was still an unknown. Laurie couldn't risk revealing herself to someone unless she knew where they stood.

So where was Joe? Now that Laurie had decided to stay another night, time was of the essence. She needed an introduction to the others, something she hoped Joe would provide. Where was he? What had Barbara meant when she'd said: "He's been taken care of?" If Joe's visit had resulted in the very thing he feared most, then, Laurie realized, by entertaining him she might have contributed to his death...*oh stop it! Keep your mind focused on facts. Your job is to report the news, not invent it.*

What was Barbara's role in all this? She had said Joe was irrational. Laurie knew little of mental illness, but the label didn't fit. And Barbara's little speech was too...what?...too pat, too quick to have it all figured out, who was doing what to whom; it was too well-rehearsed and too defensive. Like she said, they had a policy against talking about their guests. She should have stuck to it. Barbara was the one acting paranoid.

Laurie was so busy checking out the main lobby, the scene down the hall had escaped her notice. As she awoke from her thoughts, it dawned on her what she was seeing. They were emptying Joe's apartment, the new one, the one they had just moved him into. Men in blue coveralls were carrying chairs, coffee-tables and miscellaneous boxes down the hall through a propped-open door where they were being loaded into a waiting van. Laurie's heartbeat quickened; she could feel the prickle of goosebumps rising on her arms; her shoulders ached. "Where are you taking those?" she demanded. She stood in the door blocking the exit of a man with two boxes balanced under his chin.

The worker stopped. "Stuff's going into storage, ma'am," he said.

"Why? Where's Mr. Bonner? Those things are his. They don't belong to you."

"Beats me. I was just told to load the truck."

Laurie was determined to not jump to the wrong conclusion. She had seen Bird Lady do that about the death of Ben Riggs. As a reporter, she knew there was always another side to the story. There was probably a very reasonable explanation for moving Joe's things twice in only two days. It could be anything. It could be...

"YOU'RE NOT going to believe this," she said, bursting through the door of her apartment. "They killed Joe, that old man I told you about, they killed him because he was talking to me. Peter? Peter, are you all right?"

Peter sat on the sofa, wringing his hands. His face was ashen. His eyes looked puffy and red staring off into space. "I...I'm being dumped again," he said. "Tina wants to end our relationship."

Laurie turned to close the door. She did not want Peter to be seen or heard.

He continued: "What about me? What about my feelings? Don't I mean anything? Do you have any tranquilizers? I'm a mess. How about something to drink. Do they allow liquor in here? I need something."

Laurie slumped against the wall. *Not another crisis, not now.* She laid her cane aside and padded over to the couch to sit beside her friend. "I don't blame you for being hurt," she said. "That was cruel. She should have had more consideration for your feelings. At the very least, she should have told you in person. That's not the kind of thing you tell someone over the phone. You must have shared a lot of good times together. At least she should have thanked you for that."

Laurie tried to slip a consoling arm around Peter's shoulder but he threw it off. "Is that all you think it was, kicks, a fling, a...a...a ribald romance. I love Tina. You can't understand that can you? Of course not. You've never loved anyone. You don't have feelings, you...you...oh...I don't mean that...I'm sorry, I...I...It's not your fault. It's just that...she didn't have to be so cruel, did she?"

Peter was close to tears. Laurie took his head and pulled it into to her shoulder. The sobs came in reckless gulps, air bursting like balloons on strings of saliva. She rocked the man, holding him like a child with a hurt. She had taken no offense. He was right...well sort of. It wasn't that she couldn't love. She just hadn't met the right man. She hugged Peter's shoulder. "It's okay. Go ahead and let it out. That's okay."

It took a few minutes but Peter finally rose from the couch coughing. He went to the sink for a glass of water. Another rejection, you'd think he'd be used to it, having gone through it so many times.

The minute a girl showed interest, he was all over them with cards, and flowers, and middle-of-the-night phone calls. He pushed so hard, he drove them away.

Peter started to drink but poured too fast and inadvertently sucked water down his windpipe. His shoulders rolled forward, folding in on each other as he placed a hand on his chest and heaved and choked and coughed until his face was flushed and his lungs were raw.

Laurie started to get up, "You okay?" but he cupped a fist over his mouth and waved her off. She settled onto the couch again. She liked Peter. In his own sweet way, he was handsome. But it was this very soft side that also repulsed her. Inside she tried to deny feeling queasy when he got too close. In her line of work, tolerance was vital to success—unless your name happened to be Bill! That was the exception. He was the only man she had ever known to make intolerance work, and that was because he was so uncompromising he earned people's respect even when they disagreed. But that too, made her angry. To see him strutting around like a pompous brat with that square look in his eye that said, "there's only one right, doesn't matter what anyone else thinks," was infuriating. She needed someone more sensitive, someone like Peter, only strong.

Peter returned and took a seat on the chair opposite the couch where Laurie was sitting. He folded and unfolded his hands, rubbing his palms together. He looked away, refusing to make eye contact, the moisture still shining on his face. "I'm sorry Laurie, I behaved badly," he said, wiping his flushed cheeks with a sleeve. "You started to say something when you came in. What was it you wanted?"

"That's okay, Peter, we all have our moments. Ending a relationship is hard. Anyway, I was just saying I've decided to stay another night. I know, I know, the lady can't make up her mind, but it's not like that. Something's happened. I don't know for sure, but the man I spoke to, the one with the baseball cap, he might be dead; I mean he could be dead, I don't know; I just know he told me they were going to kill him. Of course I didn't believe it, but you should have seen the look on his face when he left here. You knew he was in serious trouble. And now the sales lady tells me he's been taken care of, and I find them emptying his apartment; I just don't know what to think, but I can't leave until I find out. I need to know what's going on. I was hoping to ask you to stop by on your way to work in the morning so you could do a patch job on my face. But I guess, all things considered, I shouldn't ask."

Peter's head snapped up. The bottom of his eyes still held traces of silver. He swallowed, inhaled a shaky breath and used the back of his hand to wipe the moisture from his cheeks. "I could stay here tonight," he said. "I can't be alone, not when I'm like this, and I don't feel like going bar-hopping to find a companion; I'd rather be with someone I know. I won't be in the way, I promise. I can use the cushions off the couch and sleep on the floor, and then I'll be here in the morning to do your makeup." His mouth quivered, but formed a timid smile—wet but sincere. "I'll have you looking so good your own mother won't recognize you."

Another flawed solution. Laurie didn't particularly want Peter spending the night, but she didn't want her disguise compromised either. His offer seemed the lesser of two evils. "Okay, but you may starve. There's nothing here to cook and I have to eat in the dining hall for appearances sake. I'll try to smuggle you something out of the kitchen, but I don't know the layout, so I can't make any promises."

NINE

WHAT A DIFFERENCE a day makes. They had beaten back the storm, and it had fled. The aftermath left a river-blue sky overhead, punctuated with billowing white sails of clouds running softly downstream on an eastern breeze. The sun was as fluid as the rain and they drank it in, refreshing their souls on its liquid warmth.

Bill had reached South Dakota, dripping from the drive, red-eye-weary, stubble-cheeked and aching. He crossed the border of Sioux Falls and pulled the wagon into the parking lot of the first motel he saw. He wasn't ready to bunk down, but a shower sounded awfully good. The motel had ground-level access, and it was just down the street from a seafood restaurant where he could order surf-and-turf for himself and clam chowder for his daughter.

Angie might have regretted leaving the table scraps behind (briny bits from the salty main had always been T.J.'s favorite food), but as it happened, she dozed off during dinner and Bill was able to avoid explaining why they no longer needed a kitty-bag. Bill tucked Angie in, kissing her cheek as he swept strands of silky hair off her face with his thick fingers. *Good night little partner.* It warmed him to see her like this, innocent, not one care in the whole wide world, not a hint of the misery she endured daily without complaint. He covered his mouth with the back of his hand to stifle a *ah, ahh, ahhh-yaaawwn.* He had work to do. With Angie asleep, he could get a good start on his column. He stretched out on his own bed, only for a second he told himself, yawning again as he cocked an arm over his eyes. He just needed to rest a minute before sharpening his pencil. At one in the morning he woke up and turned out the light.

THE AIR smelled of wood-stove smoke. Bill gave one more glance around the room and stepped outside. He closed the door and tugged on the knob, making sure it was locked. Angie was already sitting in the wagon, waiting.

Bill made his way to the office with the morning sun beating down on his shoulder. What a wonderful feeling, brisk air, blue sky and yellow sun—postcard perfect! He carried his travel mug in his hand, letting it thump against his leg as he walked. He hoped the cashier would have a pot of coffee brewing. Peeling paint on windowsills and shutters, blue over green, revealed signs of age not obvious the night before. The motel had seen better days. Bill let the screen door slam and punched the counter bell. No coffee, least none he could see, or even smell. He rocked back on his heels, rubbing the sore spot on his chest. His plastic cup hung empty from his little finger. *Darn shame about T.J.,* he thought. He'd called to get a report, but it had come back negative; the missing cat hadn't been seen. He was glad he'd put Angie in the car before dialing the number. One thing she didn't need was more bad news.

FROM INSIDE the wagon, Angie could see out across the yard into the street beyond. The sun was a warm ointment on her face. She watched as the day awoke. She saw the flow of town traffic yawning and stretching, the paper boy dressed in a red flannel shirt peddling his bike, a dog snapping at his heels, and a pickup truck hauling a trailer loaded with firewood. She saw white puffs of clouds balanced on crisp currents of air, the corkscrew smoke twisting up from the rock chimney of a white clapboard house, and wet leaves plastered to a brown lawn that was slowly turning green in answer to the call of spring. She heard the car door open. Her bubble of warm air was sucked outside, *whoooosh,* as her dad climbed aboard. She felt the morning again, still chilly as snow. With the window closed, and the sun's fingers of warmth caressing her face, she'd forgotten how cold it was.

Bill's keys rattled against the dash as the engine churned, missing a few times but connecting on the third try. He revved the car to life, blue smoke chugging from the tailpipe. They were on their way, destination Deadwood, the Black Hills of South Dakota, the historic reconstruction of western life in the late 1800s, and the place where they planned to spend the night. The on-ramp was just at the end of the block. Not a mini-mart or donut shop in sight. He'd have to wait until he stopped for gas to get his coffee. The wagon rolled around the corner taking the uphill grade to the freeway with a chug and a spit, driving headlong into the wind. Their troubles were behind. The blue brightness loomed ahead. Bill responded in a loud, off-key baritone making Angie giggle:

"Oh, I'm goin' to the riv-er,
The shiv-er-y ri-ver,
The river that goes down to the sea,
I'm gonna drown my trou-bles,
And leave just the bub-bles,
To in-di-cate what us-ed to be.

Take my hat, take my coat,
I'm gonna keep a walkin' till my straw hat floats.
Oh I'm goin' to the river..."

THE DOOR opened to darkness. Louis was the last to arrive; he was pulled inside and admonished to whisper. He stood blind in the darkness, smelling like Old Spice. Ruth took him by the arm and led him into the living room. The outdoor security lights seeped through the curtain, outlining shapes without detail. As he felt his way over to a small couch reserved for him because of his size, he saw the dark shadows of the others. They were seated in a circle, awaiting his arrival.

Through a mutual friend, Ruth had passed notes to each member of the team announcing the four A.M. meeting at her new apartment. No one complained about the early hour, they weren't sleeping all that well anyway, and there was much they had to discuss. As far as anyone knew, only a nurse, two custodians, and a lone security guard worked graveyard. "It should be easy to avoid these few, but try not to be seen by anyone," the note cautioned. It went on to say the meeting would end before the kitchen staff began to arrive.

Notably absent, was Joe. He hadn't received the notice because his whereabouts were still unknown.

"C...c...can't we t...t...turn on a light?" Louis asked.

"Shhhhhhh! No, no I don't think that's a good idea. Security patrols the outside. It might tip them off that we're here." Ruth was only a silhouette but her voice was recognizable. "All right, first question: has anyone seen Joe?"

There was a low murmur and shaking of heads, but their expressions were veiled by darkness.

"That's unusual, don't you think? I saw all of you at times throughout the day. Louis, you were watching TV; Edith, you were sunning yourself by the window; Cash, I saw you in the library reading the paper. You probably all saw me. How come nobody saw Joe? When was the last time he was seen by anyone? Has anyone seen him since the meeting we had with Mr. Porter?"

Another round of invisible shaking heads and muted, ghost-like murmurs.

"Well, I hope I'm wrong, but it's beginning to look like we have a problem."

"Wait a minute," Cash said. "Don't be so hasty. He could be anywhere. Maybe he's visiting friends. He could be..."

"Yes, he could. But he could also be dead," Ruth interjected. "I don't think anyone here believes Joe would leave without saying good-bye. Besides, the colonel told me he saw some men cleaning out Joe's apartment. If Joe were alive, that wouldn't be necessary. I'm worried about him. The last time someone disappeared he ended up dead, but we didn't know about it until we read in the paper."

"I...I...I think I want out," Louis said. "I...I think we should all g...g...get out. I mean leave."

"We can't just leave," Ruth warbled. "Porter has to be stopped."

"B...b...better to leave than we all end up d...d...d...dead."

"I agree," Cash joined in. His voice was low and throaty, and his words seemed to gurgle in the loose skin of his neck. "Look, there are two possibilities. Either they're killing people, or they're not. Now I know Henry and Leonard are dead, and I guess Ben, and maybe even Joe, but we don't know how any of them died." He started to uncross his legs, but found his feet too heavy to move. He settled for rubbing the shin of his leg with the heel of his shoe. "Ruthie, you and Ben and Joe convinced the rest of us that Porter and his cronies killed Henry and Leonard, but we don't have any proof of that. We took it to the police and got nowhere. Truth is, we don't know what happened to Henry and Leonard, but the police seem satisfied that no crime was committed. Mr. Porter says Ben was killed by a car. Maybe he was, maybe he wasn't, who knows? As for Joe, we don't know if he's even dead. So we have a dilemma. If we stick around, there's a chance we could all end up in the morgue because, like you say, they really could be killers. If, on the other hand, we leave, say we take a long vacation somewhere and then nothing happens, we can always come back."

Ruth shook her head, but in the darkness the gesture couldn't be seen. Was she the only one left that fully understood what was going on? People were being murdered, and someone was getting away with it. In her mind she could see the crime. She could picture every detail. Why couldn't they? Or maybe they could, but were bowing to their fears. Ben and Joe had been able to instill courage, along with conviction. That was their forte. With them gone, a fallout was bound to happen. "I understand," she said. "If you and Louis want to leave, I won't try to stop you, but I have to stay here. How about you Edith?"

Edith tugged at her shawl. "I can't leave," she said. "I'd freeze to death outside. If I have to die, I want to die where it's warm. Besides, you'll need help."

Ruth nodded. "Sorry boys, but if we don't put a stop to it, they'll eventually kill someone else. Those are our friends out there. I don't want their souls on my conscience."

Cash didn't comment. He pulled his legs up to uncross his feet, then crossed his arms and bowed his head forward.

Ruth's voice was soft at the best of times, but now she was holding back. The others were straining to hear. "We need to get something on them," she said. "We need evidence, and I think I have the key."

95

THE SUN WAS BRIGHT, plump, and juicy as an orange, but the dust devils were kicking up such a fuss, Bill couldn't see. He yanked the steering wheel to dodge another tumbleweed. He'd played this little game of hit-and-miss across a thousand acres of windswept prairie; it was becoming tedious.

He finally pulled off at Wall, South Dakota. How could he not? For hundreds of miles he'd passed billboards reading: "Just 291 Miles To Wall Drug" *(291 miles to a drug store, what kind of message is that?)* followed by, "Wall Drug Or Bust," and, as he got closer, "150 Miles To Wall Drug," and "Everything Under The Sun, Wall Drug," and "Refreshing Free Ice Water, Wall Drug," and on, and on, and on, hundreds of signs, ad infinitum. He pulled into gas stations and saw bumper-stickers that asked, "Where The Heck Is Wall Drug?" So by the time he got to the sign that said, "Whoa-a For Wall Drug," he was hooked. He had to see what was so important about a drug store that it was worth several hundred miles of billboard advertising. Besides, he'd just crossed the tumbleweed-strewn, sod-covered prairies. Mile after mile of flat emptiness that exists to perpetuate nothing but sun, dust clouds and a straight line of horizon. Bill's bored mind needed a break from the monotony.

He pulled into town and saw it right away, but he still didn't know what it was. Was it a drug store, or was it something else? It covered a city block; it had parking spaces on both sides of the road, as well as down the middle. The western facade of the line of buildings was the focal point of the entire town. From a distance, it appeared they were entering a town right out of the 1800s. He eased the wagon up to the curb.

Bill loved history. Seeing a replica of the past filled him with anticipation. He settled Angie into her wheelchair and rolled up to the main entrance. He had to wait while his eyes adjusted to the dimmer light to determine whether he wanted to go inside. He could see crowded aisles with bins of goods stacked on old wood floors. The mid-afternoon sun grilled his shirt. It felt like he was wearing the skin of a coal-baked Idaho spud. Angie loved the sun. He decided to park her just outside the door and take a second to see what the place was all about.

"Hey little partner, it looks like a bit of a bumpy road ahead. I'm going to set you right here where you can enjoy the sun, while I see if it's worth taking you inside. Let me just back you up against the wall here, and set the brake, there you go." Bill tucked the blanket up under Angie's chin and kissed her cheek. "I'll only be a minute."

TWO DENIM-clad local boys cruised by in a Dodge Ram pickup. They were checking out the tourist action. They had their windows jammed down with their sun-browned arms stuck outside. The passenger wore a white T-shirt with bib overalls hitched over his shoulders. He reached up to crank the radio's volume so the whole street could listen to Garth Brooks. A roll of street grit spun off the tires. They pulled into a parking space, mouths watering for soda, and hopped down from the cab, slamming the doors with the sound of crashing metal. *Blamm, bamm.* It was time to scope out the babes, to smile and wink and flex a little muscle, though both boys knew the tourist girls were only passing through and weren't up for serious action.

BILL STEPPED inside the emporium and was dazed by what he found. Out in the middle of nowhere, the most remote cross-section of the western prairie, was this amazing acre of everything. He saw dry goods, wet goods, a restaurant, a soda fountain, a confectionary, and a museum with fourteen-hundred photographs of historic South Dakota, Montana and Wyoming. It was incredible. There was a whole section devoted to western art and western sculpture; there were Indian war bonnets, chaps and spurs, and fur blankets. He knew he could get lost browsing for hours, but he couldn't leave Angie alone. Besides, they had another sixty miles to go before they reached Deadwood, the stomping ground of notorious high-noon gunfighters and ace-in-the-hole gamblers like Wyatt Earp, Doc Holliday, Wild Bill Hickok and Calamity Jane. That ought to be enough to satisfy his craving for western lore.

CASH AND LOUIS didn't wait. They weren't convinced someone was going around killing people, but they didn't want to risk staying, in case they were wrong. After a brief private conference they announced they would be leaving. Then they excused themselves and left the meeting to go pack. To ensure Edith and Ruth didn't face a battery of questions about their whereabouts, Louis stopped to pin a note to the community bulletin board saying he and Cash had decided to take a long overdue vacation down in sunny, Southern California. They were out the door, slicing through the morning mist in Cash's minivan before anyone else knew they were gone.

EDITH PULLED her shawl around her shoulders as she made her way down the dimly lit hall. *Yellow-bellied turncoats,* that's what they were, but secretly, she was envious. She would have gone with the two men, if it hadn't meant leaving all her lovely things behind. She was too old to try and assemble a new collection. She was too old for practically anything. She shivered as she unlocked the door to her room. She paused to tap the thermostat. Darn thing read eighty degrees, but it couldn't be working, no matter what they said. She'd have to get someone in to fix it again. She flicked on the lights and stepped around the magazines that were piled on the floor. Even if they were killing people, she'd rather die in a familiar place, than a place unknown—but she didn't want to die. The thing she feared about death was knowing her eternal rest would be dank and cold. She'd heard enough about the cold, cold grave to know she didn't want to go there. She was reconciled to the inevitable, but she would forestall it as long as possible.

RUTH SAT alone in the dark, her eyes closed as she went before the throne of her creator. She knew it was foolish to fear death. Death was just a door through which she would one day step to meet Jesus. But she also knew that what she believed took faith, and that was something her friends didn't seem to have. No matter how many times she explained it, they looked at her with blank faces like they couldn't understand what she was saying. It was like they'd gone deaf. She recognized the problem, because she'd been there. There was a time when she would have laughed at what she now believed. She'd been on both sides of the spiritual chasm. She knew that from the one side, you couldn't see through to the other—no matter how hard you tried. The darkness was too penetrating. For those still lost in the darkness, life had to be preserved as long as possible. They had to be given every opportunity to find the light. She whispered a prayer for the safe journey of Cash and Louis, and she asked God to let her know about Joe's fate, but most of all she prayed the guilty would soon be brought to justice. Then, at the close of her prayer, she cried out for courage. God answered with words from the prophet Isaiah: "Say to them that are of a fearful heart, be strong, fear not; behold, your God will come with vengeance, even God with a recompense; he will come and save you."

Ruth opened her eyes but the room was still dark. She raised her gloveless hands. She couldn't see them, but she knew they were red and pulpy. They were such an embarrassment. The arthritis prevented her from holding small objects. She couldn't pick up her change after she'd bought something. She had to scoop it into her hand. Even the slightest task, like trying to move a hat pin, made her swollen fingers ache. Sometimes it felt like she had two useless clubs of meat dangling at the ends of her arms. And they hurt so bad. But it was always worse in the morning. She pushed herself off the chair, and went to the bathroom to find some aspirin.

Two young girls came running out of the store a minute ago. They were bowed over, holding their stomachs and giggling so hard I thought they'd shake the buns out of their hair. They wore short T-shirts that showed off their belly buttons and had their bell bottoms flapping around their ankles. I guessed them to be about my age. They didn't see me, or they pretended not to. I saw one of them hold something up, and the other said: "Oh, that's so cool." So cool? What does that mean? I hear people talk like that on TV. Why can't they just say, "that's nice," or "that's beautiful," or "I like that?" I guess it's hard for me because I've never been around other children, and grown-ups don't talk that way. When you're around adults all the time, you learn to think like they do, using words you've heard them use.

The problem is, people don't expect me to think at all. I can't communicate. I can't talk, write, or even use hand signals, but that doesn't mean I can't think. I may not have the world's highest IQ, but all things considered, my brain's in pretty good shape. I wish people could read my thoughts. At least then they'd know I have intelligence. As it is, most people assume my mind is as broken as my body. They think I need to be talked down to. It's like normal people get talked to one way, and I another. A normal person with a cold might hear: "Hey you sound sick, you'd better get some rest." But to me they say: "Ahh, there, there, poor little thing, we'll take care of that mean ol' sniffle, make it all bedda." That's what hurts. My thoughts are more adult than most kids my age, yet I'm the one they treat like a baby.

ANGIE WOBBLED her head. At first she thought it was T.J. The cat darted across the road, orange and white, tail pulled back and ears flat as it ducked behind a parked car. Angie woke from her sun warm rest, her heart pumping with the strain of elation. Her head reeled and her arm stretched out to grapple the air while her mouth let out muted groans. But the cat was gone. As her excitement waned, she realized there was no way it could have been T.J. He could not have followed them to South Dakota.

BILL FOUND his way to the front of the store. He looked at his watch. Just over ten minutes had passed. He hadn't meant to be gone so long, but he'd gotten carried away. With any luck, Angie had drifted off to sleep and lost track of time. The rest would do her good. Still, he felt the twinge of guilt a father feels when he knows he's been neglectful. He picked up his pace as he approached the door.

He could hear the jibing laughter of kids taunting and jeering in good natured banter, boys being boys: "What's a matter retard, cat got your tongue? Hee, hee, ha, ha, okay, okay, look, I'll give you an easy one. Say, my name is...come on, you can do it, tell us your name. Hee, hee, hee, this kid's brain dead..." but when Bill saw it was Angie they were teasing, he snapped. The older boy, an early teen with baggy, knee-length pants drooping from his hips, a shirt three sizes too big and a baseball cap spun around backward on his head, found himself lifted from the ground and slammed against the wall. Bill whirled and spun, holding the boy by the collar. The young man's feet were jerking and kicking as he choked in the grip of Bill's hand. "What's the matter, son, cat got your tongue? Go ahead, say what you were saying. I'd like to hear it."

A crowd was starting to form, circling the drama like spectators watching a fight. The second child found the parents and brought them squeezing through the melee to see their son pinned to the wall, dangling from the hand of a troubled man. He looked like one mean son-of-a-buck. "Get the police, Nancy, phone the police," the boy's father said, pushing his wife back. "Go, now!"

Angie sat gawking, her eyes wide. She wasn't used to seeing her father lose control. Bill was blinded by a storm of white fury. He clenched his fist, his knuckles turning white. He wanted to see the boy cry. His eyes narrowed so he could focus through the din. He heard Angie groan and out the corner of his eye, saw her shoulders jerk. Her arms began to flail and her neck and head to pivot and twist. He let go. The boy crumpled to the ground as Bill fell to his knees and grabbed his daughter, holding her in a bear hug while he stroked her hair until her twitching subsided.

Reacting to the boy's fall, the man lunged forward to help his son. "You all right? Are you hurt?"

The boy shook his head, more rattled than pained.

Bill stood again. "You the boy's father? You should teach..."

But the man held up his hand. "Don't you move! You stay right where you are."

Just then the wife returned with a uniformed officer in tow. The marshal removed his hat and stood with his feet relaxed wondering what all the fuss was about. Couldn't be a fight, wasn't a fair match, one man outweighed the other by a good sixty pounds.

"All right, what's the problem?"

The boy's father pointed an accusing finger at Bill. "This man was beating my son. I want him placed under arrest."

The officer saw the boy sitting in the dust. There wasn't any blood, and no obvious bruises, but the boy was definitely on the ground.

"I didn't beat anyone," Bill retorted. "The kid was harassing my daughter. All I did was give him a taste of his own medicine."

"Go on, arrest him. He was beating my son, ask anyone. They all saw it. Ask them."

Not wanting to become involved, the crowd began to disperse, all except one young man who stood his ground. It was the boy in bib overalls, abandoned by his friend who had gone inside to entertain the ladies. "I saw it," he said. "This man had the kid up against the wall..."

"See, put him under arrest." The father, who only came up to Bill's shoulder, wagged his finger in Bill's face. "You better find a good lawyer, Jack, cause I'm gonna sue you for everything you got."

Bill grabbed the man's wrist and squeezed. "Unless you want it broken, I suggest you point that thing somewhere else."

The man jerked away. "You heard him. He threatened me! I want him in handcuffs. Now!"

"Excuse me, sir, but I didn't finish." It was the blue-jeaned spectator again. "This guy did grab the boy and put him against the wall, that's true, but the kid deserved it. He was hassling the young lady. He was laughing at her, calling her names because she's in a wheelchair. I heard it. If anything, the little brat's the one they should lock up."

The boy had picked himself off the ground and was dusting his pants with his cap. The officer looked him over. "Are you hurt son, anything broken?"

The boy shook his head, his hair hanging in front of his eyes.

"I don't care. I'm pressing charges. There are laws against child abuse. We'll let the courts decide. My lawyer will grind you like dogmeat."

"Okay, all right, I've heard about enough." The officer was growing weary of the man's attitude. "We don't even have a jail in this town, so nobody's going to arrest anybody."

"No jail? What kind of hick town you running here? I want him under arrest. If you can't do it, find somebody who can. I'm going to sue his pants off."

The policeman turned and took a step forward so his chest was in the man's face. "Mister, I said I've heard enough. This isn't Chicago or New York or wherever the heck it is you come from. Out here we believe in justice, eye for an eye, and according to the only witness willing to speak up, your son had it coming. Now you may find some big city lawyer who can make up look like down, but in this backwater town, it's the guilty who hang. And if that ain't clear enough, let me say it straight. I think you're trouble, and I don't like trouble in my town, so I'm asking you nicely, please collect your son and the rest of your family and say good-bye."

"You can't..."

"Can't what, run you out of town? Try me."

The man's face turned three shades of crimson but he was smart, or at least intimidated enough not to further provoke the officer. "Un-freaking-believable!" The man grabbed his son by the neck and pushed him across the sidewalk. "Next time I come to your defense, you darn well better play dead or hurt or something." He smacked the kid on the back of the head.

"Guess I owe you, both of you," Bill said, extending his hand.

The officer continued to hold his hat with both hands, refusing to acknowledge the gesture. "I think it would be better if you moved along as well. We're a small town. We don't like trouble."

Bill nodded. "Well, thanks anyway. My little girl here would say thanks if she could. The boy was out of line."

The trio looked at Angie, who in all the confusion had been forgotten.

Bill turned to the young man. "Thank you too, sir," Bill said. "We certainly do appreciate your help."

They shook hands.

The car was a Lexus, dark silver-green with gold trim. The dust layered on its lacquered paint looked out of place. From behind his shield of tinted glass, the man extended his middle finger to salute Bill. *Guess I should have broke it off,* Bill thought. A dust devil bounced off the car's polished bumper causing bits of paper to scatter as the wheels whirled by. Bill caught the license plate: Michigan. *Probably Detroit,* he surmised, glad the man was from the very place he was leaving.

Bill turned back to the officer. "You mind if I do one quick thing before I go? Only take five minutes. That's my station wagon right over there. Give us five minutes and you can check; it'll be gone, and me and Angie along with it."

Bill made his way through the store, this time pushing Angie. He saw the people huddled and whispering. He'd made a scene. The rumors were starting to fly. He ignored the gossip, rolling Angie past brick wall facades with western-lettered signs, cigar-store Indians and wooden prospectors sitting on benches. He came to a stop when he reached a sign that said, "Traveler's Chapel."

He'd thought it peculiar to find a drug store that boasted a built-in church. Now he saw how it made sense. This was a tourist town. God's journeying mercy was one thing every traveler needed. He rolled Angie down through the rows of pews and up to the altar. All the excitement and hard breathing had inflamed the wound in his chest, but they were alive—and he hadn't hurt the boy. He had much to be thankful for. He rubbed his sternum and bowed his head.

TEN

LAURIE SAT on a hard chair. Her cane stood before her, her hands perched on top like a bird with folded wings. She was in a large assembly hall. The room screeched with feedback, a flaw in the sound system that pointed to the haste with which the meeting had been pulled together. Barbara Marks and Alfred Porter apologized for not having time to work out the bugs, and then launched into an explanation of the gossip going around campus. It had come to their attention that the disappearance of certain individuals was being blamed on them, and they felt they needed to set the record straight. They wanted to assure their guests that this information was totally false. Nothing untoward had happened to anyone, they avowed.

It was a weak attempt to squelch the rumors, and probably did more harm than good. In the telling they became defensive, and through the ineptness of their presentation, what they claimed was complete candor, came across as subterfuge. Most of the people hadn't even heard of the disappearances. The microphones screeched and hissed. Laurie watched as people in every part of the room turned to each other and asked what these two were talking about; the room rippled with murmurs. Instead of solving a problem, Al and Barbara were creating one. They had to be guilty of something. It was obvious by the way they were trying to cover it up: Ben Riggs had been hit by a taxi and, regrettably, had not survived; Cash Williams and Louis Wiarton were vacationing in California and would return in a few weeks—so what? Why did they feel such innocuous events warranted so grand an explanation? Laurie noticed the temperature rising. Old people wear too many clothes, and too many people were sandwiched into the room. The body heat rippled like hot sun bouncing off asphalt. Under her many layers, Laurie was beginning to perspire, and that meant her makeup might run. She began fanning her face with her fingers.

So many silver heads. A room filled with the creases and folds of old age. It was unsettling. Every time Laurie looked in the mirror she saw, blinking back through web-fractured eyes, what she was destined to become. Are we but dust? She would lean on her cane, feel the pain of her pretending, and wonder how anyone bent by the years could endure such degradation. How long before these things were her own reality? How long before she became marginalized, shut away, a memory, old and unimportant? She wasn't comfortable playing this role; she was self-conscious around old people. That's the way it had always been. To see the ravages of age everywhere, was to face her own future. It was something she was totally unprepared to deal with. It made her little self-imposed assignment all the more difficult.

Not that she hadn't made progress. In taking on the role, she could almost feel a kinship with those who were aging. She could now see that "old" wasn't a synonym for "hopeless." It was that way for some perhaps, but not all. The worst were the ancients along the wall, the ones with white, bony fingers crippled by Parkinson's disease, minds melted by Alzheimer's, and eyes cauterized by cataracts, the wheelchair bound who couldn't speak, or hear, or acknowledge anyone's presence. But even these had hope. She had observed the healthy waiting on the infirm, old friends clinging to some bygone loyalty, helping each other along the path, holding a straw so juice could be sipped without dribbling.

They conversed, albeit one-sided, but no one let cognitive loss get in the way. They spoke to the inner person. The person on the outside might be hiding behind a shield of glazed-over eyes, but that didn't change the person on the inside. The inner person still had the same emotions, values, and reasoning they'd had when they were lucid. So perhaps even these were not so desperate as they first appeared. Laurie glanced up in time to hear Barbara take another question. Most of the elderly residents she'd met so far, had more on the ball than these two. She almost felt sorry for them. They were embarrassing themselves, prancing around up there with those awful *screeeeeeching* microphones.

Laurie began fanning her face to keep it from melting. Her costume was overheating, but she was glad she'd come. One of her suspicions had been confirmed. She had surveyed the room. The tall, lanky man in the leisure suit, and the one with the mop of orange hair she'd nicknamed, Big Boy, weren't there. She was sure if it. They were the two she'd previously found huddled with that little bird woman and Joe Bonner. Now, all of a sudden, right along with Joe's disappearance, it was reported Louis Wiarton and Cash Williams had skipped town. It was logical to conclude that Big Boy and Lanky Man, were none other than Louis and Cash.

What was odd, was that Barbara and Al claimed not to know Joe had vanished. They both looked genuinely surprised when asked about it. They thought he was somewhere in the room, or so they said.

Ben Riggs was dead, and Louis Wiarton, Cash Williams and Joe Bonner, were missing—very suspicious. Barbara and Al tried to assure the guests that Lou and Cash were off enjoying the sunny California coast, but even if they were, it didn't explain why they'd decided to leave so suddenly. The timing seemed too convenient. The number of people who had signed the letter, people Laurie needed to talk to, was shrinking. The only ones left were Edith Woodhouse and Ruth Wheatly.

Laurie had spotted both women. They were seated as far away from each other as possible. The lady in the feathered cap was easy. She sat at the back of the hall, one row in front of Laurie, but a little off to the right. The other one was seated on the left, close to the front. In spite of the heat, she kept pulling her shawl up around her neck and folding her arms inside like she was cold. Then, toward the end of the meeting, her hand shot up to ask about the disappearance of Joe. That must have taken guts. With the other four gone, it was logical to assume she and the little bird woman would be next. Laurie was convinced the two ladies were Ruth and Edith, but she had yet to determine which one was which. How long would they last? She continued to fan her face. How long could anyone last in this heat?

PETER KEPT looking at his watch. Laurie had been gone a long time. He needed someone to talk to, someone to help him keep his mind off Tina. He was trying to be strong. He was trying to do what the doctor said—*think positive!* He wasn't going to kill himself, Tina wasn't worth it, though he'd been to the medicine cabinet twice to see if there was anything worth taking, just in case he changed his mind. But that was a foolish thought, and besides, the medicine cabinet was empty. *Be strong. Such thoughts come and go.* He knew what it was like to be on a mountain top one minute, and down in the valley the next, been there, done that—*manic depressive with suicidal tendencies*—so what? It wasn't a weakness. He wasn't weak. He was just—*sensitive.* Dr. Roberts told him to focus on getting through one day at a time; enjoy the good days, ignore the bad. If he'd really wanted to kill himself, he would have succeeded the first time, or the second, or the time after that. He'd get over Tina, just like he'd gotten over the others. But it hurt! It always hurt—and it took so long to heal. What was the point of going on?

He was jolted from his thoughts by a loud knock at the door. He knew enough not to answer, but a key began turning in the lock, and the door began to swing open. He could hear voices. Spanish??? The door stopped, but the conversation continued. Laurie had left the patio door open to circulate fresh air. It was his only hope. He ducked out as the cleaning lady entered through the front. He took a deep breath and stepped to the side, standing with his back to the wall. The curtains had been left open, but he heard them being closed. His heart jumped to his throat. What if the cleaning lady saw the bump of his shadow against the wall? Would she find anything of his lying around? What about the makeup? He'd left bottles and tubes of it lying on the counter.

He could hear waste baskets being emptied, pillows being fluffed, dishes being washed and toilets being cleaned. By the time he heard the front door close again he had thought of a hundred things the cleaning lady could use to prove someone was staying with Laurie, or staying with Mrs. Iversen, as she called herself. He feared he had blown her cover.

THE GATHERING was dismissed. Laurie tugged at the hem of her skirt to keep it from being stepped on as she rose from her chair. She was anxious to get moving; her nose itched but she couldn't touch it for fear of doing damage. Beneath her makeup she felt a layer of perspiration threatening to dissolve her face. She had to make contact with the two women. If Al and Barbara thought that by getting rid of the men their problem would go away, they were in for a rude awakening. The story was here, Laurie could feel it, she just needed to search it out, but for that she needed help. These two frail little old ladies were all she had. They'd have to do.

Laurie waited as the rows began to empty. The little bird lady bobbed past. She had a determined stride for such a small creature, and there was a resolute set to her eyes. They were furrowed and plowed under with a look that said: I'm not buying it. *Good,* Laurie thought, *I'm not buying it either.* Laurie reached out and took hold of the woman's elbow. "I need to talk to you," she said. "It's about Joe Bonner. Could you come by unit twenty-two as soon as possible?"

Then she felt a tug at her other sleeve. "There you are, Annie." Without looking, Laurie recognized the voice of Karla Smith. "I wondered what happened to you. I haven't seen you around. I was beginning to think you'd left us. I hope you won't let all this nonsense about people disappearing bother you. It's a buncha ba-loney. Don't know why people get so all worked up whenever somebody dies. Might as well get used to it. It happens all the time. Hello Ruthie," Karla said noticing Ruth for the first time and establishing the woman's name in Laurie's mind once and for all. "I see you two have met."

"Sorry, I have to go," Ruth said. She moved away without acknowledging either Karla or the request made by Laurie. Laurie started to reach out, but Karla pulled her back.

"Oh, let her go. She's an old fussbudget. Can't figure that one out, no I can't." Then Karla tipped her head toward Laurie to confide a secret. "A few of the people around here have trouble holding onto reality. You can't imagine the kind of crazy stuff that goes though a person's head. Ruthie is always talking about the world coming to an end. Don't pay it any mind, that's my advice. Just ignore it completely." Karla wore a yellow chiffon dress. Her dark skin was in sharp contrast to the pastel color. "Did I mention I'm waiting to be picked up by my grandson?" she asked. "He's coming to take his old nana out shopping. Would you like to join us? We'd love the company."

Laurie paused and placed both hands atop the gooseneck of her cane. "Thank you for asking, Karla, but I can't. I was just going back to my room to lie down. I feel tired. I need a nap."

"Suit yourself, but sleep is just death in small doses. We're all gonna die soon enough, honey. I figure we should live as much as we can, with whatever time we got left."

By the time Laurie was able to extricate herself from the conversation, Edith was nowhere to be seen. Laurie did her best to find the woman but she had completely vanished, and Laurie had to get back to her apartment in case Ruth stopped by. Too many opportunities were being missed. She leaned on her cane and trudged slowly back to her room.

Peter jumped up from the couch. "Oh Laurie, am I glad you're here," he said. "I almost got busted while you were gone. I heard someone knock. I tried to ignore it, but then I heard the key turn in the lock and I realized they were coming in. I panicked. I didn't know what to do. I thought, what if they catch me in here, how will I explain? The door started to open and then whoever it was stopped to talk to someone in the hall. They were speaking Spanish so I couldn't understand, but while they were talking I slipped out the patio door. Thank goodness, you left it open. She didn't see me. I'm sure of that, but she might have seen something that made her suspicious. I mean about me. I did have all my makeup out, the stuff I used on you, but I'm not sure she'd know what it was. Maybe she couldn't read English. Anyway, I'm glad you're back. I'm having a terrible day."

Laurie laid her cane against the wall and removed her sweater. It was a wonder Peter's heart didn't seize. His lips had been flapping nonstop without a breath. "I should have thought of that," she said. "You're right, slipping outside was quick thinking, way to go." She patted Peter on the shoulder and looked around the room. It had been cleaned all right, all Peter's makeup bottles were standing in a tightly organized group on the counter, dirty towels had been replaced, the trash removed and the dishes washed, dried and put away. Nothing to worry about. "I guess we better figure out what to do with you," she said.

DR. VANETTER finished his workout and slipped into the shower. It felt good to lather the sweat from his body. The heat penetrated his skin as steam billowed up and water pounded his back. Good exercise and a healthy diet were the keys to staying young. He turned the hot faucet down and let cold, ice cold, freezing cold, water shiver its way through his body to close his pores.

Then he turned off the cold tap and stepped out, reaching for a towel. He came up empty. He wiped his forehead with his arm and swept his hair back through his fingers. He shouldn't have been so hasty when he asked the cleaning lady to leave. She had taken the towels, too flustered to leave one behind. The laundry was just down the hall. Stuart used a paper towel to wipe his legs before climbing into his jogging suit.

He entered the room. Along one wall were six giant dryers spinning on a vertical axis like six giant butter churns making butter. On the other wall, a row of twelve industrial strength washing machines chugged and gurgled and spew and spun. In front of each was a waiting pile of laundry. The linen cupboards were at the other end of the room. Dr. VanEtter stepped over the piles, ignoring the women who worked in the clouds of steam, loading and unloading the machines. In the cupboard he found a stack of towels, all clean, starched and precision folded. He wrapped one around his neck and moved back down the aisle. The room cranked and wheezed; the unbearable air was saturated with the noxious odor of chlorine bleach. One of the women forgot about the uninvited stranger and began grumbling to a friend. In one hand she held a towel and with the other she pointed. The doctor would have ignored them but the two

111

women were in his way, and the one who held the towel flung her arm back so he had to catch her wrist to keep from being hit in the face. The towel was stained with brown makeup, a lot of it. He looked in the basket and found another with even more cosmetic gunk. He held both up. "Where did these come from?" he asked.

THE TAP was so light, Laurie almost missed it. Her heart skipped as she moved toward the door. It might be Ruth, but it might also be the cleaning lady again. Putting her eye up to the peephole, she looked down on the familiar red hat. *Good!* She turned around and looked at Peter. "Well, she's here. You might as well stay. I'm going to risk letting her in on our secret." She opened the door, bending slightly in case she was seen by someone in the hall.

"Mrs. Wheatly, I presume?" Laurie said, as the woman entered.

"It is," Ruth answered. She went to take a seat without waiting to be invited. As she passed the kitchen she noticed Peter standing by the sink sipping a cup of tea. Her eyes seemed to stay with him as she settled in her chair. Laurie wondered what she was thinking. At least he was presentable—a good looking young man with short, neatly groomed hair, dressed entirely in black. His slacks were creased cotton, and his long-sleeved pullover fit snugly against his trim figure with a circle for his head instead of a collar. Ruth continued to stare. Peter's free hand fell to his belt, tinkering with the buckle.

Ruth turned her eyes away and began fiddling with her hat. Her white gloves worked at adjusting the pin until it was secure. Her hands folded and fell neatly into her lap. Laurie noted she wore a different hat than the one she had on the day before, but it was still red, and it still had feathers. The white gloves were a good idea. Laurie wished she'd thought of it. She walked over and took a seat on the couch opposite her guest.

"I know who you are too," Ruth said, "you're the new tenant. I saw you when you registered. I wanted to warn you. I would have too, but I'm in enough trouble as it is. Forgive me if I sound presumptuous. You said this was about Joe Bonner. If it's about Joe, it can only be about one thing. I assume he told you about the problem we're having."

Laurie nodded.

"What's your name, dear?"

The lady doesn't waste time, Laurie thought. She made no effort to disguise her real voice. "I'm registered here as Annie Iversen, but my real name is Laurie Best. However, while I'm here, it's important you remember to always call me Annie. Yes, Joe and I discussed some of the strange things going on around here, but now I can't seem to find him. You wouldn't have any idea where he is, would you?"

"He's probably dead. I fear they had to shut him up." Ruth said it with a tremor in her voice. Her lips were pinched together like a beak.

"You're sure?"

"Not absolutely. But I know he wouldn't leave and, as you pointed out, he doesn't seem to be around. It's become a pattern. People who are alive and healthy one minute, disappear and end up dead the next. All I know for sure is that Joe has disappeared. If he isn't dead, where is he?"

The question fell to the floor and stayed there. Laurie twisted in her seat. She brought her hand up under her neck and began to scratch, but stopped short of disturbing her makeup. Part of her wanted to reach up and pull the mask away to reveal her real face, the way she had seen it done in the movies. Another time perhaps. She decided to take a different approach. "What about Cash Williams and Louis Wiarton? Are they dead too?"

"No, Louis and Cash are fine. I can assure you of that. If your name's Laurie, why do you call yourself Annie?"

Giving the explanation again was tedious, but at least it provided an opportunity to introduce Peter. Peter nodded, mumbled how pleased he was to meet Ruth, and took a nervous sip of tea while Laurie revealed his role in their little ruse. The tiny woman sat and listened without comment, though it seemed she couldn't keep her eyes off Peter. Laurie found herself viewing Ruth in a different light. *You're not paranoid if they really are out to get you.* Today's exchange seemed perfectly normal. Perhaps it was because Laurie realized she herself had concluded Joe was dead without any more to go on than Ruth had about Ben. Or perhaps it was seeing Barbara and Al waltz around the stage in their own paranoia. *Maybe, to some degree, the whole world is paranoid.* She tried to be discreet and peek at her watch. Time was slipping away.

"The bottom line is, I came to help," she said. "I've uncovered enough to think the story's plausible, but there are serious gaps. Like motive. Joe said something about money but he never got the chance to explain. Then there's proof. Joe said he didn't have any. I have to tell you what I told him just before he disappeared. I need motive, and I need proof. If you can help me with these two things, I'll write a story that will make Emerald Valley look like a modern day Auschwitz. But if you can't, I'm afraid there's not much I can do."

Ruth looked at Peter and pursed her lips. She laced her white gloved fingers together and put her hands under her chin while her eyes darted from Peter to Laurie and back again. "Joe was right, the motive is money," she said. "Did he tell you two of our friends, Henry and Leonard, were murdered? Two men as sound in mind and body as you or I, sent off to the good Lord before their time." She reached up and grabbed her coiffure, her elbows flapping like wings as she adjusted her hat, though it seemed to Laurie it hadn't moved.

"Joe did mention those names, yes, but he didn't give any details."

"Well, let me fill you in. Emerald Valley has a program called the Equity Exchange Plan. If you sat through the sales pitch, you must have heard about it. Henry and Leonard were on this plan. They each had some property they gave to the corporation. Emerald Valley was supposed to sell it, deduct the cost of the program, and deposit the balance into their accounts for personal use. The corporation always estimates the cost of the customer's long term care on the high side to ensure the person dies before the money is used up. Only Henry and Leonard outlived the value of their asset, and that made them a liability."

"So you're saying they were murdered because they were costing Emerald Valley money?"

Ruth nodded, her bird feathers shaking in the breeze. She slipped a hand up to steady her hat, and pin it in place once again. "Happened to Henry first. He was called into the office and handed paperwork that showed his expenses had exceeded the amount of money Emerald Valley got when they sold his property. He was asked if he had any other assets the corporation could have. Of course he didn't. After his meeting, he told Ben, Joe, Leonard and me he couldn't see any way all that money could have been used up. We told him not to worry, that it was probably some kind of mistake, but a week later he was dead. They put him down, and they had the gall to say he'd requested it. They made some ridiculous excuse about his being in constant pain, unable to cope, or some nonsense like that. Only they weren't talking about the Henry we knew. Our Henry was old, but he was fit as a fiddle. He sure wasn't ready to die.

"The shame of it is, he didn't even get a proper Christian burial. He didn't have any family. The body was cremated. They said the ashes were scattered in the wind, supposedly at his request, but that's their story. They ended up in the garbage, is what I think. Of course, me, and Ben, and Joe, and Leonard all talked about it, but there wasn't anything we could do. Then, last month, Leonard was called in and told the same thing. You should have seen him after. He wasn't the same. He made me and Ben and Joe swear to keep an eye on him. He was very clear about it. He said he didn't want what happened to Henry, happening to him. We tried, we really did, but you can't watch a man twenty-four hours a day. Next thing you know he just disappeared. We never saw him again. A few days later, Joe found his obituary in the paper. It was supposed to have been written by Leonard himself. It was a short note saying good-bye to all his friends and explaining how he had decided to leave this world of pain for a better place." Ruth was picking at the fingertips of her gloves. "That's when we decided to go to the police," she concluded.

While Ruth was still talking, Laurie found a sheet of paper and began taking notes. She was finally getting somewhere. "Wait a minute, who's the we? So far you've mentioned yourself, Joe, Ben, Henry and Leonard. What about Louis Wiarton and Cash Williams? Their names were on the letter, and what about the other one, Edith Woodhouse, what part does she play?"

"We asked Edith to help us because she has a legal background. She didn't know anything about what had happened, but after we explained it, she got right on board. Cash and Louis joined because they're both on the Equity Exchange Plan. Both of them are scared out of their wits. They don't know how much the corporation got for their assets, or how much of it is left. They're afraid someone will come looking for more, and they don't have it, and once they become a liability...well, you get the picture. That's why they're in hiding, spending what little money they do have, when they should be staying here free of charge."

"So they're down in California?"

"No. They decided to leave, but they're not in California. That's just a cover. They've got themselves checked into a motel just a few blocks from here. We'll be keeping in touch by phone."

The lady sounded credible, far more lucid than Laurie would have thought, but it was still difficult to imagine a suit and tie businessman taking someone out and killing them in cold blood. That was a script written for Mafia dons, not the corporate business types she'd met so far. Laurie tapped her pencil on her open palm. Her lips twisted into a knot. Okay, these were old people, they were probably going to die soon anyway, so perhaps you could rationalize an early exit if it were painless, and if it could be shown the person suffered a history of poor health. Anything else was too bizarre. There had to be an explanation. Ruth's account had further convinced her that there was a story here, but would she be able to gather enough information to write it? "I already asked Joe but I didn't get a satisfactory answer. Can you prove any of this? If I'm going to write about it, I'll need proof. You claim these men didn't want to die. That's fine, but I'm willing to bet somebody has a document that says otherwise. Something had to convince the police that everything was done on the up-and-up. I need more than your word."

Ruth fidgeted in her chair. One hand flew up to her hat, but upon finding it secure, floated back down. "I'm afraid proof is the one thing we don't have. We were hoping the police would investigate and come up with whatever evidence they needed. Well, that didn't happen, so we're back to square one. I had an idea, but I shared it with the others and they thought it was too dangerous. That's why Cash and Louis decided to leave. I think Edith can still be counted on to help, but..."

"I'm listening."

"I have a key, a master key; I stole it from a cleaning lady when she wasn't looking, may God forgive me, but it opens everything. I was planning to use it to sneak in and take a look at the corporation's balance sheet. I'd like to see what happened to Henry and Leonard's money. They were both surprised to find their accounts were empty. Chances are, that's where we'll find our motive. But the problem is, Louis and Cash said the information I needed would be stored in a computer and I don't know a single thing about computers."

The curtains had been drawn, but not sealed tight. The afternoon light streamed through a crack revealing cosmic dust filtering through the air. Bill used to say that man is made of dust; from dust we come, and to dust we return...

"Maybe I can help," Laurie said, "I know a little something about computers."

ELEVEN

I hate it when my body goes berserk. I feel like an idiot with my arms jerking and my head rolling side to side. What those boys did was mean, but I don't hold it against them. They were laughing at a freak. Remember the hunchback of Notre Dame? That's what people do. I'm not saying it doesn't hurt, but I'm used to it. It wasn't anything I hadn't seen before.

I was glad the drive to Deadwood was short because it gave me less time to think, and since I was thinking mostly about T.J., it was hard. The cat I saw wasn't ours, of course. It dashed across the road so fast I'm not even sure it was a calico, but seeing it reminded me that T.J. was gone, and that sent my body out of control. My poor dad had to pull over to readjust my seat belt and pillow, and I had to force myself to think about something else. I tried to occupy my mind with the future, our dream, the boat, the golden days and silvery nights, sea gull skies, and wisps of salty air. All the way to Deadwood I stared out the window and tried to dream of the good days that lie ahead. Eventually, my shaking settled down.

BILL WAS in a bright mood as he wheeled Angie down the main street of town. He was mesmerized by the yellow magic of the street lamps weaving their golden halos into the cobalt-blue sky. The crowded lane was hopping with banjos and tin pianos, and honky-tonk clatter that echoed from clay brick saloons. In some mystical way, Bill felt like he'd been born there, like a part of his soul had its beginning there, long before he appeared in the flesh at the western end of the Oregon Trail.

Bill didn't like being thought of as a tourist, but as a sightseeing visitor he fit the description, and he didn't like gambling, though one-arm bandits were everywhere; what he did like was the history. This was a slice of South Dakota's past, a badlands refuge where claim jumpers, cattle rustlers and other horse-thieving desperados had fled to spend their stolen money on poker, whiskey and women. Deadwood: the notorious outlaw town that grew out of gunfights and gold strikes, and the very place where Wild Bill Hickok, master of guns and aces, was shot dead during a poker game. How could a man of western breeding not like a place like that?

He pushed Angie up to the doors of the Franklin Hotel. It had been a delicious evening and, because they had to head out early in the morning, Bill had made the most of it. The dining room burned with amber Tiffany, heavy brown tables and oak parquet floors. It was the best darn buffalo steak he'd ever had. Angie, bless her heart, though as plum tuckered out as a bear in hibernation, had been as bright-eyed and cheery as her woebegone life would allow.

He tucked his daughter into bed, in the room where Poker Alice had slept, pulling the cool sheets up to cover her nightgown. Bill picked up the photograph from the quilt. It was made to look old, a coffee-brown print of himself standing in a fake saloon, leaning on the bar with his foot on the rail. He was dressed in chaps, spurs and bandanna, with a sheriff's star pinned to his vest. On his head he wore a white, ten gallon hat. Angie was seated beside him. She had an Indian blanket laid across her lap covering the wheels of her chair. She reclined like a burlesque dancer in a frilly silk ensemble with a crowning feathered hat. The smiles were priceless. Bill slapped the photograph against his palm, slid it onto the dresser and turned to kiss his daughter's cheek. She was already asleep. He stroked her silken hair. Daddy's little cowgirl. It was good she'd found rest; these were grueling days and she needed her strength. Tomorrow's tour would include Mount Rushmore. He hoped Angie was enjoying the trip as much as he was. He leaned over and said good-night with a butterfly kiss.

He moved to his own bed and sat down, tugging at his boot, dragging it off. His sock slid down around his ankle. He dropped the boot with a thud and jerked the sock back on, then paused to let his toes wiggle with renewed freedom. His portable computer lay on the bed beside him. He removed his other boot and leaned back on his elbow to zip the computer case open. Ideas had been swirling in his head all afternoon. A new topic was taking shape. It was time to write his column.

I'm sick and tired of tolerance. I'm sick and tired of other people telling me what is and what is not acceptable behavior. And I'm sick and tired of pretending that everything is hunky-dory okay, when even a blind man can see our country's on a fast track to destruction.

I can agree to live and let live. As long as you don't get in my face, I won't get in yours. This is the essence of the freedom granted each of us by our Constitution. It is in defense of this constitutional right that I frequently criticize advocacy groups. Their objectives might be sincere, all well and good, but in an effort to sell their particular cause, in their drive to convert as many as possible to their point of view, they run ramshackle over anyone who gets in their way. And that "anyone" is quite often me.

Since I oppose America's headlong rush toward the pit, I'm classified as backward and narrow-minded. I don't agree with gay rights advocates when they say schoolchildren should be encouraged to explore the feelings they have for those of their own sex. And I don't agree with well-meaning educators who tell kids intercourse is a normal, healthy part of growing up, while showing them how it's done. Nor do I agree with feminist groups telling young girls that men have exploited women for centuries, and that men can't be trusted. I take a different stand on all these issues.

That, of course, makes me a bigot. Open disagreement used to be defined as freedom of speech, but in today's world, opposing the rhetoric of the political left makes you either homophobic, a sexist, a racist or some other form of extremist. Believe me, I've been called them all.

Never mind that society is in a moral tailspin, and that pregnancies among thirteen-year-old girls, mere babies themselves, have reached record numbers. Never mind that sexually transmitted diseases are out of control and that many of these are incurable. Forget that pedophiles and other porno kings peddle sex to kids on the Internet. And never mind that all these things combine to weaken the fabric of our society. None of this matters, I'm told, because now we live in a more tolerant, accepting society that holds every form of sexual practice to be healthy and normal. And this, supposedly, makes us a better people.

We are a new generation, they say, more understanding, more caring, and more concerned about the needs of others. These are good things, but at what cost have they been achieved? To be tolerant of every avowed lifestyle, is to deny that we need self-control. We may have acquired more tolerance, but we've lost an equal measure of discipline. We've traded one for the other. Discipline is what it takes to say no. It means not giving place to wanton desires and obsessions. It means showing restraint. But we've forsaken discipline to obtain tolerance. We quote the Bible: "Judge not that ye be not judged," and use it to justify our toleration of anything and everything. We forget that the Bible also gave us the Ten Commandments, wherein we find that some things are not to be tolerated.

As I travel across this once great land of ours, I continually see evidence of our surrender to such folly. At a tourist stop in the most remote region of the Badlands of South Dakota (how appropriately named), I found a teenage boy harassing my daughter, calling her a retard, simply because she's confined to a wheelchair. I admit, I became very intolerant. If it were not for the age of the young man, I might have hurt him. He needed a lesson; when you harm innocent people, there's a penalty to pay.

The boy's father refused to reprimand his son. Instead, he threatened to sue me because I stopped the boy from picking on my daughter. The Good Book says spare the rod and spoil the child. This child was truly spoiled. I was tempted to turn the rascal over my own knee, but I had to choose between two Judeo-Christian virtues: justice and mercy. Justice might have required that the boy suffer a consequence. I decided to show mercy. I chose to walk away.

I wish I could say that's where it ended, but I can't. As I wheeled my daughter down the sidewalk past the audience that witnessed the affair, I saw frowns of disapproval. People were condemning my actions, not because I didn't give the boy what he deserved, but because I dared to confront his behavior at all.

I've discovered that it's no longer permissible to exhibit righteous indignation. We must be tolerant of every type of behavior, except moral outrage; that alone must not be tolerated. Those who refuse to fall in line like good little cardboard soldiers marching in step to the beat of this politically correct drum are in for a rough ride.

I'm willing to accept that fact. I'm willing to stand up for what is right, the truth passed down from generation to generation, even if by today's standards that makes me a bigot. In this confused, mixed-up world, I will still try to live and let live. I say, don't get in my face and I won't get in yours. But if for some reason you do get in my face, don't be surprised if you discover that I'm not really a very tolerant person.

LAURIE TOUCHED her cheek. What a wonderful feeling, smooth, fresh, a feather of cool air touching her skin. Do pores really breathe? It felt like hers had been suffocating for days. Peter stood at the mirror combing out tangles of hair which now fell blonde and loose over her shoulders. And my, look at those eyes, as clear and deep as a crystal-blue river. She wanted to scream, *NO MORE WRINKLES, EMANCIPATION, FREEDOM!* She checked her watch: two A.M. Time to begin. She felt a tinge of anticipation, an edge of caffeine nipping at the walls of her stomach.

Ruth and Edith sat in quiet awe of the transformation. The cracking of the cocoon had released youth and beauty from the vestiges of antiquity. If only such could be done for them. Ruth wore her standard red crest and white gloves, looking as bird-like as ever. Edith took another sip of tea, and sat back in her shawl, wondering how they were going to pull this off without getting caught.

The curtains had been drawn and blankets spread over the windows so light wouldn't leak. Laurie stared at herself in the mirror. *Like drinking from the fountain of youth,* she thought. Peter finished smoothing her hair. "Now that's more like it," he said. "Good to have you back."

"Good to be back," Laurie responded. "And here's hoping we'll find what we need tonight so I won't have to..." she started to say, "keep pretending to be old," but quickly rephrased "...go undercover again."

"I'd give fifty bucks if he could do that for me," Edith grumbled.

Peter patted the back of the chair. "Well sit down and we'll give it a try."

"Some other time," Laurie quipped. "Right now we have work to do. I need both you ladies on lookout."

Laurie stood and tugged at the slim waist of her blue denim slacks. In her gray cotton sweat shirt and white sneakers, she was dressed for comfort. She turned to the mirror, popped a bobby pin into her mouth, and rolled her hair into a bun so it wouldn't be in the way.

"This may be the only chance we have to get what we need." She pulled the hair clip from her teeth and fixed the bun in place. "You both know the plan. If anyone comes toward the office, create a diversion, act like one of you is sick and wail and moan until I can get away, got it?"

Ruth bobbed her head and stood. Then she turned to reach down and help Edith off the sofa, but Edith shook her arm free. "I'm not so old as I can't get up without help," she cackled. She leaned on the table and pushed herself up. "I hope you know what you're doing. We'll probably all end up in jail." She crossed her arms over her bosom tightening her shawl around her shoulders. "Aw, what the heck? It can't be much colder there than it is in here."

Ruth just smiled.

Laurie walked to the door. It felt so good to be her young self again, tall and erect, confident—well almost but, realistically, even if she were caught, what could they do, shoot her? "I'm ready, but I want you both to stay here until you're sure I've had enough time to get inside, then sneak out and take up your positions. If anyone heads my way, you know what to do." She nodded at the two elderly women and slipped into the hall, closing the door behind her.

Ruth smiled weakly and turned around. Now was the time to pray. She glanced at the others in the room. It wouldn't be with these two. Edith said God was poppycock, and this Peter fellow—*a makeup artist?*—well, you couldn't always tell, but she was pretty sure he was gay. She could hear it in his voice. He looked sad behind the smile he was trying to fake. She couldn't help feeling sorry for him, but that was a sentiment he probably wouldn't appreciate. After all, Eric never wanted anyone feeling sorry for him. The bigger question was whether or not the man could be trusted. She hoped Annie knew what she was doing. She tried not to be obvious as she sent an SOS to the Father.

The hall was dimly lit, making it hard to see, even for someone with good eyes. But that was to be expected. Turning down the lights saved energy. Good thing a few lights had to be left on for the insomniacs who wandered the floors at night. Laurie made her way cautiously down the corridor, trying to see far enough ahead to spot movement. She stopped where the passage spilled into the lobby. A light in Barbara Marks' office broke the dimness and painted the furnishings dull gray. Laurie looked at her watch twisting her wrist toward the light to see the numbers. Two-twelve in the morning, the light had to have been left on by accident. The accounting office was next door. Laurie held the key, gripping it tight enough to feel its saw-toothed edges biting her skin. She glided silently across the carpeted floor, weaving through the deeply cushioned lounge chairs, around the coffee table and up to the door. She scanned the empty room, a chill caressing her neck. Turning, she took one last look over her shoulder, sipped in her breath and slipped the key into the lock. The knob turned without effort. She slid inside.

The room was murky but she dared not flick the lights. Instead, she wiggled a key chain penlight from her pocket and squeezed it on. The dim yellow light faltered, blinking, weak as an old battery. She bounced it on the palm of her hand and saw its intensity increase momentarily, but it diminished just as quickly. The faded beam was dull and short. It would have to do. She could see workstations on both sides of the room with an aisle down the middle. Another door, on the opposite wall, bore a brass nameplate. She moved closer, aiming her light. The plaque read, George Bergen - V.P. Finance. Anything of consequence would be in there.

Laurie's key turned the lock. *Perfect!* The cleaning staff had unrestricted access. She went inside and closed the door. The narrow beam scanned the dark paneled room sweeping across objects until it came to a large desk. The wave of light bounced off the smooth, polished surface onto a computer screen. Bingo! That's what she wanted.

She could see tiny flickering yellow and green lights underneath the desk, indicating the computer was on. *Good.* But was this a personal machine, used only by Mr. Bergen, or was it the hub of a networked system? Probably networked—*had to be*—the accounting people would need access. She stood over the monitor, clicked it on, and waited for the screen to illuminate. She had to access the accounts of the now deceased Henry and Leonard, and also the accounts of Cash and Louis and anyone else on the equity exchange plan. If Ruth's theories were correct, those who paid monthly from an outside bank account weren't in danger. Their demise would only curtail a source of revenue for the company. With a little luck, she might also uncover what had happened to Joe. If he'd been eliminated, there should be a record of it somewhere, along with a document stating that he'd died of his own free will. She also wanted to see any e-mails, memos or notes written about Ben, Ruth, or Edith.

The accounting files were easy to access. Using an explore program, she pointed the mouse and with a few clicks, was staring at financial spreadsheet going back several years. Laurie slipped a high density diskette out of her hip pocket and slid it into the floppy drive. The *thunk* of the disk being captured and the *whirrrrr* of the machine as it analyzed the insertion caused her to swallow her breath. The absolute silence of the room had been broken. Did anyone hear? She could feel the pounding in her breast, *ththuump, ththuump, ththuump*. She raised her eyes expecting to see someone come charging through the door but stillness settled in the room again. Her finger began quietly click, click, clicking the keyboard, command given, copy all marked files. The lights under the desk blinked and flickered as data was acquired and downloaded to disk. It was a large file; it would take a few minutes; she would print and study the information back in her apartment. She wondered how Ruth and Edith were doing. They should be in their watch positions by now, each at separate ends of the lobby.

Laurie sent the beam of her penlight around the room searching for a file cabinet. She found it behind her, a rosewood credenza with two lateral file drawers. She reached over and pulled the handle, but it was locked. She sat in Mr. Bergen's executive leather chair. What kind of man was this? Judging by the framed photo on his desk, a family man, assuming this was his wife, two boys and daughter, a nicely posed professional portrait all in all. But Hitler probably had a picture of Eva Braun on his desk. And everyone knew Goebbels was a family man, but Nazi party leader Gregor Strasser had called him, "Satan in human form." Loving your family didn't necessarily make you a nice person.

She opened the desk. The penlight did not provide adequate light but she hoped the shiny, stainless-steel key would stand out. The drawers were neatly organized and easy to comb through, but...nothing. Now what? She had no experience whatsoever in picking locks, totally out of her league. The computer completed its task. She removed the disk and slipped it into her pocket. She went back to the explore program and found a folder marked "Guests," clicked and found two more files, one marked "Contracts," and the other marked "Histories." Bingo! This was almost too easy. She pointed the mouse and clicked but instead of opening the file the action initiated a password prompt. Drat! She tried the second file...same thing.

Of course she'd anticipated this, but she'd hoped it wouldn't be a problem. She didn't have any way of getting around it. She wished she had the support of her home office. The hackers there could get into anything. They had programs that cycled through millions of passwords. But knowing this did not help Laurie now. She was entirely incapable of breaking into a computer without assistance. And she couldn't solicit office help because she didn't want anyone knowing where she was. She stared at the protected file, willing it to open. She tried entering familiar words, George, Bergen, Finance, Emerald, Valley, Histories, Contracts, Guests, nothing worked. She leaned back in the chair. She pointed the penlight at her watch, two forty-eight. Every passing minute was a minute closer to discovery. She had to do something, but what? She wouldn't get another chance. How to crack a password, *come on girl—think!*

A noise in the outer office arrested her thoughts. Ruth? Edith? A cleaning lady? A yellow shaft spread under the door. Someone had turned on the light, someone not afraid of being exposed. Hide in a closet? Duck under the desk? She was paralyzed. It all came down to this: if it wasn't Ruth or Edith, she was busted. Her job...no, her life was about to explode, guilty of breaking and entering, of trespass, of corporate espionage. How much time do you get for a first offense? The key turned, the door opened, the light flicked on and a face jolted, as startled as Laurie's own. The two people stared at each other, silenced by the unexpected encounter. "Who are you?" Barbara demanded. "What are you doing in here?"

TWELVE

A THOUSAND THOUGHTS flashing, a video arcade of sequenced ideas ripping like film through a projector, bursts of photographic images forming a series of questions, outlining Laurie's options. *Where are Ruth and Edith? Why wasn't there warning?* She could run. Barbara was no match for a younger woman's strength. She could burst through and escape into the night without revealing her identity. What about Peter? Would Ruth and Edith warn him? What about fingerprints? She could lie. She could claim she was Mr. Bergen's mistress. She could say she couldn't sleep, that she let herself in with a key he'd given her. She was waiting for him. Better still, she had decided to end the relationship. She wanted to leave a note. She couldn't risk calling him at home. She was struggling with the words. *Where are Ruth and Edith?* Or, she could confess. She could tell the truth and wait for Barbara's reaction, be it friend or foe, a fifty/fifty proposition at best. Would she be held for prosecution or given grace to go? Either way, it would mean the end of her investigation, which would mean the bad guys had won...rapid fire thoughts projected on the blank screen of her mind at a million frames a second. Her temples were throbbing. She blinked to relieve the burning in her eyes. It felt like sour milk was curdling in her stomach.

"Who let you in?"

There had to be a reasonable explanation but...but what? She'd been caught with a smoking gun—game over. *Think girl, think!* She was there undercover, dear Mrs. Iversen, doing a human interest story on what it's like to be elderly. She could say she was with some other

128

paper, a small, low-circulation tabloid. *No, no, no, no, no, avoid the papers.* She could say she was visiting one of the guests. She only slipped into the office to use the phone so she wouldn't disturb her sleeping host. The door wasn't locked. But why was she awake at three A.M.? And for that matter, why was Barbara?

"I could ask you the same question? Who are you, and what are you doing in Mr. Bergen's office at this hour of the morning?" she challenged, taking the offensive. *Why not? When you ain't got nothing, you got nothing to lose!*

"I'm the one asking the questions," Barbara shot back. "I work here, that's all you need to know."

"Not quite. Mr. Bergen suspects someone's been tampering with his computer, stealing confidential files. He hired me to investigate and bingo, first night on the job you show up. I find that suspicious. I think you'd better explain."

"Oh for the love of...Mr. Bergen was the one who insisted I have these sales projections on his desk by morning." Barbara waved the folder in her hand. "He needs them for his board meeting."

Ruth stumbled huffing and puffing into the room, followed by Edith a few seconds after. They were panting, marathon runners, gasping to catch their breath. Laurie noticed how short they both were. They barely reached Barbara's shoulder.

"Laurie, *huh-ah-huh-ah-huh,* you all right? *huh-ah-huh. Whhhew.* We, *huh-ah-huh,* couldn't stop her." Ruth wheezed.

"We were, *whew, huh-ah-huh,* stuck at opposite ends of the lobby," the throaty voice of Mrs. Woodhouse added.

"She came out, *wheeeze,* out of her office, *huh-ah-huh,* right in the middle."

"What the devil is going on?" Barbara's shrill voice demanded.

Ruth took a deep breath and raised a white-gloved finger. "Be careful what you say. We know who's responsible for the deaths of Henry, Leonard, Ben, and Joe." She panted. She paused to catch her breath again, looking at Laurie for support. "We've got evidence. You should probably keep quiet until you talk to a lawyer."

Laurie's eyes narrowed and darted from Ruth to Edith to Barbara. *Ru-uth, what are you saying? I haven't got anything yet. Don't blow my cover.*

"Yeah, you and the rest of these hooligans are going to jail."

Ed-ith!

"Evidence? That's what this is about? You...whoever you are, can't you see how crazy this is? They're delusional."

Barbara's eyes wrinkled, the olive green saucers quivering with the realization that something was amiss—but not something she knew about. If Laurie had to guess, she'd say the lady didn't have a clue. "Oh, there's evidence all right. You might want to think about cooperating with us. It may mean a lighter sentence."

"You people are crazy. All of you."

"Maybe, maybe not, but things aren't kosher around here. Why were you defending the disappearance of Mr. Wiarton and Mr. Williams yesterday?"

"People on vacation?"

"Perhaps, but why go to such great lengths to explain? You want me to believe everything's copacetic, tell me this, where's Joe Bonner?"

Barbara's mouth opened. Her chapped lips formed a small "O" but no words came out. The crow's feet tucked away at the corner of her eyes revealed tension. She brought her hand to her throat, her painted fingernails massaging the loose skin as if trying to prime her vocal cords.

As Laurie recalled, this was the same question Edith had asked at the meeting. Barbara didn't have an answer then, and it was apparent she didn't have one now, and from the look of it, Joe's disappearance was troubling Barbara as much as the rest of them.

"I don't know anything," Barbara finally said. "If you have something the police can use, take it to them. It doesn't concern me. I'm only paid to sell a service."

"Uh-huh," Laurie intoned. "Well, as I said, we do have evidence and we're gaining more all the time. I believe there's information in this computer that can prove people are being murdered here."

"Nonsense! We've been through all this. They filled out the proper authorization. They wanted to die with dignity. Why can't you let them rest in peace?"

"Authorization? Hardly! They didn't know what was coming.

You want to prove your innocence, give me Mr. Bergen's password. I need access to one of his files."

"I can't."

"Because your name's in there, along with whatever part you played?"

"Because I don't know it, and even if I did I wouldn't give it to you, a total stranger, unless I was absolutely convinced that what you're saying is true. And at this point, I'm not."

"So you're saying if you knew for sure someone had done something illegal, you'd help? Because if that's what you're saying, I'll give you the proof. All I need is twenty-four hours. We've acquired a fair amount of evidence. Let me put it together for you. Just don't say anything till then. Is that fair?"

The silence was long and daunting. Ruth blinked and put her hands to her head to adjust her hat. Odd she would wear it at three in the morning. Edith spread her fingers over her chest and stooped slightly, still trying to catch her breath. Laurie stared into the eyes of Barbara and waited.

Barbara wrapped her arm around her file and held Laurie's gaze. They were bulls, pawing the ground, locking horns, ready for combat. You could feel the steamy tension. Barbara finally broke. "Twenty-four hours," she said, and walked out.

THEY STOOD IN AWE, staring into eyes of wisdom, decades old, but as resolute as the rock from which they were carved.

"The preservation of the sacred fire of liberty and the destiny of the Republican model of government are justly considered as deeply, perhaps as finally staked, on the experiment entrusted to the hands of the American people." George Washington - Commander of the Revolutionary army, First U.S. President.

"We hold these truths to be self-evident, that all men are created equal, that they are endowed by their

Creator with certain inalienable rights, that among these are Life, Liberty, and the Pursuit of Happiness." Thomas Jefferson - Author of the Declaration of Independence, Third U.S. President.

"Let us have faith that right makes might and in that faith let us dare to do our duty as we understand it." Abraham Lincoln - Commander and Chief of the Union Army, war between the states, Sixteenth U.S. President.

"We, here in America, hold in our hands the hopes of the world, the fate of the coming years; and shame and disgrace will be ours if in our eyes the light of high resolve is dimmed, if we trail in the dust the golden hopes of men." Theodore Roosevelt - Commander of the U.S. Calvary, Spanish-American war, Twenty-sixth U.S. President.

And their faces were smiling down upon Bill. He was overwhelmed by the splendor of it all, how such a tribute could be carved in stone. How much he wanted to sing "America, America, God shed his grace on thee," but he dared not. That grace was being withdrawn. The people had forsaken the God of their fathers and like Israel before them, had gone chasing after the false gods of pride, materialism, and sexual gratification.

Bill felt a flick of breeze toss his hair. He listened to a blue jay chattering in the nearby trees. The air was thick with the scent of pine. The majesty of Mt. Rushmore was staggering. It was cause to reflect on everything that had made America great, but such thoughts also made him sad. Most Americans were guilty of rejecting the wisdom of their forefathers. Their words had been trampled in the dust. He recalled a quote from George Washington's inaugural address, an excerpt so insightful, he'd committed it to memory:

"It would be peculiarly improper to omit, in this first official act, my fervent supplication to that Almighty Being, who rules over the universe, who presides in the councils of nations, and whose providential aids can supply every human defect...We ought to be no less persuaded that the smiles of heaven can never be expected on a nation that disregards the eternal rules of order and right which heaven itself has ordained."

Bill stared up into the rock solid eyes of Abraham Lincoln. He'd memorized the words of this president as well:

"It is the duty of nations, as well as of men, to owe their dependence upon the overruling power of God, and to confess this truth announced in the Holy Scriptures, proven by all history, that those nations only are blessed whose God is the Lord."

The wisdom and greatness of men like Washington and Lincoln was dependent upon yielding to the will of Almighty God. If only men could believe today what the country's founding fathers believed, that only those who put their faith in God could hope to receive his blessing. God himself promised it when he said: "If my people, who are called by my name, shall humble themselves and pray, and seek my face, and turn from their wicked ways, then I will hear from heaven, and will forgive their sin, and will heal their land."

It was a brilliant blue-sky day. The granite faces were shining with the sun's favor, slick, polished, and timeless as stone. Bill loved history, perhaps because by looking at the past he saw hope for the future. He could see things the way they were meant to be. But thoughts of yesterday served to manifest the errors of today, and thinking about that made him weak in the knees. They had to be moving on. A song came to mind, one he could still sing. He turned Angie's wheelchair around and began crooning as they bumped over the tiles: "This is my Father's world, O let me ne'er forget, That though the wrong seems oft so strong, God is the ruler yet," all the way down the Avenue of Flags, back to the parking lot.

LAURIE AWOKE. The room was awash in midday sun. She rubbed her eyes and felt the sandpaper dryness of her tongue. Then she heard it again, three rapid knocks. Where was Peter? She rose and felt the aching in her bones as she stood and willed her legs to move. She saw Ruth through the peephole, her head flicking back and forth, a skittish bird trying to avoid capture. Laurie opened the door to find a skinny limb raised to her face, knuckles forward, ready to strike. She took hold of Ruth's arm and pulled her inside.

"What time is it?" She glanced at her watch, "Oh gosh, I overslept, it's already noon. I'm glad you woke me. It's getting late..."

"We've found Joe."

"Whaaa...Joe? Alive?"

"Yes. No. I mean, sort of."

Peter came from around behind the kitchen divider. "Did I hear you say Joe's alive? Well that's good news, isn't it?"

But Ruth was too flustered to answer. "I can't stay," she said. "They've done something to him, something terrible. Go see for yourself." She turned to the door, tilting up on the toes of her red patent shoes to see through the peephole. Her head tipped back so far Laurie thought she might lose her hat. Her heels clicked on the tile as she popped down and turned to deliver her final message, her hands flying around her head like little birds. "Hurry!" Ruth opened the door and stuck her head out.

"Wait," Laurie said.

But seeing the coast clear, Ruth skittered into the hall and headed toward the lobby, where she'd indicated Joe could be found.

"Peter, I need you to make me up again," Laurie said.

LAURIE LEANED on her cane, supporting herself. Each step was forceful, designed to appear slow while in a hurry. Ruth had delivered the most cryptic message so far. Joe was alive—but not really? Ruth was obviously shaken by it. Things were developing fast, but not fast enough. Laurie had stayed up till five-thirty reviewing the

134

information she'd pirated from Mr. Bergen's office. It verified what she'd been told. Every time someone on the prepaid plan died, the balance of their money was placed into corporate coffers and the company netted a tidy profit. But there were shortfalls whenever a guest outlived their endowment, which resulted in corporate loss, a deficit that was eventually corrected when the person died. The problem was, the spreadsheet showed only numbers, there weren't any names attached, so the evidence was purely circumstantial.

There was one other discovery that had caught her attention. The home had been operating in the red for several years. Whether it was because of slow business or bad management wasn't clear, but they were losing money, so they certainly had motive to get rid of people who couldn't pay their way. She e-mailed the entire file to Bill and asked him to review it. Perhaps he would spot something she had missed.

Laurie slowed as she entered the lobby. She could feel her pulse in her fingertips, a sure sign her heart was working overtime. She realized she was holding her breath. She exhaled and drew in air through her nose making a fluttering sound. She waited a moment to collect herself. Thankfully, the ladies, in their mishandling of Barbara Marks, had failed to mention her alter ego. Her identity as Annie Iversen was secure, or was it? If Barbara saw her now, would she see through the disguise? She hoped not; she still needed to use it.

She couldn't see Joe at first because he was roped off by a knot of people. She took one deliberate, plodding step at a time until she squeezed through the periphery and stood within the circle. It was Joe, all right. But then again it wasn't. The man confined to the wheelchair looked as lifeless as a cotton-headed doll, a huge bald Raggedy Andy in a baseball cap. The eyes were parched and unblinking, focused on life in another dimension. His head was lobbed over. His face was white except where his lips curled out. Oddly, his lips were blood red, and a string of clear saliva drooled from his open mouth making a dark wet stain where it came to rest on his collar. Ruth, the fuzzy little songbird, knelt beside him. She didn't acknowledge the others; her eyes were closed; she simply held Joe's hand and mumbled a litany of soft words.

A group of a dozen people stared at the grotesque scene in silence. For seconds that seemed to stretch into minutes, no one budged. Laurie wondered how long they had been there. What were their thoughts? Here was a man they all knew well, a man they had played cards with, had laughed with, and had swapped stories with, suddenly struck down, a lump of breathing meat. How could it happen?

"Poor fellow had a stroke."

Laurie turned to acknowledge Karla standing behind her. "Is that what it was?"

"What else, honey? The man was a junk food junkie. Can't say I didn't warn him. I told him it would kill him. The man ate potato chips by the bagful. All that oil finally clogged up his arteries and, *wham,* he seized up, just like that."

The little colonel peeked out from behind Karla's bountiful skirt. "That ain't it," he said. "Weren't no stroke. He was done in." He stepped out and pointed his finger at Joe. "I told him to watch his flank, but he wouldn't listen. Stubborn as an army mule. I told him."

"And I tol' you to hush. You keep foolin' where you don't belong and you're gonna be in a mess a trouble."

"And if you don't wake up to what's going on, you're gonna end up just like him!"

Karla turned to Laurie in wide-eyed frustration. "Just ignore him," she said, her ruby lips sparkling in the light.

"I will not be ignored," the little colonel stammered, pounding his fist into the palm of his hand. "You watch your flank. Watch your flank I say. Many a good man died on the field of battle 'cause they didn't listen."

IT WASN'T Colonel Jack's imagination. It happened just that way, back in forty-four, in the blood and guts of war. He'd been at the Normandy Invasion: Omaha Beach. His landing craft had taken a shell from a large coastal gun installed on the cliffs. Half his men were blown away before they hit land. Others were thrown clear but, in their marching boots, helmets and packs, had drowned. He'd survived by hanging on to a floating box. He'd crawled up on the beach, breathing smoke and dust so thick, he couldn't see a dozen feet in front of his nose. He'd crawled over the dead and wounded, inching his way forward while waiting for the smoke to clear. All around him, men were falling. They fell on his right, and on his left, in front and behind. Each time he looked up, more men were gone. But the one thing that stuck in Colonel Rosen's mind was the image of a surly sergeant bleeding from the head and covered in dust who wouldn't stop yelling at his men: "WATCH YOUR FLANK! WATCH YOUR FLANK!" he'd screamed over and over. But death came out of nowhere, and took them away, one by one, even those who watched.

KARLA TURNED the little colonel around and rested her arm over his collar. "Just don't pay him any mind," she said, and then she escorted the colonel off through the lobby. He continued to jabber and pound his fist as they moved away.

That was a surprise. Apparently the colonel's conclusions were the same as her friends, but he wasn't part of the group. How many others knew the truth, or at least suspected something was wrong? And why was Karla trying to keep it quiet? For her own protection? Or was she a mole for the corporation?

Laurie turned back to Joe. The sight of Ruth kneeling, holding his hand, whispering words to the empty shell, his tomb-like visage, the sense of loss, the failure, all of it troubled her. Something stirred inside—a twinge of guilt? Had their one brief conversation led to Joe's undoing? She recognized the feeling. Was it Joe, or something else? Her own daughter probably looked like this, drooling and wetting herself. But that was Bill's fault. He was the one who insisted she carry the child full term.

She was sanding in the nursery, looking down into the crib. She wanted so desperately to pick the baby up so she could hold her, but she couldn't, and she couldn't understand why. What cosmic force prevented her from reaching down and lifting the child into her arms? What invisible tape kept her arms bound to her side? It wasn't her fault—was it? She hadn't wanted the child to be born. How was she supposed to live with the fact that her disease was causing her child to suffer?

There were too many questions, with too few answers. She pictured Angie on the day she left, unable to walk or talk, not like a normal three year old, a tiny, hapless soul, twisting around in her chair as her father wheeled her away. The eyes had said it all: *Come with us mommy. You come too!*

So much guilt. She was guilty of abandoning not only her child, but also her husband. She loved Bill, even if she couldn't agree with him. What Peter said wasn't true. She could love. She just hadn't found anyone better than Bill to give her love to. But loving him didn't mean he wasn't still the root of her problem. Imposing his will on hers had resulted in the guilt she now felt. It created a living paradox; she both loved and hated the man, and it made her emotions a confused mess. Bill said he'd sold the house and bought a boat. He and Angie would be back in Seattle around the first of May. That was just a few days away. The thought burned in the hollow of her chest. She wasn't sure if the feeling was anticipation, or dread, but she knew she'd soon find out. She would see them again. It was inevitable. Had Angie received her birthday card? What was she supposed to say to a daughter she hadn't seen in ten years? What excuses would she make? *Questions, questions, questions!*

Laurie looked at the silent, gurgling figure in the wheelchair. Poor old Joe. Such an awful end to what seemed like a decent man, but at least he'd lived a full, healthy life. Angie didn't deserve the kind of life Bill had condemned her to. Wouldn't it have been better if she hadn't been born? That was the question Laurie was still trying to answer. Maybe seeing Angie again was exactly what she needed. It would either prove she'd been right—or...?

Another voice, rankled and sharp, spoke in her ear and something was pushed into her hand. "Do what you can. This is too much for me." Then Edith pulled away and Laurie was left holding a scrap of paper. She took a step back and unfurled the note. "I'm no part of this," it read. "Tell your friend the password is 'candy,' as in stealing from a baby."

The note was unsigned.

THIRTEEN

I think my dad has some kind of special gift, a sixth sense, call it what you will, but he can say out loud exactly what I'm thinking without my having to say it. He's like some kind of mind reader. Of course, he has an edge when it comes to understanding me. He sees me through eyes of love.

Some people have peculiar eyes. When they look at me, they see something different, something subhuman. They act like if they get too close, they'll catch whatever it is I've got. Seeing me makes them think of themselves and how awful it would be if they were in my place, and that makes them uncomfortable.

Dad showed me in the Bible where it says that man looks on the outward appearance, but God looks on the heart. In the same way, Dad looks past my palsy and sees the real me. He pretends not to notice the difference between me and everyone else. He knows that inside this twisted body is a human soul—and every human soul has worth!

BILL LEANED against the car, counting to ten, breathing slowly. The black tar rippled at the edge of the road, chipped and broken. A withered dandelion poked its head through a jagged crack. If there was some good in all this, he would find it. The sun was translucent, like light shining through a thin slice of lemon, and the air was sagebrush sweet, thick and heavy, like honey in his lungs. Life was too short to waste time fretting over things he couldn't change.

He kicked the tire, leaving a black rubber streak on the side of his already dusty boot. The gravel crunched underfoot, and the sun shimmered off the asphalt in waves of corrugated heat. Bill mopped his brow with his sleeve. He should have changed into something lighter. It wasn't until he'd dragged every single box out of the back of the station wagon, leaving them stacked helter skelter by the side of the road, that he'd discovered another oversight the car's previous owner had failed to mention: there was no spare tire!

Cheap retread, it wasn't able to survive the long haul; it had withered under the pressure of unending miles. Buyer beware, impulse decisions usually lead to remorse. At least his cell phone worked. He hadn't had a chance to charge it. What if it had been dead, or what if there hadn't been enough cell sites on this deserted stretch of road to make a connection? He couldn't have left Angie and gone hitchhiking thirty-six miles back to the nearest town, and he couldn't have taken her with him. At least the tire blew in a place where he could call for help.

The delay was his primary concern. He'd planned to make Yellowstone by nightfall, but he was beginning to doubt it would happen. He'd put in a call for a tow truck. They'd said they'd be there in half an hour. He looked down at the melted tire. By the time the driver got the call, stopped whatever he was doing, and drove all the way out, Bill knew it would be at least an hour.

Breathe deep, smell the air, this too shall pass. The romance of the high plains dissolved his anxiety. At least it wasn't raining, it wasn't snowing, it wasn't even blowing, it was just sunning. He leaned against his dirty vehicle, crossed his arms and considered that maybe it wasn't such a good idea to be speeding willy-nilly cross country like a lemming looking for water. He might be headed for a cliff. He brought his knee up and rested the heel of his boot on the side of the car. They'd lost their van, they'd lost their cat, they'd survived the worst deluge he'd ever seen, he'd almost been arrested, his new car had only one wiper and no radio, and now this double whammy: a flat and no spare tire. It didn't do much to affirm his west coast plans. Doubts had been creeping in ever since he'd left. Wanting to reunite Angie with her mother was a good thing. Why did doing something good have to be so hard?

DR. VANETTER accompanied the cleaning lady on her rounds. She filtered through the halls taking the same route and cleaning the same rooms as she had the day before, in and out, same routine, day after day, month upon month, year after year. Her fretful glance revealed she was intimidated by the doctor's presence.

He didn't explain what he was doing there. It was none of her business. Besides, he wasn't sure why he was there himself. Someone could have spilled a bottle of skin tone and used the towel to clean it up. But not knowing bothered him. He had to satisfy his curiosity.

He watched as the maid emptied the trash and filled her laundry cart with dirty linens. The canvas bag was full to overflowing: washcloths, bed sheets, towels in pairs of matching colors, all embroidered with the green Emerald Valley logo. He sifted through the pile, occasionally separating a few towels, holding them up for inspection and tossing them into the basket again.

The maid disappeared to do her cleaning, leaving the doctor standing alone in the corridor. Only the maids were allowed to enter the rooms without being invited. He had no intention of breaking the rules.

The cleaning lady came back with the trash, emptying it into the large canvas bag at the end of her cart. A magazine tumbled from the rubbish. Dr. VanEtter picked it up. "Fashionable Fitness," it read. Well, at least someone saw the value of staying in shape, though he couldn't imagine who. They practically had to drag people into the fitness center. He leaned against the wall, flipping through the pages, his white lab smock rustling against the flat painted surface. If they wanted good muscle tone, why not use the exercise room? That's why it was there. He tossed the magazine back into the trash and looked at his watch. How many rooms were left to clean?

THE BOARD MEETING had convened. The dimmer was low. The directors sat around the table, a dull yellow light glowing on the crowns of their heads; their faces subdued by shadow. In front of each man was a scuffle of printed sheets, plotted, diagramed, two-side copied and wire bound.

Charts and graphs illuminated the white board, but their brilliant colors couldn't mask another year of red ink. George Bergen, V.P. of Finance, was on the spot. His presentation was flawed. He'd barely shown the first slide when Gabe Solomon commented that he needed to see improvement, or he'd be forced to divest.

George didn't have what Mr. Solomon wanted. Every financial projection he'd put together indicated further losses. He'd padded Barbara's sales forecast ten percent, which was at his insistence, already over inflated. The numbers still didn't add up. He cleared his throat. He was stalling. He wanted to hold back the next slide, the one that showed the five-year forecast. He looked at Carl Shiffer, the company's president and fair-haired boy wonder, for a cue to continue.

Mr. Solomon coughed. He grew impatient waiting for the next slide and picked up the printed copy to get a preview of what was coming.

George fumbled, raising his finger over the button. If only he could avoid showing this one. It was bound to upset Solomon. It wasn't his fault, he kept telling himself. They'd tried everything. They'd simply run out of options. They needed to increase their income, but people weren't standing in line to purchase a unit, and they'd already raised the rent to the point where they were no longer competitive. People on a fixed income wouldn't pay more, no matter how many additional services they provided. Besides, additional services meant additional cost.

The concept had looked great on paper. He and his young partner Carl, had optimistically forecast a fifty percent split between those who purchased a unit outright, and those who paid a monthly lease. You needed a certain amount of lease tenants to provide a steady flow of cash. The revenue stream was required to make the mortgage payment and cover the cost of operation and maintenance. But the real strategy was focused on selling the units outright. Each lump sum was added to a cumulative total and set aside for reinvestment which, because of the ever ballooning size of the amount, was projected to bring shareholders a maximum return.

The original prospectus had proposed this facility as a pilot, a prototype to be followed by the opening of another new facility each year for five years. Based on a plan to achieve exponential growth, they had raised seed capital and had taken the company public. George and Carl had rewarded themselves with a half million shares each. But their shares were being held in escrow until predetermined levels of profitability were reached. Because they had not yet reached their profitability targets, none of their shares had been released.

The failure was marketing's fault. George knew his numbers were sound, it was marketing's inability to sell the program that crippled their success. All they needed was a fully utilized campus of three hundred residents. If half paid fifteen hundred a month, it would provide over two hundred thousand toward operating expenses, which was more than enough. If the other hundred and fifty residents each paid an average of three hundred thousand for an outright purchase, or supplied the corporation with an asset of equal value, it would provide nearly fifty million for investment. And that was only one facility. They should be making money hand over fist. But the marketing types couldn't deliver. Barbara was their third salesperson. Granted, she was doing better than her younger, fast-talking, predecessors, but it wasn't good enough.

After five years, the facility was only half leased. Since it took a hundred and fifty residents to sustain enough cash flow for monthly maintenance, all revenues were being used just to keep the facility in operation, and they were still in the red. Those few who'd paid up front didn't contribute enough to provide the returns promised to shareholders, most of whom had bailed long ago. Trading was at an all time low, and disenchanted brokers were discouraging investment by referring to EVC shares as "penny stock." George punched the key to bring up the next slide, but before the screen filled with color, Solomon stood.

"I've seen what I came to see," he said. "I apologize, but I can't afford more time. I need to begin offloading before the market closes. Assuming, of course, my broker can find someone to purchase my shares."

"Mr. Solomon, Gabriel, please, let me finish, I have…"

"I'm sorry. I don't mean to be rude, but I have to protect my investments." Solomon nodded at the screen. "I believe that slide shows your five-year forecast. And that forecast, which I'm sure is based on the most positive and favorable market conditions, says you won't see profit in this company for at least another three years. I can do a lot with my money in that amount of time. I don't need to have it tied up here doing nothing."

"But..."

"Mr. Bergen, I've waited five years for you and Mr. Shiffer to make good on your promises. I've been more than patient. You were supposed to have three to five operations running by now, all of them profitable. You promised my shares would be worth ten times my original investment. Instead, they're worth nothing. I can absorb the loss to this point, use it for a tax write-off, but no more. When your quarterly report is published, I expect your shares will dip even further, and I don't plan to be around to see it." He reached into the inner pocket of his jacket. "You have my resignation," he said, tossing a sealed envelope onto the boardroom table, "effective immediately. I apologize to the other members of the board. I hope you won't be hurt by what's to follow, but I must do what I must. Good day gentlemen."

CHARLOTTE McKIDRY sat in the dining hall sipping steamy coffee and chewing the last bite of an oat-bran muffin. She looked at her watch. She had specific instructions to leave Joe in the lobby for one hour, and then take him back to the hospice. She didn't like it. The patient needed rest. The idea of putting him on display was absurd. But her objection had been overruled. It was ivory tower madness. *Those idiots do the dumbest things.* She had to wait another fifteen minutes.

THE WHEELCHAIR-restricted guests sat alone on their shining chrome thrones. Owen Lowell occupied one of those chairs, minding his own business. His thoughts were trapped in a layer of ozone, tethered to the ethereal world of space. Suddenly, a pair of hands gripped the back of Owen's chair and began rolling him forward. His co-regents, the other listless nobles, feigned not to notice as Owen was wheeled across the floor. They remained crunched over and huddled in their blankets. Owen, with his eyes hanging down, saw only the passing weave of carpet.

The wall of people parted to let the chair pass, and closed again once it was on the other side. Owen was backed against another wall. The brake on his chair was set. The blanket was removed from his body and a baseball cap squeezed onto his head. The blanket was then wrapped over the shoulders of a second man, seated in a wheelchair to Owen's right. Owen's face fell forward as though the bill of the baseball cap was too heavy for him to sustain. Someone in the group passed another hat into the inner circle and the broad-brimmed fedora was used to cover the other man's bald head. The hands took hold of the second wheelchair and began rolling it forward. The circle parted letting the wheelchair pass through. Then the circle closed again.

CHARLOTTE GOT UP and walked to the door. She could see the group of people still surrounding her patient. The milling of parted legs revealed sporadic flashes of chrome. The patient was in good hands. If something was wrong, they would call her. She went back to her coffee.

THE WHEELCHAIR came to the lobby and stopped. The room, usually a bustle of activity, appeared deserted. The wheels began rolling again, taking a sharp right at the first corridor. *Stop!* The occupant fell forward but was pulled back by the collar. Down the hall, Dr. VanEtter stood in the dim fluorescent light. The wheelchair jerked back. The chair was spun around and shoved in the opposite direction. It moved quickly along the wall, but was slowed as it approached the corner. *Listen.* Down the hall, a lilt of conversation could be heard. The wheelchair was thrust through an unlocked door, a storage closet smelling of acetone and floor wax. The only sound was that of breathing. The man listed to the side, drooling on his shirt. His attendant took hold of a long-handled mop and mumbled a quick prayer. They waited in the dark for the voices to pass.

LAURIE ENTERED her apartment to find Peter all worked up

again. Same reason as before, the invasion of another cleaning lady. He'd been forced to duck outside, and he wasn't happy, though he was glad to see Laurie again. He needed to tell her about it.

"Calm down Peter. She didn't see you, did she? Why are you so upset?"

"You don't have to go through it Laurie. I do. I almost had a heart attack," but Laurie rolled her eyes, and Peter took the hint. "Okay, okay, I guess you're right. I guess I'm being silly."

Laurie's face was itching again, it felt like lumps of clay were dripping from her skin. She set her cane aside, used the palm of her hand to straighten her back, and went to the bathroom. She flicked on the light and stood starring at her reflection, the haunting ghost of Christmas future. How do people grow old? What causes wrinkles that twist and destroy the skin, biting deep into the flesh to leave indelible scars? What if, when Peter finally removed her mask once and for all, those lines were permanently etched into her face? What a scary thought.

She brought her finger up to feel the mask, and realized she still had the note wadded in her hand. She unfurled the message and considered it again. It was scrawled in blue ink in a pretentious style with high arching loops and long meandering tails on a plain white piece of paper torn from a pad. The upper corner of the note had been ripped off. Laurie figured if she found the tablet with this piece still attached, it would say: "From the desk of Barbara Marks." The note had to have come from Barbara. Who else knew they needed Bergen's password? Barbara must have thought it over and decided to do something to prove her innocence. Or, it could be a trap. What if Barbara was trying to lure Laurie back into Mr. Bergen's office, to have her arrested for trespassing. It wasn't an exciting thought, but if that's what Barbara was up to, her plan just might backfire. Once the police were called in, they might be persuaded to reopen their investigation.

Laurie was being enticed to commit a second act of corporate espionage. She didn't want to do it, but she knew she would. She had to find out. People's lives depended on it, and even if they didn't, she would do it for Joe. She had left him in the community center surrounded by his anguished and bewildered friends. Those that knew him, knew his condition couldn't be so easily explained. Poor Ruth had held Joe's hand, stroking it, her face wet with compassion. It was pathetic. Who could have done such a thing? Joe hadn't been killed, true, but he'd been silenced, and judging by what he was having to suffer, the crematorium would have been kinder.

Crematorium? Funny she should think of it that way. She favored euthanasia. When animals get old, people put them down, not because they want to kill a beloved pet, but out of mercy and compassion. No decent human being wants to see an animal suffer. When they no longer served any purpose, when they were reduced to the pain of mere existence, putting an animal to sleep was the decent thing to do. Why should it be different with humans? When there's nothing left but misery, when there's no cure and all hope is gone and all that lies ahead is slow, sure death, why prolong the suffering?

How could anyone think otherwise? Bill? Right, okay, but he belonged to the lunatic fringe. It was just one more wall between them. Like with everything else, they had their feet firmly planted on opposite sides of the euthanasia issue. He would be appalled by what was going on. She remembered the articles. He and his sanctimonious right to life: "I won't sanction unnatural death of any kind, not abortion, not mercy killing, nothing except the electric chair, because God said to kill the malefactors; but with everyone else, let God have the final say." Laurie grinned at her mimicry, but her smile faded as she began to think it through.

In a series of articles, Bill had cited what happened in Nazi Germany when Hitler began promoting forced sterilization, eugenics they called it, for those with inferior, or undesirable, blood. That's where it started, Bill maintained. Before long the Nazi party was busy goose-stepping in glossy boots while six million people were being forced to inhale Zyklon-B. That's why she'd likened Joe's escape from death, as his having been pulled from a crematorium. Bill had planted that seed.

She remembered the article because she'd so strongly opposed it. Bill argued that Hitler's eugenics program had paved the way for the holocaust. He tried to show how, under the supervision of S.S.

doctor, Lt. General Karl Brandt, the eugenics program was expanded to include the killing of deformed and retarded children (they had nothing to live for anyway) and in special cases, to the killing of adult undesirables like Gypsies and homosexuals. On and on, step by step, arm extended, "Sieg Heil," on to the master race, smash the window of the dirty little Jew and throw his disease riddled bones into the purifying ovens.

She'd read it, fumed, stewed, reread, and picked it apart. Then she sat down and wrote Bill a long nasty e-mail, lambasting his oversimplification of a very complex issue. "The boogie man is not always out to get you, Bill," she wrote. It was just another case of right-wing fear mongering, and she told him so. But was it? Right now, at this very moment, she wasn't so sure.

She touched her face. She wanted to poke it out of shape. She wanted to rip it from her skull. Getting old meant certain, unavoidable death. She didn't want to die. Ever! She withdrew to the living room.

"Excuse me Peter, I need to do a little work, and I need to be alone. I have to disappear for a few minutes. You can watch TV or listen to the radio. I'll close the door."

"Laurie, you just got back. I was hoping we'd have a chance to talk. You haven't even told me what happened to Joe. Is he alive?"

"Yes Peter, he's alive, but I can't talk about it now. I'll be out in a few minutes. We'll discuss it then." The door closed.

Peter shrugged and shuffled to the sofa to sit down. He crossed his legs and fiddled with the toe of his shoe. It wasn't fair. He was there to help Laurie, but he needed help too. He needed someone to talk to, someone to console him and reconcile his hurt. Being jilted by Tina was bad enough, but to be ignored by Laurie, the one he wanted to share his pain with, was unbearable. She'd been up most of the night reviewing her story while he slept; then she'd slept late so they weren't able to talk in the morning; then she'd run off the minute she woke up to go see Joe. They hadn't had time to sit down and discuss how much he was hurting inside. Now she was back but refusing to talk. She'd run off to her room and closed the door, while he sat there all alone aching for comfort.

It wasn't just about Tina. Tina was only one in a long chain of rejections. It was about feeling inadequate. He wasn't good enough for anyone. Women came and went with the wind. Each one said he was handsome. But he didn't feel that way. He looked at himself in the mirror and saw only a freak with dishwater hair, and an anorexic jaw, and...and a blazing red zit. That's what he was, an unwanted zit, a pimple on the face of humanity. And they were all liars, because if he were as handsome as they all said, they wouldn't all leave. He couldn't please anyone, not even Laurie.

LAURIE DREW the window shade. She had her computer hidden beneath the dresser. If she'd put it under the bed, a maid might have seen it when cleaning, but even the thin head of a vacuum couldn't reach under the dresser, it was barely high enough to permit passage by her ultra-slim electronic notebook. She slid the computer out, set it on a small writing desk, and unplugged the phone so she could insert the computer's modem jack in its place. She flicked the switch and waited for the programs to load, then went immediately to her web crawler and found Bill's home page. How nice it must be to have all your articles posted on the web so they can be read by anyone at any time. Such is the life of a columnist. No one would want to read one of her articles a day after the fact—it would be old news. Of course Bill only posted his nationally syndicated column, the daily items were too localized to be of widespread interest. She tried to recall when he had written the series on euthanasia, had to be at least a year ago...there it was!

She scanned the first article but didn't find what she was looking for. Ditto the second. She found it in the third. The article was entitled "Going Dutch" and dealt specifically with what happened in the Netherlands after the legalization of assisted suicide. It was Bill's contention that the same thing would soon happen in the U.S.

Laurie's eyes ran back and forth across the page, speed-reading to capture the highlights. The Netherlands had begun by sanctioning euthanasia for the terminally ill, those with no hope for a cure and less than six months to live. *Okay,* the same criteria were used to get the law passed in Oregon, *so what?* The Dutch didn't stop there, *uh huh,* neither would Oregonians, *hummm?* Once established for the terminally ill, the scope was quickly broadened to include those who were chronically ill, *uh huh,* and then broadened again to include those with psychological disorders, *right,* and finally to include those who were suffering only from depression. Each progressive case had been argued before the Dutch Supreme Court on the grounds of human rights. If one person was granted the right to die, then all people had to be given that right. *Sure, but...*

Ah, there it is. This was what she wanted. Bill claimed the Dutch government recorded more than a thousand cases each year, where doctors had administered euthanasia without first consulting with their patients. They were ending the lives of competent people without asking their permission. *And what was their justification? Ahhh,* they either felt the person would be unable to enjoy a reasonable quality of life, or, they felt the cost of keeping the patient alive was too high. Noble reasons, but it didn't change the fact that it was the doctor, not the patient, who made the decision. According to Bill, elderly Dutch people were beginning to resist being sent to the hospital for fear of being unwittingly put to sleep, and that meant they weren't getting treatment when they needed it.

Laurie leaned back in her chair. She recalled how the piece had raised her hackles. How dare Bill assume that the same thing would happen in the U.S. Just because doctors in the Netherlands took advantage of the law, didn't mean American doctors would. American doctors were far more concerned about keeping people alive.

She crossed her arms and twiddled her fingers on the sides of her stomach, pursing her lips as she rolled her eyes to the ceiling. Here she was, smack dab in the middle of a nursing home where the limits of the law were already being tested. She herself had discovered it right here in the good old USA. Somebody was ending the lives of people who were not terminally ill, who certainly hadn't requested they be allowed to die, who hadn't even been consulted. Someone assumed they had little to live for, and decided that since they had run out of cash, they should be killed. The parallels were obvious.

Laurie felt her stomach tighten. She was not a Nazi butcher! Euthanasia and abortion were two entirely different things. A deformed fetus had to be terminated for its own good. Bill had cut her heart when he'd said she was like one of those Nazi doctors that euthanized deformed, imperfect babies because they wanted to rid the population of the unfit. She hated him for that. She hated him for being right.

She wished she'd never met Joe, or Ruth, or Edith, but she had, and they were decent people, and their friends had probably been decent people too. They deserved to live. When she looked at herself in the mirror, she realized she would one day be just like them. Would the next generation of doctors be licensed to put the old and infirm down without asking their permission? She was pro-choice. When the time came, she would choose. No one had the right to make that decision for her, even if it was deemed to be in her own best interest. No one had that right...except...but that was different...you can't ask an unborn child to make such decisions. *Hypocrite!* She sat staring at the monitor, eyes burning, condemned by her own rationale.

FOURTEEN

THE CLOSET was silent, so silent the person standing behind the wheelchair felt as though their breathing, and the loud thumping of their heart, could be heard. The smooth wooden-handled mop was set aside. Only minutes had passed, but each heartbeat felt like a minute in itself, so the passage of time seemed like hours. Light was streaming under the door, illuminating objects in gray silhouettes: the bucket on wheels with its metal basket, a stack of cardboard boxes filled with paper towels, a chemically stained shelf full of randomly stacked cleaning solutions, an upright vacuum, and in the middle of it all, a chrome chair with large spoked wheels. A man wearing a floppy brimmed fedora was seated in the chair, his head sagging to the side.

Cloaked in the shadows, Ruth stepped out from behind the wheelchair and made her way cautiously to the door. She pressed in and placed an ear against the cool surface of wood. *Nothing.* She slipped a hand around the knob, holding it like a fragile egg, and turned with slow determination until it stopped. Then, drawing in a breath, she gave the door a tug, just enough to allow a thread of light to spill inside. Her eye filled the gap, prying and apprehensive. *Nothing out there, least not that direction.* The door still had to be opened; if someone were standing at the other end of the hall, both kidnapper and kidnappee would be caught. *It's now or never.*

Slipping behind the chair again, hands firmly locked on the grips, Ruth readied to make her escape. *Oh Lord thou art my shield and my salvation.* Breathe deep, natural as taking a Sunday stroll. Leaning around the bowed head, heart pounding like a hammer, the door was pulled slowly open and the fugitives entered the hall. *Keep moving. Don't look back.* The wheels bounced as they lunged forward. The runner expected to hear someone yell, "STOP!" but the walls remained silent. They rounded the corner and were gone.

GEORGE BERGEN, Vice President of Finance, propped his elbows on his desk and buried his face in his hands. He needed an excuse, a credible strategy for fending off shareholders. Emerald Valley Corporation shares were in the tank, and irate investors were demanding to know why. He pursed his lips and riddled his fingers against his cheek. *What to do, what to do, what to do?* He wished he could shut the phones off. One thing was certain, Carl wasn't going to be of any help. It seemed the young president was good for only one thing—*hype!* Hype and enthusiasm, that's how George had been sucked into the deal. He was making good money at the bank before Carl filled his head with all his over-inflated hype. The kid had seemed so credible with all those neatly organized spreadsheets in their index tab folders and that raw look of determination on his face. The plan had looked good on paper, an opportunity to make millions. George took Carl's numbers and embellished them, convinced he was sitting on gold. He recommended the bank approve the loan and then, to avoid a conflict of interest, resigned before the decision was made. By that time he and Carl had formed a partnership. Hype! That's what it was then, and that's what it was now, but this was reality; this was worse than their worst case scenario. There was no contingency plan, they were going down without a parachute, and Carl was nowhere to be found.

He leaned in close, eyes fixed on the monitor. Each time he asked the computer to do an update, the shares hit another low. The phones continued to ring. Solomon must be dumping huge blocks on the market. With the price of EVC shares continuing to plummet, they were in danger of a hostile takeover.

George removed a piece of lint from his coat. Then he moved the mouse and clicked update again. "The man's killing us," he groaned. *He has to quit sometime. Pretty soon we'll drop to a price even he won't accept. Either that, or he'll run out of shares. The market has to correct itself. We just have to wait.* George slipped a finger under the knot of his tie, pulling it loose as he unbuttoned his collar. He leaned back in his fine, Moroccan leather chair, his shoulders melting into the padding. *We'll bounce back. We just have to convince the shareholders to hang tight.* But even as he held the thought, the computer beeped, updated the file, and showed another nickel drop.

The telephone intercom buzzed. "Yes?"

"Dr. VanEtter to see you, Mr. Bergen."

"Tell him I'm in conference."

"I did sir. He says it's important."

George took a sip of water and placed the glass back on its coaster. "All right. Send him in."

Dr. VanEtter entered the room carrying a leather satchel, which he set on Mr. Bergen's desk. He popped the clasp open, reached inside and withdrew two folded towels, obviously soiled, and held them out. "We could have a problem," he said.

George rolled his chair back, lacing his fingers over his stomach. "Yes we do. The whole world is dumping our shares; we can be bought for a song, and I'm sitting here watching my future go down the tubes. We have problems, real problems, but they don't include your dirty laundry. If the washing machine is broken, have someone fix it, and please remove that, that, whatever it is..." but before he could finish, the intercom buzzed again.

"WHAT!"

"Call for you on line three."

"I'm not taking calls."

"It's Charlotte McKidry. She says it's urgent."

Urgent? Urgent! Why all of a sudden is everything urgent? George rocked back his chair still holding his stomach. He punched the button and picked up the line. "Yes, what is it? What? Say it again, slowly. How could he just—*disappear?*"

LAURIE'S MIND was whirling. She fiddled with the blinds, lowering them to block the light, but then she opened the louvers so light could stream in. She turned the thermostat up, then down, then up again, and went to the kitchen to make some coffee, just to keep busy, anything to avoid Peter's incessant questions. *I don't want to talk about it, Peter, not now.* But Peter went on asking, and Laurie went on pretending to be distracted.

"But Laurie, you haven't said a thing about Joe. When will I meet him? Why don't you invite him over?"

"Uh huh, uh, I think perhaps some other time. I'm busy right now."

When the door flew open, Laurie and Peter cranked their heads around, startled, teetering off balance. Peter swallowed his tea and slammed down the cup turning to run. There was no way he could make the terrace in time. Laurie held her ground, ready to challenge the intruders. "What are you doing? Hey, wait a minute. Slow down. Stop!"

Ruth placed a hand on the shoulder of the man seated in the wheelchair and pulled him to an upright position, her elbow knocking his hat to the floor. His lip hung from his chin like a rubber cup from which spittle drooled.

"I had to get him out of there. I couldn't let them take him," Ruth said.

Laurie closed her eyes and inhaled deeply. *No, not this, not now, a person can only handle so much.* The man in the wheelchair was Joe, or, at least the remains of what used to be Joe. It was Joe's body, but different, more like a stuffed scarecrow, lifelike—but lifeless, not the same man who only a few days ago had bluffed his way into her apartment to use the phone. Ruth looked different too. She'd changed clothes. It was the first time Laurie had seen her in anything but red. This dress was blue, and she wasn't wearing her hat, an obvious attempt to draw less attention to herself. Ruth bent over, wiping Joe's mouth with her handkerchief, revealing why the hat had been such a necessary part of her attire. There was a small, shiny, bald spot on the crown of her head.

"I need the key," she said, "the one I gave you, the one that gets in everywhere. I've got to find Joe an empty apartment to hide in."

Peter spied the key on the counter and picked it up. He held it out to Ruth. "Want me to push? Might make it easier for you check out the empty apartments," he volunteered.

Ruth looked at Peter. She appeared distracted. Her eyes were small and red, and her lips pale. "Thanks for offering, but I think it would be better if I just leave Joe here while I go looking. If that's all right with you?" she said, turning to Laurie.

Laurie nodded, noticing again just how tiny Ruth was. She had an aspect about her that made her seem larger than life. Or maybe it was her hat that made her appear tall. With her hat missing, she looked small again.

"I'm going to try and get something close by." Ruth's gloveless hand reached for the door.

"I'd be glad to help," Peter volunteered again.

"Thanks, but this should only take a few minutes, and you shouldn't be seen outside," Ruth said. Then she darted out, flitting down the hall like a little bird in search of a nest.

The closing door fanned Peter's face. His short hair stayed in place, but still he smoothed it with the palm of his hand as he staggered over and dropped onto the couch.

Laurie looked at Joe. It was hard to believe he'd been in this very room only a few days before, an animated specimen of health. He'd said something like this would happen. Now, here he was, his only sign of life the constant wheezing that accompanied the rise and fall of his chest.

Peter took a pillow from the couch and tucked it under his chin, wrapping his arms around it like a teddy bear.

The door opened and Ruth was back. "Ran into some luck," she said. "The room right next door is empty. I thought it might be. I know where folks live. Hasn't been anyone in there for a long time. Say hi to your new neighbor." She gripped the back of the wheelchair and spun it around.

Peter jumped up to help. "You're going to need a hand getting him into bed," he said. He opened the door and held it. Ruth nodded and pushed the wheelchair into the hall.

At the very next door, Ruth passed Peter the key and he ushered them inside. The unit was similar to Laurie's own, but smaller. There were only three rooms: a kitchenette, a bath, and a living room that also served as a bedroom. Peter went to the couch and removed the cushions. Then he pulled on the bottom of the convertible sofa, unfolding it into a bed. He helped Ruth slide Joe onto the sheets. There were no blankets.

Ruth pulled the wheelchair back out of the way, and Peter went to the bathroom for a tissue to wipe Joe's face. The old man seemed to constantly drool. Ruth watched as Peter waited on her friend. She could see a tenderness in his actions. She recognized it for what it was—both a blessing, and a curse. Homosexuals were often criticized for being too sensitive, but it was the kind of compassion straight men needed more of. *Look at him...so much like my Er...*she wanted to hold back, but it came too quickly.

Peter looked up and saw Ruth standing there with tears streaming down her face. "He'll be all right, Mrs. Wheatly. He'll be fine. We'll take good care of him."

Ruth looked down, puckering her chapped lips until they turned white. She wiped her cheek on her sleeve. "I'm sorry," she said. "You'll have to excuse me. It's just...everything's so...there's a lot going on right now, with Ben and Joe and...it's hard with you here because..."

Peter waited. "Yes?"

Ruth turned and went to the bathroom for a tissue. She blew her nose and came back into the living room. "It's been ten years. You'd think I'd be over it, but then I see you standing there...you're so much like him, Eric I mean, my son...he died of AIDS."

"Your son was gay?"

"Yes...no, not really. He was homosexual, but he wasn't gay." Her hand came up to adjust her hat but it wasn't there so she ended up dragging her red knobby fingers through her brittle hair. She took a deep breath, the air fluttering in her chest. "Eric was a homosexual. There's no denying that, but he wasn't happy. I define gay as being happy. He just dealt with it as best he could. By the time he got around to seeking help, he was dying. Sorry," she said wiping her nose. "It's not your problem. Please don't think I'm blaming you. I don't mean to offend."

"No offense taken, Mrs. Wheatly," Peter backed up and went to the sofa to wipe Joe's mouth, "but I think you're making a wrong assumption. I'm not gay. I mean, sometimes people think I am because of the way I act, but that's just me. It's something I've had to put up with all my life." He looked up again, wadding the wet tissue into a ball. "Ask anyone who knows me. They'll tell you. I've always been a sissy. Even when I was a kid, I ran like a girl, I threw like a girl, and when other boys called me a queer and a fag, I ran home and cried like a girl. Truth is, I still do. But I know I'm not gay. I'm not even comfortable around other men. Practically all my friends are female."

Ruth smoothed the folds of her dress and stiffened her back, looking Peter straight in the face. "Okay, I understand. My mistake. Sorry. Sometimes I'm just an old busybody." She put the hand holding the tissue to her chest, cleared her throat, and closed her eyes. She heard Joe coughing. When she opened her eyes again, Peter had turned away.

THE PHONES were ringing incessantly. George's administrative assistant, Abbie, had to recruit several accounting clerks to help juggle calls. "No, we don't know why the shares are dropping but there's been no material change. No sir, no change in corporate direction. No, there hasn't been any announcement. Yes, yes, everything is fine, business as usual. No, I'm sorry. I'm afraid you can't talk to the president. He's out of the office. That's right. No, no, please, everything is fine. Just hang in there," repeated over and over, ad infinitum, creating a roar of confusion in the usually quiet office. Her desk was a pile of pink messages strewn in cluttered disarray, and so was her mind. Her coffee was cold, but the ringing wouldn't stop long enough to pour a refill. "Go away!" she muttered as she picked up the line. "Mr. Bergen's office, how may I help you?"

George Bergen and Stuart VanEtter were in conference. George had unplugged his phone and was refusing to talk to anyone. Even with the door closed, he could hear the drone of phones and chattering voices. It sounded like the trading floor of a stock exchange. There was no point in taking calls. They had been round and round the problem, attacking it from every possible side, but the fact was, there was nothing they could do.

The situation with their newest tenant, Annie Iversen, was

another matter. Dr. VanEtter was concerned. He'd invented an entire scenario, a spy among us, an undercover cop, a cheesy soap opera with an over-developed plot, and all of it based on a dirty towel. It was good to be cautious, but not paranoid. Old ladies can use too much makeup for a lot of reasons. It was much more likely she was concerned about hiding her wrinkles, or perhaps she was trying to mask a few ugly scars—old people do crazy things. Still, it did warrant observation.

"All right, we agree, the market will correct itself," George said. He wanted to instill confidence, but he had to fake it; he certainly didn't feel it. He could only hope Stuart wouldn't see through his facade. "Now, about this other problem. You can keep an eye on Mrs. Iversen, if it makes you feel better, but do it from a distance. See if you can dig up anything on her background, like where she comes from. I doubt she's here under false pretense, but if she is, I want to know about it. Just don't get too close. I don't want to scare her off unnecessarily. We need the business. As for Joe, I haven't quite figured out what to do about him, but I wouldn't worry about it, he'll turn up. Charlotte said a number of residents were involved in the swap. She wrote down their names. It shouldn't be hard to get one of them talking. We'll find out what we need to know." George leaned back in his swivel chair, folding his hands over his stomach. "I expect this whole mess will be cleared up by tomorrow," he said, trying to sound positive. "Now, we both have a lot to do, so if there's nothing else, let's get back to work."

TWO AM. Laurie slipped down the dimly lit hall pretending to be invisible. She had shed her disguise again. It felt good to be free of makeup, to let her skin breathe. If she were stopped, she would not be recognized, but she would have to do some fast talking. The low fluorescent, eerie-green light was bugging her. It wasn't bright enough to help her clearly see her way, and it wasn't low enough to keep her hidden. She felt the give of the carpet through the thin soles of her sneakers, and the rough surface of the paint as her fingertips rode along the wall.

She stared across the lobby at the dark portals leading to other corridors, at the empty couch and chairs, and at the mind-boggling distance she must cover. Being caught last night made her wary about tonight. She had to be extra careful. She was pleased to see the light was off in Mrs. Marks' office.

She was wearing the same outfit as the night before, casual clothes so she could make a mad dash for the front door if confronted. Would it be locked? Surely they didn't lock the doors at night. What if there was a fire, people had to get out, didn't they? What if she got arrested, who would she contact? She couldn't call the newspaper, that would only get her fired. She wouldn't know where Peter was. He wouldn't hang around after she was caught. She could try to reach Bill, but he might still be in Detroit, or he could already be on the road. Either way, there wouldn't be much he could do.

She realized she'd been thinking a lot about Bill lately, never to the point of welcoming his return, but at least she was getting used to the idea. She had to concede the change. There was a time, not that long ago, when the thought of ever seeing Bill again would have sent her into a depression. She didn't want to confront that part of her past which, rightly or wrongly, had forced her to choose between two evils. She'd been forced to choose between carrying around a load of guilt (because her illness condemned her daughter to a life of pain) or cutting her husband and daughter loose to fend for themselves. She still maintained she'd made the right choice. She'd convinced herself it was for the best. Her husband was strong, he could live without her, and her daughter was too muddled to care. She, on the other hand, needed time alone to heal. The trouble was, no matter how hard she pushed, they never went completely away. Angie was in her blood. Her daughter was weak and imperfect, but in some way, wasn't that true of everyone? Perhaps Angie only showed outwardly, what everyone else felt inwardly. And Bill had always been there when she needed him. That's why she was thinking of him now—but that didn't mean she was ready to see him in person! That was the crux of it. E-mail was one thing, but his being there might reopen old wounds. Perhaps Seattle was far enough away not to pose a problem. It might be okay, as long as they kept their distance. But would they? She wasn't ready to let bygones be bygones, but she couldn't help herself, she ached to see her daughter. And she knew, though she didn't want to admit it, that for whatever agonizing, inexplicable reason, she wanted to see Bill, too. She'd been through it over and over in her mind, but no amount of self analysis, the constant rehashing of the good, the bad and the ugly, could change the way she felt. Bill was easily the most attractive and repulsive man she had ever known.

Her mind wandered back to their courtship, to the office Christmas party, the tinselled tree, the silver place settings, and the gift exchange. He had bought her that silly mug, the one that claimed a woman had to be twice as good as a man, to make it in a man's world. She still had it on her desk, even after all these years. She recalled the festive greetings and warm feelings as Bill romanced her under the stars. It had been a wonderful evening, the warm music, the Christmas cheer, the bright dancing and ballroom laughter, everything had been perfect. They'd swooned across the dance floor, Bill's arm holding her close, his warm breath on her cheek, both of them lost in a moment of passion, and in their light-headed frivolity...he'd kissed her...kissing her neck and...she felt herself beginning to burn. *Stop! Get a grip!* He was also the man who'd tried to suppress her will; he wanted to mold her into his image, and make her thoughts like his own. He'd choked and smothered her and...now he'd turned religious and...and...why was she so angry? Had he really been that bad, or was she making him out to be a villain so she could justify pushing him away?

What was he really? Devil? Angel? Something in between? One thing he was, he was a good friend. She couldn't talk to other men. Whenever she let her guard down and let a flicker of her emotions show, they'd steer her toward the bedroom. It was like they thought all the world's problems could be solved by hopping in the sack— *make love not war*—how trite! Bill, on the other hand, just answered her questions and let it go at that. Of course they communicated by e-mail, so sex wasn't an issue. She definitely liked it that way, so much less personal, everything kept at a safe, cool distance. She could tell him anything without fear of being misunderstood. And there was nothing wrong with that. Perhaps this was the most puzzling part.

She rarely agreed with his advice, and she rarely ever took it, but she valued his opinion above all others. How do you explain a conundrum like that?

What would Bill say about what she was doing right now? She knew he would agree with her purpose, but would he also agree with her plan? No, he would never allow the end to justify the means. Illegal entry was a crime, even when done for the right reason. It was a perfect example. She would explain what she proposed to do, he would object to the idea, and she would go ahead and do it anyway, yet she still valued his opinion. *Uh huh.* There wasn't any point in dwelling on it. It was too late to ask his advice. Besides, this time she needed more than words. She needed his physical presence, and he was somewhere else. She had to get through this one on her own.

The route was familiar. She purged Bill from her mind. *Dwell on the present, not the past.* She took each step thinking buoyant thoughts, just a stealthy, prowling cat lifting one soft, weightless paw after the other.

Laurie used her penlight to navigate her way around the dark room. She clicked on the monitor and within half a minute she was staring at the folder with the two files she had been unable to retrieve the night before. The screen requested a password. Slowly she typed in the word "candy," each click of the keys echoing loud enough to attract someone's attention, at least in her mind, but the sound went unnoticed. The file opened. *Yes!* There in front of her was a log of names listed alphabetically, and under each name was what appeared to be the guest's complete historical record, page after page of notes, charts and diagrams. She didn't try to interpret the data. That would take time. It had to be what she was looking for. Why else would Mr. Bergen keep it protected? She slipped her diskette into the drive and instructed the program to copy. She repeated the same process for the file marked "contracts." She'd been there less than ten minutes and was almost done.

She pushed the eject button to retrieve her disk, but the clatter of the spring-loaded mechanism caused her to freeze. She envisioned an army of storm troopers descending on her with guns and grenades. Her pulse quickened and the vein over her temple throbbed. She made a quick decision. She could be caught here tonight. She could be walking back to her room and be stopped by a roaming security guard, or a nurse dispensing medicine, or someone walking the halls who couldn't sleep. She decided she couldn't risk losing this information. It was too important, and too hard come by. She brought up the e-mail program, transferred a copy of both files to the template and addressed it to Bill, sending it with a click of the mouse. Besides, she deserved to have him recognize her achievement. *Wait till he sees this. This is good stuff.* Then she deleted the message from the sent items file, erasing the record of what she'd done. She shut down the program and turned off the monitor. She let herself out and returned to her room.

Her heart was bouncing like a ping-pong ball as she locked the door behind her. *Mission impossible, aaaaand, mission accomplished, noooo problem. This super-sleuth stuff is easy.* She slipped the disk from her back pocket and brought it to her lips giving it an overly dramatic kiss. Then she took it to the bedroom, flung her arms wide, and fell backwards onto the bed. She waited until the mattress stopped bouncing, then brought the disk up where she could see it, holding it clasped in a victory salute over her head. *Kudos, kudos, congratulations all around. Job well done.* She rolled off the bed and slipped her computer out from its hiding place beneath the dresser. Time to get to work.

BILL COULDN'T SLEEP. It had been a restless night of twisting, turning, stretching, scratching and staring at the ceiling. So many things plagued his mind, making it difficult to keep his eyes closed. He rolled over. Red digital numbers burned through the night. It was five A.M. They hadn't made Yellowstone. The tow-truck driver showed up, but he wouldn't patch the tire. It wasn't something he did on the road, he explained. He could change the tire, providing Bill had a spare, but he couldn't fix a flat. He hitched Bill's rust covered, copper-brown station wagon to his truck and hauled them to a garage where Bill had to pay for both the towing service and a new tire. He had the flat tire fixed and kept it for a spare. It was midnight when they pulled into a motel on the outskirts of Buffalo,

Wyoming.

He thrust an arm under his pillow and looked over at Angie, peaceful as heaven itself. He didn't want to disturb her, at least not yet. They had to get an early start to make up for lost time, but it wouldn't be fair to rouse her at this hour. Six was early enough. Why couldn't he sleep? Even as the thought came, Bill knew the answer. It was that unsettling feeling in his gut that he was doing something wrong. Not one thing had gone right since they'd left Detroit. It was beginning to feel like God was against the move. It didn't seem fair. He'd sought divine counsel, but, for whatever reason, God chose to remain silent, leaving Bill to assume the decision was his own. How can a mere mortal know the mind of an infinite God? Especially regarding trivial matters. So the decision was made; only now it appeared God was throwing up roadblocks to send him home. If he was, it was too late. The boat was bought and paid for, and he'd quit his job and sold the house. There was nothing to go back to.

The bruise in his chest throbbed, his eyes burned, and his mind ached from too much thought. He didn't need to stay awake trying to second-guess God. Sometimes things just happen. The measure of the man is in the response. Wasn't he doing everything he could to make the best of a bad situation? He was doing just what he thought God would want him to do. *For I have learned, in whatsoever state I am, therewith to be content.* That's what the Apostle Paul had said. It was the principal Bill was trying to live by. He kept grinning through it all, looking for the good that comes from tribulation, the refiner's gold. But sometimes, in his private thoughts, he wondered if he had enough strength to rustle up even one more smile. He felt beaten. He couldn't let Angie see his problems, she had her own to deal with, but it was becoming harder and harder to mask his uncertainty. How could he smile when he'd just lost his only vehicle, and along with it, his daughter's best friend? He'd made a bad deal on a hunk-of-junk car that probably didn't have the guts to get him where he was going. He'd had to endure flat tires, busted wipers, broken radios, and storms, and they weren't even half way to Washington yet. He wanted to scream: "Okay God, I give up. Stop the slow torture." He was defeated, too weak to go on. His smile was turning upside down.

He rolled onto his back and cocked an arm over his eyes to shut out the encroaching dawn, but his mind wouldn't stop racing. Finally he gave up and tossed the covers aside. Maybe there was a donut shop within walking distance, where he could buy a coffee and a newspaper and get back before Angie stirred. He put a hand against the door and quietly pulled it open to check the weather. A thin brush of purple light was painting the soft horizon. It looked clear, a few diehard stars were still blinking in the open sky, another beautiful, sunny day on the way. Early birds were chattering in the trees, high on a morning that smelled as sweet as desert sage. Perhaps the storms were behind them.

Maybe the whole thing was just another test to see if he could endure hardship. What a laugh. What did he think the past thirteen years had been? More irksome was the thought that this might be some kind of punishment for his making this move with the wrong motivation. He wanted to believe he was doing it for Angie, to give her a better life, to free up more of his time so he could spend it with her, and hopefully create a situation where distance couldn't be used as an excuse for not receiving visits from her mother. Was his desire to arrange those visits really for the benefit of his daughter, or was it for himself? That was the nagging question. Truth was, it was probably for both. He needed to see Laurie again, face to face. He had to tell her what had been gnawing at his insides for the past ten years. He needed to explain. Allowing Angie to live had been the right thing to do, but the way he had handled it had been all wrong. He needed to apologize for cramming the truth down her throat, instead of trying to understand what it was she was feeling. He'd shut her out; he'd refused to listen. It was his pride, not Angie, that had driven Laurie away. Being right was all that had mattered. Well he'd been right—and now he was alone.

The sun sent a sliver of yellow light into the picture. Early morning editions would be out. Speaking of reading, he still hadn't read yesterday's e-mail. Might as well kill some time. He closed the door, slowly, careful not to make a sound.

The screen dazzled with the active matrix, color display, providing its own light as the electrons pulsated across the dark room. There were only two messages waiting for him, one from Laurie, which had no explanation but was obviously hours and hours of reading material. *Be kinda nice to receive a friendly hello now and then.* He gave the document a cursory glance and quickly determined it was not of immediate interest.

The second message was from the police department in Milwaukee. As Bill read it, the corners of his mouth curled into a grin. *Well, bless my socks, they found T.J. Maybe God isn't mad after all.*

Bill jerked his jeans off the back of the chair and spun around to recheck the time. Wisconsin was an hour ahead. That would make it six in Milwaukee. Didn't matter, it was a police station, they'd be open twenty-four hours. He hopped on one foot pulling on his pants. Then he leaned over and took his jacket from the bed, patting the pocket for his cell phone, but found he'd left it in the car. Just as well, he couldn't make the call from the room without disturbing Angie. There was no sense in getting her all excited until he had more information, and maybe not even after that. He stuffed the tail of his shirt into his waist as he stooped to read the phone number off the screen, committing it to memory. He would call and make arrangements to have the cat sent out on the first plane headed west. All he had to do was figure out where they'd be staying, so he could give the courier a shipping address. They had to do it; it was for his little girl. The smile of God was beaming down on him. He could feel it radiating from his own cat-grinning face. *Thank you Lord!*

FIFTEEN

INCESSANT TAPPING from the terrace door. Laurie pried one eye open; a hot knife of raw white light pierced through the slit; she clamped the eye shut again, *burning, burrrrning*. She tried to open it one more time. *Ouch!* She forced the eye to scan the room. *Who's there?* Her tongue was stuck to the roof of her mouth, a hard sponge, devoid of moisture. She pushed her tongue against her teeth to produce saliva, but it was too dry. Her other eye remained sealed. The tapping continued, an echo hammering inside her skull. *Stop it! Please!* Who dared beat down her door at this hour? She pulled the glued eye open, rubbing the sleep away with her finger. She tried to stand but her legs were rubber. She teetered, wobbled and dropped back down. Why was she asleep in a chair? Why was she still in front of her computer? Had she been there all night? She remembered writing her story, a first draft, she remembered sending it to Bill. A screensaver ball was skittering across her monitor, *bouncing, bouncing, bouncing*. What time was it? *Stop that knocking!*

Liquid began to flow into the pits and cracks of her mouth. The dry sponge began to soften, and her thoughts began to gather. Her analysis of the stolen information had been disappointing. There was plenty of innuendo, but nothing concrete. She needed more. She needed hard, factual, indisputable evidence. Otherwise, they'd never get a conviction. Joe, the team's star witness, had been neutralized, and that only left the word of one person, Ruth, whose testimony without Joe's collaboration would be weak. Perhaps by fitting all the pieces together, the picture would be clear enough to warrant another investigation by the police. They still had one witness. Ruth had talked to Henry before he was taken. According to her, he was as healthy as a man his age could expect to be. He'd never mentioned wanting to die, which had led Ruth to conclude he'd been murdered. She'd witnessed Leonard saying he was afraid the same thing might happen to him, and then it did, and Leonard had specifically told Ruth he wanted to live.

It would be hard to prove he hadn't changed his mind. Laurie had found a document scanned into his file, presumably bearing his signature, stating that a peaceful exit was his express will and intent. The reason: an incurable tumor had been discovered in his lung which gave him less than three months to live. Of course there were X-rays of a chest, someone's chest, showing the suspicious tumor in the lung—but whose lung? You couldn't exhume Leonard's body and prove the tumor was his because his body had been cremated.

Funny, Leonard never mentioned having a tumor. In fact, he'd said he was enjoying his retirement, that he planned to live to a ripe old age, but that was before he'd learned his bank account was empty and that his ongoing care was putting a drain on the corporation. He'd come away from the meeting with the distinct impression he was living on borrowed time. Now he was dead. It seemed, after five years of losses, the corporation couldn't afford to keep people around unless they paid their own way—which went to motive!

The story of Henry followed the same pattern. His medical history showed he had a spreading cancer that kept him in constant pain. His file said he had requested the lethal drugs to avoid putting his friends through the long, drawn-out process of watching him die by inches. But those closest to him seemed totally unaware of his condition, so he either hid his suffering well, or he wasn't suffering at all.

The cases were too similar. Both men appeared to be healthy and happy, at least to their friends, and yet both had requested they be allowed to die "with dignity" because, according to their files, they were incurable and in constant pain.

Ben, Ruth, and Joe had drawn the same conclusion any logical, opened-minded person would, the same conclusion Laurie herself had drawn: these were wrongful deaths. They had presented the evidence to Cash, Louis and Edith, and found agreement. The group had taken the information to the authorities, but there they'd hit a stone wall. When the police investigated, they were shown the files containing the two men's medical histories, and paperwork, ostensibly bearing each man's signature, requesting they be allowed to die. Then the officers were handed documents showing that the people who filed the complaint were emotionally unstable. Who were the police to believe?

Only now they could prove the corporation was in financial trouble, that it couldn't afford to carry freeloaders, and it couldn't ask them to leave because each man had a contract guaranteeing them a lifetime of care—so there was motive.

One other oddity Laurie had discovered was worth further investigation. Ruth had claimed that both Henry and Leonard were surprised to learn their money was gone, yet each man's account clearly showed several large—no not large, huge—withdrawals. Amounts as much as twenty, thirty and even fifty thousand dollars had been removed and transferred to other places. Of course, each transfer required a personal signature, which was always there, legal and proper, so the transfers had been authorized. It made Laurie wonder why, if they were spending such large sums, they would be surprised to learn their money had run out. She needed to ask Ruth what she knew about this.

Something was definitely wrong, but that didn't change the fact that all the evidence was circumstantial. Any good lawyer could provide a reasonable alternative to her theory. All they had to do was establish reasonable doubt. She needed something solid. She'd gone ahead and written her article, but she knew it was thin. If the evidence wasn't compelling enough to get the case reopened, her career as an investigative reporter would be ruined. She'd have little chance of relocation. She cringed at the thought. She might end up working for some community rag: the weekly neighborhood gossip a la advertising supplement.

Surely what she had was enough to call for a proper investigation. There was Ruth's eyewitness account, which was in strong contradiction to the story told by the corporation. Of course, Ruth would have to undergo a competency hearing to determine her mental health, but she'd pass. Perhaps she could testify that Joe had also been an eyewitness, *unless that was hearsay.* She could suggest that what had happened to him was nothing more than damage control, *or was that conjecture?* They could find a competent doctor to testify that Joe hadn't suffered a stroke, *but what if he really had? No way...unless it was induced by artificial means.* What if Ruth started running off at the mouth about Ben being murdered? That would be easy to disprove. There would be a flurry of smirks from the lawyers at the corporate table, and then one of them would get up and use the statement to assassinate her credibility. Laurie had to use Ruth. She had no other choice. Other than Ruth's testimony, all she had was the corporation's long-term debt. Well, she also had the missing money, but as yet she hadn't proved the money was really missing. *Circumstantial, circumstantial, circumstantial!*

She was about to take the biggest gamble of her life. If they opened an inquest and the police were unable to find enough evidence to make an arrest, let alone get a conviction, her career as an investigative reporter was toast. Was it worth it? If she walked away, she might be assured of picking up her career again, no harm done. But over time, as things settled down, the killings would continue, beginning with Ruth and Joe, and that would make her partly responsible for their deaths, and possibly the deaths of others as well. She wished she had never become involved.

She inhaled deeply and tried to stand. Her legs wobbled and she started to hyperventilate, her brain spinning into blackness. She bent over, placing her hands on her knees until her head cleared. Why had she allowed herself to fall asleep at the computer? She was only a few feet from her bedroom and a nice soft bed, yet she'd laid her head on her arms and faded into zombie-land, just like she'd done a thousand times before. She always paid for it when she awoke. She squeezed her tongue against the roof of her mouth to stimulate the flow of moisture. Her eyes adjusted to the blinding light. She took a staggering step, pushed the heel of her palm into the small of her back to straighten herself, and walked to the terrace door to stop the person with the hammering fist. She had to put an end to that incessant rapping.

Laurie pulled back the drape and saw Peter standing there with his hands cupped against the glass trying to peer inside. He jerked back, startled. She opened the door, squinting to block the blaring light and turned to walk away leaving Peter to make his own way into the room. Her body ached. She combed her hair with her fingers and brought her wrist around to look at her watch. Already afternoon. How could she have slept in an upright position for so long? She used her knuckles to knead the small of her back as she walked to the sink. *Coffee.* She needed a heavy dose, and she needed it now!

Laurie could hear Peter babbling in the background, but her mind couldn't focus. Water poured from the tap, filling the pot to overflowing. She wondered if Bill had a chance to read her story yet, then decided it was too early. He always read his e-mail at night, didn't he? At least that was his old routine. No need to check for a response. Whatever he had to say would only upset her anyway. They'd spent the last ten years criticizing each other's work. Of course, they were usually on opposite sides of an issue. He should at least compliment her on writing something he agreed with. Who cared anyway? What Bill did or did not think was irrelevant. The only thing that mattered was whether or not she thought it was good. With all the evidence being so blatantly circumstantial, she questioned whether any reputable paper would run the story in the first place. Of course, she could always insist on another police investigation. If she presented what little evidence she had, and then proceeded to make enough noise, someone would have to listen. But if she waited until after the inquest, when the facts were established, she'd lose her scoop. By that time, every news journal would have someone assigned to the story. Maybe Bill's comments would help her decide. He might be brutal, but at least he was brutally honest. She could always count on him for that. She shut down the tap, poured the water into the coffee maker, slid the pot onto the hot plate, and flipped the switch to on. The red brew light illuminated as the pot began to gurgle. Peter was asking something. She turned around to face him, wiping a string of yellow hair from her eye with the back of a wet hand.

"Sorry, I'm a little slow this morning. What did you say?"

"I said you have to get your makeup on and get out of here. Something funny is going on. Ruth thinks they're watching your place. Your staying inside doesn't look good. You need to get out and circulate and act like everything is normal. They may be getting suspicious. I'm supposed to get a report on how it went last night; so while I'm fixing you up, you need to fill me in. How did it go? Did you have any luck?"

Laurie grimaced. Did she have any luck? Yes, no, maybe so...how could she explain? *Read the article?* And how could she sit down and put on a whole new face when her body wasn't awake yet. Maybe it was time to quit the whole charade. If Bill wrote and said the article was fine, she'd pack it up and leave. Even if he didn't, what else could she do? This seemed to be all the information they were going to get, and every day she stayed she chanced further risk of discovery. "What do you mean you think they're watching me?"

"It's not me, it's Ruth. She saw Dr. VanEtter outside in the hall. She thinks he's looking for Joe. Well, duh-ah. Anyway, we've been using the terrace door so we won't be seen coming in and out. These units have small backyards with privacy fences on either side, but they're open at the rear. It encourages people to take a walk in the park. Ruth goes out the back and around the outside to her own unit and enters through the terrace door, the way I just did. When she wants to be seen, she exits through her front door, like she was always inside. Pretty clever, huh? But things are heating up. Dr. VanEtter has already been to her place with some excuse about wanting to check a prescription. He said there was a mix up at the pharmacy and that several people complained about receiving the wrong medicine. He asked if he could check her drug cabinet to make sure she hadn't received something intended for someone else. Well, he looked in her bathroom all right, but he also went through her bedroom and kitchen. Guess who he was really looking for? Anyway, it was lucky Ruth happened to be home at the time. Everything went okay, but Ruth thinks, since the doctor saw you and Joe together, he might want to check your place too, so you have to be ready. Hop in the chair girl. I'm going to do you up. Then I have to get rid of all my stuff in case he does come poking his nose around here."

Laurie resigned herself. The aroma of fresh brewed coffee filled the air, waking the still sleeping portion of her brain. The pot was only half full, it would be strong but she needed it. She took a fragile china cup from the shelf, poured it full, and sat down. "Can you wait just a second?" she said. "I have to have this or I'll die."

Something's up! My dad's acting strange. He won't say anything, he refuses to even hint, but something has happened, because he's sitting there with that big cow grin on his face driving me nuts. We just crossed miles of rolling prairie with the scenery sweeping by in a blur of tiny yellow and blue flowers. And all the way Dad was singing, "Count Your Many Blessings," while beating his big thumbs on the steering wheel. He's acting like he doesn't have a care in the world. I haven't seen him this happy since we left Detroit.

I've gone over every possibility, but only one makes sense. I'm betting they've found T.J., but he can't tell me because he thinks I'll get too excited and start twitching. He's probably right. I get jittery just thinking about it. Of course it could be something else. Whatever it is, it's got him so happy he's about to bust at the seams.

There's not one cloud in the sky; it's a sunshine perfect day. Dad's happy, and I'm happy, and somewhere out there in the not too distant future, I'm thinking I'll see my little T.J. again. Okay Dad, I'm countin' my blessings. Just you keep on singing, because I'm counting them—one by one!

BILL STOOD in a phone booth, with his road map in hand, trying to decide where they should stop for the night. The glass was smudged. The glare made it difficult to see Angie, though she was sitting in the car only a few feet away. Bill reached into his pocket for change. Using a pay phone was necessary. He didn't want Angie overhearing this particular conversation. He had to make a reservation, and it had to be at a place where they could not only spend the night, but a place willing to accept receipt of T.J.

They'd already been on the road for an hour. Bill hated to stop, but making sure Angie and T.J. were reunited was important, and that meant pulling off in Dayton to use the phone. He'd been in touch with a regional courier service and the police department in Milwaukee while Angie was still asleep. He'd been able to use his cell phone for that, but it had been too early to wake the proprietor of a bed and breakfast, and he didn't want to call a motel, because motels usually had rules about pets. Bed and breakfasts were operated out of people's homes. He needed to find one willing to let him have the cat shipped to their address.

He held up the map. The town of Gardiner was at the northern end of Yellowstone. It was as good a place to stay as any. Bill glanced at the tattered phone book dangling from a chain. Gardiner was across the border in Montana. They were still in Wyoming. The directory would be useless. He dropped a quarter into the slot, waited for the tone, and dialed long distance information. Mustering all his charm he explained to the operator that he couldn't give her the name of the place he wanted her to look up, because he didn't know it. He asked if she'd be kind enough to provide him with the numbers of any three bed and breakfasts located in Gardiner, Montana. He sighed, rubbed the itch of his nose with the back of his hand, and folded his map while he waited. Then he thanked the operator and wrote down the numbers.

The first call didn't answer, which Bill found odd. If they were serving breakfast, they should be up. He dialed the second number. The line was picked up on the first ring. "Hutchinson House, Mary speaking, how may I help you?"

"We're looking to make a reservation—two people, separate beds if possible, for one night. Any chance you have a vacancy?"

"We might. When would you be arriving?"

"Tonight. I know it's short notice. We can double up and use the same bed if we have to."

Mary looked over her shoulder. The man was busy assembling the pipes. His tools covered the kitchen floor. "I'll have to check. Can I put you on hold a moment?"

"Sure." Bill tried to make out the silhouette of his daughter, but the glare was too bright.

Mary put the phone down and went to speak with her employer. "I have a man on the line who wants to make a reservation for this evening. Can we handle it?"

Mr. Hutchinson nodded. "Don't see why not. I just spoke with the serviceman. He says he'll be out of here in an hour."

Bill pushed on the accordion door and let it pop closed behind him. It couldn't have gone better. Hutchinson House had a room with two double beds, perfect for himself and Angie. The courier service said they'd try to get the cat on a morning flight and make the delivery later that day, but failing that, they guaranteed it overnight. Mary, the woman Bill had spoken with, volunteered to keep an eye on T.J. if he arrived early. She even offered to provide Bill and Angie with dinner.

Bill opened the car door. The hinges *screeeched*, crying for oil. He slid onto the seat beside his daughter, closing the door with a *blam*. His grin was spreading as he began to hum. He brought the engine to life, smoke puffing from the tailpipe. The floorboards rumbled with anticipation. Bill slipped the wagon into reverse. By this time tomorrow, Angie would be reunited with her friend. *Yes-sir-ee, Billy-Bob, count your many blessings—see what God has done!*

LAURIE OPENED the door and stepped forward. If Dr. VanEtter was lurking in the hall, she couldn't see him. She had to stay bent over. She moved slowly, in case he was there, to give him a chance to duck out of sight. Her stomach fluttered. It was too late for lunch and too early for dinner, so eating would have to wait. She didn't know where exactly she was headed, she only knew that Ruth had conveyed through Peter that she should get out and socialize. Dr. VanEtter should be given an opportunity to search her apartment and prove to himself that Joe wasn't there—if that's what he wanted to do. She took another deliberate step, her pace slow and difficult. *Step, place the cane, pull forward, step, place the cane, pull forward, step.* She was determined to put on a good show. She'd checked her e-mail before she left. There was nothing from Bill, and that left her article in limbo. For the moment, she had to keep up the charade. But time was running out; she wouldn't be able to keep it up much longer.

The community center was quiet. People were standing around in small groups but the buzz of animated talk was missing. Several were seated around the card table. They were usually laughing and jeering, trying to prod an opponent into playing a sucker's hand, but now they were seated in chairs staring at each other, their faces void of expression. There were no cards on the table. Even the television was off. A death-like pallor hung over the room. She was supposed to mingle, but how could she, the new kid on the block, go in there and start a conversation when those who had known each other for years weren't talking. She passed by without stopping. She wasn't about to make some kind of grand entrance, and then stand there like a statue waiting for a pigeon to land.

She continued down the hall. The sound of silence coming from the lobby was even more pervasive. The impact of Joe's demise was being felt even in the empty corridors, corridors that usually bristled and bustled with life. And why not? Joe was a friend, he would have warned of what was coming. They might have excused his ramblings as an early sign of senility, but now his predictions were coming true. Now the reality was sinking in. Their lives were in danger, and there wasn't a thing they could do about it.

Well, that's what they thought. They didn't know the real Laurie Best; they only knew her alter ego, Annie Iversen. They didn't know that a super hero walked among them, ready at any moment to shed her disguise and save them. Laurie smiled at the analogy. Superman had been a super hero disguised as a mild mannered reporter. She was a super reporter disguised as a mild mannered old lady. She wished she could fling off her costume and stand before them with pad and pen in hand, revealing herself in all her super glory. They needed to see they were not alone, that someone had come to their rescue. She gripped her cane. That day would come, but not yet. *Step, poke the cane forward, pull yourself up, step, poke the cane forward, pull yourself up, step...*

Mrs. Marks came plunging across the lobby, reading from a sheath of papers. She held the folio in front of her eyes. She was so engrossed, she nearly bumped into Laurie before looking up. She stopped short, startled for a moment, but then paused to study Laurie more closely. A glint of recognition caught her eye, and her brassy lips opened to smile.

"Mrs. Iversen, Annie, I was just thinking about you. Could I see you in my office for a minute?"

Laurie felt a moment of reluctance, but nodded. Ever since the encounter in George's office, she'd avoided this part of the building. She didn't want to be questioned. Now she was trapped. Any quick excuse would sound contrived. She turned to step through the door.

The office was neat, as usual. In fact it was so neat it shined: the phone was shiny, the lamp was shiny, the desktop was shiny. Three loose paper clips looked like six because they were so shiny they duplicated themselves on the desk's mirrored surface. Laurie sat in the wing-back chair, propping her cane up between her legs so both hands could perch on its flamingo neck. Her face was beginning to itch; it seemed to happen whenever she got nervous. She could only imagine what this was all about. She did not want to be presented with a contract. She could never sign such a document. Was Barbara so callous as to continue signing up victims even after being told the corporation's dirty little secret? Maybe she had to conduct business as usual to avoid suspicion, to keep her bosses at bay and keep them from finding out about how she'd been helping the enemy.

Barbara closed the door, indicating she wanted privacy. She set her file on the desk and walked around to her chair.

"I had an unusual experience the other night," she said. Her copper hair gleamed. It was hard and unnatural, fixed in place like the hair of a plastic doll. She placed both hands flat on her desk as she sat down. Her hands were mirrored on the desktop, her arms extended, lying flat as she interlaced her fingers. "I bumped into someone— someone in a place they shouldn't have been. I was wondering if you knew anything about it? Ah, I thought so. Don't look surprised. Your disguise is excellent. I had to look really close to tell. That's not what gave you away," Barbara brought her arms up to where they rested on her elbows, tapping her fingertips lightly together, "but I've been through every other possibility and frankly, I'm left with only you.

"Like I said, I'm not part of whatever's going on. If you're building a case against the company, maybe I can help. I've had my own doubts about the way certain things have been handled, but up till now I haven't had a reason to say anything. Well, seeing Joe has changed that.

"There's something I need to tell you. If you've been into George's computer, you've found files with signed affidavits from people requesting they be allowed to die. But you've been told those people didn't actually make the request, and if that's true, you must wonder how the company got those signatures on those documents. I was perplexed about that one myself, but after I thought about it awhile, the answer dawned on me.

"You may have noticed we run a clean, organized office here. It is, for the most part, a paperless office. This is something our Vice President, George Bergen, insists on. We don't keep file cabinets full of paper. Every document is scanned and stored electronically. Much more efficient. If you need to see a file for any particular reason, we print a hard copy. What you may not be aware of, because you haven't signed on with us yet, is that we also use something called biometrics. If you don't know what that is, don't worry, I'll explain in a minute.

"See, we set up accounts for many of our guests; we hold their money and invest it for them, and because it's combined with the investments of other guests, their money grows at a faster rate. I'm not sure that's entirely true, but it is what our guests are told. It's part of our sales pitch. These are retiring elderly people, not savvy business types. They usually want us to manage their money for them. They trust us. They rarely ask to see a statement. As long as the bills are being paid and their needs are being taken care of, they have nothing to question. They're told, of course, that their account is protected and that no one has access to their money without their signed consent. Then we set up an authorization procedure.

"That's where biometrics are used. We employ digital signature analysis. Every guest is asked to sign their name five times on a plain white sheet of paper. The five signatures are scanned and digitized. Then the unique characteristics of each signature are combined to form a single template that takes into account all the various ways the person might sign their name. This template, which is not a signature itself but a digital representation, is what we keep on file. When someone requests a withdrawal, they sign a slip and the computer checks the new signature against the template to verify whether or not the signature is legit. Of course, the guest is told we do this for their own security. You wouldn't want someone to forge your signature and take money from your account, would you? Apparently, the electronic analysis is very good at picking out forgeries. I gather banks use it all the time. It's becoming a standard procedure.

"As I recall, when we bought the system we were told we needed a digital pad and pencil to enter the signatures electronically, but George said no. He said our guests would sign the old-fashioned way, using a regular pen and sheet of paper. He suggested we scan their signatures into the system. The sales person argued with him about it, but George was firm. He said we were dealing with elderly people who were intimidated by technology. He didn't want to force any more electronic gadgets on them than necessary.

"Of course, after the process is complete, the sheet of paper containing the original signatures is supposed to be destroyed, but that's the part I wonder about. What if it isn't? When you think about it, the company has all these legal signatures which can be lifted and scanned into other documents. That may be how the signatures of Henry and Leonard appeared on those forms requesting they be allowed to die. Their signatures could have been used without their knowing about it."

Laurie wrinkled her eyes as if trying to focus. She kept her expression deadpan in an effort to appear confused. She wasn't ready to confirm Barbara's suspicion about who she really was, at least not yet, but her mind was whirling. It explained so much. If those signatures could be used to authorize a mercy killing, they could also be used to authorize the transfer of money...but to where? That's what she had to find out. This was getting good. Someone had conceived the perfect crime. All signatures vary slightly; using the same one over and over would be a dead giveaway, but if they had five original signatures, by using a different one each time, they could access the person's account, make up to four withdrawals and still use the fifth signature to authorize the final exit request. That was it! The large withdrawals from Leonard's and Henry's accounts, and the forms both men allegedly signed stipulating they wanted to die, were counterfeit.

They had the mother of all scams going. The same process was most certainly being used to forge the phony health records, which probably bore the signatures of unwitting physicians lifted from other documents. It would also explain the collaborating doctor's signature that had to be appended to the consent form. Most of all, it raised another possible motive. Up till now, Laurie had bought into Ruth's theory; she assumed Henry and Leonard were sacrificed to save the corporation from financial ruin, but it could be they were killed to cover a theft. Were they victims of corporate mismanagement—or personal greed?

"I'm not saying this is what they're doing," Barbara continued, "that's for you to prove, but it does fall within the realm of possibility. You look dumbfounded. Well, maybe it's a crazy idea, I just thought I'd pass it along, food for thought, know what I mean? But if it is what they're doing, then I've been duped into being part of their little scheme, and I'd appreciate your bearing in mind that I had nothing to do with it. I may be the one they use to collect all these signatures, but I pass them right on up to corporate. In fact, far as I know, the only person who has access to the signatures after that, is Mr. Bergen."

Laurie's mind raced over the possibilities. Barbara had just painted a scenario that included both motive and opportunity, but what if she couldn't be trusted? The confidential bond between a writer and a source was tenuous at best. She knew she didn't trust Barbara the insolent, smooth-talking salesperson. She might say anything to get a sale: "don't worry about a thing, I'm here for you, trust-me." It made Laurie want to pretend she didn't know what Barbara was talking about. On the other hand, Barbara had supplied Mr. Bergen's password, allowing her access to data she would not otherwise have been able to acquire. And thanks to this new information, she could now demonstrate how Henry and Leonard's signatures may have been used without their knowing. They might even be able to trace the missing money to someone's bank account. It was obvious Barbara was trying to distance herself from the corporation. Sometimes you just have to trust people. "I'm grateful for your help," Laurie said, dropping any effort to sound old. "It's too bad it couldn't have come sooner. We might have saved Joe. But the main thing now is to put an end to it. All those people out there are depending on us. Have you seen their faces? They know something's up. They look like they're waiting for the axe to fall."

"Yes, I'm sure they do know something's up," Barbara responded, "as did I, but I didn't know how serious it was until I saw what they did. Joe and his group have been going around swearing something like this was going to happen, but nobody, including me, wanted to believe it. That doesn't mean it didn't stay on everyone's mind, though. You saw us trying to explain the sudden disappearance of Cash and Louis. We weren't told to do that. We just felt we had to say something. We wanted to prevent what's going on out there right now, but I guess it was too little, too late. Whatever they did to Joe has everyone in a state of panic."

Panic? Hardly! They're caught in the headlights—too frightened to move. "I don't know if I'd call it panic," Laurie said. "It's more like resignation. Frankly, it's beyond me. They look like they're in a vacuum. Why do you suppose they just sit there? Why don't they get up and do something?"

"Like what? What would you have them do?"

"I don't know, stand up and fight, go to the police, insist on an investigation, do something. Maybe Joe failed, but there are more of them now. If all of them went together, someone would have to listen."

Barbara lifted her hand and, for a moment, fingered her scarf, then she thrust her palm forward. "We had a lady staying with us awhile back who had a number tattooed right there," she said, pointing at her upturned wrist. "A Holocaust survivor. I asked her that question. I had always wondered. Why, if there were so many of them, and they knew they were being killed by the hundreds each day, why did they just let them do it? Why didn't they fight back? They outnumbered them a hundred to one. Why didn't they charge the soldiers and take away their guns and take over the camp? You know how she answered me? She shrugged her shoulders, like she didn't know, or didn't have a good answer. She just shrugged. That's what you're seeing out there."

SIXTEEN

THE JET OF WATER hit the windshield. The wiper flapped, scraping dirt from the glass on Bill's side, leaving him a transparent tunnel to see through. Bill was adamant about not washing that car. The only bath he planned to give it was when he drove it into the Pacific Ocean, but he did have to clean the windshield every now and then. They had been through some of the grandest wilderness on the face of the good old U.S. of A. And some of the dirtiest, but that's what wilderness was, *wild-dirty-mess,* and any son of a buck who didn't understand that had no place being there. You get to see it the way God intended it to be, like the Garden of Eden: man, animals and plants in their natural habitat, down and dirty in the high country—God's country!

And with perfect weather too. Yellowstone was just another name for the sun. The sky: proud, big and open, breathed in clean and pure; the waterways tumbled and fell in cascades of virgin white; the mountains sang the song of the wind, while each and every tree pointed a finger at its creator. Bill welcomed the freedom. After so many years held captive in the city, he felt his soul had been released. Just look at that sun! It poured through the window warming his skin, causing the hairs on his arm to stand up and dance in the light. Okay, outside a chill was still in the air, but that just made the freshness crisp. The ranger at the east entrance had warned that April temperatures could fall to near freezing and snowfalls a foot deep could collect overnight, all of which proved that God was still smiling on them. They had hit an incredibly warm spring. The temperature hovered in the mid-sixties.

The engine hissed and spat like a steam locomotive. At times Bill wondered if they would make it over and around all the hills and curves surrounding Yellowstone Lake, but the car kept on chugging. The views had been worth every shaky minute of it. The blue of the water was deeper than an indigo sea. Flecked with yellow glints of sun, it was at times so resplendent it took his breath. Bill pulled into turnout after turnout so they could capture the sights from every angle. They spotted a herd of muddy mule deer kicking along a cold mountain trail, a grizzly foraging through cans of garbage at Fishing Bridge, a bony coyote shagging across the road right in front of their bumper, and a twelve-point elk pausing to bray at a pasturing doe and her spring calf.

But what really made Bill's day was the sighting of a bald eagle. He hadn't seen one since he left the Oregon coast, so many years ago. It was symbolic of his newfound freedom. The bald eagle, ensign of the nation, emblem of patriotism, the essence and spirit of the free. He recalled a verse of scripture: "They that wait upon the Lord shall renew their strength; they shall mount up with wings as eagles; they shall run and not be weary; they shall walk and not faint." It was a favorite because it revealed, in a few succinct words, the universal source of all energy. Seeing the eagle play on the morning breeze, the broad sweep of wings circling the star-studded water, the sudden stoop and splash of fury, the retrieval of prey, a glistening speckled lake trout twisting in those powerful yellow claws, made Bill feel proud to be an American. It was a feeling life in Detroit had denied him. Tramping through the asphalt jungle, through the muck and mire of the daily newswire, only made him feel dirty. The eagle turned and, catching a favorable current, took a cutting drive toward a steep walled embankment at the far side of the lake. Bill imagined it heading for its nest built high into the rocky crags on the side of a cliff. The eagle would disdain the comfort zone. Cages were for songbirds; the eagle lived out on the edge, clinging to the highest heights, crying *freedom, freedom, freedom* to all who would be free.

That was the sad thing about America, wasn't it? America had fallen into the comfort zone. It had lost the pioneer spirit of exploration and survival, man against the elements, the day-to-day struggle to conquer fear. Only those who took life head on, those who despised complacency and fought against the sweeping moral morass could know that freedom, because only those few had the guts to stand up and speak the truth: that "righteousness exalteth a nation, but sin is a reproach to any people." America the beautiful was becoming America the ugly. Only those few who stood strong to fight against her decline deserved to wave the flag. Bill knew he was one of those few and, dad-gum, that's why he felt so good right now. He was truly free, heading into an uncertain future, yes, but with God on his side, he knew he'd overcome whatever obstacles got in his way. He inhaled deeply, filling his lungs with solid blue air. Man that's heaven!

They were approaching one of the most incredible natural sights in the western world. The geothermal phenomenon of Old Faithful drew people from around the globe, though Bill had read how Old Faithful was known more for its dependability than its majesty. A number of other geysers eclipsed Old Faithful in size and length of eruption. Yellowstone was full of them. There were more geysers in Yellowstone than anywhere else on planet earth, but they were moody, they couldn't always be counted on to provide a show just when you wanted it. For people on a clock, like Bill, the predictability of Old Faithful was important.

They rolled down out of the forests that surrounded Yellowstone Lake into the lowlands of bubbling yellow mud and geysers. The trees there were crusted in white, mineralized, and the meadows were woven in a steamy ochre mist. It was a hostile environment that made seeing wildlife scarce. A misty vapor saturated the air, leaving behind a light sulfuric smell that pinched Bill's nostrils. He rubbed a forefinger against the side of his nose, wondering if the acrid odor was bothering Angie. It didn't appear so. Her eyes were closed against the sun. She looked at peace. Her hair shone honey brown, as silken and shiny as cellophane, and she had just a smattering of rust brown flecks across the bridge of her nose. She was stunning: the spitting image of her mother. Were it not for her disability, young bucks would lock horns for the privilege of courting this doe. Perhaps her condition was for the best, who's to say? Bill shuddered at the thought of giving advice to the lovelorn. It wasn't his bailiwick; affairs of the heart were a mother's job. His big thumbs began tapping the steering wheel. *Man-oh-man, if her mother could only see her now, she'd beg to take Angie in her arms, wouldn't she?* There had to be some invisible link, some genetic tie, some...instinct, call it what you will, but there had to be something that made Laurie, as a mother, want to be nurturing and protective of her child. If only she could stare into the bubbling blue brilliance of Angie's eyes, eyes so much like her own, why, tossing Angie aside would be the furthest thing from her mind. Bill was sure of that. Angie had grown up to be what every mother wanted for their daughter, beautiful, uncomplaining, far more giving than taking, a real class act. It did his heart proud. He didn't have to feel sorry for his daughter, because his daughter didn't feel sorry for herself. If anything she was...what?...self-satisfied?...no, she was happy, that's what she was, she was just plain happy. In the midst of her impediment, Angie had learned what few people with all good health and prosperity ever learn, that happiness is a state of mind. It flows from within, like a wellspring of the soul. It isn't something you manufacture, it can't be bought or earned, and has little to do with circumstance or surroundings. Happiness is the result of contentment. There was no point in wondering what Laurie would or would not do. They were on a grand adventure, soon to set out on the high seas, father and daughter sailing off into the sunset. If Laurie was afraid of getting her feet wet, she deserved to be left behind, simple as that. His mind fashioned an image of Laurie standing on the dock, with her hair down and flowing, her handkerchief flapping in the breeze as she waved good-bye with kisses borne across the water on salty currents of air: Bon voyage and hurry home. He shook his head. Must be the sulfuric heat. His brain was beginning to melt.

He pulled the station wagon into the parking area, his mind still waving good-bye to Laurie on the shore. He shoved the shift lever into park and watched a cloud of brown dust float by. He opened the door, planted a dusty boot on the ground, and raised himself to full height, towering over the car. A few people were milling around the entrance to the visitor center while one or two others meandered out across the barren plateau toward the viewing site. Bill would have expected bigger crowds, but it was early in the season. The tourist depot had only been open a week. Again he considered himself lucky. They were due to take possession of the boat on the first of May, which was Saturday. Yellowstone opened to full use mid-April. The timing had been perfect. They had fabulous weather, and no crowds; what could be better?

A man with a porkpie hat shuffled by, scuffing the dirt as he read a brochure without looking up. The hat had a dozen shiny gold tourist pins stuck to the band, advertising the places the man had been.

"Excuse me, sir. You know when the geyser's set to go off next?" Bill started to lay his arm across the top of the station wagon but realized the faded copper paint was covered with road film. He drew his arm back, rubbing it up and down.

The man stopped to look around, his wide eyes puzzled. His silver hair rode shaggy over his collar and his glasses were thick rimmed and black. "They said it could go at any minute," he said, blinking as he brought a weathered hand up over his eyes. "Their predictions are always give or take ten minutes either way, so if you don't want to miss it, you have to get out there and wait."

Bill thanked the man and thumped the tin roof of the wagon, raising dust. He looked at his hand, wiped it on his pants, and went around the car to free Angie, taking her in his arms. He wouldn't bother with the wheelchair; it was a short distance.

The observation area was three hundred feet from the geyser, a distance far enough back to keep tourists from being burned by the boiling-hot spray. Maybe there were bigger and better geysers, but Bill knew that seeing a fountain slightly higher or wider or longer lasting wouldn't be more impressive. All that steam power, compressed like hot water blowing from a kettle, spewing into the air in a rainbow of color presented an awesome sight. Besides, they couldn't see everything. Bill wanted to hike into the high country, to camp with the mountain wolf and bighorn sheep, carry Angie if he had to, but there wasn't enough time. They were on a schedule. They had to be in Seattle on Saturday. They'd lost time with that blasted flat tire. They'd got an early start, but it had taken five hours to get from Buffalo to the park's western entrance, and the drive around

Yellowstone Lake had proved incredibly slow. Then they had to wait for Old Faithful to gush, and now they needed to grab a quick lunch. It was already early afternoon and Bill had to make it all the way up to the north park entrance, up through Mammoth Hot Springs, and all the sightseeing along the way, in order to be out of the park in time to find the lodgings he'd reserved for the night. At least the lady who'd helped him with the reservation had had a sympathetic ear. Through the phone he'd heard her coaching the owner of the bed-and-breakfast to let their address be used for the delivery of T.J. Bill tried to build an image of the woman from her voice. *Mary, wasn't it?* Thanks to her, they would soon be back on schedule with Angie grinning ear to ear at the return of her lost friend, but it meant they had to rush their tour of the park, and that niggled him. So much for the call of freedom, the cry of the eagle in the sky, sailing on a breeze without constraint. Bill couldn't fly. He was bound by the ropes of time, obligation and circumstance.

STEP, CANE OUT FRONT, pull forward, step, cane out front, pull forward, step, it was slow slugging, infinitely slow, but Laurie held the pace, careful not to draw undue attention to herself. She would have continued, would have plodded on, and on, and on, until she reached the door of her apartment, but she had to pass by the community center. The silence contained within those walls stopped her cold. It was eerie, the sound of static air looming over an amplified mike, a cadaverous sound. In it she saw defeat, the surrendering of the will, the result of giving up; it was the sound of death. She could only wonder if this was what it was like for despairing Jews sent to Nazi death camps, awaiting their turn, hoping it would never come but at the same time having a sixth sense that told them it most definitely would. People shouldn't be so fatalistic. You can't just sit and wait to die, not with help so close by; the allies were on the way, but she couldn't tell them that. Her secret was already known by too many, and the more that knew, the more chance it had of getting back to the wrong people.

Colonel Rosen sat by himself, staring at the ground, his shoulders hunched as he slumped in his chair. Laurie might have been reading his thoughts when she likened the mood of the room to that of a concentration camp. Jack had been there. It was, he felt, to his shame, though his government called him a hero.

IT WAS LATE 1944. The mood of the troops was optimistic. The war was almost over. Jack had been placed in command of a company attached to the First Army, sweeping their way across France. They had been successful in pushing the Germans back in one battle after another. It seemed they were invincible. The Allied front was five hundred miles long. It spanned the entire country. Jack's division moved into Belgium, advancing quickly through the Ardennes region. The Allies did not place particular importance on this sector, so it was one place where the line was stretched thin. Unbeknownst to army intelligence, Hitler had amassed three German armies to attack and penetrate the line held by the allies at this, its weakest point.

At five-thirty A.M. on December sixth, thirteen German infantry divisions, supported by eight German armored divisions launched their attack on a line held by five divisions of the American First Army. They pounded the battlefield with howitzers, rocket launchers and heavy cannon, allowing the fifth and sixth German Panzer armies to squeeze into the Ardennes through the Loshein Gap, at precisely the point where Colonel Jack and his regiment were positioned.

Jack couldn't remember much about the engagement, though history would label it, "The Battle of the Bulge," and give it the distinction of being the hardest fought battle of the war in Europe. All he remembered was that it was December, and freezing cold. The men under his command were stuffing newspapers into their uniforms to provide insulation against the snow, and trying to thaw their fingers over cans of Sterno so they'd be able to pull the trigger, when the time came.

When the pounding of the guns began, Jack scrambled to his Jeep and ordered Corporal Jerry Knapp to drive him to the front so he could assess the situation. A shell lobbed over the heads of his men landed right to the side of his jeep, overturning the vehicle and throwing the unconscious colonel into the bush. Corporal Knapp was killed instantly.

Jack woke up in hell. More literally, he found himself in a Jewish concentration camp known as Buchenwald, but the description fit. When his eyes opened, the ghoulish, skeletal faces looming over him reminded him of a passage from Dante's Inferno. The dispirited zombies even spoke an unknown tongue. They meandered aimlessly overhead, wearing black and white striped pajamas, looking like lost souls of the netherworld.

He was not offered medical assistance, though he had a severe concussion. He was left bleeding on the floor where he had been dumped by his captors. The sullen faces must have thought him delirious when he began asking questions. It took two days before someone recognized he was speaking English. The interpreter, who had been a student of languages at the Frankfurt University, had only recently been in the extermination camp at Auschwitz. He had narrowly escaped death when the Russians advancing through Poland forced the Germans to abandon the camp and retreat back into Germany, taking their prisoners with them.

Under the terms of the Geneva Convention, Jack knew he should have been taken to a POW camp, not a concentration camp filled with German Jews. He should be receiving medical attention from the Red Cross. This was some kind of mistake. He tried to convince his multilingual friend to help him explain this to Commandant Pister, the camp's senior officer, but his interpreter urged him to keep quiet. He was there because he was a Jew. Nazis didn't distinguish between German, Polish, or American Jews. A Jew was a Jew, period! To make a complaint of any kind meant certain death.

He was asked to lay low, and to stay out of trouble. The camp was not an extermination camp, though dozens were hung every day, and hundreds more died of disease and starvation. But it was a place where people could survive, if they kept to themselves. As Jack's strength returned, he began to explore his surroundings, but he saw little evidence of the alleged survival. Even working around the clock, the camp incinerators couldn't consume the bodies of all those who died every day. Naked corpses had to be piled in the yard to sit and rot. The camp reeked with the smell of death. General Eisenhower once acknowledged that most of the boys sent over to fight the war didn't know what they were fighting for. Jack wished they could see what he was seeing. At least then they would know what they were fighting against.

He finally agreed to keep quiet, but only, he said, because the Army was on the way. He was ignorant of the battle that had ensued after he'd been taken prisoner. He knew nothing of the nineteen thousand Americans that had been killed, or the twenty-three thousand that had been captured and carted off as prisoners of war. He only assumed, based on the allies previous advance, that the Nazis had been routed, and that liberation was at hand. Fortunately, he'd been right. Through his interpreter he began explaining to his fellow inmates how the Allies had retaken France and Belgium, and how the Russians had already swept across Poland, and how the German Army was in retreat on every front, and how the war was sure to be over within a matter of months. Thus, he brought hope to those who had no hope.

Colonel Jack Rosen spent two months in that place. He saw what Laurie now saw: dejected, despairing people. And he understood how the loss of hope, the refusal to laugh, or even speak, was a form of death in itself. He pondered what he could do to bring comfort to the dying spirits of those around him. But this time he didn't have good news to share.

LAURIE SAW the same somber faces, and recognized the same despair as Jack, but though she knew help was on the way, she couldn't say anything. Why get involved anyway? She wasn't responsible for the morale of the place. She was there to get a story, a front page story if possible, with her name on it, something to show the unbelieving back at the office what good reporting was all about, the risk, the uncompromising defense of the truth regardless of the cost—her name in lights! The people themselves were not the issue, the story was the issue, but as she stared into the room, peering, as it were, into the very souls of the downtrodden, she knew it was more than that. Whether she liked it or not, she was there to help people in need, defenseless people, people without hope, resigned to an undeserved fate, who, without her help, were doomed to die.

Curse it all, now she was thinking like Bill! Defending the helpless, the down and out, the oppressed, those were his lines. What right did he have to take credit for her idea? Or maybe it wasn't Bill, maybe it was just virtue; it was doing what was right, and as much as she hated to admit it, it was the side Bill was usually on. So maybe, just this once, she was on the same side as him, but she'd arrived there on her own, which proved she didn't need his help. She probably would have come to the same conclusion about Angie, if Bill hadn't put her under so much pressure. Okay, she was ready to admit it; letting Angie live had been the right thing to do. She didn't buy into eugenics, the purification of the gene-pool by the elimination of bad seed. It was just that the raising of a disabled child was more than she could bear. It wasn't a desire to weed out the imperfect and build a master race. It was a desire to want normal children, to want them to have normal lives; was that asking too much? She'd paid for her decision. Bill would never know how many tortured nights she'd spent wondering about her daughter. She would never tell. He would only encourage her to become involved with the child, and that was something she couldn't do, because...well, because she was afraid she would fail, and failure was something she could not allow. But that didn't mean she didn't lie awake at night thinking about it. She knew it would end up like this. The weight had to rest on Bill's shoulders. The damage was done and it was his fault, and that was that!

But these folks were another matter. It might have been Bill's lead that brought her here, but she had taken up the cause, and that gave her ownership. It was hers; she was the one running the show. He was just a bystander, a recipient of the glory she alone deserved. She would share it with him because his name carried more weight. This story deserved a broader audience than her own paper could afford. But it was still her story—not his! What would he do in this situation?

Her mind wandered back to the miserable Christmas Eve they'd spent stuck in O'Hare, and the awful trauma of being stranded for five unbearable hours in a stuffy, smoke-filled airport waiting for a flight delayed by weather. The room was rude. Those hoping to enjoy

Christmas with arriving loved ones, and those trying to get home to friends and family, were at each other's throats. Altercations broke out over stolen airport seats—the most uncomfortable seats in the world—and over the fumes caused by smokers who refused to go to the smoker's lounge because they might lose their airport seats, and over popcorn spillage, and soda pop dribble, and over snoring and bad breath and body odor. Complaints were made to the airline staff who scratched their heads, keeping their smiles in place over clenched teeth, because they could do nothing but keep assuring those waiting that the plane would eventually make it, as soon as the weather cleared.

Bill was right in the middle of it, doing his usual positive attitude thing, wanting to cheer everyone up because, doggone-it-all, it just wasn't right for folks to be quarreling at Christmas. Then he'd hit on an idea. He went to the coffee shop, handed them his credit card and got one of the employees to bring out a rolling cart of coffee, tea, eggnog and cookies for everyone. Wouldn't you know it? That one single act of kindness got everybody in such a good mood, not only did they stop squabbling, they started singing carols together and the mood in the airport changed from rancorous animosity, to one of peace on earth and good will toward men.

Laurie, for her part, remembered how embarrassed she'd been when they started singing, how she wanted to crawl under a table and hide. She'd accused Bill of foolishly spending their money at a time when money was tight, and of not thinking of her needs first: the need for privacy and quiet. She did not want to sing. They were not the Mormon Tabernacle Choir. It was an airport, a public facility. She hated having all eyes focused on her choral-master husband. She resented it. Just as she resented the letters and Christmas cards that came, for several years after, from people who had been there and still wanted to thank Bill for making it one of the most memorable Christmases they'd ever had. Looking back now, she had to admit the stunt made quite an impression. It had changed the mood of an entire airport.

She pushed her cane forward, *plant the cane, first foot forward, bring the second foot to join the first, plant the cane, first foot forward, bring the second foot to join the first, plant the cane,* and moved past the community center until she came to the dining hall—too early for dinner, too late for lunch. There had to be something she could do.

The tray rattled, rolling on a cart pushed by a server dressed in a white kitchen jacket. Silver service coffee and tea pots glistened in the overhead lights, and the juice containers clinked with ice. The people in the room gave little notice; whatever it was, it wasn't for them, though a few curious eyes posted hope. The man approached a stooped woman and asked if he could provide her with something. He assured her there was no cost as he poured her a cup of tea. Steam rose from the cup's rim in robust swirls. Then he passed around a plate of coconut macaroons, and went on to serve a beverage to the next person, and the next, and the next, and the next, until the entire room was served and people who had been mute began to converse. The beverages had lubricated their vocal cords. If nothing else, people had to ask each other where the treat had come from.

Laurie kept silent, nibbling her own cookie between sips of hot coffee. Her head was nodding, and her lips were rolled up at the corners, having caught a contagious smile. Her toe began to tap out a beat on the carpet. A maple console rested along the wall, presumably housing a stereo of some sort. Maybe it wasn't the season for carols, but that didn't mean they couldn't have music. She raised the lid and realized she was looking at a vintage sound system. There were no CDs. There weren't even cassette tapes. She was staring at something almost unfamiliar. It was a phonograph. Beside it, held upright by little wire racks, was a collection of dog-eared record albums. The music was right out of the forties and fifties, music that had passed into history, with titles she didn't recognize by recording artists she'd never heard of—*Billy Bo Jo and the Flim Flam Band? Oh, what the heck, when in Rome*...she dropped the disc onto the spindle placing the changer arm on top the record to hold it flat and tweaked the knob until the vinyl album fell onto the turntable and began to spin. The sound was from a bygone era, scratchy, popping and hissing through low-fidelity speakers, but it was music. It waltzed out of the box like a Jimmy Stewart romance, slow and easy. She would have preferred something a little more upbeat, but she didn't know one record from another, so this would have to do.

She crooked her hand on the small of her back, and turned to find herself nose to nose with Jack Rosen, the little colonel.   He extended his arms in her direction, his right hand reaching out past his torso, and his left circling around like it was holding the waist of an invisible person.

"Ma'am, I'd be honored if you'd do me the pleasure," he said.

SEVENTEEN

THEY HAD BEEN driving all day. Angie's head was nodding, falling forward and rolling to the side. Bill was fighting to keep alert and hoping to find a roadside stand where he could get a quick cup of coffee. The grace of purple mountain's majesty, the spacious skies and amber waves of grain, were becoming tedious. They were ready for civilization: a hot bath, a hearty meal, and a warm bed.

A dark purple dusk had overtaken the sky by the time they arrived in Gardiner, Montana. Bill stopped for gas. The driver's side door had developed a hideous screech. The hinges had been invaded by rust after the torrential rains, and scoured by sand as they crossed the Dakota plains. He plopped the nozzle into the tank and set about playing squeegee-kid. It wasn't fair that Angie couldn't see. He wiped the rubber blade on the brown paper towel before streaking it across the window, and repeated the process over and over until her vision was restored. When the tank was full, he hung the nozzle back on the pump and went inside to pay.

The station was a discolored roadside establishment Bill figured to have been built in the fifties. The paint was dingy. Chunks of soiled white stucco crumbled from the corners, exposing tarpaper and chicken-wire. He stepped over and around a mountain of mess. Stacks of engine parts, batteries, carburetors, air cleaners, belts and hoses were mixed with racks of chewing gum, chips, and bars of candy sheathed in oil-smudged wrappers. He saw dregs of coffee in a pot, but it looked like it had been floating in its tallow skin since morning. They were only minutes from their destination; he decided he could wait. He handed his credit card to a young man in coveralls who, though standing behind the counter, smelled more like gasoline than the pump outside. Too bushed to consult a map, Bill asked directions. The boy pointed down the street, "Take your first left, then go left again, 'bout half way down on the right," he answered, his hand snaking through the air as he pantomimed the route.

They were rolling slowly down the road. The trees stretched above them like a canopy of dark silhouettes. Their inky overhead branches merged to form dark rivers that flowed down to massive murky trunks. Bill kept his eyes focused on the tiny names above the roadside mailboxes, but he found them difficult, if not impossible, to read. They were looking for Hutchinson House, their reserved lodgings, trying to make it before the night's purple hat covered them with darkness. Bill was carrying on a one-sided conversation, explaining to Angie how he hoped their hosts hadn't already served dinner because he was too tired to go find a restaurant, and besides, he was weary of restaurant food, and did she know that one of the things their host had bragged about was the fact that they offered home cooked meals, which sounded mighty fine to him; was she as hungry as he was? Then an unusual flash caught his eye. One house, set back off the road, stood out brightly. He rolled up slowly, looking to the right. Standing out of the blackness, the house was aglow. Warm light was bursting from behind the curtains. The whole left side of the house was lit on the inside by a thousand-kilowatt lamp. Then the front door blew open and several people raced out, one seemingly holding a young child and one trailing light from his back. Bill could see inside the house now. There were flames—the house was on fire—the man's back was on fire! He hit the brakes. The station wagon skidded onto the curbless lawn leaving wheel tracks in the muddy grass. "WAIT HERE!" he barked as he rammed his shoulder against the door, popping it open. *Screech, bamm, pow!* it slammed, and he was gone. The wagon was left rocking with Angie alone inside. The lawn felt mushy and wet, as though spring snow had only recently melted.

Bill's feet indented footprints in the soft grass as he ran. The man was trying to twist out of his jacket, a dancing marionette—*get on the ground, roll around*—Bill closed the distance. The man continued to hop and bop, his elbows jackknifed behind him trying to slap the flame, his feet dancing as though they were landing on hot coals. Bill was close now. Revisiting his high school football days, (what else could he do?) he launched himself through the air and tackled the man waist high, pulling him to the ground. The old quarterback sack. Bill heard the *thud,* as they hit the turf and the, *ooofffhh,* as the man lost his wind. He lay on his side in a semi-stupor, stunned and confused by the attack. His jacket was still ablaze, but the fire was less fierce than a moment ago. Bill rose to his knees, took hold of the man and rolled him on his back. Smoke wheezed out from beneath the jacket as the flames were extinguished. Bill placed his hands on his thighs, panting and wheezing, trying to catch his breath. He could feel water soaking up through his pants where his knees were buried in the wet grass.

"*Aaah-huhh, ahh-huhh,* sorry, *aaah-huh,* to be so rough, *ah-huhh,* but we got it out." Bill could smell the man's singed hair. A few more seconds and his head might have burst aflame.

The man crawled into a sitting position, pulled his knees up, and leaned on one arm with a hand holding his stomach. He nodded, still bemoaning his loss of breath.

"You feel okay? Any pain?"

The man shook his head. "No...no, I'm okay. I think."

People were coming out of their houses attracted by the pyrotechnics. Forked tongues of fire were licking the night. The siren of a fire truck could be heard in the distance. The blaze sizzled, popped and roared, and then, over it all, a woman's voice began shrieking: "Jason, Jason, JAYSONNNN!" The woman ran toward the house and Bill, sensing this was probably not a good idea, leapt to his feet and gave chase. She was almost to the door but stopped short at the last second. Her hands went to her face, holding her cheeks, her eyes wide in terror. Bill caught her by the arm and pulled her back. "What's wrong? Is somebody in there?"

The lady cupped her hands over her mouth, her voice shuddered as she spoke. "I...brought him outside with me...he was right here! I had him in my arms. Oh God, please, nooooo!" She started to move forward but Bill held her back. He could feel the flames inside the house burning his forehead.

"If you had him outside, why do you think he's in there?" The woman didn't answer. Her hands were covering her mouth as hot tears, glowing with fire, washed her face. "He was right here. I brought him out. Oh no...this can't...no...noooo...nooooo!"

Bill turned and stood in front of her. He placed his hands on her shoulders and shook her lightly, forcing her to look at him. "If you had him outside, why do you think he's in there?"

The shrill pitch of her hysteria made her words hard to understand. "He asked about the cat," she sobbed. "He said, 'where's Whiskers?' but...I...I ignored him, and...he's gone, and...he can't...nooooo, it can't be..."

Bill scanned the cluster of onlookers but couldn't see a small boy among them. Somewhere in the vague distance he was aware of Angie watching through the window of the station wagon. He could see the fire reflecting off the dark glass. He turned to look at the house. The highest concentration of burning was on the left side where flames were shooting out the window. The blaze in the living room was confined to the walls. The center of the room was clear of flames. If he could just get into the house, past the door and turn right, the back half of the house seemed unaffected.

There was no time to think. Bill let the woman go and dove for the house, filling his lungs with air as he leapt over the threshold and landed in a room as hot as the pit of hell. He turned, holding his breath, his cheeks bulging, his eyes brimming with water and beginning to sting. He paused to get his bearings. He was standing in the middle of an inferno, with flames surrounding him, chewing up the wallpaper. To his left was a kitchen, most likely where the fire had started. Roaring waves of heat billowed out the door. The boy couldn't have gone in there. He turned to the right. There were two ways to go: a door leading into what was probably the dining room, and an entrance to a hall. His arms felt scorched, the hairs shriveling in the heat. He tried rubbing his sleeves to cool the burn. The trim around the door was dancing in flame, but there was less smoke in that direction. He decided to try there first. He broke through the blaze and landed against the dinette. The tablecloth was in cinders; clumps of melting material dropped to the floor around the table's circular edge. Bill ducked to see if the boy was underneath. He nearly lost his balance when he placed his hand on the floor and found it scalding hot. He jerked his hand back trying to stay crouched—*nothing!* He blinked to clear the water from his eyes so he could look again just to be sure, but saw nothing. Now he stood looking around the room, a few sticks of furniture, but no boy. There was a sliding glass door and a large window along the wall. He wanted to smash the window, let in air and catch his breath, but he knew feeding a fire oxygen was the worst thing he could do. If he opened that window the fire would explode. His feet were heating up through his boots.

Bill raised his arm up over his eyes and plowed back into the living room. He'd probably been in the house less than a minute, but he was in desperate need of air. He continued on, broad-jumping across the threshold of the front door to find solace in the night. Out of the reach of the flames again, he bent over, placing his hands on his thighs to gulp in fresh air. Liquid blurred his vision but he raised his head to find the frantic mother. The man he had helped stood beside her with a hand on her shoulder. Bill locked eyes with the woman for only a second. The distraught look on her face begged him to give it another try. He sucked in a deep breath, stood, turned, and hurled himself back into the fire, this time covering his head with both hands as he plunged down the hall. There were fewer flames in this part of the house, but the rooms were full of blinding smoke. *In a fire, most people die from smoke inhalation.* That was a comforting thought. He dared not take a breath. He turned to the right, fanning the smoke to clear the way. It was a bedroom, with a large, queen bed. He dropped to his knees looking underneath the bedframe. He saw a couple of boxes, but no boy. He thought he heard something familiar—a distant mew—the cat was in the next room. Was that where he'd find the child? He wanted to call out, but couldn't chance inhaling fumes. He ran back into the hall and turned right. There were two doors, one on each side—*which one?* Then he heard the cat again and turned to the right. The smoke was thick. He could barely see. The cat's cry was coming from under the bed, a single bed this time, *must be the boy's room.* He plopped down on his stomach and there, down low, barely visible through the thick brown haze, was the cat—but no boy. His lungs were about to burst, but he couldn't leave a defenseless animal. He reached his long arm beneath the bed trying to grab the cat, but it backed up to avoid being caught. Bill was losing his breath; the cavity of his chest felt like it was on fire; he could only afford one more try. He pushed his shoulder against the bedframe, stretched his arm as far as it would go, and grabbed the cat's paw. He didn't have time to be gentle. He yanked the cat forward, clutched the scruff of its neck, and pulled it out. No time to go all the way back down the hall. The front door was too far, and he still had the boy to rescue. A lamp sat on a bedside table. In the absence of flames, he could risk letting oxygen in. He yanked the lamp up, pulling the plug from its socket, and in one continuous motion hurled it through the window. The glass shattered. Thick black smoke funneled out in a mighty plume, blocking the window, but Bill knew where it was, or at least where it had been. He heaved the cat through the opening with such a thrust, the animal cleared the smoke, became a pretzel in the air, and twisted until all four feet were square with the ground. It landed with a, *"meowrrrow,"* and took off running across the lawn, under a neighbor's hedge, and into the next yard.

Bill had a hopeful notion that breaking the window would give him air to breathe but the exiting smoke made it futile. He turned away and headed for the room across the hall. He was running out of time. His lungs were on fire. *Please Lord, just a little longer...please.* He burst into the next room, probably the one where he and Angie would have stayed—no little boy. That was it. His lungs were seared. He tried to stumble back out the door, turning, but it was too late. He knew he had to take a breath or risk blacking out. He dropped to his knees. JAYSONNNNNN! he cried as he exhaled. He took in what he hoped was air, but wasn't. Whatever it was shredded the inside of his lungs. He went down on all fours. He tried putting his face close to the floor to breathe. Smoke rises, the cat survived by breathing low to the ground. He tried to take another breath. His lungs were peeled raw. He moved to get up. He wanted to make a lunge for the door, but his feet weren't there. He felt his shoulder crash to the floor. He tried to take another breath but only choked, hacked and coughed. He tried again as his brain swirled in pin-pricking snowflakes of white which became a cyclone of charcoal dust. He struggled to take in only the tiniest small sip of air. His brain began fading to black. He thought of Angie. He inhaled fire and swallowed his breath. He had a feeling it would be his last.

PETER SAT ALONE watching over Joe. The crinkled old man was stretched out on the bed. A pillow elevated his shiny, bald dome, and a crisp white sheet was tucked up under his chin. His face was growing stubble. A fierce gray forest of nubs poked through the rumpled mounds and crevices of his flesh, and his mouth emitted the odor of sewage through teeth as pasty and yellow as old wax. Sometimes his eyes would open, but they appeared not to see. They stared into the great cosmic void of eternity like living death, or perhaps like a man staring into the face of God. Then his eyes would close and he would appear to rest. His breathing was irregular and punctuated with coughs that convulsed his chest. Sometimes he swallowed and sometimes he drooled. Peter was there with a moist towel to wipe his mouth when it overflowed.

Ruth spent most of her time outside. They both agreed it was best if she made herself visible. Whoever did this to Joe would be looking to get him back. They would be watchful of everyone, but especially Ruth, and be suspicious of any deviation from her normal routine. They would take note of her absence. Joe couldn't be left alone. Someone had to stay with him. Peter volunteered.

He liked being needed; he rather enjoyed the compliments he received from Ruth: "I don't think we could have done without you," she'd said. What he didn't like was the austere quiet, and hollow hours of loneliness. He looked around the room for about the hundredth time. Empty, artless, beige walls, no dishes or cutlery, or towels in the bathroom, no toothbrush or toothpaste. They had chosen a vacant apartment, so there were no amenities, *no radio, no television, not even a phone,* and because it was a studio unit, designed for single living, there was no bedroom. They were lucky it came furnished with a foldout sofa and a pair of stuffed living room chairs. *No radio, no television, no phone!* And they had to keep the curtains drawn to stop anyone from looking in, and keep the lights turned off to avoid drawing attention. He could handle it during daylight hours, but last night would have been unbearable if Ruth hadn't excused herself and told the others she was turning in early. She'd made her way back over to keep Peter company. He would have gone crazy sitting alone in the dark all night.

The worst thing about the isolation, was it gave him time to think. Peter didn't like his thoughts. He didn't like thinking about Tina. *How could she just dump me like that?* He could feel a burning in his chest. Forget her. Tina was a looser, a...a creep a...a...but he knew he loved her, and he couldn't bring himself to believe such terrible things about someone he loved. It hurt too much. He wanted to get his mind off Tina, but he had too much time on his hands, and nothing to do but think. Besides, he didn't like his other thoughts any better. Why dwell on death, and what lie beyond? (Would he even be missed?) Ruth had given him something to think about—but he didn't like that either. She was such a sweet old gal. Sometimes he just wanted to squeeze her, but other times he wanted to throw her out the door.

Her answers were too simple, that was the problem. "My goodness Peter, why would you want to destroy something God has made? That's the very kind of thing we're trying to stop. God alone gives life, and God alone has the right to take it. Whoever took the lives of Henry and Leonard didn't have that right. And neither do you or I. You mustn't think about killing yourself, Peter. God wants you to live."

Wrong! Peter knew if he were to die today no one would care, and especially not God because he was not one of God's perfect creations. He was a mistake, a misfit, a square peg in a round hole. He should probably stop pretending. Just go ahead and be gay. That's what everyone thought he was anyway. All his gay friends thought he was gay. He'd been to their parties and danced and had fun, but when it came to sex, he always pulled away. They said he was in denial. *Why?* Being a makeup artist didn't make him gay. He was a makeup artist because it was fun. He didn't like working on cars. He liked the smell of shampoo, not grease. Therein lie the problem. He had the genitals of a man, and the soul of a woman, but he wasn't gay. Clingy, drippy and pathetic. That's what Tina had called him. The truth hurt. Maybe he should just make himself up to look old, and go outside and let the powers that be put him away. At least then he wouldn't be guilty of killing himself. He needed to call Dr. Roberts. His therapist wouldn't want him thinking this way. He glanced around the room, but there wasn't a phone.

Peter's hand dropped to the book in his lap. Why bother? If they didn't like him on earth, they wouldn't want him in heaven. The afternoon light was subdued by the curtains. It would be hard to read anyway. He thumbed the worn, gold leafed pages, and shook his head. It was all about help, but he wasn't sure he wanted that kind of help—been there, done that, I'm OK, you're OK, leave it alone—but he didn't want to offend Ruth. She was playing surrogate mother, bent on helping her child whether he needed it or not. Interfering, meddling, intruding, call it what you will—all right, maybe it was really caring—but who needed it? She didn't have permission to butt into his life. Still, the book was his fault. He'd asked for it. Well, maybe not for this particular book, but for something. He should have been more specific. The hours were long and lonely, and since the apartment did not have a radio, a television or a phone, he had asked Ruth if she could bring him something to read, and she'd complied. She'd brought him a Bible. A BIBLE? The lady had chutzpah, he'd give her that, but a Bible? What was he supposed to do with it?

Joe coughed, gurgling on his saliva, his chest heaving spasmodically. Peter jumped up, tossing the book into the chair as he put his hands on Joe's shoulders to hold him down and keep him from kicking off the bed. Drool washed down the side of his face. Peter grabbed a cloth to mop it away, wiping also the inside of Joe's mouth as he had seen Ruth do so many times.

If ever there was an example of Christian charity, Ruth was it. He marveled at her patience. She cared for Joe the way a mother might care for a child stricken with fever. Yet as far as he could determine, there was no physical bond between them. It was a delicate subject, and he had broached it carefully because a romance between two old people might be a private matter, but she had picked up on his meaning and immediately assured him that Joe was just a friend, a rather new one, she explained. They'd only been brought together by events of late. Then she'd wiped Joe's mouth, her eyes brimming silver, and said the most unusual thing. She'd said: "Christ commands us to love one another, Peter. Greater love hath no man than he lay down his life for a friend."

Peter was still trying to figure that one out. Be that as it may, he wasn't about to start reading this silly book. Joe seemed to settle back into oblivion. Peter sat down and picked up the Bible again, more because it was in the way than because he wanted to hold it. Ruth's heart was in the right place.

He set the book in his lap. His thumb flicked across the pages the way a card dealer flips through a deck of cards. The gilded edges were tattered and worn. He knew it was full of things he didn't want to know. Who were all these fanatics trying to save him from the flames of hell, and what business was it of theirs anyway? He thumbed the leather cover. Ruth had asked him to read the passages she'd marked. Then she'd run off to make herself conspicuous. She couldn't afford to have anyone wondering where she was.

Hope for the lost soul, that's what she had called it. Now he sat with the unopened book in his lap—*a Bible?* His curiosity was getting the best of him. Several places were flagged with yellow note paper. He opened to the first and saw she had written down the verses she wanted him to read. The page was shabby from years of use, dog-eared, soiled and worn, with pencil marks everywhere: this underlined, that referenced, the other noted. His eyes found the place: "The thief comes to steal, and to kill, and to destroy, but I am come that you might have life, and that you might have it more abundantly." The passage didn't end there, but that was enough. He closed the book and laid his head back, staring at the ceiling.

EIGHTEEN

I worry about Dad. He's a good man, the kind of man you want around when you're in trouble, because he's always ready to help, but sometimes I wonder if there isn't such a thing as being too good.

Don't misunderstand. I'm not saying he's perfect. No one is. The trick for me is to ignore his flaws, the way he ignores mine. It's the old cliché: "if you can't say something nice about someone, don't say anything at all," so I guess I shouldn't say anything at all, but the truth is, I was scared. Want another cliché? "The road to hell is paved with good intentions." I wish someone had shared that one with my dad...

THE SCENE PULSATED with swirling red lights. A fire truck stood at the shoulder of the road with piles of spaghetti hose covering the lawn. Volunteer firefighters were busy flipping the canvas pipes to get them straightened out, and scurrying about in yellow rubber jackets and black boots to establish a water connection. The terrified mother stood fixated at the front door. Her hands covered her mouth, hiding an ashen face streaked with tears and muddy soot. She had seen the cat come flying out the window—but where was her son? Where was the man who went to get him? A fireman, only seconds off the truck, hurried over. He stopped and said something to the man standing beside the woman, and then reached out to take the woman's arm.

"You better step back ma'am. The boys will need room when they come through here with the hoses."

She jerked her arm free and blurted out: "MYYYY...MYYY SON'S IN THERE!" Her voice was shrill, shrieking through her fingers.

The firefighter turned toward the house. He was padded from the bottom of his rubberized feet to the top of his helmeted head, and he had a face mask dangling from his chin. He raised his axe and gave a shout to the nearest member of his crew. "ORIN! OVER HERE. WE GOTTA DO A PRIMARY!"

Orin turned, dropped the hose he was dragging, and pulled his self-contained breathing apparatus over his face as he bolted toward the door. Both men reached the threshold at the same time, but Orin stepped aside until the man with the axe entered and was engulfed in flame, then he plunged in behind. The woman watched as both men were swallowed up in smoke, just like the man who had gone before. They didn't bother looking in the kitchen, the wall of fire was too high, nothing could survive that. They headed down the hall, pushing against smoke, waving their rubbery hands in front of their faces to see what they could see. Bill's hulking body was an unexpected obstacle on the floor. The first fireman stumbled into Bill's shoulder and tripped forward. He caught himself but his sudden stop caused his partner to bump into him from behind, which threw his feet off balance so that he had to pirouette to avoid stepping on Bill's head. He struggled to regain equilibrium and stooped into a crouch, fanning away the smoke to get a better look at what he'd found. It was a massive unconscious body. *Could this be the son?* No time to figure it out. He pointed at Bill and motioned toward the door indicating he wanted Orin to shoulder the man while he continued the search in case there was anyone else. They grabbed Bill's arms and hoisted him up so his body could be flopped like a saddlebag over Orin's collarbone. Bill was unwieldy but Orin was big and adept at moving dead weight. He turned and tramped heavy-footed down the hall into the living room. He was almost to the door when a section of ceiling pulled away from the rafters and fell into his path, erupting in flame. He swiveled around stepping the other way into the dining room. He saw the sliding glass door. Its wooden frame, consumed by fire, had come apart. The intense heat had cracked the glass, and the upper half had fallen out. He kicked the remaining piece letting it shatter, and walked through. They were in the back yard. Orin was tempted to put Bill down and go get help, this boy was heavy, but every second was crucial. He forced himself to continue, step after plodding step. As soon as he reached the front of the house where he could see the others, he dropped to his knees and rolled Bill off his back onto the lawn. Bill's lungs began to heave as he choked on the poison gas. "I NEED AN E.M.T. OVER HERE," Orin screamed to no one in particular, but the volunteer fire crew had only themselves just arrived. The Emergency Medical Technicians weren't there yet.

NO ONE saw Angie inside the station wagon. She was strapped in, which restricted her movements, but she was moving. Her arms were writhing and her torso was twisting and her head was windmilling around on her neck. She had just seen her dad do an incredibly stupid, and incredibly brave, thing. She had watched him disappear into that inferno and not come out. Now he was lying dead on the lawn. "Daaaaaaaaa!" Her anxious nerves were doing the grease on the frying pan sizzle. She had to get out and help, but she was trapped in a body that would not cooperate. All the windows and doors of the station wagon were shut, so in the midst of all the other commotion, no one heard her agonizing cry. Her kicking feet were raising carpet dust from the floor, but nobody came.

BILL GAGGED as oxygen reached the air-starved blood in his veins. Inside his brain, he saw red and black. Neuron synapses were pulsating, broken pictures forming into compound thoughts, but he couldn't see. He coughed and choked and broke through the wall of consciousness. His eyes popped open. The burning was so bad he had to squint. Through watery slits he peered out and saw a fireman talking to the childless mother shaking his head. The man beside her put a comforting arm around her shoulder, drawing her in as she burst into uncontrolled sobs, her chest heaving as the tears came. Was the boy dead? Then Bill saw a second woman holding the hand of a little boy. She walked up to the grieving couple and said something. The first woman bent down and took the boy in her arms, still crying, but with a wet smile on her face. "I had go bathroom, Mommy, I had to..." Bill forced himself up on one elbow.

"Hey there bud, just relax. Don't try getting up. There's an E.M.T. on the way. We'll call Life Flight and get you to a hospital."

Bill was already shaking his head. He sat up and wrapped his arms around his knees, still coughing. "No, *chughff chughf,* sorry, I can't. *Chughf, kuff,* I have someone I, *kuff,* I have to take care of. But thanks, *Chughff.* I guess you guys saved my life."

Orin was not to be deterred. He placed a hand on Bill's shoulder. "Don't worry. It'll get taken care of. Lie back down and relax."

Bill rolled his shoulders and rubbed the back of his neck, shucking off the fireman's hand. He could feel a headache pounding in his skull; his neck was stiff. It had been less than a week since he'd survived the accident and his chest still ached. Now he'd inhaled too much smoke. He struggled to his feet. "I'm fine," he said, dusting the side of his wet pant leg, "just fine, *chuff-chghuff-chuff,* don't waste your time on me." He placed a closed fist over his mouth, *chghuff-chuff.* Fire hoses were spewing water, their white streams crisscrossing over the roof of the house. The men who held them were professionals. They'd soon have the blaze under control. The mother and son were reunited. That was all that mattered. He turned and began walking away.

Orin balled his fists and placed his knuckles on his hips. "Okay bud, I can't force you to stay, but I highly recommend you let an E.M.T check you out. Your throat could be swelling; cut off your air before you know it."

Bill's head was pounding, but his throat didn't feel sore. His headache would be one lalapalooza. What he needed was aspirin, not a doctor. That's all a doctor would say anyway—*take two aspirin and call me in the morning.* Bill turned and waved the fireman off without stopping. "Thanks, *chugff,* you guys did a great job, *kuff.* I'll be okay."

He walked back toward his car, passing by a group of onlookers who began to applaud. He turned, surprised, a bit nonplused by the action. He hadn't done anything special. Any one of 'em would have done the same thing. Thank God, the little boy wasn't even inside. All he'd saved was a cat. They should be applauding the firemen that just saved *his* life. They were the real heroes.

"Anybody, *chughff-chughf,* know where I can find Hutchinson House?" he said, acknowledging their presence while turning the spotlight away from himself. He coughed and blocked the spray with the back of his hand. Seemed every time he tried to talk he triggered some kind of tickle in his throat. He tried to clear the phlegm by hawking. Sweat from the fire and the damp evening air had combined to weld his hair to his forehead. He pushed the thick mat aside. His hand fell back moist and sooty.

"You found it, mister. This *is* Hutchinson House." Bill turned to see who was speaking. The woman pointed her finger and continued. "That man over there, the one who ran out of the house with his jacket on fire, the man you helped, that's Mr. Hutchinson. He's my boss. The woman who thought she lost her little boy is his wife, Violet. Only her son, Jason, was with me. I'm sorry, really sorry, I didn't mean to cause so much trouble. He had to relieve himself. I was only trying to help. I had no idea she'd think he went back inside."

"No trouble, *kuff,* at all," Bill said.

The look the woman gave Bill let him know she wasn't buying it. Bill took it in stride. No point in making something out of nothing. "My name's Bill Best. My daughter and I..."

"...we're supposed to stay here tonight," she said. "I know. We were expecting you. I'm glad you're all right. If you'd been hurt, I don't think I could have lived with myself. My name's Mary," the lady extended her hand, "maid, cook and chief bottle washer. Least I was. I guess I'm out of a job until they get things back together."

Bill started to take her fingers and then remembered how charred his were. He held them up, "Ah, I think I should wash up first. Anyway, pleased to make your acquaintance. We spoke on the phone."

The woman nodded and tried to smile, but it was weak. She withdrew her hand. "I understand you were able to save your cat. I'm glad about that."

"My cat...?" Then Bill understood. He looked out across the yard. Now where would that cat be? The darn thing had been frightened out of his wits for the second time. He might never come out of hiding. "Right. T.J. made it. I'm glad about that too. You didn't happen to see which way he went?"

"Sorry. I was with Jason at the time. But don't worry. He can't have gone far."

Bill would have to search for the cat, but he needed to take care of his daughter first. Perhaps he could ask Mary to have the neighbors keep an eye out. Nice lady. He guessed her to be in her early thirties, perhaps younger, it was hard to tell. She was brunette, but highlights from the fire caused individual strands of hair to appear red. She wore blue slacks with a white cotton blouse under a denim vest. Her figure was slim, but not skinny. Bill assumed it was a body that got a fair amount of exercise. Natural as the great outdoors. Bill wiped his face with the back of his hand, leaving a streak of charcoal on his cheek. He tried to comb his hair by plowing it with his fingers. "In that case, you know where my daughter and I can find a place to spend the night?"

The man standing next to Mary spoke up. "I can be of help there," he said. "We own the lodge down the road. We're empty this time of year. It would be a pleasure to have you stay with us. You too, Mary," he said turning to the woman. "I suppose you'll be needing a room as well. No charge to either of you. I, ah, I'd ask the Hutchinsons but they have family in town. I'm sure they'll be taken care of."

"It's generous of you to offer," Bill said, covering his mouth with the back of his hand to cough again, "but I don't mind paying. Just getting a room is enough."

"Think nothing of it. Name's Thompson, Ed Thompson, I'd offer to shake your hand but, well, you know." The man nodded, affirming what Bill had already pointed out, that his hand was black as night. Ed was a tall man, tall and thin, perhaps even taller than Bill, and he was wearing a ten gallon, buff colored Stetson, that made him seem even taller than he already was.

"Bill Best," Bill said. "It's a pleasure to make your acquaintance. I, ah, I have a special situation you need to know about. I have my daughter with me; she has cerebral palsy; she can't talk, but sometimes she groans and it can put people off, and she has difficulty controlling her motor reflexes, so if that's a problem..."

"No problem. Look, here come the Hutchinsons," the man said, nodding in the direction of the approaching couple. The woman was holding a young boy. "I imagine they want to say their thanks. Why don't I get out of the way? I'll go up the road and get everything ready. Mary, you stay and introduce Bill. Let Rick and Vi know everything is taken care of, and then bring Bill along with you so he can find our place. That's if you don't mind giving her a ride," he said, looking at Bill again, and then added, "Mary doesn't own a car."

"It would be a pleasure," Bill said.

BILL COULD hear dinner already being prepared in the kitchen by the time they arrived and were standing in the vestibule of Ed and Emily Thompson's TimberView Lodge. Angie was restless. Her feet kept stomping the floor and her neck went rotating in wild concentric circles until her head finally grew tired and fell lobbing over to the side. Bill understood why; at least he thought he did. The fire had been a traumatic event. He didn't know if she'd seen T.J. come flying through the window or not. It wasn't likely. She couldn't sit still long enough to catch things that happened quickly, not with her head rolling the way it did when she got excited, and it was dark, and she was a good distance away. But then why was she so agitated? Maybe it had something to do with the presence of Mary. Angie had never had another woman sit between her and her father. Bill would have changed the arrangements if he could, but there was no back seat. The rear of the station wagon was full of boxes. Angie had to sit by the door where she could wear the seatbelt. That meant Mary had to sit in the middle, right next to Bill. She didn't appear to be wearing perfume, but something...some kind of mystical musk, maybe just the scent of her hair, or maybe it was her choice of body lotion, but something about her...was appealing. By comparison, he figured he smelled like a pile of charcoal briquettes doused in lighter fluid. He wondered why he felt sheepish about motoring around in a door-creaking, chrome-pitted, hunk-a-junk car. He wasn't a taxi. She hadn't called a limo. Why was he worried about what she thought?

They stood in the entry as Ed introduced them to his wife, Emily. She wiped her hand on her apron and insisted on shaking Bill's hand in spite of the grime, and then wiped her hand on her apron again leaving a dark stain. Mary asked if she could help in the kitchen and walked back with Emily while Bill stood and listened to Ed, who held his beige cowboy hat in his hand while he explained why the house was empty. "Our bookings don't really get going until June," he said. "All we have in between are folks like yourselves traveling in the off-season, and darn few of those. I don't know, it was Em's idea to buy this place and I swear, by the end of each season, I've had enough eighteen hour days to sell the place for a dollar. But then, after we sit idle through a long winter, I always get excited about meeting our first guests. Course, we're not technically open yet, which is why I'm not gonna charge you. You won't get full use of everything. Did you know we have horses? Can't let you ride 'em because they're not here. We have 'em grazing up where the land is better suited for winter pasture. Can't use the pool yet either, be too cold, but you get the picture. TimberView is what some folks call a dude ranch. It's really just a place where city folks can relax and breathe a little fresh air."

Bill could hear dinner being prepared in the kitchen, pots clanking, the rake and rattle of silver, the clink of glasses and clatter of dishware. He knew Ed wanted to talk, but he couldn't imagine being called to eat without first taking a shower. Rude or not, he asked to be shown to his room.

LOOKING BACK from the mirror was a sweaty, soot-speckled face. His hair was wet, matted and flecked with ashes. The veins in his eyes were a web of red; only the deep blue centers were his. The image was even worse than he'd anticipated. Bill popped two aspirins into his mouth and stepped into the already running shower, slurping in water so he could swallow the pills.

He let the hot water roll over every inch of his skin, melting into his pores, massaging tight muscles, stimulating circulation; a shower never felt so good. He spread the bubbly-rich lather with the scouring cloth, scrubbed under his arm and, rub-a-dub-dub, splashed in the tub. The steam rolled up in cascading clouds, fogging the mirror.

"Ohhhhh, When peace like a river, *chuff-chghuff-chuff,* attendeth my way, *chuff, chuff,* when sorrow, *chuff,* like, *kuff.*" Bill ran out of air. He was feeling better, but his lungs weren't ready for song. He lifted his jaw and let hot water splash off his teeth. "Dum, dum dum dum, *chuff.*" He gave up. It would take time for his lungs to heal. He slapped a towel around his waist and stepped out onto the cold tile. The shower had been just what he needed. He wiped an oval in the mirror to comb his hair back in wet coily waves, and ran water over his razor so he could shave. By golly, he'd put on a whole new face. "Hey there little partner, get yourself ready, you're next."

BILL FELT as spit-clean as new polished silver, as he made his way back to the lobby. A whole feast of smells captivated his nose. The scent was heavenly, real food, home cooked on a stove, over a fire, not some prepackaged ground beef dinner warmed in a microwave. He could smell rolls, and some kind of beefy gravy, maybe beef stew, and steamed greens, and...and...dare he even think it...home-baked pie—*my oh my.* He ambled into the dining area, just to let them know he was there, in case they were waiting for him.

"Dinner won't be ready for another few minutes. Sit down in the living room and relax," Mary said. In her hands she carried a glass bowl of fresh garden salad which she set on the table.

Bill rolled Angie into the living room. He stooped to kiss her cheek and used his finger to free the hair that had become caught under her collar. Then he gently lifted her from her wheelchair and sat her on the couch, making sure she was comfortably balanced against its cushioned back. She wiggled and started to tilt, but Bill caught and straightened her. He kept his hand on her collar as he turned to take a paper from the magazine rack and spun around to sit down beside her. It was a thick paper, not from this little town. Bill didn't recognize the banner. He didn't know if it was one of the papers that ran his column or not. He couldn't keep track. He unfurled the paper, shaking out the front page folds. The headlines summarized the usual bad news—the chronicle of a world filled with pain and death. It wasn't worth the aggravation. This was, after all, supposed to be a vacation. He folded the paper and tossed it aside. His mind wandered back to the kitchen. The smell of sizzling beef and gravy and cinnamon and spice and...and...whatever else it was she had cooking in there, was fabulous. He could see Mary in the next room filling glasses with cold milk. He loved cold milk. "Know what partner? I'm so hungry, I could eat a cow." He smoothed Angie's silken hair. She giggled and let her head fall to the side, rocking back and forth. The clock on the wall rang seven bells. "They're putting food on the table now, and don't it smell guuu-uud?" he said, just to confirm that dinner was on the way.

Angie groaned and shot her fist out, her jaw slipping to the side like it had become unhinged. Bill recognized it as impatience. He wanted to tell her about T.J., about how close they were to seeing him, but he knew if he did, her sleep would be restless, and she needed her rest. He would wait until she was in bed and then go see if he could find T.J., and if not, try again in the morning. Perhaps he could get Mrs. Thompson, or maybe Mary, to watch Angie. No point in making her sit in the car if it could be avoided. He wondered if Mary liked kids, and then wondered why he wondered that. Oh for crying out loud. Why was he feeling drawn to this woman? It made him edgy. He needed to stay focused. However absurd, his goal was to reconcile with Laurie. It was best for Angie. They were leaving in the morning, and that was final. Twelve wild horses couldn't hold him back. Besides, he didn't know anything about this Mary, whoever she was, so there was no reason to give her another thought. No, that wasn't quite true. There was a reason. It just wasn't a good one. It was based on his unfulfilled yearnings. It was based on lust of the flesh. Mary seemed like a breath of mountain air. What put him off about city ladies was their highfalutin fashion dress, with all that headwind howling hair and rubbery-slick shiny lips, and those vogue mannequin mannerisms...and attitude—that's what turned him off most, was attitude—and metro girls were attitude girls right from the tips of their painted plastic toenails to their painted plastic hair. But this was his beloved west, and he was Best in the west, and so were the ladies because out here they grew them as natural as wildflowers. Out here, painted-on makeup was for hookers. The clean fresh test of the unblemished west was having skin as clear as mountain water.

He caught himself. Why entertain such thoughts? It was a waste of time. He was on his way to see Laurie, or so he hoped, and yes, she had an attitude, but it was different. She had an attitude of strength, which of course was why they were apart, because her strength and his strength were always pushing against each other. What they needed to do was get together and push from the same side, which they someday would, or so he hoped. Boy wouldn't that be something, if they could just learn to push together, their combined strength might move mountains...his thoughts were interrupted by Mary, who entered the room to announce that dinner was ready. He didn't even know if the woman was married.

Bill rolled Angie's wheelchair up and tied one of Mrs. Thompson's checkered kitchen towels around her neck. The table was set with so much food Bill wondered if they planned to feed a small army. There were peas in a mounded bowl with a huge pat of butter melting on top. Another bowl, wrapped in a red checkered cloth just like the one he had placed around Angie's neck, was filled with hot biscuits, and another bowl held breaded, fried squash. Still another bowl steamed with a humongous pile of mashed potatoes, which Bill just knew had to be Idaho spuds fresh from the neighboring state. Emily entered the room with potholder hands, holding a great silver platter of Salisbury steak covered in a brown spice gravy. The table was set for entertaining, not your everyday, run-of-the-mill, chip-edged plates. No sir, these dishes were ornate with fine gold edges, and the engraved, scrolled flatware was polished silver. They couldn't do this for everyone. The dishes wouldn't last. In the middle of the table, glowing effervescent on silver holders, were two white candles—and it wasn't even Thanksgiving.

Mr. Thompson sat down at the head of the table. His wife, Emily, came back from the kitchen after removing her potholder gloves and apron and sat beside him looking incongruently small. Bill sat at the other end, beset on both sides by beautiful women, his daughter on one side, and Mary on the other.

"We don't usually sit down and eat with our guests," said Ed, planting his elbow on the table, "but then, we weren't planning on having any guests. Well, don't be shy. Help yourselves. Dig in."

Bill hesitated. "Angie and I always say grace at the table, if that's all right with you..." He looked to Ed for a sign of approval.

Ed nodded. "Suit yourselves," he said, laying his fork and knife aside.

They lowered their heads. Sensing this wasn't the custom of the house, Bill kept it short. He thanked the good Lord for keeping little Jason safe, and for bringing the firemen to his own rescue. Then he asked God to help the Hutchinsons during this difficult time, and asked a blessing on the Thompson home and on the food they had prepared, and closed with a quick, "Amen."

Mr. Thompson opened his eyes, picked up the heavy bowl of potatoes, scooped a fistful onto his plate and passed it to his wife. "I don't normally get a feast like this," he said. "It's always extra nice when we have company. I reap the benefit, if you know what I mean."

Bill refrained from comment. Looking out across all the steamy platters of food, he wondered if he'd be able to save room for pie.

Ed took the greens, piled on a mountain of garden vegetables, and passed it to Mary. Bowls were moving in both directions—no phony protocol, no pseudo etiquette, everybody just eat. Bill liked that. Mary handed Bill the bowl and he scooped salad onto his plate and passed it across to Emily, taking the potatoes. Angie wouldn't eat salad, but she loved mashed potatoes.

Ed reached for another bowl. "What you did over there at the Hutchinson's, that took real guts. I admire you, Mr. Best."

"Please, call me Bill," Bill said as he tried to get a spoonful of potatoes into Angie's mouth. She twisted her head, rolling it to the side, causing him to miss. He patiently took the corner of her bib and wiped the glob that had stuck to her cheek where the spoon hit, and then wiped his fingers and tried again, gently, but firmly, holding her head. This time he succeeded. "It's kind of you to say so, and I don't mean to show false humility, but I really don't deserve to take credit for what happened. I just reacted to a situation. In some ways, it was foolhardy. If the firemen hadn't shown up when they did, I wouldn't be sitting here eating this wonderful meal. I've always had a bad habit of acting first and thinking later. It would have been hard on my little girl if things had turned out different."

"That's exactly my point. You could have been killed. Going in there took courage. A coward would have pretended there was nothing he could do, or waited until it was too late. A coward's concern would be to save his own skin. Your concern was for others. What you did was heroic."

Bill nodded as he lifted a good-sized saucy steak off the platter and asked Mary if she could pass the rolls.

Mr. Thompson changed the subject. "Where you headed Mr. Bes...sorry, Bill?"

"Well, I'll tell you sir. My daughter and I are off on an adventure. We're on our way to Washington. We just bought ourselves a boat and intend to spend the summer motoring up and down the coast of Canada, through the gulf islands that border Vancouver, all the way up to Desolation Cove and back down again. I figure it'll take us about four months if we stop to see all the sights along the way. Always been a dream of ours."

"Sounds romantic."

"It does. But then so do most dreams, until they become reality. I suppose it will be more hard work than fun. I have to earn a living. The boat may be paid for, but we still need gas and we still have to eat." Bill took a fork full of the only thing he hadn't yet tried, fried zucchini, and passed the bowl to Mary. He took a bite and let it rest on his tongue and then began to slowly chew. The squash was breaded in a crispy batter and deep fried in a lemon and butter sauce, uuummmm. "Well now, I believe that's the best darn zucchini I ever tasted."

"Mr. Best. Did I hear you say you're on the way up to Washington? Are you going anywhere near Seattle by any chance?"

Bill looked over and found Mary's dark eyes staring at him, eyes black as obsidian, volcanic glass, burning with fire. Man, he did not need this! "Actually, that's where our boat is moored. Why, is that where you're from?"

"No, but I do have a sister who lives there..."

NINETEEN

BILL'S STATION WAGON sat parked on the road's shoulder with beads of moisture accumulating on the hood and windows. A gray cotton fog swirled through the air, making the day seem hazy and unclear.

Up on the lawn, hiding behind a shroud of mist, Bill could see the carnage of last night's fire. The bulky fog billowed around the house in a smoky haze, the charred skeletal remains rising out of the vapor. The entire left side was a black cinder with bits of wall dangling in place. A section of the roof was caved in. There were clumps of charcoal strewn about the lawn, and the grass wore a sooty film. It was sad, really, thinking how what seemed like a nice family would now encounter the frustration of dealing with insurance claims, the hassle of rebuilding, lost income, and the general disruption of their lives. God forbid he should add insult to injury, but Bill couldn't help taking a note of encouragement from it all. The words: "misery loves company," came to mind. He wasn't the only person on earth to experience the trials and tribulations of Job. He felt a pinch of shame for thinking such a thing. He wouldn't wish discomfort on anyone, and particularly not just to make himself feel better.

He gripped the steering wheel until his knuckles turned white. So many questions, and no easy answers. He could justify his actions. On the surface, helping Mary seemed right, but underneath, he wasn't so sure. He'd made the commitment without thinking it through. Now he couldn't back out without feeling embarrassed.

He pulled himself from the car, turned to the back seat and retrieved a stack of fliers which he folded and slipped into his back pocket. He walked toward the house, leaving tracks on the dewy lawn as he cupped his hands to his mouth. "TeeJayyyyyyy. TeeJayyyyyyy. Come-mere boy, let's go," he called, trying to be loud enough to be heard, but not loud enough to disturb the neighbors. "Here kitty, kitty, kitty, come on T.J." He waited, hoping to hear a telltale meow, or see a streak of movement, but there was no response. Bill decided to go inside. The walls of the living room were a charcoal mess. A large section of the ceiling was burned through, and the kitchen was completely destroyed. The house would need substantial repairs, but it wasn't a total loss. Bill kicked a loose board out of his way. What a shame. The Hutchinsons were led to believe the gas shut-off valve had been fixed. They'd given little thought to the odor they still smelled. The repairman said it would take a few hours to clear up. It wasn't until Mr. Hutchinson walked into the kitchen, set his lit cigarette in the ashtray, and went back and get his newspaper, that the gas exploded.

Bill made his way to the back of the house. The carpet squished under his feet. It was laden with water from the fire hoses. Things looked a lot worse today than they had last night when he and Mary explored the damage with a flashlight. *Mary?* Now what was he going to do about her? He wrestled with his uncertainty. He hadn't changed his mind. He still wanted to work things out with Laurie, but Mary kept intruding on his thoughts. It was foolishness. He'd cautioned himself to not become involved, but that was before he began talking to her. Their conversation seemed to flow like water from a spring, until he noticed that the Thompsons had gone to bed, and his lying watch said it was well past midnight. He yawned, using the back of his hand to cover his mouth, and stretched with his elbows angled out. That was the problem. His lack of sleep was clouding his mind. At least Emily had been kind enough to see he had a hot cup of coffee before heading out the door. What's a morning without a wake-up coffee? Especially a morning as muddled as this one. No, the problem wasn't sleep, or the lack of it. The problem was Mary. She was the cause of his confusion. Throughout the ten years of his separation he'd been totally autonomous, unencumbered, and free. Not once, not even one single time, could he recall feeling the recklessly intense, pitter-patter cravings he'd felt last night. Strange that such a significant change could occur so fast. Especially since all they'd done was talk—for five long hours—with only a brief time out to drive back to Hutchinson House to look for T.J., and collect Mary's things, all of which fit into one suitcase. It may have been a silver lining on a black cloud that her clothes had not been ruined. They would smell like smoke until they were washed, but the firemen got the blaze out before they were destroyed. A blessing, however small, was still a blessing.

He was standing in Jason's room. There was no doubt about it. The baseball-print bedspread, the pants and dirty socks still on the floor, the tractor-truck toys, all said so. The window was broken, smashed by the lamp Bill had thrown. He got down on his knees to look under the bed. That's where T.J. had hidden before. He lifted the dust cover and waited for his eyes to adjust. It was dark, but he could see the space under the bed was empty. He stood looking around the room. Other than the window, there was surprisingly little damage. The closet was closed, so T.J. couldn't be in there, not behind the lamp-table either. He turned and went across the hall into the next room. This one was Mary's. He knew, because this was where they'd come to get her things. *Mary—quite contrary.* If they were going to be traveling together, he'd have to keep his guard up—*be friendly, not flirtatious.* He wasn't obligated to take responsibility for someone he didn't know, but now that she was familiar, helping was no longer an option, it was a requirement. He had to be charitable. Ed and Em had done as much for him. He'd needed a place to stay, and they'd offered him a room. Mary needed a ride. He was compelled to reciprocate. Or was he just trying to justify doing something he wanted to do anyway?

Bill put his hands on his hips. He'd checked every room. Where could that cat be? He'd looked under every bed, in every open closet, around pieces of furniture and behind open doors. The only place he didn't look was the kitchen. There was no point in getting dirty. Cats were clean animals. T.J. wouldn't choose to hide in a pile of soot and ashes, not as long as other options were available. And he would have mewed when Bill called his name. All this hassle for a cat. Bill caught himself: T.J. was not just any cat; T.J. was Angie's friend, and that made it worth the trouble. He went outside, kicking loose pieces of blackened wood out of his way as he strolled down the drive. It was too early to go knocking on doors. Last night they had prepared a flier asking the neighbors to call Ed or Emily Thompson if the cat showed up. Bill walked along the curb, stopping at the first mailbox he came to. He opened the lid and slipped a leaflet inside.

He was glad he'd refused Mary's offer to help. It wouldn't take him long to walk up one side of the street and down the other, stuffing fliers into each box. T.J. would turn up sooner or later. This was a small town. A stray cat was bound to be noticed. He hadn't told Angie yet, not about T.J., or about Mary. Angie had fallen asleep right after dinner, and had still been asleep when he'd left in the morning. Emily promised to see she got breakfast, if she woke up. Unless the cat showed, it was probably best to avoid mentioning T.J., but about Mary, that was another matter. He took a breath and felt the raw soreness of his lungs. *Chuff, chuff.* What was he supposed to tell Angie? What possible reason could he give? Mary was all-alone; perhaps that was reason enough. If she were married, her care would fall to her husband. She had been married—had, as in the past—to a park ranger, married for three years and saving toward the purchase of their first home. But it was not to be. With a flood in the forecast, her husband, Tom, had been called upon to rescue a half-dozen campers believed to be trapped in the canyon. It was expected they would be swamped by the descending wall of water. It was decided the search would be made by helicopter. They made several unsuccessful passes, rotoring up and down the canyon, but with the thunderhead building, and darkness upon them, they were called back in. They refused to quit. After the fact, it was theorized the pilot had hovered too close to the canyon wall, catching a blade. They were never certain. Fitting all the pieces of the downed aircraft together would have cost too much. The important thing was, the six campers survived. They were found, waterlogged and weary, after climbing to safety on their own.

The Boydes, that was Mary's married name, were not insured. All the money they'd saved was soaked up by the funeral. Abandoned and alone, Mary lost her sense of purpose. She was left to drift without direction, aimless on an ocean of questions: *Why God, if you're really there...why?* She didn't receive an answer; she concluded no one was listening. It was only the intervention of the Hutchinsons that prevented her from stepping across the great divide to join her husband in the cosmic void of eternity. They saw her distress and offered to take her in. She became their cook and cleaning lady, a position created more out of charity than need. The bed and breakfast didn't pay for itself. Mr. and Mrs. Hutchinson, Rick and Violet, also owned a small café in town, which consumed a great deal of their time. Mary became a live-in maid serving to keep Hutchinson House clean, a sitter to satisfy the day-care needs of their infant son, a call-in waitress whenever needed, as well as a hostess tending to the comfort of the occasional guest. In other words, she moved in and became part of the family. She agreed to work for room and board, though the Hutchinson's also gave her fifty dollars a week to help with personal necessities. They couldn't afford more. It had become a comfortable arrangement. But that was three years ago, and now it appeared to be over.

Bill was at the end of the road. The fog was beginning to lift. There was an open field in front of him with plenty of places to hide. He called T.J.'s name several times and waited and called again. He didn't want to dwell on Mary and her problems. He needed to get his mind on something else. An old Sunday School tune crept into his head.

> *"So let the Son shine in,*
> *Face it with a grin,*
> *Smilers never lose*
> *And frowners never win..."*

That's the spirit. He needed sunshine. *Enough of this dismal dank. Give me sun, Lord!* A smile trickled across his lips. Funny how a beat up old kid's song could repair his adult attitude. A smile could get him through anything. He turned and headed back down the street, popping a flier into the next box he came to, and the next, and the next, and the next, as he moved along.

GEORGE SAT in his office frustrated by the apparent collapse of the corporation. The whole thing was upsetting his constitution. What had gotten into Gabe? Why was he showing such a lack of faith? He hadn't griped when they'd quadrupled his seed capital by taking the company public at a dollar. Nor had he complained when, to excite the market, they'd issued one fluff-filled press release after another, driving trading to up over three dollars. How dare he bail out now, after he'd made his money back in spades. How dare he hurt the corporation that way. Was he, George, responsible for the public's lack of confidence?

He reached for a tissue. It never rained but it poured. On top of Gabe's knee-jerk sell-off, the exchange was now threatening to halt trading. They were demanding an announcement. They wanted stockholders to know why EVC shares were in a tailspin. *Not a good idea. You want decline, wait till you announce the reason for the slump is that the company's biggest shareholder, and now ex-chairman of the board, is dumping his shares.* This was only a small anomaly, a mere hiccup. George had to convince the exchange to let them see it through.

At least Carl Shiffer was still pumped. Perhaps his enthusiasm could be used to convince others to hang on. He was still a believer. He had to be, the whole thing was his idea. His only problem was, he didn't think big enough. Carl had presented the skeletal concept, but it was George who fleshed it out. George had written the prospectus. He had developed convincing spreadsheets that confirmed a surefire and rapid R.O.I. and he had shown, through protracted charts and graphs, exponential long-term profitability. If things weren't happening as fast as planned it didn't mean they wouldn't, it just meant they had to adjust their strategy, make a few corrections and move on. Investors had to be patient; nothing happened overnight.

Two things were clear: George had to convince the exchange to hold off their demand for an announcement, and he had to convince Carl to keep pumping the company's shares. If they bottomed out, someone was bound to scrutinize the books. So far, he had been successful in convincing the auditors that the cash transfers made by people who were now deceased were gifts they chose to confer upon loved ones. If you've already determined the exact date you're going to die, why hold on to what you don't need? Since there was no reason to suspect foul play, no one challenged the assertion, not even Carl. But if the company went belly up, someone might decide to look more closely at where all that money actually went. That was one thing he simply could not allow.

He rolled his eyes around his office, the one tiny piece of property where he was ruler of the realm. He swiveled in his oxblood red leather chair, so luscious, so smooth. The pictures on his walls were originals. His was the only office in the building that had original art, a luxury even Carl didn't know about. Carl thought they were lithographs, like everyone else's. But George wasn't about to stare at prints all day. One of the many perks afforded the lord of finance was the ability to bury subtle cost differences in between the lines.

He glanced at his Rolex. Dr. VanEtter was supposed to be meeting with him at eight sharp to discuss their two newest problems: the questionable identity of Annie Iversen, and the unexplained kidnapping of Joe Bonner. That was the real mystery. An incapacitated old man couldn't just disappear. As for Mrs. Iversen, she'd better be on the up and up. George was watching. He didn't need another problem right now. The market was crashing, Joe was gone, and Ruth was blabbing her mouth off. She had the other residents so upset, they were moping about like a bunch of zombies. They had to get Joe back. The whole thing was posing a massive breach to security.

George reached into his drawer for a bottle of antacids, only eight in the morning and already he felt fire in his chest. He had to relax. *This too shall pass.* No point in getting all worked up. *Relax, relax, relax, relax, relax,* but his stomach bubbled with acid. He needed something to dilute it. He picked up the phone and hit the intercom button, paging his secretary. "Abbie," he said, "could you get me a glass of water?" The page was heard by others in the accounting office, but they feigned not to notice. Servitude came with the job. Abbie moved her cursor to the icon and clicked. A password-protected screen saver jumped onto her monitor. The dolphins began sailing up and over the crests of waves, up and down, up and down, as though pinned to the rods of a carousel. It was a security device Mr. Bergen insisted all his employees use when away from their desks. He wanted to keep passers-by from seeing private corporate data. She pushed her chair away from the desk and went to assist Mr. Bergen.

Dr. Stuart VanEtter walked in as Abbie was pouring. She placed the charcoal-filtered decanter back into the refrigerator.

"Please close the door on your way out," George said. He waited until the door was shut before speaking to the doctor. "You're late. We were supposed to meet at eight."

Stuart looked at his watch. "Sorry. I got stopped on my way over. Florence claims her medication isn't working. Of course it isn't. It's a placebo. There's nothing wrong with her, but there's no telling her that." He sat in the woven tapestry chair, leaning forward with his hands folded between his knees.

George waved him off. "Florence isn't the problem. How'd you make out with the others?"

Dr. VanEtter sank back into the upholstery. He rubbed his palms together. Warm moisture was shining on his smooth skin. "Not so good. I've been asking about Joe and getting nowhere," he said. "No one will say anything. They're scared to death. They're all afraid what happened to Joe might happen to them. Which is, of course, what you wanted, but I don't like it. We shouldn't have to scare people. This whole thing has gotten out of hand."

"That may be so, but I don't have to remind you of what will happen if our secret gets out."

"No, you don't, and that's what bothers me. We wouldn't be having this problem if you hadn't taken advantage..."

"Hold on, Doctor. As I recall, it was you who came to me, suggesting we euthanize patients without their consent. I only devised a way of doing it, so..."

"That was totally different," Stuart interrupted. His face was pinched; his eyes focused on his nose. "They were suffering. And they weren't lucid. They couldn't make the decision for themselves. People shouldn't have to suffer. In the Netherlands, they'd have..."

"This isn't the Netherlands, Doctor. Besides, you told me your reason for terminating these particular patients was that it was costing us money to keep them alive."

The doctor began massaging his nose with a thumb and forefinger as though stung by Mr. Bergen's words. He leaned forward again. "That wasn't the real reason, and you know it. They were suffering. I wanted to end their pain. And what I said applied only to Gus Olson and Blanch Albright. I never wanted to terminate Mr. Hobbs, or Mr. Miller. That was your idea."

"Let's not argue about it, doctor. The point is, if you end the life of a patient without first getting their permission, it's called murder, regardless of the reason. You may think you're altruistic, and I'm just some greedy S.O.B., but in the eyes of the law, we're the same. And we'll both go to jail if we're caught. So let's not waste any more time. What did you find out?"

The doctor tried to relax, settling back into his chair again, his finger still rubbing his nose. "Not a whole lot. At least not about Joe."

George began to drum his fingers on his desk.

"Okay. I got Charlotte to give me the names of the people she remembered who were there when Joe disappeared. I interviewed every one, but they're not saying anything. They're clammed up tight. Like I said, they're afraid."

George leaned back and closed his eyes. His hands were folded behind his head with his elbows winged out. He could see dots of white light on the backside of his eyelids. He snuffed his nose as though trying to clear a passage. It broke his meditative spell. He leaned forward and took a tissue from a solid crystal dispenser. His eyes felt as gooey as egg whites. He dabbed them with a tissue. Maybe he should get Stuart to prescribe something. He pressed his hand against his stomach to ease the pressure. Why were so many negative influences converging on him all at this one particular point in time? "What about their behavior? Notice anything unusual?" he said, wiping his nose.

"This isn't really my area of expertise. I'm a doctor, not a private eye," Stuart said. "I don't see these people often enough to know what

226

to look for. Everyone seems pretty normal to me, except for the brooding, but I don't think anyone's acting suspicious, not even Ruth. I've been watching her close as any, closer in fact. I've even been inside her apartment, with her permission of course, but there was nothing there. She hasn't done anything unusual. If she's hiding Joe, you wouldn't know it by her actions."

Stuart unfolded his hands and placed them on his knees. Then he scratched under his chin, and leaned forward to plant his elbows on the desk, rubbing his palms together. "You know what I think," he said, "I think it has something to do with that Iversen lady. I still think she's a plant. I know old people do crazy things, but I can't help thinking she's hiding more than wrinkles behind all that makeup."

The doctor waited. George raised his eyebrows in a look that implied both curiosity and impatience. Stuart met his glare. "I checked into her background, just like you said. I started by looking in the phone book to find her address, but there is no Annie Iversen, at least not in the local listings. Then I checked her application to see what address she gave us, to see if she came from out of town. I found she'd used a local address, but the odd thing was, it was the address of an industrial park. One of my medical suppliers has an address on that block. I called just to be sure, and they told me there isn't a house or apartment on the entire street. I don't know what to make of it exactly, but it is suspicious."

George leaned back in his chair, the fine Moroccan leather squeaking with the shifting of his weight. He massaged his agitated stomach. The whole thing was utterly absurd. The idea that some bent little old lady was responsible for the disappearance of a man she probably didn't even know, was...ludicrous. Stuart was becoming paranoid—or was he? And could he, George, risk not finding out? "That's good work, doctor. You're more of a private eye than you think. I guess if we want to know, we'll have to search her apartment. It's a little after eight. She should be eating her breakfast about now. Why don't you pop over and see what else you can find?"

"You want *me* to search her place? I'm not..."

"You're the one who thinks she's hiding something. It's up to you to prove it." George took another antacid from the bottle and popped it into his mouth. He crunched down on the chalky pill, hoping the calcium would, just this once, do what it was advertised to do.

TWENTY

STUART'S WHITE LAB COAT rustled as he sauntered back into George's office. He was trying to refrain from smiling as he placed his leather satchel on the desk. He opened it to remove a small computer.

George looked at the gray, high-impact case, a sleek looking notebook, light weight, thin and very expensive. He raised his head and rubbed his palms together. "Okay, I give. What am I supposed to do with it?"

Stuart placed his hands in his pockets and rocked back on his heels until his jaw pointed at the plastic box. "You're looking at the key to Mrs. Iversen's real identity," he said. Then he sat down, tugging on the material of his slacks as he crossed one leg over the other. "I did what you said," he continued. "I went through her place with a fine tooth comb, but I didn't find a thing, not even the makeup I expected to see. I went through every drawer; I went through the closet; I checked the bathroom; I checked the cupboards. I was expecting her to walk in at any second. I had to work fast, but I was thorough. The place was clean. I was about to leave, but something kept bugging me. I knew there had to be something I'd missed. Finally it occurred to me to check under the dresser. I almost ignored the thought. The space was only about an inch high, but I figured she could have been hiding a file of some kind, so I looked, and that's what I found.

"Now the first question is: why would a lady as old as our Mrs. Iversen is supposed to be, need a state-of-the-art business machine like that? That's assuming this little old lady is computer literate in the first place. And why is she hiding it under her dresser? I couldn't help myself. My curiosity got the best of me. I sat down and turned it on, and guess what I discovered? She's a reporter. Her real name is Laurie Best. She works for that Portland newspaper. The one you threatened to sue."

George picked up the small computer, opened the lid, pressed the tiny "on" button and began loading the word program. *Good thing these little units come with batteries.* He didn't bother plugging it in. There it was, under a file labeled "Dutch Treat." George scanned the article. His heart thudded like a basketball on a hardwood floor. How had she uncovered all this? He kept scanning. Line by line, her commentary nailed him to the wall. Oh, she didn't know everything, and she lacked hard evidence so her case was spurious at best, but she knew enough. It was clear she believed the story told by Ruth and Joe. Only she wasn't some crazy old fool to be ignored. It only took two reporters to bring down the Nixon administration—*two people against an entire government!* George couldn't afford to let that happen. He turned to the address book of his own computer, reached for the phone, and began to dial.

"So?"

But George raised a finger, cutting the doctor off. One ring...two rings...the receptionist answered.

"Hello, can I please speak with Laurie Best?"

There was a pause. He put his hand over the mouthpiece. "We need to find out what she's doing here. Bob assured me they'd drop the story. It's his newspaper but..." He was put through to Laurie's voice mail, which only confirmed she wasn't in the office. He waited until the end of the message and pushed "O" to be returned to reception. This time he asked to speak with Laurie's editor.

"Jack Hardy," the voice said.

"Good morning, I understand one of your writers, a Laurie Best, is, ah, doing a story on Emerald Valley. I have information she asked me to look into. I was wondering if you could tell me how I can get in touch with her?"

"Emerald Valley? The retirement home? Got your facts wrong, bud. She wanted to do a piece out there, but we pulled the plug. Hope she didn't waste your time. If you need her, she's down in Salem covering a conference on women's issues. Can't say I know exactly where she's staying, but I can give you her pager. I'm sure she'll be in touch."

"You sure she's in Salem? It's important I track her down."

"Sure I'm sure. Got an e-mail from her yesterday. Said she was going to need a few more days. You wanna try her pager, or not?"

George wrote the number down and hung up the phone. "Interesting. If Laurie Best is here, she's on her own. Her editor told her to back off the story." He paused, biting his lip. "Where is our mysterious Annie Iversen right now?"

"Still in the dining hall, far as I know."

"Good. First things first." George blocked the story and pressed the delete key. "There, she can't publish a story she doesn't have."

"But she'll know we're on to her."

"Not necessarily. Computers do funny things. Files go missing, you know how it is, technical glitches happen." George went to his own computer to retrieve an encrypted file. It looked like programming data, page after page of meaningless symbols. Without an encryption key, which Laurie would not have, it would be impossible to translate the text. It was pure gibberish. He copied several pages and installed them on Laurie's computer under the file that contained her story. "What you're going to do, is leave the computer running. With any luck, she won't try to use it until the battery runs dead. Then she'll assume she accidentally left it on, and because the computer died while the file was still open, the story got corrupted. She'll likely blame the computer before she suspects tampering. I need you to get this computer back into her unit and get out without being seen."

George waited but the doctor didn't move. "I would suggest you hurry doctor. You don't know how long it will take her to eat. You don't want to be caught in the act."

"What about you? You got me taking all the risks. What are you going to do?"

"I'm going to stay right here and figure out what to do about Laurie Best," George answered.

BILL GUIDED the sluggish, oxidized, dull, copper-brown station wagon with its imitation wood side panels, up the U-shaped drive of TimberView Lodge. Mary waved with her fingers as he approached. Her other hand remained on the grip of Angie's wheelchair. He'd been gone just over an hour. They must have figured he'd be returning soon, to be waiting outside. Or maybe Mary decided to take Angie out for a morning stroll. Didn't matter, he was glad to see them. The sun had burned a hole through the fog and the day was beginning to warm. Didn't she look lovely standing there...they...they looked lovely...Angie and Mary, both. He noticed how the light streamed over her shoulder highlighting her hair...*their hair,* both of them, honey and chocolate, beautiful hair. Bill felt his chest burn. It wasn't the pain caused by his recent auto accident, nor was it the fire he had breathed the night before, this was a burning of the soul, the kind of burn that makes a man's chest tremble and his hairs stand on end. It was the slow burn of passion, and it was a burn he did not want to feel right now.

He opened the creaking door and planted his boot on the ground.

"Hi girls. Out enjoying a walk?"

"No, just waiting." Mary brushed her hair back with her hand. "You said you wanted to get on the road as early as possible. We're ready to go. Have any luck?"

Bill shook his head quickly, narrowing his eyes, but it was enough to let Mary know he didn't want to discuss the subject in front of Angie. "I have the suitcases just inside the door," she said. "Give me a minute, and I'll bring them out." She turned and walked toward the house.

Bill knew he should offer to help. He had to go inside to say good-bye to the Thompsons, but he let Mary go alone because he wanted to talk to Angie. He squatted down on his haunches so he could look her in the eye. "I didn't get a chance to tell you," he said, taking her hand, "but Mary is coming with us. She needs a ride to her sister's, and it's right on our way. I hope you don't mind."

Angie twisted in her chair, pulled back, and let out a groan. Bill couldn't tell if she was trying to say "no," she didn't mind, or "yes," she did.

The front door opened. Mary and Emily began strolling down the walk arm in arm, followed by Ed, carrying the two suitcases. He looked the consummate rancher. His denim shirt was faded and his blue jeans were soiled. His cowboy hat was seated squarely on his head. He was dressed for roping horses, an effect spoiled only by the luggage.

Bill walked over to meet them, taking one of the bags from Ed. "Morning Folks," he said. Then he lowered his voice. "I couldn't find the cat. I didn't really expect to, but he'll turn up sooner of later. I appreciate you're offering to let me know when he does. You've got my number, right?"

Ed nodded. They were at the curb now. Bill looked at his watch. "Well, this whole thing has put us way behind schedule. Thanks again for your hospitality. You both have been exceptionally kind." Bill stuck out his hand and shook Ed's. The hand felt callused, stiff as old leather. "You take care of yourselves, you hear? Good folks are hard to come by these days."

"Thanks young fella. You do the same. Send us a postcard when you get on that boat of yours. We'd like to hear from you."

"You bet-cha," Bill said, releasing Ed's hand. He wasn't into emotional partings but something made him grab the tiny little gray-cotton Auntie Em and almost swallow her up in his big arms. "That had to be the best darn meal I've had since I can remember. Thank you so much."

"Oh stop it. You'll spoil her to death with that kinda talk," Ed said.

Mary held out an envelope. "I would appreciate your giving this to Violet. It explains why I've decided to leave. I wanted to call, but I'm not sure where they're staying. Tell her I'll try to reach her when I get to Seattle." Mary leaned over and hugged Emily, bending down to wrap her arms around the shorter woman's neck.

Bill took Angie in his arms, wondering how this was going to work, and how the seating should be arranged, not that there was any choice. Having an adult companion, especially such a pretty one, would be a treat, but also a temptation. He'd have to be careful. "Okay everybody, climb aboard."

Mary crawled across the seat to the middle, and Bill strapped Angie in next to the window. It was cramped, but they only had to put up with it for two days. He walked around behind the vehicle, noticing that the rear end drooped sadly under all the weight. The shocks had had it. He loaded the suitcases and climbed in, closing the door with a screech and a crunch. He fired up the engine, waved a final good-bye to Ed and Em, and slid the transmission into drive. They pulled away with a loud...*BANG!* It was the first time the engine had backfired. What the heck, the old hunk-a-junk was destined for a baptism in the Pacific. All it had to do was get them there. The brown paint was covered in road dust, the faded simulated wood panels creaked, the rust pitted chrome held a bountiful collection of bugs, but the vehicle slowly picked up speed as it moved down the block, backfiring again just to protest being overloaded. Bill could smell the faint odor of car exhaust. "We're off," he said, as they chugged, spit and huffed down the road.

DR. VANETTER slid the computer under the dresser. He looked to make sure it was still on, and that it was positioned just the way he'd found it. Now all he had to do was exit without being seen. He had knocked before entering, making sure no one was home. The corridor had been empty. No one had seen him go inside. But getting out was another matter. He'd been lucky the first time; no one had seen him come or go. Would he be lucky twice?

What a demeaning situation. Here he was, the senior physician of a modern, luxury retirement home, sneaking around like a common crook. This was not the way it was supposed to be. He should have refused the money. He didn't want it, and had said so. Mr. Bergen had agreed that the patients needed to be euthanized. They were mortally sick, and in great pain, and it was costing the company to keep them alive. But there was also the matter of the money that would be left in their personal accounts. The question was: should they leave it alone, or keep it for themselves? He'd only done what he felt was prudent. It didn't make sense to throw perfectly good money away. The people were going to die anyway, and they didn't have the wherewithal to decree where their money should go. What harm was there in keeping it? It had seemed so innocent, and so easy. But it had been the first step down a slippery slope. He felt like he was still sliding, *down, down, downnnnn* into the pit.

It might have been okay, if they had quit while they were ahead, but George had come to him later, suggesting they do it again. This time, of course, Stuart had done the right thing; he'd absolutely refused. The person George named was healthy, or at least someone with a few good years left to live. Stuart stood firm, until George threatened to expose him. It was, after all, the doctor's idea. He was the one who'd performed the procedure. Stuart found himself trapped. He'd acquiesced on the promise that it would be the last. They were, after all, only terminating an elderly person, someone who had already lived a good life. Old man Miller would have died in a few years anyway. He had nothing left to offer, and only the pain of life's final moments ahead. But no matter how many times he tried to rationalize his decision, he knew in his heart he'd slipped a little further down the slope. Then George had come to him again, this time claiming Leonard Hobbs knew what they'd done to Henry and had to be euthanized to keep him quiet. One slippery step after another. Now this female reporter was onto them, and he was cowering inside her apartment, afraid to step outside.

Maybe it was all for the best. With all the pressure building, George wouldn't dare risk doing it again—*ever!* If they could get this reporter to leave without a story, maybe things would settle down. But how were they going to do that? He'd have to think of something, but first things first. He still had to find a way to get out of her apartment without being seen. Then it hit him. The rear door. Funny how it was so easy to overlook the obvious. He pulled the drapes aside, looking out into the yard to see if he could leave without being noticed. He saw what Ruth before him had seen—a walled escape. The privacy fences would hide him on both sides until he reached the park. From there he could step onto the walkway and appear to be taking a casual stroll.

He closed the door and made his way across the lawn, his leather shoes squeaking on the wet grass. The morning wore an apron of clouds, but they were thin. They were sure to burn off by noon.

When he got to the end of the fence he paused, not wanting to be seen entering the park from Annie's yard, no need to raise questions, but suddenly he was surprised by Ruth coming around the opposite side of the fence at precisely the same moment. Only it was not the Ruth he knew, this Ruth was oddly different. She wasn't wearing red. She put her hand to her mouth, *"Ohhhh,"* and turned, scurrying away in the opposite direction. At first Stuart thought he'd blown it. Ruth had seen him coming out of Annie's yard. When Annie complained about her computer being tampered with, he would be fingered. Then he realized how inane that thought was. Ruth was the one in trouble—not him! What was she doing in a backyard right next to the one being rented by Annie Iversen?

So that's how they did it! He decided to take a closer look. He thought he saw movement behind the curtains as he approached, but it was hard to tell. As he reached for the knob, he heard a distinct click. Stuart knew the sound of a deadbolt turning. Someone had just locked the door. Someone was inside that apartment, an apartment that was supposed to be empty.

He tried looking dignified, as he zipped back to George's office with his nylon coat rustling and his heart in fast fibrillation. Hurry did not become a professional. There was moisture on his forehead, and his voice trembled as he tried to explain what he'd found. It appeared Mrs. Iversen, the reporter, was hiding Joe in the apartment next to her own. Apparently Ruth was in on it too. Everything was falling apart. Too many people knew, and there wasn't much they could do about it.

TWENTY-ONE

RUTH PUT A HAND over her heart to still the tremor. Her knuckles were on fire. The arthritis was acting up again. And the rapid-fire staccato in her chest wasn't healthy. *Tap, tap, tap, tap, tap.* She was too old for playing hide and seek; this much excitement was sure to raise her blood-pressure. She closed her eyes and tried to visualize the rate of her heart slowing down. She collected a deep composing breath. The pungent smell of lilac helped soothe her nerves. The perfume came from the flowers budding on the bush behind which she hid, purple lilac, purple thoughts, pastoral tranquillity. *Thou art my rock and my shield, in thee do I put my trust.* She opened her eyes, still alone; she hadn't been followed. Good! She tried to peek through the branches to see what had become of Dr. VanEtter. Once again, her heart began to race, *pitter, tap, tap, tap, tap, tap. There! There he goes, back into the building.* She took another refreshing lilac breath and stepped out from behind the bush, turning around. Her flight had carried her to the end of the condominium, down to the very last apartment. *Isn't it also empty?* She couldn't recall who, if anyone, was living there.

She closed her eyes, took a deep breath, slowly exhaled, and opened her eyes again. With her hand still covering her chest, she moved to the window. She tried to be quick, but her old bones were aching. She put her hands up to the glass. Drapes covered the terrace door, preventing her from seeing inside. She hurried across the lawn, around the corner, and into the parking lot. There was a door at the end of the building. It was supposed to be an emergency exit, but people were always using it to bring things in from their cars. She

237

tried the latch handle and found it unlocked. *So far so good.* She stood in the corridor with lines of doors stretching down both sides toward the lobby. It would be the first one on her right. Her heart continued to hammer, *tap, tap, tap, tap, tap.* She thumped on the door and waited, and waited, and thumped again, using the palm of her hand because her knuckles couldn't stand the beating. No answer, but they could be at breakfast. Only one way to find out. She used her master key to let herself in. She moved quietly through the rooms, cupboards, closets, cabinets, *check, check, check,* everything empty, no sign of habitation. *Good!* She let herself out and flew down the hall to Joe's room.

She slipped the key in the door and popped it open to find Annie and Peter inside. Peter turned on his heel, ready to run. His eyes mirrored fear; his voice stammered: "You...you scared me to death. That doctor was just here...and...and he was trying to get in, and...What are you trying to do, give me a heart attack?"

Ruth scurried over to inspect Joe. "Not now Peter. We don't have time. They're on to us. Annie, I'll explain later. Right now I need you to clean this place up. Peter, you and I have to move Joe down the hall. Annie, make the bed into a couch, arrange the chairs and collect all our personal things. You have to make it look like we haven't been here. Soon as you're done, come down and meet us and I'll explain. Last door on the left, and be quick about it. Let's go."

Peter's hands quivered. He found the wheelchair and bumped it up to the mattress. He slid his arms around Joe's shoulders and hoisted him to a sitting position. "I'll need some help getting him into the chair," he said, his jaw trembling involuntarily. Laurie took one of Joe's arms and Peter the other and together they tried lifting him, but they bumped the armrest and the chair rolled back out of reach. Ruth caught the rolling chair and held it until Laurie and Peter, each taking an arm and leg, were able to lug Joe onto the seat and draw him upright. Peter took the grips from Ruth and turned the chair toward the door. He stopped and went to the counter for Joe's hat, and returned plopping it on the old man's head. "Oh...okay, I...I guess we're ready," he said, but his faltering voice said otherwise.

Ruth opened the door a crack, sweeping the hall with her eye, and then opened it all the way. Turning to Laurie she said, "Hurry, they could be here any minute. Don't forget, last door on your left." Then she, and Peter, and Joe were gone.

Laurie pulled the sheet tight and folded the bed away, nudging the cushions into place. Then she hoisted the chairs into position in front of the sofa. A Bible sat in one of the chairs; she recognized it by its worn black cover and glittery gold edge. Only one book looked like that. Bill had sent her one, though she couldn't fathom why. The mystery of what he found so meaningful, eluded her. It had to be written in code, because on those few occasions she'd tried to read it, it hadn't made sense; it was just a bunch of religious mumbo-jumbo. This most definitely belonged to Ruth. Peter wouldn't waste his time.

She found her makeup in the bathroom. After wiping down the counter, she scooped up the containers of brown paste and putty and dropped them clattering into the chair with the book. She went to the small kitchenette and started to put an empty cup into the cupboard but realized there were no other dishes. The cup must belong to Ruth. She yanked the plastic bag from the waste can, tossed the cup inside and continued filling it with the remains of Peter's dinner of bread, apples and cheese. She wiped down the kitchen sink and paused to look around. Spic and span. She was ready to go, but she had too much to carry. She couldn't juggle the jars, the bag and the Bible, and still stoop, lean on her cane, and pretend to be old. The garbage wasn't pasty or wet. She tossed the Bible into the sack along with a half dozen jars, tubes and bottles of colored cosmetics and creams. She twisted the top and clenched it in one hand. Then she hunched over, pulled her sweater up around her shoulders, and reached for her cane, ready to hobble away in retreat.

Down the hall, behind the last door on the left, a plan was being forged. Laurie entered to find the seventy-something year-old Ruth pacing the floor. They'd been discovered. Dr. VanEtter had no business being in Laurie's backyard. And he'd seen Ruth in her dress-down browns, and subsequently attempted to enter the very room where they'd been hiding Joe. The bad guys were closing in. They had to get Joe out of Emerald Valley, permanently, and they had to do it now. If they waited any longer, it might be too late. But they couldn't just wheel him out into the parking lot in broad daylight. They'd be stopped. They had to create a diversion.

Laurie had an idea.

I did not want to share my dad with Miss Boyde. I did not want to give her a ride. I thought part of our reason for moving west was so we could be closer to Mom. Already, I was wondering how I was going to be able to share my dad with her, but at least they were both in my blood. I had grown up without my mother. I needed to know she loved me. It was like there was a hole inside me that needed to be filled, so I was determined to make it work—one way or another. And we were almost there. Then, right out of the blue, along comes this other woman—a total stranger.

This was not a good idea. The three of us would be uncomfortable, crammed together on the front seat of the car. Miss Boyde would be seated next to my dad, taking my place. She would be doing the talking, I couldn't, and stopping him from talking to me because talking to me would mean he would have to talk over her, and that would be rude. I wasn't one bit happy with the arrangement. And if dad and this woman started getting close, he might forget about Mom, and that would spoil everything.

THE STATION WAGON pulled into a small diner just outside Butte, Montana. The treescape looked like the pop-up foreground of a 3-D greeting card, with a watercolor blue background and white cotton clouds. The knot in Bill's chest made it hard for him to breathe, and the tickle in his throat made him cough more than he liked, but overall he was feeling good. He gave the turn indicator a flip and rolled his creaky vehicle up to a wooden bumper, gravel crunching beneath the tires as road-dust floated by. The station wagon coasted to a stop. Theirs was the only car in the lot, yet the place appeared to be doing a healthy business. The other vehicles were lining the road in convoy formation, a long chain of extension-cab fitted, overhead piped, polished chrome eighteen wheelers, which suited Bill fine. He tended to stay away from anything advertised as family fast-food-'n-fun. He had a philosophy: if you want a good meal, go where the truckers go.

"Whew-eee, pit stop." Bill said, pounding the steering wheel with the palm of his hand. "Girls, I'm shootin' to make Missoula by nightfall. Let's see if we can't use the facilities, get ourselves some lunch, and be back on the road in less than an hour." He opened the door, *screeeeech,* and stepped out onto a crushed rock parking lot. The wagon eased back at the shedding of his weight; the door closed with a metal crunch. Bill stood tall as timber against the bold Montana sky. He stretched to smooth the kinks out of his back, and tucked in the back of his shirt as he paced to the other side of the car. He had to get Angie out before Mary could move. He opened the rear door on Angie's side and tugged at her compressed wheelchair, pulling it out and snapping it open before it hit the ground. He clicked the locks and eased the chair up to where he could lift Angie onto its seat. She nodded sleepily. She had dozed off. For more than an hour her head had rested against the window. There was a flattened white patch on her cheek surrounded by a blush of red.

Mary finished checking her makeup, let go of the rear view mirror, and slid out to stretch her legs. She tightened both fists and raised her arms, wrists up, as she rolled her shoulders forward, closing her eyes against the sun, her lips forming a dimpled smile. Her chocolate brown hair was spun in long kinky locks that hung down on the shoulders of her faded red cotton shirt. The blouse was tucked neatly into her slim waist. Her form-fitting blue denim pants followed the tight curve of her thigh, flattering the trim shape of her legs. She continued to drink in the sun, unaware she was being admired. Bill caught himself staring and looked away. He stooped to fasten Angie into the chair.

"There you go partner, all buckled up. Let's go see what kinda chuck this place has to offer."

They rolled into the diner. Bill could see at a glance that it was a typical truck stop, heavy on calories, coffee and conversation. The floors were undecorated brown linoleum in a fake tile print. Bud, Coors and Miller signs glowed off the dark paneled walls in neon bright colors. There were two stuffed trout and a few trophies on a shelf behind a glass case full of gum, tobacco and candy bars. The case also supported a cash register. Three overhead fans turned to keep the air moving, but it was a futile endeavor. They might have had a non-smoking section, but faint streams of smoke wafted into every nook and cranny. A few heads turned to check out the new arrivals, casual faces lifting from plates of grease-fried potatoes and mugs of steam brewed coffee. There would be little interest coming from those roadie, water-red eyes, and even fewer comments made by those wind-burned, cigarette totin' lips.

One thing Bill liked about truck stops was that truck drivers kept pretty much to themselves. He'd had his fill of family feeding frenzies where it was inevitable some wild-legged imp that should have been on a leash would bolt up to his daughter and pin her with a hard, gawking, *what kind of freak are you?* stare. Not so in truck stops, no sir, these were good old boys, coffee nerved, two-way radio brained, and zoned out on the white line. They were down-to-earth, and for the most part, a darn considerate group. Under normal circumstances, he'd pull into a stop like this and hardly get a second glance. This time, however, Bill, who was sensitive to such things, thought he noticed more than casual interest as he wheeled Angie through the rows of tables. It took a moment, but then he realized their eyes weren't following Angie, they were watching Mary, the way she walked, poised and erect, with an athletic, purposeful stride. They were captivated by all that wild hair, or was it the spell of her dark, riveting eyes? Bill found himself wondering if she was enjoying the attention. Was she flattered enough to flirt back, exchanging their glances? He rebuked himself. It was an inappropriate thought, one worthy of a jealous high-school jock.

The entourage paraded past row after row of full tables, empty tables and tables being bussed, past T-shirted, baseball-capped, denim wearing, smokers, chewers and abstainers, the ever present clatter of dishes, silverware and glasses and the din of low grade conversation and throat clearing coughs. They headed straight to the back to take care of business. Mary volunteered to take Angie into the ladies' room but Bill declined. It wouldn't be the first time Angie suffered the indignity of being changed in the men's room, nor would it be the last, and while he appreciated the offer, there was a certain routine he had perfected that made the job easier for him. Bill wheeled Angie into the tiled facility, thankful Mary hadn't argued. Changing Angie's diaper could be a challenge, especially when she was upset about something, as she appeared to be now. There were certain techniques he'd developed to make the operation go smoothly.

Mary found a booth down by the front window and settled in. She began eyeing the long line of trucks moored at the road's edge.

"Mary?"

Mary? She looked up at the sound of her name, but her expression was blank.

"It's me, Hank Hall, remember? We went to school together. I was fullback on our high school team, the fighting Comanche. I was the one everybody called 'the wall.' It rhymed with my name, remember? Hank 'The Wall' Hall."

"Hank!" Mary said. "Of course I remember. It's been a long time. How have you been?"

"Fine, just fine. I saw you come in. I knew it had to be you; you haven't changed a bit. So how are things? You still living in that little town you moved to, Gardiner, I think it was? As I recall you married that Tom Boyde fella and moved up there."

"Boy, you do have a good memory." She raised her forearm and flicked her wrist at Bill and Angie, emerging from the bathroom at the other end of the building. Bill raised his chin in an almost imperceptible nod, and she relaxed her hand. "Yes, well, not quite. I did, up until last night. Tom died a few years back."

"Sorry, I hadn't heard."

"No reason you would. And no reason to be sorry. Things just happen. Anyway, yes, I was working for a guest home in Gardiner, but we had a fire last night and it burned down, which kinda leaves me without a job or a place to live, so I hitched a ride with this man and his daughter here. They're taking me up to Seattle to stay with my sister."

Bill had reached the table. The two men eyed each other. Bill extended his hand. "Bill Best, pleased to meet you," he said, taking stock of the man's appearance: heavy steel-toed amber boots laced half way up but untied, blue jeans, forest green plaid wool shirt and blue diamond stitched vest, hair a bit long but neat, well-trimmed Grizzly Adams beard, obviously a driver. A burly man, too good-looking to make Bill thrilled he was talking to Mary.

Hank took the hand. "Hank Hall, back at ya," he said. Then he turned to Mary. "I drive through Seattle on my regular route. I run logs between mills in Washington, Oregon, Idaho and Montana. See that rig out there? The one loaded with coastal redwoods? Big honkin' trees those are. I'm taking them out to Three Rivers. Then I have to pick up a load of pine. I should be back in Seattle by Monday or Tuesday. Maybe I could give you a call and we could catch up on old times?" He caught himself, realizing he might be being presumptuous. He looked at Bill, then at Mary, "that is...I mean, if you two aren't..."

"No, no, nothing like that," Mary said, coming to his rescue. "Here, I'll give you my sister's number." She looked around for something to write with. Bill helped her by providing a pen, but part of him regretted doing so. Mary wrote the number on a napkin.

Bill stood back, reminding himself that, in spite of Laurie's absence, he was still a married man. His feelings were totally inappropriate. His goal, if given the opportunity, was to mend fences with his wife.

Hank took the napkin, folded it neatly into his vest pocket and turned to go. "Nice meeting you, Bill. Mary, I'll call you later." He shuffled away, his shoelaces trailing on the floor as his heavy boots thudded down the aisle.

Bill could find a lot of reasons for not liking a guy like that, not the least of which was he'd completely ignored Angie, as though she somehow didn't exist. He rolled Angie's wheelchair up to the end of the table and sat down across from Mary, telling himself how unfair it was to dislike a guy for being friendly with a woman he himself had no interest in.

Angie was in reckless motion. Her arms tweaked, twisted and rolled in and out. Her head whirled and her eyes folded back into her scalp with her jaw jutting side to side sputtering moans and groans. Bill knew she was anxious. She'd been hard to change, and it would be even harder getting her to eat.

"Old friend of yours?" Bill asked. He picked up the menu and flopped it open on the table, glancing up and down at pictures of roast beef covered in brown gravy, ham with pineapple slices, and eggs smothered in chili.

"We went to high school together," Mary said, reaching for her own menu.

They didn't speak for a few minutes. The waitress, a fortyish, graying redhead with her hair roped in a long braid and more freckles than Anne of Green Gables, brought water to the table and set out napkins and silverware. Bill lifted his menu so she could slide his cutlery underneath. Mary held hers in her lap. The waitress poured coffee, explained the lunch specials and promised a few minutes to let them decide.

Bill could hear a thunderous motor warming up outside; he could feel the rumble coming through the floor. He glanced up and found Mary staring out the window, no doubt at her friend Hank, as he checked his load. Bill looked at his menu and fought his emotions. This was not his woman, he told himself. She was free to seek companionship with anyone she chose. In fact, he should encourage her to do so. He was on a mission to reunite Angie with her mother. This woman was attractive, no doubt about it; she'd turned every head in the place, had that poor trucker sucking up like a tick on a hound, but who needed a woman like that? That was one of the problems he'd had with Laurie. She always caught every man's eye. On the one hand it made him proud, but on the other, it made his life uncertain, especially with a lady like Laurie, because with Laurie you never knew quite where you stood. Jealousy was such a destructive thing. No, Bill didn't need another situation. One woman was handful enough, *thank-you-very-much,* but what if he failed to recapture Laurie's heart, or what if he couldn't hold on? Then his hands would be empty. Then what? *A bird in the hand is worth...* For the first time in years he found himself thinking it might be better if he tried to accept the fact that Laurie had emphatically said: "No!"

TWENTY-TWO

LAURIE LOOKED at her watch, straightened the white cuff of her long sleeve polyester blouse and stood. "Well, it's quarter till. I guess we better be getting down there. Peter, you stay here with Joe. Edith will come back, soon as the coast is clear. I'm going outside and enter through the back. Edith, you and Ruth should wait five minutes, then enter from opposite sides of the building so you won't be seen together. They'll probably be watching us a lot closer now. With any luck, this will be the last time we have to take such precautions. I'll be in the community center. The boys said they'd try to make it by two. Everyone know what they're supposed to do?"

Laurie inspected her troops. Ruth, the valiant soldier, had already proved herself. She could be counted on to do her part, particularly since her part required the least activity. Edith had resigned her commission, but she'd stepped forward like an eager volunteer when asked to join in this one last battle to save Joe. Would they be able to count on her? Her role was crucial. Ruth would be too closely watched. And Peter...well, what could she say about Peter? He was weak, but he had a willing heart. Now all three stood nodding their readiness to serve. "Okay, everything is set to go. See you in fifteen minutes."

LAURIE ENTERED the main lobby. *Thunk, pull forward, thunk,* her cane hobbled out front, the glass doors shutting behind. She crossed the heavy Mexican tile onto the carpet, aware that Al Porter was watching her every move. Was he simply curious, or was he told to keep an eye on her? She didn't know. She still wasn't sure

246

about his role in all this. Barbara seemed to think he was an unwitting pawn, but his stare gave her goosebumps. She shuffled across the carpet with her white orthopedic shoes brushing up such a static she could feel it raising the hairs on her neck. Her temples throbbed. *Just keep moving. Long as he doesn't say anything, don't stop.* She was almost out of the room. The community center was just ahead.

"Mrs. Iversen?"

Her pulse froze. It was Mr. Porter. She stopped to acknowledge the man.

He walked patiently over and looked down at her, the teacher rebuking a misbehaving child.

"How are you finding your stay with us? Is everything to your liking?"

Is everything to my liking? There's a loaded question. She blinked a few times, formulating her answer. "I had a few concerns, but they were taken care of. I suppose it is, young man. Yes, I suppose it is." She swallowed hard, washing the evil taste of her lie down her throat. Just then an itch started poking at her eye. She blinked, twisting the skin around her nose. She couldn't touch it for fear of smearing her makeup. She kept both hands firmly gripping her cane.

Al's expression narrowed as if to say, *what are you doing?* but what he said was, "Ah, good then. I hope that means you'll be staying with us. Your week is up tomorrow. Have you scheduled time to sit down with Barbara and go over our program?"

Al appeared to be trying to stall, or had he just chosen this moment to make light conversation? Either way, she had to get into the community center; she had to make sure the door was unlocked. From where she stood she could see all three of the corridors that funneled into the lobby. Off to her right, over Al's left shoulder, she saw Ruth enter the hall. She was in her red chiffon outfit, complete with feathered hat. A few seconds later, Edith turned a corner, entering the corridor off to the left. She was plowing ahead with her back hunched and wrapped in her shawl. She snuggled the soft knit cotton around her neck. Her shoulders sloped forward. She seemed to be having trouble breathing. Laurie could hear her gasping with each step.

The pause in their conversation caused Al to turn and see what had distracted Annie. *Good, he too was taking note.* Both ladies were walking slowly, and their faces were dour. The whole ward had gone sullen, and these two were right in character. Ruth looked like her wings had been clipped, and her throat sagged like a songbird without a song. Laurie hoped they would see she had been detained. They might have to go on without her. Al turned toward Laurie again, still waiting for an answer.

"No...no I haven't, but I'll do that, young man. I'll just have to do that."

OUTSIDE, a blue minivan pulled into the parking lot. The driver took a speed bump a little too fast. His passengers began to bark and yelp in unified protest. "Haaeey! Ta...ta...take it easy."

"Keep those dogs quiet back there. We're on the property now. Don't announce our arrival." The driver, a tall, thin man dressed in a mint-green leisure suit, glanced over his shoulder at his overweight friend who was hopelessly snarled in a tangle of leashes. "Just let 'em go. I'll help you get them straightened out when we stop."

ANNIE excused herself, promising Mr. Porter she wouldn't fail to set an appointment with Mrs. Marks. She tried to hurry without looking out of place, *thunk, swish, thunk, swish, thunk, swish, thunk.* The bending over continued to crimp her back. She poked a finger at the place on her face where it itched hoping it wouldn't leave a mark. As she turned the corner, she took a peek over her shoulder and saw Mr. Porter enter the accounting office. *Perfect, let Mr. Bergen know we're all in here together.*

The community center was death-camp quiet. Ruth and Edith sat opposite each other, separated by distance and the wall of people and furniture in between. Laurie glanced at the curtained glass on the far side of the room. She had never been out that way, but she'd been told the door led to a summer patio. She caught Ruth's eye. The woman nodded, lifting her fingers with a half twist like she was turning a key, letting Laurie know the door had already been unlocked.

Other folks were cloistered in chairs arranged for conversation, but no one was talking. The television droned on, but no one was watching. The daytime talk show host's mouth was flapping but he couldn't be heard because someone had turned down the volume. There were at least a dozen people in the room, assembled by habit, but grim in thought. Laurie saw Karla, still brightly dressed, but even this island flower seemed uncharacteristically dormant.

The colonel stood off by himself. He didn't seem very soldierly. His shoulders drooped around his narrow, military style tie. Where was his fighting spirit? *Never, never, never, give up!* Laurie had the sudden urge to ask him to dance, swing daddy—*the boogie-woogie bugle boy of Company B.* This place needed cheering up, and it needed it bad. Someone needed to show these folks that every single moment of life, even when short, was worth living, and living meant more than just breathing. It meant activity, it meant movement, it meant...life! Well, that somebody was her, and yes, it meant she was borrowing yet another page from Bill. His opinion was well known. He'd written several columns about the benefits of animal therapy, never mentioning their daughter by name, but making it painfully clear that Angie was the one he was writing about. *Thank-you, Bill, for that.* Laurie heard the barking outside growing louder. *Okay, we'll test your theory. Let the show begin.*

The door swung open and suddenly there was one, two, three dogs and a man holding them on a triad of leashes, and then four, five six, and another man. Cash and Louis were doing their best to keep the dogs at bay, but the excited animals were going crazy. Ruth and Edith jumped up to help. They hurried from their chairs, each taking a leash, but the leather straps were becoming so entangled, they had to let go. A cocker spaniel broke loose and ran to the nearest couch, sniffing the legs of each person, one after the other, up and down the row. His tail swept the carpet as he sat on his haunches and placed his hairy paws on the cushions, panting and licking.

The two men weren't able to contain the others. They found themselves being dragged across the floor. Ruth and Edith tried to unhitch the dogs one at a time. A poodle raced across the carpet, jumped into an easy chair, vaulted over the chair's back and raced out the door, heading toward the lobby. The other animals were piling over each other, tangling their tethers. The beagle broke free of the pack, dragging its leash behind. One by one the dogs were released, a terrier, a Scottie, a sheltie, and sprang forward, finding legs to sniff and laps upon which to climb.

Cash and Louis disengaged themselves. Cash tapped Louis on the shoulder and caught the eye of Edith. The three gathered the empty leashes and backed out the patio door unnoticed, closing it behind them.

THE COLONEL had been reminiscing about the war. In all the quiet, he found himself revisiting the march of death—the forced march of silence that took place two months after he'd arrived at Buchenwald. The soldiers had rounded up everyone they could and, after making them stand for hours in the freezing cold, made them exit the camp, walking at gunpoint in ranks of five. By the thousands, the sick, the lame and the malnourished filed out onto a road heading north. Patton's Third Army was advancing through the middle of Germany. The Soviets were approaching from the east. The inmates could hear the cannonade, the constant exchange of gunfire, mortar and grenade as the liberating armies approached. Allied planes could be seen flying overhead, on route to bomb Berlin. They expected to be set free any day.

Then orders came to evacuate the camp. With the war almost over, the Nazis had to destroy the evidence of their crimes, or face execution themselves. If there had been time, they would have killed everyone, but Buchenwald wasn't facilitated for mass murder so they marched thousands upon thousands out of the camp, away from the advancing armies. Out into the frozen streets they marched. Anyone who couldn't keep up was shot on the spot. Jack watched as hundreds were cut down, simply because they were too weak to move fast enough. It appeared the death march was designed to do what the ovens could not—kill them all, kill a few here, kill a few there, until all the witnesses were dead.

ONE OF THE DOGS, the beagle with the leash still attached, wagged his way over to the colonel, waking him from his thoughts.

Jack's eyes seemed to take on light, and a smile played across his lips. Jack took the beagle up and held him in his arms. The dog slobbered on his face. "Hey there fella, hey, hey, good dog, yeah, you look like our old company mascot. Ever been in a war?"

The terrier raced over to a woman that was knitting, grabbed her ball of yarn off the floor and ran away. The string unraveled from her lap. The dog crawled underneath a chair and positioned the yarn beside his nose, challenging anyone to try and take it.

The three ladies on the couch grabbed the spaniel and pulled him into their laps. He raced up and down the couch, sniffing each of his captors, getting his floppy ears scratched by one and his wagging tail by another. "Oh, you are so adorable. Aw, give mamma a kiss. You're so cute, kiss, kiss, kiss." The ecstatic dog turned round and around to lick his new fingernail-scratching friends, all the while dancing on the lap of the lady in the middle. Finally he laid down, his tongue hanging out, eyes closed as he embraced the three pairs of fondling hands.

The colonel sat down in a chair with the beagle. "Yep, fella, right by squads by right, hep, right by squads by right, hep. You remember, don't cha boy?"

Laurie watched as Karla picked up the sheltie. The dog assaulted Karla's face with its tongue, which was the very reason Laurie herself did not try to pick up a dog. She marveled at the difference a few dogs had brought. The shadow of death was lifted, and in its wake, mirth had settled on the room. Which was exactly what she'd hoped for. Bill's animal therapy worked.

The Scottie was sniffing the leg of a gentleman Laurie recognized as one of the card players. He was a boisterous man who seemed particularly skilled at goading his opponents into playing foolish hands. The man tried to shake the dog off, but the Scottie was persistent. The man finally gave in and reached down to pat the dog's head. "Oh, cut it out, stop that, stop it." He picked the dog up and tried to hold its muzzle to keep it from licking his face but after a few seconds gave up. "Ya like me do ya? You like me boy? Okay, all right, I guess I like you too."

Karla took the sheltie over to a man seated in a chair in front of the silent TV. The man was a curmudgeon known to the locals as Big Elmer. Laurie couldn't recall having ever heard him speak. Day after day he sat with his long arms extended on the armrests of his chair, his eyes glued to the set, his face void of expression. His lower lip hung out past the upper. The sandbags under his eyes were heavy and emphasized the deep lines that flowed downward to divide his cheeks. He was one of the few people in the room that did not try to commandeer a pet. Now he ignored the one Karla placed in his lap. The sheltie was a gentle, intelligent dog. The dog tried to lick the man's face, but he didn't respond. Karla put a hand on the dog's back and forced the animal to lie down. She massaged the Sheltie's head until it relaxed. The dog laid its muzzle on the man's arm. Karla took Elmer's other hand and used it to stroke the dog's head. She did this four or five times and then let go. The petting continued as though Elmer's motor, once wound, was set in motion. The man, without acknowledging there was even an animal in his lap, kept kneading the dog's fur, his hand moving from the dog's ears across its back, up to its tail and back to the head in circular motion, repeated over and over and over again. His eyes were still glued to the television, watching a program he couldn't possibly hear because the volume was so low.

The woman whose ball of yarn had been seized, finally caught up to the thief. She began rolling the slackened blue string around the ball, which brought the terrier crawling out from beneath the chair. He began bouncing around and barking, laying his nose flat on the ground with his front legs outstretched and his tail high in the air. *Yip, yip, yip, yip, yip.* "Hush, be quiet," said the woman, still coiling her ball. The dog tried to snatch the string in his teeth but the woman saw it coming and jerked it out of reach. The dog jumped and jumped and jumped until the woman sat down and then he jumped into her lap and tried to steal the ball again. "Now you quit that. Come here. Lie down and be quiet," but the frisky dog said no. In exasperation, she finally stuffed the ball and her knitting down into the cushions. The dog tried to retrieve them by needling his nose around the woman's waist.

The man with the Scottie sat down at the empty card table. He held the dog in his lap and began shuffling cards. "Ever play casino?

I bet I could show you a trick or two. Hey, anyone want to play? I got a dog here says he can beat all of us. I'll bet this animal knows when to draw." Two other men and a woman, of those who had not been able to seize a pet for themselves, took up the challenge and joined him, taking seats around the table.

"Let me see that mutt. You probably got him trained to help you cheat," one of the men said.

"What for? He don't need help. He cheats good enough on his own." They all laughed.

It was good to hear laughter again. Laurie, standing by the old phonograph, reached in to put on some music. The tune didn't matter. They were all unknowns to her. She grabbed a record, pulled it from its jacket and plopped it on the turntable. The sound hissed, scratched, and popped from the speakers. The only thing recognizable was the smooth mood of swing time.

Now the once silent room was full of noise and music and activity. A card game was going full tilt with a fifth taker, the Scottie, sitting in. The dealer raised his hand in the air and slapped down three cards, "Come on, play that queen!" The three ladies seated on the couch were fawning over the spaniel, ogling and goo-goo talking. "You're the cute one, aren't-cha, yes you are." The terrier was snapping as the lady held out the roll of yarn, letting him have it one moment and taking it away the next. "Want it? Can't have it. Here it is. Missed again." The colonel, with leash in hand, was up teaching his beagle to walk in formation, "go-to-yo lep, yo rite, yo lep, hep," and the sheltie was almost asleep in Big Elmer's lap. Karla stood in the middle of the room with her hands on her hips, bright as a parrot, saying: "Not bad. Not bad at all. It would appear my mamma was right. There is life after death."

The poodle finally finished his exploration of the lobby and came skimming around the corner with legs splayed out, barely missing the door. The dog recovered and sniffed two or three people, its tail wagging as it went from leg to leg to leg. Al Porter was in hot pursuit. He leapt toward the dog but the poodle whirled about and skipped out of the way, leaving Al crashing to his knees, empty handed. *"Oouuffff!"* He picked himself up, dusted his pants and limped away with a hand on his thigh. "Will somebody please tell me how these dogs got in here. What's going on?"

Dr. VanEtter and George Bergen followed Al into the pandemonium. They stood in the entry, blocking the door, watching Al's interrogation. "Where'd all these animals come from? We don't allow pets in Emerald Valley." He stormed over to take possession of the terrier, but the dog sensed his hostility and snapped at his hand. Al pulled his fingers back to avoid getting nipped. Big Elmer was on his left, still staring at the tube. Al reached for the sheltie but the old man, who in Laurie's presence had never so much as blinked, instinctively grabbed Al's wrist. Elmer stood, cradling the sheltie in one arm and gripping Al with the other. Laurie had never seen the man standing before. No wonder they called him Big Elmer; he was huge. With his bottom lip sticking out, deep lines etched like scars across his face, his pale gray skin and those droopy bag-dead eyes, he looked downright menacing. He let go of Al and hugged the dog, clearly challenging Al to try to take it away.

Al backed off. "I want to know what's going on. Who let these animals in here?"

George looked around the room. This had to be the doings of Ruth and that Best lady. He gave the two women a brassy stare, his eyes shifting from one to the other. These two were getting on his nerves. They had Joe somewhere, that much he knew. He'd investigated Stuart's discovery of the secret apartment within minutes of being told about it, but he'd been too late. They'd already gone. Still, the doctor had been right. The apartment may have been vacant, but it was evident they'd been there. A faint smell of body odor still hung in the air. And an empty apartment would have been vacuumed. The carpet in that room had its pile crushed. There were dozens of footprints. The wheelchair even left tracks rolling out the door but the low pile commercial weave carpet in the hallway gave no indication as to whether it had turned right or left. Didn't matter, they couldn't have gone far. He had just apprised Al of the situation. "We have to locate Mr. Bonner," he'd said, "for his own good, you understand. We can't leave a sick man unaccounted for. Too much liability." The door-to-door search was about to commence when all this commotion broke loose in the community center. Where had these dogs come from? Wheatly and Best were somehow responsible, of that he was sure, but Al had just reported seeing both ladies in the lobby, and they didn't have any dogs with them then. Who let the dogs in?

Now there were two priorities: the search for Joe, and getting rid of these animals, but the animals had to come first. If they let the guests carry them off to their rooms, they might never get them back. He pointed to the pack of hounds. "Al, round up these dogs and get them out of here," he said. "And find out how they got in."

Laurie wasn't worried. The tenants wouldn't say anything, and even if they did, by the time the dogs were harnessed and under control, Cash and Louis would be gone.

THE BLUE minivan pulled up to the west wing, and the three old friends piled out. Cash hurried toward the door, taking long, lanky strides. Edith tried to keep pace, her rounded shoulders leaning forward. Louis waddled up behind.

Edith paused. She pulled her shawl up and snuggled in to ward off the chill. "They're right in here, just through the door."

Cash leaned in and grabbed the handle, pressing down with his thumb on the latch. *Click.* The door opened.

Edith went inside, moved forward a few paces, and stopped at the first door, giving three loud distinct raps as some kind of prearranged signal. The door came swinging open and Peter ushered the trio in.

"You were gone so long. You had me worried," he said to Edith.

Louis looked around the room. "Wa...wa...where's he at? Ja...Ja...Joe, I mean."

"He's here. I've got him ready. You'd better go." Peter ducked around the corner and rolled Joe out into the foyer.

Cash blinked back his repugnance. Louis found himself becoming nauseated and put his puffy hand to his mouth. They'd been told what to expect, Joe had been silenced, but hearing and seeing were two different things. Joe sat listing to the side. His skin was a faint mustard-yellow, his eyes were open and void, and a spill of saliva washed over his lower lip, spiraling down in a smooth clear stream all the way to his collar. It smelled like he'd wet his pants.

"Oh man..." Cash said.

"You two better go. We don't have time to waste." Peter took hold of the wheelchair and rolled it to the door.

"Can you handle getting him into the van by yourselves?"

"No problem Edith, it's empty, we'll slide him in on his back. The floor's carpeted and we have a pillow for his head. Louis will stay with him until we get to the hospital."

Edith nodded and brought a hand up to tighten her shawl. "I have to be getting back now. If I'm gone too long, it'll look suspicious." She placed her hand over her heart. "Peter, you have to get over to my place. Remember, you're my nephew. You can use your real name, in case they ask for I.D. You're supposed to be my sister's boy so having a different last name won't matter. Just wait for me there."

Louis opened the door. Cash took hold of the grips and wheeled Joe outside.

A chilly breeze swept across the parking lot. Edith shivered in her shawl. A wall of gray clouds was blocking the sun. "It's cold out here. I have to get back inside or I'll freeze to death. You two better go."

Peter and Edith watched as Cash and Louis rolled Joe up to the van and eased him through the side door. Louis lifted his short stubby leg and crawled in on his knees. He grabbed the pillow and placed it under Joe's head as Cash slid the door shut. Peter turned to head off toward Edith's apartment, but Edith lingered another few seconds. Gripping her shawl with one hand, she raised the other to her shoulder. Her fingers curled in toward her neck as she tried to wave good-bye.

Cash fired up the engine, kicked the van into reverse and rolled back, arcing left, then turned the wheels to the right. He eased the van into drive, and pulled away.

TWENTY-THREE

BILL FOUND HIMSELF with a car full of awake passengers. Angie and Mary had risen from a deep sleep induced by vibrating tires and draining road hum. Eyes were blinking and mouths yawning and hands stretching, all wondering how far they had traveled and where they were on the map. Bill outlined their journey. They had made Missoula ahead of schedule and, since he was feeling good and everyone was asleep, he'd just kept going. It was only five o'clock, well, actually it was six, he explained, but they'd lost an hour when they crossed the time-line into Idaho. They needed to set their watches back. They were on west coast time now, hallelujah, back to the land of the western setting sun, an hour earlier than it had been in Montana, and yes, you heard right, this was Idaho. And not just the border either, they were coming into Coeur d'Alene, and darn if it wasn't pretty.

For a while it looked like they might push all the way into Washington, but the road-weary look of Mary and his daughter made Bill decide against it. Mary's hair was frazzled and Angie's heavily lidded eyes, though only just awake, were already beginning to droop. What they needed was to get out of the car, get some exercise, and enjoy the scenery. He'd already gone half again further than he thought he would. Making Seattle by tomorrow evening would be easy. Coeur d'Alene was the perfect stop, downright romantic, though he was careful not to describe it that way for fear of being misunderstood.

They wound their way down through the tree-lined streets. It was paradise, small and remote, a casual town on the banks of its own multi-fingered lake. Bill could hear the siren's singing as he steered his vessel toward the rocky shore. It was a good sized basin too. Bill judged the distance across the water to be at least equal to that of Yellowstone Lake, only deeper blue, if that were possible.

He found lodging in a unit of small cabins and rented one with two queen-size beds and a balcony overlooking the water. As he brought in their suitcases, he wrestled with his conscience. He'd worked hard at teaching Angie the difference between right and wrong. Spending the night in a room with a woman who was not his wife was opening the door to temptation, and that couldn't be construed as right. What was his daughter to think? He would have changed the arrangements if he could, but it seemed accommodations were in short supply. The spring sportsman's show was in town. Boaters and fishermen, excited about the upcoming season, were everywhere. They'd already passed two motels with glowing neon signs reading: "No Vacancy." And this place only had one available suite. Chances were they wouldn't find anything else. As long as Mary had her own bed, and as long as everyone dressed behind closed doors, what was the harm? It was only for one night. Still, he couldn't shake his apprehension. If it was the right thing to do, he shouldn't have to justify doing it. He threw the suitcases on the bed. What was he supposed to do, sleep in the car?

He went to the window, tugging the cord to open the clattering Venetian blinds and caught a glorious view of the late afternoon sun sitting off to the right, twenty degrees above the water's horizon, ready to explode into a wonderful western sunset. The temperature was mild, especially for this time of year. He decided to bundle Angie up so she could sit out on the balcony and enjoy the clean crisp air, the way she used to back in Detroit.

He felt an obligation to entertain Mary, but he also had work to do. He hadn't checked his e-mail in two days, a real no-no for a journalist. Bill already had his computer out when Mary entered the room. He apologized and suggested she sit down and relax, watch TV, or read something, while he got caught up. With luck, it wouldn't take him more than an hour and by then they would be ready for dinner. He recommended she use the time to peruse a restaurant guide. They needed to find a good place to eat.

Mary disappeared into the bathroom with her suitcase and returned wearing a skirt and blouse looking fresh and beautiful again. Bill was determined not to become distracted by the faint scent of her perfume or the striking shine of her hair. He plunged into his computer, dialing up his server to retrieve his mail. *Well, what do you know, something from Laurie.* He brought it to the screen, disheartened once again to find the message lacked even a cordial "hello." But what did he expect, radical change in a woman that hadn't changed in the fifteen years he'd known her?

Mary strolled over to the window and looked out. "Beautiful evening. Your daughter looks like she's enjoying it. Maybe we should join her."

"In a minute," Bill responded. "I have something I have to read first."

Mary sat on the bed, her long fingers smoothing the folds of her skirt. She had a mother's touch, patient and tender, the kind needed for raising children. She was good with Angie. The three of them were good together. But what was he thinking? He was married to Laurie, for better or for worse. In that finite moment, caught between lust and commitment, he wondered just how much worse it could get.

He continued scanning the document. It was a draft of the story Laurie proposed they jointly author. His eyes were speed reading the text and logging highlights. He came to the end, squinting and pursing his lips. Was that all she had? He certainly hoped not. She was a reporter. Reporters report news. They don't create news through innuendo. Bill was disappointed. This wasn't the caliber he expected of Laurie. There was a note tagged to the end soliciting his comments, demanding brutal honesty, but he knew Laurie well enough to know she was seeking his praise, not his criticism. What was he supposed to say?

Dad parked my wheelchair on the balcony and went back inside. I was left all alone, while she, that Mary person, was allowed to be in there with him. I didn't want to think about it, negative thoughts make my body go haywire, so instead, I let my mind wander out across the lake. It

*was beautiful, a dark blue encompassed by a river of rolling hills that
stood out smoky and gray-green.*

*With so much beauty surrounding me, I couldn't stay mad. I think
that's why Dad put me out there. He knew once I got my eyes off myself,
and onto the beauty of God's creation, I'd forget whatever was troubling
me. My heart began to hum one of my favorite songs, How Great Thou
Art: "...ta da da da, from lofty mountain grandeur, and hear the brook
and feel the gentle breeze. Then sings my soul..." That did the trick. A
soul can't pout when it's singing.*

THE ROOM was stiflingly hot and cluttered. The thermostat
read eighty degrees, but the annoyance was overshadowed by a roll of
good-natured laughter. At times the laughter got so loud, they had to
work at choking it down. But they were having fun, and they
deserved it. They'd outfoxed the enemy, and it was cause for
celebration. They could ignore the mess. When the five co-
conspirators were separated, Edith was the only one not moved to a
new apartment. She had her mess to thank. There was simply too
much to haul away.

Edith was a collector, and she collected everything. The room
overflowed with an assortment of bottles, and plates, and vases. There
were so many, she couldn't keep them on the shelves, so the collection
of odd shaped receptacles spilled over onto tables and chairs and
popped up like sprouting flowers in various corners around the room.
She also fancied knitted coasters of every conceivable shape, color and
size, umbrellas, clocks, books, rubber dolls and glass figurines. But
mostly she collected magazines, tons and tons of magazines. Sun-
yellowed copies of *Life, Look* and *Post,* publications that were no
longer in print, were piled in so many places it was hard to find a clear
path between rooms. You had to wonder if she ever threw a magazine
away. And recent publications, like *People, Better Homes and Gardens,
National Geographic* and *Modern Health,* were scattered everywhere.
Edith was one of those people who never failed to enter the Publisher's
Clearinghouse Sweepstakes, at which time she always ordered a few
more magazines to improve her chances of winning. They had to give
better odds to those who purchased, she was sure of it, and she never

canceled a subscription. She couldn't bear to let them think she'd stopped reading their wonderful articles. What else did she have to spend her money on, anyway? The stacks of magazines were so many and stacked so high they actually served to deaden sound, which helped muffle the noise of the party going on inside. They had been trying to contain their laughter but they were so high on success, the effort was in vain.

"You...you, tee, hee, hee, should have seen the look on his face," Ruth tittered as her white-gloved hand smoothed her dress. "Elmer stood there defying Mr. Porter to take his puppy. I was trying so hard not to laugh, I almost swallowed my tongue."

"You should have seen them searching my room," Laurie added. "They were so disappointed. Mr. Porter even looked under the bed, as if I could squeeze Joe under there. It was hilarious." A bolt of lightning rocked the room. "Uh oh, looks like we're in for a storm."

Releasing the pent up nerves they all felt, the laughter had become contagious but the clap of white light sobered the group. They had noticed the sky becoming gray, but now it appeared night had fallen. "I would like to have seen it, but someone had to stay with Joe," Peter said, not taking his eyes from the window. "At least we got him out."

"We couldn't have done it without you," said Edith.

"We sure couldn't have," Ruth added. "We owe you a big hug."

"Ohh Pleeease. No hugs and kisses. You guys are getting sappy on me," Laurie's stomach fluttered; all the giggling had filled her tummy with air. She felt like she needed to burp. She was still dressed as Annie Iversen, and would be for at least one more day. She tugged at her ruffled cuff to find her watch. "What time did the boys say they'd call?"

Edith searched the room for one of her many clocks. They didn't all work. Some needed to be wound, others required batteries, and several of the electric clocks weren't plugged in, but she knew which ones kept time and which ones didn't. "It's six," she said, spotting one hanging on the wall in the kitchen. "They should have already called. It's time for our dinner."

The phone sat on a table in the center of the room, surrounded by stacks of magazines. Four pairs of eyes shifted to the pink device, willing it to ring, but it remained silent. *Rummmble-Brummmble-Boom!* came the thunder. It was so loud it rattled the window. Rain began pelting the glass.

"Mercy, what a time for a storm," Ruth said. Her cotton-gloved hands adjusted her hat. "Glad we got Joe out before it hit."

"So, what do we do now?" Peter asked.

They looked to Laurie for an answer, but she didn't know. Her investigation had reached an impasse. Joe was safe, but in his muddled state he made a lousy witness, and Ruth alone might not be convincing. "I hate to say it," she said, "but I think we've gone about as far as we can, at least for now. We still can't prove what's going on, and if I go out and make unsubstantiated accusations, I could be sued for libel. I don't know what kind of power these guys have, but they were able to get the story suppressed once, and I have no doubt they'll try again. Unless we come up with some hard evidence, I think we have to consider what we've achieved and be satisfied with that. At least for the moment."

"What?" Ruth's smile fell away. "We can't give up now. Henry, Leonard and Ben are dead, and maybe even a few others, and what they did to Joe was as bad as killing him. He'll never be the same. We can't just let them get away with it."

"I'm not saying that. What I'm saying is, we've run out of time. I was only given a week, and it's up tomorrow. They want me to make a decision. Mr. Porter as much as said so, and if I don't want to buy one of these units, which I don't, I'm out of here. All I can do is become Laurie Best again, go back to my office and analyze the information we took from George's computer. Maybe I can track down where all of Henry and Leonard's money went. It's all I have to go on. I don't want them getting away with it any more than you, but we have to have proof; otherwise, we'll just be guilty of making libelous accusations. That's the way it is. Anyway, we still have twenty-four hours. Maybe something will turn up. But if it doesn't, I recommend the two of you do what Cash and Louis have done. Find somewhere else to stay until this whole thing blows over."

Ruth's mouth was pinched. Her eyes fell from Laurie, focusing for a moment on her hands, then she shot a glance at Edith. "That's a good idea. You should do that. There's no point in your taking chances."

"And what about you?"

Ruth didn't hesitate. "I can't," she said, "it wouldn't be right. I have to be here in case they try it again. I have to put a stop to it." Then she softened her tone and smiled. "Don't worry. Jesus will send his angels to protect me."

Laurie knotted her lips. This woman was facing a loaded gun and didn't have the sense to duck. "That's all well and good Ruth, but I..."

The phone rang, jolting the room to silence.

Edith pulled a skinny arm out from beneath her shawl and reached over an off-kilter stack of magazines to answer. "Hello. Well, it's about time. You could have called sooner. We're still...what? Uh huh. You sure? Okay, I'll let them know." She stretched over the heap of paper and dropped the handset onto its cradle. Her arm dove under her shawl as she slumped back into the chair. Everyone continued staring. Her face puckered.

"Well?"

"They don't know anything. They got him admitted. Said he's in good hands, but they're not allowed to see him. They're just waiting."

"Well, I guess no news is good news," Laurie acknowledged. She thought about getting Ruth to reconsider, but decided to let it go. She slapped her hand on the arm of her chair. "It's time for dinner. I'm going back to my room. I need to check my e-mail and freshen up a bit. Peter, I guess they think you're visiting Edith, so you better stay here. I'll stop by and bring you something to eat. In fact, I suggest we all try to smuggle something out for Peter. I wouldn't want him to starve to death. I still need a ride home tomorrow." Laurie stood and picked up her cane. She shifted her weight around the clutter, stepping over piles of paper as she carved a path to the door. Then she turned, pulling her sweater around her neck and stooped over, planting her cane, preparing to exit. "I'll see you ladies in a few minutes."

Ruth pushed herself out of her chair. "I have to be going too," she announced, "but we can't all leave together. We're still being watched. Annie, since you're headed out the front, I'll go out the back. Edith,

I'll need one of your umbrellas."

Laurie started to object, but Ruth was firm. She was determined to take the outside route. She insisted she enjoyed walking in the rain; she implied she took to foul weather the way a duck took to water. Besides, she emphasized, if Laurie were to go outside her face might get wet which could cause her makeup to run. Peter rose to his feet nodding in agreement, and that was that.

LAURIE ENTERED the corridor, *poke, pull, step forward, lean on the cane, poke, pull, step forward,* making her way toward the dining room. She had been back to her room to check her e-mail, but the message she wanted, the one from Bill, wasn't there. In this case, she decided no news wasn't necessarily good news. He must have read her article and hated it, not that she could say she blamed him.

The community center had a few stragglers still milling about but it seemed, with the removal of the dogs, and the demonstration of power it represented, the people had reverted back to a compliant, do-nothing, say-nothing, no-life routine. That part hurt. She wished there was something she could do—*anything.* If there were, she would gladly stay and do it, but there was nothing, so she would leave, and they would stay and succumb to a program of living death.

She didn't doubt that Bill would know how to cheer these people up. He'd been right about the dogs. The animals had lifted spirits in the room. What he'd said about death with dignity, and the abuses that would follow its legalization, he'd been right about that too. She was witness to the fact. And he'd been right about Angie. It hurt to admit it, even to herself, but it was something she had to face. They would be here in a few days. Oddly enough, she found herself looking forward to it. She was curious to see what kind of young lady Angie had become.

Bill, Bill, Bill, Bill, Bill, what to do about Bill? That's the question. There had always been a chance he might one day return. She lived with it. Over the years, she'd steeled herself against the possibility. Her thoughts had run the gamut, from realizing she might flee in a nervous panic, to hoping she'd be able to stand tall and confront him. But the one thing she'd never considered was that she might somehow welcome his arrival. Such a thought was so foreign, she found it impossible to fathom.

She had to be careful. She would not bow to her emotions—ever again! She was nobody's fool. She wasn't ready to reconcile with Bill. There was too much about which they still disagreed. They were as different as black and white—as opposite as night and day. But even black and white could mix and become gray, and didn't night and day overlap at dawn and dusk, melding into one, and...why was she thinking that way? It was pointless. They were doomed to repel each other. They were magnets of the same pole, forever pushing each other away. But it only took turning one of the magnets around and the poles would attract. Only one of them had to turn, but which one? She'd turned some, she could feel it, but she wasn't about to turn all the way. Would Bill be open to changing his views? *Never!* They were polar opposites, and doomed for eternity to stay that way. It was magnets of opposite poles that attracted anyway, not magnets of the same pole. And she and Bill were about as opposite as two people could get, so maybe? But why was she thinking that way? Such speculations were a waste of time. *Put the cane forward, pull yourself up, put the cane forward, pull yourself up.* Why think about it at all? Que sera sera, whatever will be, will be...

TWENTY-FOUR

B ILL AND MARY sat in a booth across from each other, with Angie rolled up to the table's open end. Her neck reeled from side to side while her shoulders gyrated, her hands ascending and descending like pails on ropes. She was anxious, and Bill knew why. Mary was a good person, she had been trying patiently to help soothe and comfort Angie, but Angie would have none of it. She was rejecting this beautiful, kind, sweet woman without giving her a chance. In her voice-disabled way, Angie was sending the message that Mary wasn't wanted, and that was disappointing. Bill expected better of his daughter. He was thankful Mary hadn't been around Angie long enough to read the signals. Bill could see compassion in Mary's eyes every time Angie made a clumsy move. All Mary wanted was to help the poor suffering child cope with her problem.

The waiter brought a huge deep-dish pizza to the table. Holding it off to one side, he cleared a glass, a few pieces of silverware and a Parmesan shaker out of the way. "One large Super Deluxe, three quarters with the works, one quarter cheese only. There you go, folks. Enjoy your meal," he said, setting the pizza down on the heavy wood surface.

A cut glass lamp in mellow shades of brown hovered above, casting a warm glow over the pizza from which steam rolled. Bill dug a spatula in under the crust and hefted a slice with nine different toppings onto a plate for Mary. He turned the pizza tin, taking a slice from the cheese-only side, which he slipped onto a plate for Angie. Then he took another fully dressed slice for himself. "Looks good to me," he said. "Let's say grace."

Bill bowed his head. "Lord for that which we are about to eat we are truly thankful. Bless it in Jesus' name. Amen. Okay ladies, dig in while it's hot." He leaned over and picked up Angie's piece, blowing across the gooey cheese to cool the steamy bread. Then he put a finger under the slice to keep it from drooping as he held it to her lips, but she turned her head, refusing to take a bite. It would be nice if she could be on her best behavior in front of their guest, but no such luck. She was being a pill.

Bill could see he was in trouble. Angie still seemed upset about his leaving her outside for so long. He couldn't help it. He'd had work to do, and yes, perhaps he had got caught up in conversation with Mary and lost track of time, and, okay, it was almost dark by the time he remembered to wheel Angie in, but he was only human. He was trying to be the best father he could, in spite of the circumstances. Angie was his number one priority, always had been, always would be. Didn't she know that? Her happiness was more important than anything. That wasn't going to change. She shouldn't object to his enjoying a little female companionship.

He felt Mary's smile burning deep in his chest. The attraction was mutual. The eye contact was there. It was so strong it proved embarrassing. Seemed he was the one always in retreat, not because he was shy, but because he had to keep from moving too fast. The situation with Laurie was still unresolved, but he could feel his *resolve* weakening.

How could things have changed so fast? A week ago, he wouldn't have considered anyone but Laurie. He held the vows of marriage to be sacred. But the situation was impossible. Was he supposed to keep pounding his head against a wall? He had to weigh the feasibility of forming a lasting relationship with Mary, against any hope of reconciling with Laurie. On the one hand, things looked pretty good, on the other, pretty dim. About the only thing he and Laurie had in common, was their daughter. And Laurie didn't want either of them. Everything depended on Angie. Her happiness was paramount. She needed to accept Mary, if not as a mother, at least as a friend. He needed her approval, and right now, she wasn't cooperating. He tried to act as though his daughter's refusal to eat was the most natural thing in the world. "What's the matter lil' darlin', not hungry? I'd a thought you'd be famished by now." He held the slice up again but she turned her head the other way. "Okay, not hungry, I get the picture." He laid the pizza on the plate, looking at Mary. "She can be finicky at times, but I usually find whenever she misses dinner, you have to be on guard the next morning, 'cause she'll try to eat a horse."

"Maybe it's too hot. Perhaps if you let it cool down and try again in a minute."

"Oh, I will. I'm not giving up, just pausing to eat my own. I like it hot. Bon appétit," he said, lifting a slice to his mouth. The melted cheese dripped as he pulled the slice away, leaving strings of creamy goo on his chin. Mary smiled as he grabbed a napkin. He loved that smile, two dimples sitting on the fringe of her upturned apple-berry lips, so juicy, so natural, so inviting. Her dark eyes caught his and lingered. He could see tiny flecks of the golden overhead lamps dancing like suns in their reflection. Goosebumps caused his hairs to stand on end. His chest felt sultry and hot. Those eyes were beckoning him. Once again his eyes skittered away.

"I...ah...how's your pizza?" Bill offered, scrambling for something to say.

"Delicious, how's yours?"

Bill nodded taking another bite. He hated to admit it, even to himself, but he was smitten. He, the master wordsmith, was at a loss for words. Mary came to his rescue. "When do you plan to leave on your voyage north?"

"Don't rightly know. It'll take maybe a month to get our sea legs. We have to rehearse emergency procedures; we have to be ready for anything nature throws at us. I wouldn't want to be caught in a summer storm out on the ocean without practice. We bought a motor launch, which is easier to handle than a sailboat. I'm told it's a solid craft with good carriage. I shouldn't have any trouble keeping it stable, even in rough seas. And it's supposed to have a comfortable ride, even for Angie, but I had them install special devices in the cabin so I can lock her wheelchair down, just in case. I guess the only thing we're missing is a couple of deck hands. I'll have to pilot the boat alone, but I'll manage."

"Looking for volunteers. For a crew, I mean?"

Bill would have liked to answer; it appeared Mary was ready to enlist, but Angie began writhing and twisting and putting up such a fuss Bill had to stop so he could soothe his daughter's jangled nerves. "Hey there, little partner, what's the matter? Whoa, slow down, you're gonna hurt yourself," but she continued yowling and corkscrewing and working her way loose, until Bill finally had to unbuckle her security belt and take her in his arms.

"Perhaps we better go," Mary said. Her eyes were uneasy and tight, showing little crow's feet at the corners.

"But you haven't eaten your pizza."

"That's okay. Have the waiter bring a box and we'll take it with us."

Bill couldn't argue. So much wriggling made Angie hard to hold. If he loosened his grip, she'd squirm free, but if he squeezed too hard she might be hurt. He had to be careful. He hoped the inconvenience wouldn't ruin the evening. Was that empathy in Mary's eyes, or was it embarrassment? If Mary was embarrassed, she more than likely wouldn't make a good soul mate. He wasn't looking to find a mother for Angie, but Angie was part of the package and if her actions embarrassed Mary...but no, he could see it in her eyes, she was expressing genuine concern.

I feel bad about what happened. I wasn't trying to embarrass my father—or his female friend. I didn't like the attention he was giving her. I didn't like feeling pushed aside. And my dad was acting like he'd swallowed silly pills. But even with all that, I wish I could have sat quietly through dinner. These things are out of my control. I can tell myself to relax and not get excited, but my nerves have a mind of their own, and when they start to pop, my body goes haywire and my arms fling out and the next thing you know I'm causing a scene. It may have seemed that I was trying to embarrass my dad, but in truth, the only one embarrassed—was me.

ANGIE SEEMED to calm down once they were in the car. Bill was pleased. He hoped he could get Angie into bed without trouble.

She had to be weary from all the driving; it was probably the reason for her discontent. The wagon bumped over a dirt washboard at the edge of the driveway and squeaked to a stop in front of the cabin. Bill slid out and stuffed the keys into his pocket. It was a magnificent evening, not too cool, smelling of wood-stove smoke and evergreens. The fresh air helped to clear his head, which had wandered into all kinds of foolish imaginations under the spell of Mary's perfume. He looked up into the star-laced sky and wondered where this game of romance would eventually lead.

He gently pulled Angie into his arms and shouldered her across the porch with his boots clapping on the boards as he carried her inside. Mary followed, holding the pizza, which she set down on the lowboy dresser. Bill carried Angie to her bed and tucked her in. Her tremors had quieted down. He stroked her forehead and spoke soothingly, causing her to melt into calm repose. Before long, her eyes grew heavy and she slipped into that land between wow and worry known as sleep.

Mary went outside. The air was mild, though chill enough to raise goosebumps under her sleeves. She strolled across the deck overlooking the water. Bill followed, closing the door quietly so as not to disturb his sleeping daughter. He drifted over to the rail and leaned against its rough frame, savoring the moment.

"Beautiful, isn't it?" Mary finally said, breaking the spell of silence.

"Uh-huh." Bill had to admit it was beautiful. The moon had risen to dance over the water, shimmering above the lake's dark inky spill. The night was a starscape of swirling nebula, with twinkling coronas of pink and blue hanging on a black velvet curtain. Truly the heavens did declare the glory of God. Bill turned so he could see Mary. The ethereal beauty of the heavens paled when compared to the woman standing at his side. Bill was mesmerized by the faint trail of her perfume. His chest was burning with desire. He knew she felt it too, because it wasn't the kind of thing a person feels alone; it was the kind of feeling a person has when they send out a signal and an even stronger signal comes back. Problem was, Bill was still married, which meant his heart should not be running wild and free, it should be grazing in the green pastures of domestic life. Who was he trying to kid? He wasn't married. He was estranged. The fences had been broken down.

Mary turned and leaned back, resting her arms on the rail. Bill could see her face shining in the moonlight's faint glow, a dusting of rose blush touching her cheek. The crickets were chirping, frogs provided a chorus from the banks of the lapping lake and an owl hooted in the dark wooden distance, the nighttime sounds of spring returning to the shores of Coeur d'Alene.

Mary turned to look at Bill, her eyes as deep as the night, her hair glittering under the moon, her lips full, moist, and tempting. "This is going to sound really bad," she said, "but I'm glad we've had this opportunity to get to know one another."

Bill raised an eyebrow. It seemed an odd thing to say. "Why should that sound bad?"

"Oh, I don't know, I guess I feel kind of guilty about being thankful for something that was so devastating to the Hutchinsons."

"You needn't feel guilty. You didn't start that fire. If something good can come out of it, then be happy."

"How'd I know you'd say something like that? Bill, this is crazy. I shouldn't be here with you. I'm finding myself thinking thoughts...feeling things I haven't felt in years. Actually, three years, not since Tom was killed. I'm sorry, I'm babbling. I...I...would you mind holding me?"

Bill drew her warm body into his arms. He nuzzled his chin in her hair, the smell titillating his senses, his emotions lost in lust. The blood was racing in his veins, causing him to be reckless. He recognized the warning. A combination of speed and recklessness was fodder for an accident, but his mind was wanton, and his head pulsated with aberrant thought. *Too fast, too fast, too fast.* If he didn't slow this pony down, he'd ride over a cliff.

Mary trembled. Bill caught a moonlit tear running down the side of her cheek as she broke into gentle sobs.

"Hey there. What's the matter? I say something to get you upset?"

Mary swallowed, tightening her arms around his waist. "No, you're fine. You're a good man, Bill. I wish...It's just that I...I guess

I'm mixed up, that's all." Her voice faltered as though the words were coming hard. She brought her head out from under Bill's chin and turned to kiss him full on the mouth. He started to respond, his lips softening at the touch of hers, his mouth wet with desire, but he pulled away. He was a married man. Even if his wife said she no longer wanted him, even if she said she would never return, until they had a written divorce, he was still obligated to keep his commitment. That was what was meant by, for better, or for worse. "I'm sorry Mary. I can't."

Mary stiffened and shrank back. Bill could feel her quaking, the tremor running down her arms. "No, I'm the one who's sorry," she said. She pulled her sweater around her shoulder and backed away. Bill saw her moist eyes and the tracks of her tears shining in the moonlight. She turned and fled to the cabin, letting the door slide closed gently behind her, leaving Bill standing alone, cooling off in the now chilly night.

TWENTY-FIVE

P ETER SAT in Edith's overstuffed easy chair staring at the television. A stunning blonde paced back and forth, her polished teeth shining like porcelain as she smiled at the camera. Her job was to illuminate letters for the show's host who auctioned them to contestants bidding on prizes. He stifled a yawn. The show was a bore, a mere time killer, a Band-Aid over the wound of his loneliness.

Peter struggled to resist calling Tina. He wanted to hear endearing words about how he'd been missed, but he'd already used Edith's phone to check his answering machine and there were no new messages. Tina hadn't tried to reach him—not even once! Hadn't their love meant anything?

Peter didn't know how to play the love game to his advantage. He was always the one hurt. He was the weaker vessel, exploited, stepped on, and abused. At times like these, he wanted to act more like a man, roll up his fists and fight—don't get mad, get even—but that would mean conflict, and he hated conflict. He ached to feel the potency of raw masculine strength. He wanted to know he could stand on his own two feet, rise to a challenge, and even (dare he say it?) fight for what's right. Big laugh. The very thought of confrontation made him want to hide, though he had to admit the act of saving Joe had been therapeutic. He'd had to face his fear several times. He'd stood his ground, even when that snoopy doctor was standing right outside the door, trying to get in. What a terrible episode that was. The door was rattling so hard, he thought it was going to break off its hinges. His palms were sweaty, and he felt his heart failing, but he'd held fast, and the doctor had gone away. It made him wonder how Ruth could be so brave. She'd walked right in and fearlessly taken charge. She acted like she was invincible. "Jesus will send his angels to protect me." That's what she'd said. He wanted to ask her what she meant, but this was their last night. They would be leaving tomorrow, and he was trapped here with Edith.

It wasn't going to work. He didn't want to hurt Edith's feelings but he couldn't stay here. There wasn't enough room. He wanted to put his feet up, but even if he could have found a stool to put his feet up on, there wouldn't have been any place to put the stool. He had to continually shuffle stacks of paper back and forth, just to get from one place to another. How could anyone live like this? He couldn't breathe. The oppressive heat clogged his lungs. He could ascribe to clichés like: "each to their own," "live and let live," and, "do your own thing," but this was ridiculous. Where was he supposed to sleep in all this mess? He couldn't wait to hear Edith say he was to stretch out on the couch because, the trouble was, it wasn't a couch, it was a love-seat; it was about two feet too short and covered in magazines. No, it simply wasn't going to work.

The show host appeared to be talking to his viewing audience (though Peter knew he was reading from a teleprompter) and the blonde hostess was waltzing back and forth, pointing at letters that lit up with the sound of bells. Her fashion label clothes were designed to show off her natural endowments. The screen vibrated with one singular, sizzling, titillating message: sex sells!

It was boring. He'd already flipped through the channels three times, but unless he was willing to settle for game shows, sitcoms, sports, or travelogues, he was stuck. He took a moment to scan for something to read. Hundreds of outdated magazines washed through the room like shipwrecked planks on a storm-tossed sea, but they all had the same problem, they were all yesterday's news. He looked deeper into the crevices and cracks hoping to find an interesting book. How 'bout a Bible? She must have a Bible somewhere. He got out of his chair and went rifling through a bookshelf, tilting books back to see if any of them had those telltale glittery edges, but what he found was: "Moby-Dick," "Atlas Shrugged," and "Hawaii." It seemed she had everything but.

He sat down, planting his elbow on the arm of the chair, resting his chin on the back of his hand. Who needed a Bible anyway? It was just that he and Ruth had unfinished business. If he could understand her point of view before they got into it, he could prepare a better defense.

Another likelihood came to mind. He got up and went to the bedroom. It too was piled high with magazines, more than in the living room. The place was a fire hazard. There were also dolls, thirty or forty of the plastic, stuffed and stitched creatures lying in a heap on the bedspread and propped up against pillow shams. There were bald infants in diapers, and little girls with their pretty toy purses, and mature young women with silky hair and frilly dresses, and dozens of cuddly cute, furry animals. The chair beside the bed was covered in a heap of pillows surrounded by stacks of magazines. There was a dresser against the wall with an oval mirror that swung back and forth on pins. But there weren't any books on the dresser. It was covered in bottles, combs and brushes. A sea of Bibleless clutter. Even motels have Bibles! Where were the Gideons when you needed them?

He heard the door opening and froze. Mr. Porter again? He wanted to run and hide, bury his head under a pillow so he couldn't be seen. His heart filled with terror. Were they coming to question him again? He knew the manager hadn't bought the story about his being Edith's nephew. He didn't look anything like Edith. He bit his lower lip, only seconds from his doom, waiting in the ticking of a dozen clocks for the trap to spring. They would drag him off to be scourged and beaten, and then call the police. At least it solved the problem about where he would sleep. He'd rest on the cold, rat-infested floor of a cell tonight.

Edith closed the door and turned to find Peter standing in her bedroom, pale and trembling. The encounter startled her for a moment. She didn't recognize the man standing there. Her mind was playing tricks on her, fading in and out like a poorly tuned receiver picking up a weak signal. "What are you standing there for?" she finally said.

Peter forced himself to move. He brought a hand up to mop his forehead. Another close call. All part of his therapy. "I...I thought you were someone else."

Edith nodded. She set her knit purse in the chair and shuffled in, barely lifting her feet. She clutched her shawl and shivered. "You turned the heat down didn't you? It's cold in here." She plodded over to tweak the thermostat, and then turned to enter the bedroom. "Don't just stand there. You're in the way. I have to turn in early. I missed my nap today."

Great! Peter was now stuck in a stuffy junk dealer's apartment, breathing musty, stale air that reminded him of death, without anybody to even talk to. "Sure. I understand. Don't worry about me. Okay if I just sit out here and watch TV?"

Edith didn't answer. She sat down on her bed, pushing the piles of dolls aside. Peter glanced away as she began to unbutton her blouse as though he wasn't there. "Would it be all right if I called Ruth? I have a question to ask her." Peter kept his eyes averted in spite of the fact that Edith seemed unabashed about disrobing in front of him. *See, even she thinks I'm a girl.*

"Suite yourself, but it won't do any good. They took our phones. I had that one stashed away. Never hurts to have two of everything. That's what I always say. Course, I suppose Ruth could have had a spare too. You might as well try. Dial nine, and then her room number, like in a hotel. She's in number fifty-three, least that's where they moved her after they split us up." Edith leaned back and used the toe of one foot to pop the shoe off the other.

"Thanks. Rest well." Peter pulled the door closed so Edith could undress in private.

Well, now what? Peter stared at the luminous, flickering light of the TV. The voluptuous blonde with perfect teeth was still prancing about, while her penguin-suited host promised the world to would-be riddle solvers. Peter carved a path through the stacks of paper, making his way over to the table to use the phone. He pressed button nine, and then five, and then three, and heard a rapid *bep, bep, bep, bep, bep, bep, bep,* letting him know the number was out of service.

He set the receiver back in its cradle. The studio audience cheered at a contestant's correct answer. She now had nine thousand, two hundred, sixty-four dollars and a new red Camaro, though Peter couldn't imagine what the matronly schoolteacher would want with a car like that.

He clicked off the set. He had to get out. Dare he? Yes, but he couldn't go wandering down the halls. That would be dangerous. He had to go out through the back. Peter turned out the lights to prevent anyone from seeing his escape. He pulled the terrace door back and stuck his head out, sniffing the air. He could feel the rain spitting in the wind. At least it wasn't pouring. There seemed to be a lull in the storm. The night smelled heavy, like sultry grass. There were flashes of white off the horizon, accompanied by distant rumblings, but they appeared far away. He tiptoed onto the lawn, feeling a brisk chill. He closed the door behind him, making sure it wasn't locked so he could get back in.

He paused, biting down on his lip, considering the best route to take. Ruth was in the string of units on the other side. He would have to go around. His heart was pounding, but more from excitement than fear. He knew it wasn't fear. If it had been fear, he would have stayed inside where it was safe, and the fact that he didn't feel afraid, made him feel even more excited. He turned, looking up into the nighttime sky. There was a hazy break in the clouds where a few faint stars flickered, and behind them were billions more he knew he couldn't see. Who really threw all those stars into space...the Big Bang...God? Was man God's creation, or was God the invention of man? So many questions with no apparent answers. He wanted to know how a tiny little woman like Ruth could exude such power, while he felt compelled to flee his own shadow. Perhaps Ruth would know. The wet lawn smelled freshly cut. He hoped the little blades of grass weren't sticking to the cuffs of his pants. Green always showed up on black. *How embarrassing.* He would have to remember to wipe his feet before entering Ruth's apartment. He'd be mortified if she caught him tracking wet clods across her carpet.

The Emerald Valley complex was patterned after the spokes of a wheel. The three sections of units extended from a semicircular hub containing the lobby and administrative offices, with the community room and dining hall nestled in between. Ruth had once pointed out her apartment. It was in the branch off to his right, but without being able to see the numbers, he didn't know exactly which suite it was, which meant he couldn't approach from the yard. He'd have to risk going inside. His heart raced at the thought. It would be best if he could avoid the lobby, too much traffic. If he followed the wall around to where it bordered the parking lot, he should find a door like the one they'd used to help Joe escape.

It took him a few minutes to get there. He tried the door and found it unlocked. His heart was snapping but the adrenaline made him feel oddly in control as he slipped down the corridor leaving wet, grassy footprints on the carpet behind him. He scanned the numbers...*sixty, fifty-nine, fifty-eight*...and prayed no one would open one of those doors and find him lurking in the hall and get the bright idea to call security...*fifty-five, fifty-four, fifty-three*...there it was. He knocked, and waited a moment and knocked again. A shadow covered the peephole and the door opened.

"Peter? What in heaven's name are you doing here? Get inside, quick."

Peter stepped in so Ruth could close the door. "I wanted to talk to someone, that's all. Edith was tired and went to bed. I thought maybe I could talk to you."

Ruth had her hat and gloves off, obviously the way she relaxed at home. She always seemed shorter without her hat. "Well, of course, come in," she said. "Never hurts to have a little company."

BILL'S HEAD bumped the roof of the station wagon, as he climbed in behind the wheel. *Thud, ouch!* One big hand rubbed his cranium, while the other pushed down on the seat. The fabric yielded to his weight as he slid inside. He pulled himself comfortable, lifting his rear and tugging on his blue denims to keep them from binding. The car was parked in a space next to the cabin with a view overlooking the lake. Bill settled both hands on the wheel and contemplated what to do next. His libido had been in overdrive, amorous and sensual, sending out and receiving signals. The windows began to fog—and *she* wasn't even there! He had to cool off.

There were times when he questioned his sanity. This woman was something special. He could list her attributes: she was attractive, athletic and articulate, ready for adventure, not afraid of risks, she was everything he might look for in a woman, except he wasn't supposed to be looking. He was married!

Or was he? Because if he was, where was his wife? Where was the little darlin' he'd wed? Good fences might make good neighbors, but not good marriages. He needed to be close to someone. But here he sat, staring at a magnificent star-filled sky—alone. And Mary was in there curled up with her pillow—alone. And he was cooling off, out in the cold car staring off into space—alone. And they were alone because he couldn't let himself become involved until things were settled once and for all with Laurie, when it was Laurie who wanted to be alone in the first place, not him! So who cared if pursuing this relationship meant curtailing any chance he had of mending fences with Laurie? He was through blaming her. At least he'd come that far. He was ready to concede that he'd been the one who wouldn't listen. He had his confession all worked out, but if he walked in arm-in-arm with Mary, he knew he'd blow any chance he had of asking Laurie's forgiveness. Dang-it-all, she didn't seem willing to work at it anyway.

His fist pounded the steering wheel. Nice try, but that wasn't the point. The point was, he'd made a lifelong commitment, a vow, a contract that couldn't be broken. That was love, and he loved her, always had, which was why he'd given her the space she needed when she'd asked for it. He'd waited ten years, and he'd gladly wait another ten, if that's what it took. Jacob worked fourteen years to make Rachel his wife. That's love! Bill had a sudden urge to lean on the horn. Let it scream! Why did life have to be so complicated? At least Jacob had a promise of getting Rachel. There was no assurance he'd ever be with Laurie again.

It would have been simpler if she had asked for a divorce. The fact that she hadn't was the one thing that kept him hanging on. They'd never even talked about it. Neither of them seemed anxious to take that first step. To Bill's way of thinking, not insisting on a divorce was Laurie's way of telling him she wasn't serious about anyone else. If she were, she'd want this little detail taken care of. She'd want to remove all impediments in case she and the man she was seeing wanted to get themselves hitched. No, it seemed pretty obvious Laurie was still alone, and happy that way.

That was the problem. He had spent the last ten years waiting for Laurie's return. Okay, perhaps it was more correct to say he would have to return. He was the one who had traveled east, but that was just semantics. If she'd given even the slightest indication she was thinking they might get back together, he and Angie would have been on the first plane west quicker than a jackrabbit. Now he'd made up his mind to do it anyway. He was almost there. Why even consider the notion of courting someone else? *Talk about being fickle.* He'd made it ten years. Ten years that had gone by in a blink, but ten years all the same.

The bird in the hand, or the bird in the bush, which way to go? He wanted to march right back into that cabin and find Mary. He wanted to hold her, and caress her, and get lost in the fragrance of her hair. Therein lie the rub, because he knew that would only be the start. She was no virgin, and neither was he, and lost in the throes of passion, once begun, it would be hard to stop. Sexual union was designed for marriage. That's why he couldn't go back inside. He would uphold the injunction: *flee fornication.* But that aside, why was he struggling with the idea of becoming involved in a normal, healthy relationship? Why? He knew the answer. In spite of everything, in spite of difference, distance and dissolution, he knew he loved Laurie. Like it or not, Mary, for all her charms, was a mere infatuation. *Love requires commitment—for better or for worse.* He placed his elbows on the wheel and buried his head in his hands, letting his fingers massage his scalp. Here he was, alone again, waiting for the day when he and Laurie would be together again...and there would be no more hunger, no more death, no more disease, and no more war—and hell would freeze over!

TWENTY-SIX

S TUART VANETTER, doctor, healer, sworn upholder of the Hippocratic oath, sworn to do everything in his power to bring life and health to his patients, struggled to gather the instruments he would need to take another person's life. He should never have taken the oath if he didn't mean it: *"I will neither give a deadly drug to anybody, if asked for, nor will I make a suggestion to this effect."* He moved through the peaceful slumber room like a zombie. It was no longer the Hippocratic Oath he observed. His was the oath of a hypocrite!

Lightning brightened the room, followed by a sonic boom. A perfect night for Dr. Frankenstein to do his sinister work. This was not "death with dignity," this was murder, something he once felt himself incapable of, and yet was now forced by circumstance into doing. How had he fallen from innocently helping a few suffering old people find their rest, to out and out murder?

He went to the refrigerator, reaching in his pocket for the key. Pentobarbital was a controlled substance. Both the door to the room, and the refrigerator, had to be kept locked at all times. He removed a plastic container of 100-milligram tablets, counted out thirty, and held them in his hand. He considered taking them himself. But, if he did, he wouldn't be around to help others. He was the doctor. Someone had to put an end to their pain. There comes a point in the life of every living thing when it no longer functions, when all that remains of life, is an arduous wait for the final stroke of death. For the fortunate, the process could be painless. They could wait out their days in relative comfort. But for most, plagued by cancers,

Alzheimer's disease, advanced multiple sclerosis, and other afflictions too numerous to mention, the process was one of abject pain. And sometimes the indignity suffered was worse than the pain itself. He hated watching human beings waste away, their dry shriveled bodies having to be rolled every few hours to ease the pressure on their bedsores, their uncontrolled bladders soiling their clothes, every day accompanied by shortness of breath, excessive salivation, nausea and vomiting. It was more than he could bear. For these he had compassion. Hippocratic oath notwithstanding, something had to be done.

The room flashed, throwing strobes of stark shadows against the walls. There were no windows in the room. People usually wanted privacy. But to give a last glimpse of sun to those who wished it, several long vertical skylights were built into the ceiling. Stuart looked up and saw lightning peeling back the sky. It may have stopped raining, but the thunderheads remained. The clouds were black, the very black of his soul. He began to dissolve the tablets in a saline solution. He would use a standard IV and lock, injecting the mixture with a syringe. Once in the bloodstream, the solution would act immediately, putting the woman to sleep, and subsequently, to death, within minutes. It would be totally painless.

Murder, in the first degree! The thought made him feel numb. How could he, a man of letters, a respected professional within the community, have stooped so low? It was the system. Oregon's Death with Dignity Act was flawed. The law required a patient not only be able to ask their doctor to provide them with a lethal drug, but that they be able to take the drug orally, without assistance from the physician. That was fine for those who were able-bodied, but many weren't, and for them it wasn't fair. Blanche and Gus were too far gone. Their pain was evident, but they were physically incapable of asking for the prescription, let alone swallowing the pills themselves. In conversation with George, Dr. VanEtter expressed his desire to relieve their suffering, but he needed a signed request before the procedure could be done. George had come up with a foolproof plan, a way of obtaining the patient's full authorization, without their having to give it.

Helping Gus Olson, and Blanch Albright, had been the right thing to do. He was convinced of it. He'd done exactly what he knew, as a doctor, his patients would have expected of him. He'd ended their suffering. He'd let them die with dignity.

He walked over to inspect the cardiograph monitor. Electrodes would be placed on the woman's arms and legs to confirm her death. Everything seemed in order. The doctor went back to the counter and removed a syringe from a stainless steel tray, took a new needle from the supply cabinet, fixed it to the end, and drew the solution up into the tube. He placed a cap on the tip of the needle, and put the hypodermic into the refrigerator, locking the door once again. Why were his hands shaking? Because he was preparing to kill a healthy human being, that's why.

He couldn't justify terminating the lives of Mr. Hobbs or Mr. Miller. Their premature deaths weighed heavy on his conscience. Once on the slippery slope, there was no turning back. He tried using every rationalization he could think of. All he'd done was eliminate a few useless old people who were taking up space on a planet to which they were no longer contributing, people with nothing to live for and probably only a year or two remaining. What harm was there in that? He was helping them peacefully exit a world in which they no longer had a place. In many ways it was an act of compassion. But he knew he didn't believe it—not for one minute!

Now he was being called on to murder someone—*murder in the first degree*—and his hands were trembling. But he couldn't back out. He was trapped. He feared going to jail. What would they do to him there? And the trial would be humiliating. They'd make his actions public. Revealing what he'd done could set the "right to die" movement back a decade. He'd just proved the validity of an argument made against physician-assisted suicide: the argument that doctors, faced with difficult decisions, might not bother to obtain a terminally ill patient's consent before taking their life. If some pro-life group were to vilify his actions, they might bring the whole movement down like a house of cards. At the very least they would circulate petitions to have the law repealed. He wasn't about to let that happen. It had been his mistake. He would fix it. Better that one should die, than many should suffer.

GEORGE SAT in the privacy of his office, staring out the window. His skin was tense around his temples, throbbing when he gritted his teeth. He found himself digging his nails into the palms of his hands. *Relax, breathe deep, calm down.* He began rapping his fingers on his desk. *Calm down, calm down, calm down, relax.* He took a tissue and used it to clear his watery vision. His conscience was seared with the great evil of the task that lay ahead.

The murky air outside was swirling into blackness. A wind swept down the valley, scattering bits of paper and broken leaves across the lawn as the clouds piled on top of each other. A storm of black, vile proportion was building, a metaphor accentuating his mood. What was it about weather that always seemed to influence his disposition? A flash streaked across the shadowy sky, followed by a bass drum's rumbling boom.

Earlier in the day the stock exchange had halted trading of the company's shares. They insisted on knowing why the company was in a tailspin. Corporation president, Carl Shiffer, complied by issuing a statement announcing Gabe Solomon's resignation. The world was left to speculate as to why the chairman of the board had quit, and speculation was grist for the rumor mill. Web chat lines had been buzzing all day. Everyone had an opinion, but most saw the move as a vote of no confidence. Panic was setting in. By the time the wire service made the release, it was too late to resume trading, but when the market reopened, EVC shares were sure to take another dive. The company was in the tank, swirling in a vortex of rapid decline and gurgling down the drain. Carl had packed his briefcase and fled. He couldn't take the calls. "Everything is okay," he'd tried to explain. "Just hang tough." But the shareholders wouldn't listen. They wanted someone's head. He decided it wouldn't be his.

Carl's exit was to George's advantage. George had some tidying up to do and Carl would only have been in the way. At least the dogs were under control. Five of the beasts were contained in the fenced yard that housed the facility's propane tanks and back-up generator. A loud crash of thunder told him the dogs were in for another shower.

Just desserts, to his way of thinking. Only the mutt held by Elmer remained at large. As soon as he was caught, the whole pack was off to the pound.

More lightning, more pounding thunder, responding to his thoughts. If things had gone right, by now they'd have Joe in custody. How could they go through every unit, every closet, kitchen, bathroom, recreational facility, every cupboard big enough to hold a man and not find Joe? People don't just vanish.

From bad to worse: the corporation was crumbling, Joe was still at large, and a reporter was threatening to make them front-page news. His eyes drifted to the photograph on his desk. The problem stared back, wearing an insidious smile: his wife and three children. That was his undoing. Correction—not the kids—it was *her!* He loved his children, his boys, his daughter; they were the reason he'd given up the house. He didn't mind paying support, that was the least a father could do, but she was asking too much. If he'd come home drunk, if he'd beaten her black and blue, or even threatened to, or if he'd had an affair and then shamed her by flaunting his infidelity, he could understand her anger. But he had done nothing. She was claiming emotional abuse. What kind of reason was that? It was legal insanity, a catchall phrase that included anything and everything from the fact that he insisted they roll, rather than squeeze, the toothpaste tube, to the fourteen-hour days he'd spent cultivating his unprofitable business. Trivial grounds for a divorce. Emotional abuse was the flimsy excuse used to end a marriage when a person didn't have a legitimate reason, and because it was so vague, so all-encompassing and so sinister sounding, the "injured party" usually got everything. She wanted the house, free and clear, no payments, the car, paid in full, and it was less than a year old, and two thousand dollars a month for each child. That's seventy-two thousand a year for the kids alone. Not that he was complaining, they were his kids, but then she wanted income for herself because she claimed raising the kids had prevented her from pursuing a career and developing the necessary skills she needed to earn a decent living. After taxes, the total package came to more than he took home. What was he supposed to live on? That was why he'd had to do it—had to—had no other choice. He had to

285

secure a nest egg for himself that neither she, nor Uncle Tax Man Sam, knew about.

It wasn't an issue of ethics. The practice of sacrificing one life to profit another was a time-honored tradition. It was the consequence of innumerable wars. Men of every generation had been called upon to pay the ultimate price, to conquer and subdue, all for the greater good. One man died that another might obtain greater wealth. Sovereigns sent their armies into battle under a banner of conquest, to increase the borders of their land. People were starved, maimed and blown apart in every part of the globe, just so someone could claim a bigger piece of dirt, for God and king! Worse, people were butchered over philosophical differences. If you don't think like I do, you're dead! That's the way it worked. He wasn't saying it was right, just that it was man's nature to do such things.

And not just men, but women too, tens of thousands each day were called upon to make life and death decisions. A woman had the right to end an undesired pregnancy. If her baby was unwanted, if it proved to be too much of a burden, or was too inconvenient, she could get rid of it. Old people were like babies, dependent, incoherent and unintelligible, so what was the difference? It was the evolution game, survival of the fittest. One died that another might live, or at least live more comfortably. *They shoot horses, don't they?* It was only civil to put an animal out of its misery. Why should it be different with people? Man was just an animal, albeit, a more sophisticated breed, but an animal all the same. The world was continually being cleansed of its unwanted. Men killed their enemies, babies were aborted, animals put to sleep, why should the elderly be exempt?

He put a hand to his chest. The knot was on fire, his heartburn raging out of control. It felt like his lungs were imploding. He reached into his drawer for a bottle of antacids. Every forecast he'd put together showed the corporation losing money for at least another five years. By then, he'd be bankrupt. He'd be on skid row, while his highfalutin ex-wife was hobnobbing in style. That's why he'd had to do what he'd done. He hadn't wanted to; it was necessary for his survival. He'd needed something to carry him through. Dr. VanEtter was right: old people with nothing to live for should be put to sleep. And if they just happened to have money they couldn't use, then making good use of that money was the right thing to do. He needed it, and they didn't. It was that simple. He was willing to bet anyone else faced with the same situation, given the same set of circumstances, and the same opportunity, would do the same thing. Death was inevitable. They'd only helped it along. Everything would have been fine if Joe, Ben, and Ruth had kept their noses out of it.

Pitchforks of bright white stabbed the ground, causing the lights in his office to flicker. He had crossed the line: no turning back. In war, spies were shot. The reporter was here under a presumed name. Her last communication with her office was believed to have come from Salem. They had no choice. They couldn't let this little newspaper lady go. She wasn't supposed to be there, and according to her editor, nobody knew she was. She was down in Salem. That's where she apparently ran into trouble. *Salem does have its seedy side.* They would do a search, the paper would run stories about their missing reporter, maybe they'd even offer a reward, and finally, after enough time, be left to conclude she had fallen victim to foul play, kidnapped, raped, and murdered. A tragic mishap. Eulogies would be written; she would be sorely missed. There was no connection, no way to trace her back to Emerald Valley.

He popped the lid off the bottle, tilted his head back, and tossed three of the chalky pills into his mouth. The body would, of course, be cremated and the ashes scattered in the wind. Without a body there was no murder. It was habeas corpus, the rule of law: without a body they couldn't prove the lady was dead. As for Annie Iversen, she didn't exist. No one would come looking for her. The guests would be told she'd decided not to stay. Her exit would seem perfectly normal. People declined to purchase all the time, nothing unusual about that. The lady had to disappear.

The black hole in his chest ached, sending streams of fire to his belly. Old people eventually die anyway, but this was someone young, someone with her whole life ahead of her. He struggled to find vindication. The sacrifice had to be made. The death of one would benefit the other. But his head wobbled under a weight of confusion, and he remained unconvinced. Pilfering the money had been easy. Who could have known it would lead to this? He placed his hand on his stomach, groaning under his breath. He didn't have the constitution for murder. He chewed the tablets and swallowed, but it was a futile endeavor. He allowed his grip to relax, his fingers curling open as the bottle left his palm. The plastic bounced on the hard surface of the desk and rolled to the edge, spilling the tablets onto the floor. He made no move to pick them up. In the silence of the storm, he could feel the weight of his oppressive conscience, a violation of morals so severe it would have paralyzed a lesser man, but he was George Bergen, a man of inner strength, risk-taker extraordinaire. If he wanted success, he took it. He was a man of action, not of thought. Thoughts were the destroyer. He had to get away from the tyranny of his mind.

LAURIE HADN'T meant to fall asleep, but she'd been up till dawn two nights in a row. She'd come back from dinner feeling sluggish, and decided to peel off her makeup so she could take a hot bath. She didn't want to sleep in all that gunk again. Peter would be over early in the morning to help her get into costume. She'd drop in on Barbara to explain why she was leaving. Barbara would play along to keep up appearances, and Peter would wait in the car and give her a ride home.

The hot bath had seeped into the pores of her skin like a muscle relaxer, dissolving her tension. She stepped out, toweled off, and dressed again, planning to spend some time polishing her story, but when she tried to retrieve the file, she found it scrambled. She was too tired to try and figure out what had happened. Bill would have a copy. She might as well wait to see what he had to say before making changes. She'd only laid down and closed her eyes for a second, but she'd found her mind reeling in the blackness of a deep, deep slumber.

If she could have awakened herself she would have, for this was not a peaceful repose, this was restless upheaval. She was floating. She tried to grasp the emptiness of air, hoping to find something to hang onto, but it was no use, there was nothing. She could feel herself spinning, the unsettling queasiness in her stomach like the whirling dervish of a carnival ride. It turned her stomach upside down. Why was she falling? The dream had no meaning because she couldn't see anything except an expansive void of blackness, and the blackness had no meaning because it was just an empty hole in space.

She knew she was old. She didn't know how she knew it, she just felt it, the wrinkles digging deep into her skin, ancient lines carving her face, her hair matted and gray. No, no, no, it was the costume, not reality; her hands thrashed trying to pull it off but it wouldn't come.

Was this death? Had she somehow been transported to the other side? That's how it felt, empty and alone, separation from all form of human existence, a godless void, outer darkness, weeping and gnashing of teeth. She didn't deserve this. She saw a face, the face of God? No, it was the face of Bill. He thrust out his arm, his fingers curling, beckoning her to take hold. She couldn't. And she didn't understand why. She heard his words echoing across the black emptiness of space: *"The wages of sin is death."* The face disappeared as she continued to fall. *Don't refuse God's forgiveness. Pray for mercy!* She was in free-fall. At least there weren't any flames, or at least, not yet!

How had she died? She couldn't remember. There was no memory, not of life, nor of death, or of anything in between, just a terrible emptiness, an awful swirling through a thick black soup of nothingness. This could not be death. It had to be a dream. She reached out to pinch herself; she squeezed hard and felt the bite. She was awake and alive, had to be, there was no pain in sleep, and there was no pain in death. But that begged the question, if she was alive and not asleep, where was she? Falling into a hole of unfathomable dimensions, into a realm that she could not describe, a vast vacuum, and still falling further. This was not within the domain of conscious understanding; she had to be outside the confines of space and time; she had to have slipped into the great null of eternity, but that again would mean she was dead. Maybe all the sages of time immortal had been right. There was no death; there was only a door through which a soul passed from one dimension into the next, from one life into another. Maybe she could still feel and experience pain because she had died in the mortal sense, but in the infinite, celestial, eternal sense, her spirit had survived and was still alive. And still she was falling, falling, falling, down to what, a bottomless pit?

Then the light began. She could see it as a pinprick only, at first. It was taking time to grow, but here it seemed time was irrelevant, no beginning, no end, only continuing forever and the light was growing brighter; she could tell. What did light shining out of darkness mean? It had to be God. Once again she didn't understand how she knew it, but she knew. The tiny hole of light had grown into a huge ball so blindingly brilliant she could not look upon it. It was too awesome to behold, absolute, unadulterated, unapproachable pureness. She was being sucked in, closer and closer, minute by minute, as though the light was determined to consume her. For some indescribable reason, she knew she feared the light more than she had the darkness. Why? Why be afraid of light? And then she knew. If the light was God, she had much to fear. No, impossible, it couldn't be, because God was dead. Not dead, there was never any God to begin with. She knew that. All the great minds had told her so: Kant, Rousseau, Shelley, Bertrand Russell, Jean-Paul Sartre, intellectuals of such persuasive argument, to think they could be wrong was beyond reason. Besides, science had proved it. Man was an animal evolved out of the great primordial stew, not fashioned by some invisible creator's hand. Darwin and Huxley and Leakey and Patterson, great men of science, had to know more than a bunch of silly preachers. Why wouldn't Bill listen? He had an answer for everything. She found it uncanny that he actually believed the Bible's mythological version of man's origin over the wisdom of great men who spent their whole lives studying the subject. He was pitted against men like Dr. Hawking, a pithy journalist against someone who held the secret of the cosmos in the palm of his hand.

Or was she the one who hadn't listened? Here she was at the edge of eternity and the great white gob was about to consume her, and she was terrified. And that too presented a paradox. Why should she be afraid? Even if there were a God, wasn't he supposed to epitomize love? God wasn't about to shove her down the throat of an all-consuming fire. She hadn't done anything to deserve punishment; she hadn't murdered anyone. Well, she might have, would have, if Bill hadn't stopped her. No, abortion wasn't murder because you weren't killing a living sentient being; you were just expelling a blob of unborn protoplasm. And that's all Angie had been at that point. But then, if God were out there in the infinite, he might be of a different opinion.

She was still *falling*, or was she rising now? In the black hole there was no up or down. The light was growing more intense. Now all she could think of was escape, but the light was drawing her in. No God, no! *God have mercy on my soul*...why would she think that? She'd done nothing wrong...*God have mercy on my soul*...but it seemed the immense brightness of that pure white light exposed the fact that she was flawed. The light seemed to demand perfection and she could see clearly now, perhaps for the first time, she was anything but. She viewed the innermost depth of her soul and saw it was entirely black. And the closer she got to the light, the darker it became...*God have mercy on my soul...God have mercy on my soul, God have mercy on my soul, God have mercy on my soul*...

Her eyes popped open and she snapped upright, her heart pounding in the empty vacuum of her chest, sweat itching the line of her scalp. She paused, taking a breath, glad to be awake. She tried to get up, but her bottom was too heavy and her top too weak, so she plopped back down. She drank in air and tried again, this time succeeding. She took a feeble step and began pacing the floor, trying to cool down, *just a dream, just a dream, just a dream.*

She was walking in circles. She paused and bent over, placing her hands on her knees, inhaling deeply. She was hyperventilating. *Thump, thump, thump, thump, thump,* went her heart. For a second she couldn't remember who she was. Was she Laurie, or Annie? Then the pieces of her fragmented memory fell back into place. She was Laurie, pretending to be Annie. Her head was pounding. She put a hand to the back of her neck, and checked her watch. It was eleven. She wasn't ready for sleep. The room had become haunted. She didn't want to be revisited by whatever mysterious ghost *(or was it the angel of death?)* that had brought that terrible dream. She remembered how Joe had looked the day the doctor came to get him. It was like he'd been visited by a specter from another realm. Had he received some sort of cryptic warning? Had she...? The whole thing was unsettling. She sat down and picked up the phone. She needed to dispel the grizzly nightmare and prevent its return. She needed someone to tell her she wasn't going crazy.

BILL BUMPED his head on the armrest as he jerked awake. *Ouchhhh!* What had startled him from his sleep? *Biiiilllllllleeep.* There it was again. *Biiiilllllllleeep.* He began patting down the sides of his coat. *Biiiilllllllleeep.* The sound was coming from the glove box. He flicked it open and found his phone jammed inside. He'd put it there to make room for Mary.

"Hello," he said, still groggy, realizing he was in his car, and that his back ached. Who would be calling in the middle of the night?

"Bill?"

"Laurie?"

"Hi. I'm not disturbing you am I?"

Bill rubbed his back. The voice at the other end sounded out of breath. "No, of course not. What's up?"

"Well...I...ahhh. When are you and Angie supposed to be arriving?"

He reached for the steering wheel to pull himself up, collecting his thoughts. "We'll be in Seattle tomorrow. Why?"

"I don't know. I...I was thinking about Angie."

Bill waited. It was her nickel. If she had something to say, let her say it.

"I guess I'm looking forward to seeing her," Laurie said, filling in the silence. "You too, I'd like to see you too, I guess. I..." The air filled with a long sustained pause.

"What?"

"Nothing, I guess I just wanted to hear your voice. I better go. Call me when you get settled. There's a lot we need to discuss."

"Like?"

"It'll wait. See you in a few days. Bye."

The phone went dead. Suddenly Bill found himself wide-awake. He stared out the windshield at the night. The stars were fewer in number than before, and their twinkling was subdued. *What was that all about?* He tried to swallow, but his mouth was dry. His heart was beating like a hammer, swelling the inside of his already sore chest. Something about the call, something he couldn't quite put his finger on, bothered him. He'd be lucky to get back to sleep.

LAURIE PUT the phone back into its cradle, and went to her computer. She had to write down what she was feeling. She needed to feel release. Her fingers clicked away, pulling thoughts from the air onto the screen. She'd probably wake up regretting she'd made the call, but if she wanted any kind of peace, she had to do what she was doing right now. She stared at her words for a moment. Then, before she could change her mind, she inserted Bill's e-mail address and hit the send key. Writing was so much easier than speaking. She walked back over to the bed, laid down, and for the second time that night, fell asleep without removing her clothes. She slipped into such a sound sleep, when the bumps and thuds and jostling took place, she thought it was all part of another dream. Except that funny smell, that part seemed real.

TWENTY-SEVEN

PETER SAT ON THE COUCH beside Ruth, who was skipping through her book, trying to convince him that he needed God, which was something he didn't understand. He didn't feel the need, and even if he did, the way this book said to find God, was too simple. Golden edges aside, it didn't look any more authoritative than any one of a dozen other holy books. Too bad he hadn't found a copy at Edith's. He would like to have been better prepared for this conversation. He was paying attention, but only because beneath Ruth's ill-advised attempt at saving his soul, her heart bled genuine concern. She may have been misdirected, but she was well intentioned.

The paradox was the verse he'd read about Christ dying for the weak. Ruth had been on target there. It was something he could relate to. He was weak—weak and meek. There wasn't a macho bone in his body. Okay, they called it effeminate, but to him it was the same thing. Being effeminate was just a euphemism for being weak. It all boiled down to the fact that he couldn't play football. He wasn't big, strong, or fast enough. The only running he did was from kids who wanted to rearrange his face for being different. Imagine getting beat up for liking nice clothes, and wanting to keep them clean. He liked classical music. He liked books. They built forts and threw rocks. And when they all grew up, the boys who once threw rocks, instead threw insults: *faggot, queer, homo!* And they quoted Ruth's book to justify their actions. But the book said Christ died for the weak, and that the meek would inherit the earth. Didn't they know that? Ruth's religion was based on a contradiction. The book said

Jesus loved the meek and lowly, (like being weak was some kind of blessing) but it also said his effeminate ways were wrong, when it was his femininity that made him weak. It was a catch twenty-two, and he told Ruth so. She just opened her Bible and showed him another verse: "Therefore I take pleasure in my infirmities, in reproaches, in necessities, in persecutions, in distresses for Christ's sake: for when I am weak, then am I strong." Now there was a paradox!

Ruth didn't belabor the point; she closed her Bible and stood. "You know God loves you Peter. He will help you, and he will give you strength. All you have to do is ask. Just don't wait too long. By the time my son got around to seeking help, it was too late." She brought a tissue up and wiped her nose. Her eyes were starting to mist. "Sorry. I don't mean to get emotional."

"That's okay, Mrs. Wheatly. Don't worry about it. It's not your fault. I'm a mess, but it's nothing you or God can fix. I ought to know. I've been seeing a shrink for years, and even that hasn't helped."

Ruth was shaking her head. "You sound so much like Eric. He would have said the same thing. Maybe you didn't choose to be born different, Peter, but how you deal with that difference is up to you. And God *can* help. You just have to let him. Excuse me for a moment, will you?" she said. Then she disappeared into her bedroom.

Peter rubbed his hands together. How in the world had he ever gotten so screwed up? Was he a genetic abnormality, or were there developmental reasons. His therapist, Dr. Roberts, felt it was the latter. He attributed Peter's feminine tendencies to his being raised by his mother. But the real problem, he said, was Peter's feeling of inadequacy, which went all the way back to the day his father left, never to be seen or heard from again. The pain of that rejection, along with his mother's non-stop castigation of her husband's character, made him spurn the idea of ever becoming like his father, and by extension, ever becoming a man. It all started with rejection, and that, according to the doctor, was why he found rejection so hard to take. It made him feel worthless. When you have no worth, you have no reason to live.

Dr. Roberts never suggested Peter undergo behavior modification. He felt the tendencies were too ingrained. He, in fact, encouraged

Peter to stop denying his homosexuality. "It's okay to be gay," he said, suggesting that Peter's problem was his repression of an obvious fact. But in trying to discover what would make him want to commit suicide, Dr. Roberts had discovered that Peter's femininity had more to do with his upbringing, than an aberrant gene. He'd hidden behind his mother's skirt to shield himself from pain, but it had led to an alienation from other boys. He'd missed the camaraderie and male bonding that were typically part of a child's development.

Knowing what he knew now, Peter wished he could climb back into his mother's womb and start over. Maybe being "born again" wasn't such a bad idea. He'd focus on developing his manly side, but it was too late for that.

Ruth reentered the room. Peter looked up to see her standing there with something in her hand. It looked like a letter.

"I've been debating on whether or not to give you this," she said. "It's kind of personal, but I think you should have it." She held it out. "You don't have to read it now. Save it for later, when you're alone."

Peter's hands were moist again. He wiped them on his slacks before taking the envelope. It felt like the walls were closing in, like the room was suddenly smaller than a moment ago. He slipped the envelope into his pocket. He wanted to ask what was inside, but another question might involve a ten-minute response. He wanted attention, not pontification. He needed to get outside, breathe some fresh air, clear his head, and think. "I...uh . . . Thank you . . . I guess. Look, don't get me wrong. I'm interested in all this stuff, I really am, but can we continue it another time. I have to be getting back. If Edith wakes up, she'll wonder where I went. I wouldn't want her to worry. Besides," he yawned, "it's getting late and I'm tired."

Ruth picked her big black book off the sofa, her knobby red hands gripping the spine gingerly to lessen the pain in her joints. She folded the cover and set it aside. "Of course," she said.

BILL REALIZED he'd been sweating. The moisture had soaked through his shirt while he was asleep, and now felt cool on his skin. His hand rubbed his grizzly jaw, bristling the stubby spikes of hair. He put his other hand on the wheel and scratched his scalp. He itched all over. Hearing Laurie's voice had been a wake-up call. He smiled at the pun, but his humor was quick to fade. What could he say? He'd made light of his wedding vows. He'd stepped over the line. If he didn't know it before, he knew it now.

His hands gripped the steering wheel, head pounding, wrestling with the emotional drain. He'd messed up. How could he explain that he'd decided not to pursue the relationship, that he hadn't been thinking clearly, and that while he had enjoyed it, it was time say adieu, arrivederci, adios—*it's nothing personal. You're a fine lady, just not right for me. I'm sure you'll find a good man someday.* It sounded so shallow. He'd run through a dozen scenarios, but no matter how he couched it, his words fell short. He stared at the dusty dashboard, feeling as old and shabby as the car. She was a terrific lady, a real catch. She had the qualities he'd look for in a woman, if he were looking. And yesterday he'd almost convinced himself he was, but Laurie's call had changed all that. He reached into his glove box, retrieved his map, did a mental calculation of the distance, and looked at his watch. If they left now, they could be in Portland by morning, but it would mean dropping Mary in Spokane, finding her a motel, and giving her bus fare so she could continue on alone. He owed her that much. His fingers drummed the steering wheel.

He found the handle and let the door groan open. Not many miles left on the old rust-bucket. Only a little bit further, that was all they needed, then the whole thing could take a bath in the ocean for all he cared—*good-bye car*—*adios. He raised his eyes to the dingy liner. Please Lord, just five hundred miles, that's all I ask.* He tugged on the steering wheel, pulling himself out. Actually, all things considered, it had been a good car, cheap transportation. He pushed the door closed, *shrieeeek, crunch,* and stretched, rolling his shoulders up, pushing his hands into the small of his back. They'd probably think he was crazy, wanting to leave in the middle of the night.

His boots cobbled across the porch, thudding on the wooden planks, which he didn't mind because he wanted to wake the girls anyway. It didn't hurt to let them know he was coming. He knocked, and stood there a moment. Then he knocked again. A light came on, but he waited until he heard Mary's voice before opening the door.

There she was, sitting up in bed, holding her covers up under her chin, her face squinting in the amber glow of the bedside lamp. Her eyes looked slightly red, which was probably because she was tired, but her cheeks also seemed to glisten with the residue of tears. This wouldn't be easy. Angie's eyes rolled open, responding to the intrusion of light.

"Sorry to wake you girls, but we're going to have to leave," Bill said. "It's kind of an emergency, so I need you to hurry. I'll explain once were on the way. Mary, I'd appreciate your seeing how fast you can dress and get your things together. I'll get Angie and meet you in the car."

PETER CROSSED Laurie's back yard, breathing the stormy night. He trundled across the wet lawn, his shoes dangling a shoelace that had become untied. Blades of cut grass were sticking to his cuffs. He wasn't tired, but he didn't dare stay at Ruth's any longer. She was working her way up to the big question. It was a question he wasn't ready to answer. He wanted to change. He'd love nothing more than to be the man he was born to be, but he simply wasn't able. Never mind what she said—being *weak* did not make him *feel* strong! Laurie's place looked dark. He hoped she wasn't asleep. He couldn't go back to Edith's. There wasn't any place to lie down. And he needed someone to talk to.

He was sure this was the right door, but the lights were out. He tapped gently on the glass, hoping to summon Laurie from her bed. He needed to hear a different point of view. Laurie wasn't out to change him. She liked him just the way he was. *No answer.* He wiped his wet knuckles on his pants and tried again, this time a little louder. *Still no answer.* He tried again, calling Laurie's name. This time half a dozen dogs answered from somewhere out in the yard. They were yipping and barking. Peter turned and tiptoed back across the lawn until he was standing in the park. He could see another building off in the distance. A light snapped on. The dogs hurled themselves against a chain link fence, howling in delirium. A door opened and a shadow appeared at the threshold. The light cast back a silhouette surrounded by an edge of yellow. "Hey, quiet down. You'll wake everyone up!" It was the voice of Dr. VanEtter.

Peter froze. He was on his toes, ready to flee, but something told him to stay. It was too dark to be seen. He was, after all, dressed in black. The light went out and the door closed again. Amazingly, Peter had held his ground; he hadn't run; he'd stood there daring the doctor to come and get him. He stuck his thumbs in his ears and wiggled his fingers. *Chicken! Brraaak, cluck, cluck, cluck, brraaak!*

Laurie's apartment was still dark, no sign of life. There was no point in returning to the door. He couldn't knock again without getting the dogs all riled up, but it bothered him that Laurie hadn't answered. She shouldn't be in bed this early. It appeared she wasn't home. Something didn't feel right about it. He wished he could go inside but the door was locked. Then it occurred to him: Ruth had a key.

BILL HAD to keep reminding himself to back off the accelerator. He kept his window open a notch, even though he could feel moisture in the nighttime air. His wipers were set on intermittent. The old Country Squire moaned and wheezed, but kept on moving. Bill checked the instrument panel. Pushing seventy again. He eased his foot off the throttle. The needle on the gas gauge was down to a quarter tank, but the oil pressure was good, and the temperature was normal. Over a hundred thousand miles on the odometer and going strong. He moved his left leg to improve circulation and rolled his shoulders. The bruise in his chest was on the mend, but there was still a rasp in his throat from the smoke he'd inhaled. He covered his mouth with his fist and coughed lightly. It was only a mild discomfort. He checked his watch. Almost midnight. They were making good time. They were on the outskirts of Spokane. They'd make it with gas to spare.

Bill looked over at his passengers. Angie was asleep but Mary stirred and caught his eye. Without a radio, the car had been quiet. The constant drone of the tires was hypnotic, and the late hour made it hard to stay awake. She closed her fists, yawned and straightened herself.

"How far are we?" she asked.

"Practically there. Just another few minutes."

Mary rubbed her neck and settled back, making herself comfortable. Her lips glowed in the dashboard's dim light, full and inviting. Bill was tempted to reconsider his decision. Doing the right thing wasn't always easy—but it *was* always right! "You have a nice rest?"

Mary nodded, "Uh huh."

Bill cleared his throat and swallowed, mustering his courage. Angie was asleep; the car was quiet; there wouldn't be a better time. "There's something we need to talk about," he said.

Silence filled the air. Bill began to think Mary might not have heard. He cleared his throat, considering carefully his words, and how to begin, but she beat him to it. "Yes we do, but I need to say something first."

He turned his head, one hand perched over the rim of the steering wheel, and nodded. "Go ahead."

"It's about what happened earlier."

"Uh huh."

"I was out of line, throwing myself at you like that. You caught me at a weak moment, but that's no excuse. I need to apologize."

"There's nothing to apologize for..."

"Yes there is. I wasn't being fair, not to myself, or to you. You're a good man Bill. You've got a big heart, but it's only big enough for one person at a time, and right now that place is taken."

"I..."

Mary raised her hand, cutting him off. "No. Don't try to deny it. I don't know if your wife needs you as much as you seem to think she does, but the fact that you're willing to rush off in the middle of the night to go be at her side, speaks volumes. Anyway, you know where to find me. You can always call if things don't work out."

Bill reached over and picked up Mary's hand, interlacing their fingers as he brought it to his lips and gave it a gentle kiss. "You're one special lady," he said. It was done. The truth was out, with no hard feelings. But why then, he had to wonder, did his heart still feel so heavy?

THE LIGHT was a ball of fuzz, a pale distant sun withering on the horizon. Laurie could hear voices, indistinct chatter, gruff with grunts, and clanking tools, the sound of metal on tin plates, implements of unknown origin and purpose. Her body was numb as she faded in and out of the light. Her limbs were locked down. She could feel straps holding them in place, though she wouldn't have had the strength to move, even if she wasn't restrained. She could feel more going on internally, than externally. She could feel her heart *pump, pump, pumping* blood through her veins, feel the ebb and flow of life itself, steady but irregular. She tried opening her mouth, but her lips were stuck. She used her tongue to explore the smooth enamel of her teeth. What's going on? Her head felt numb, fading in and out, somewhere between life and death but hanging on, and yet slipping? Where was she going? The light was *fading, fading, fading,* but she called it back, she willed it back, *never give up, never give up, never give up!* And for whom were the words spoken, words from the gods? No! They were words spoken by harsh, hurried men.

"I think she's coming to. Hurry and get it over with. I couldn't stand to have her looking at me."

"You'll have to be patient, George. These things take time." The doctor began daubing the suction cups of an array of electrodes with a cold, slippery lubricant and sticking them to Laurie's arms and legs. He was trying to maintain an air of ambivalence, but he could feel his hands trembling. "I don't like it any more than you do, but you're the one who got us into this; it's only fair you see it through."

Slipping into darkness, ebbing away, past the halls of light, down the black tunnel toward...what?...toward death...toward hell? NO!...*No, No, No, No, No!* Now she found herself wanting the light. Better the swift, severe, searing judgment of bright white light than the slow reception of an eternally damning dark. But how does one approach the unapproachable? How does one petition the Lord of Light when no just reason for such an approach could be given? She was unworthy. There, she'd said it! She was unworthy, and all the benevolence bestowed by the Almighty did not make saying those words any easier. She tried flexing her arms. *Forget that!* What else could she do? Pray? She didn't know any prayers. Correction. She knew one:

"Now I lay me down to sleep,
I pray the Lord my soul to keep,
If I should die, before I wake,
I pray the Lord my soul to take . . . "

PETER WAS PANTING as he tried to explain to Ruth why he needed the key. He couldn't help it. While standing outside Laurie's apartment he'd suddenly been overtaken by a feeling of dread. It wasn't something he could explain; he just knew something was terribly wrong. He'd hurried back to Ruth's to catch her before she went to bed, but he found her still awake, reading her Bible. She stood listening, inclining her ear so she could hear better, and finally said: "Then, let's go."

"What? You don't have to come."

"Of course I'm coming. You can't go wandering the halls alone. Fact, you should go back the way you came. You need to wait outside where no one can see you. I'll wake Laurie up and we'll let you in."

Ruth went to the closet and slipped into her hat and gloves, like going out without them was akin to being undressed. She reached up again and yanked a sweater from its hanger. The garment sprang away, covering her head, but she quickly pulled it down and looped her arms through its sleeves, slipping it up over her shoulders. She opened the door and stood waiting. Peter glanced down at his slacks, peeved by the green stain he saw circling his cuffs and the shoelace dangling from his Italian leather shoe. Ruth was already on the move. The shoelace would have to wait.

THE WINDSHIELD WIPER, the one on Bill's side, flapped incessantly, *cah-chunk, cah-chunk, cah-chunk,* clearing away the rain, at least on his half of the window. If he was going to live in the great northwest, frequent rain was something he'd have to get used to. But the storm dampened spirits, adding to the melancholy mood of the car. Everyone was awake. Angie was rolling her head side to side looking through the rain-streaked glass at the wash of neon colors.

Bill pulled to a stop at the light. *Cah-chunk, cah-chunk, cah-chunk.* He wanted to say something, but what was there to say?

He could see the hotel just up ahead, an easy walk to the bus station in the morning, just like the man said. They'd stopped for gas, and had called ahead to make a reservation. Mary's hands were folded in her lap, holding the money Bill had given her to pay for her lodging and bus fair. He would drop her off, wave good-bye, and that was that. Why did he feel like such a creep? *Why?* It wasn't like he was abandoning an old friend. If he'd kept the relationship to one of driver and passenger, the Good Samaritan lending a helping hand, he wouldn't feel this way. But he'd become mixed up in her emotions. There's always a price to pay for that.

The windshield wiper worked at pushing back heaven's tears, *cah-chunk, cah-chunk, cah-chunk.* The light turned green.

Bill drove the final two blocks, pulled to the curb and stopped beneath a blinking neon sign. Mary allowed him to help her with her things, but asked that they say their good-byes before she went inside. Bill did not object.

He opened the door and stepped out, planting his boot in a thin puddle. He asked that Mary squeeze out on his side so he wouldn't have to pull Angie into the rain. Mary leaned in to kiss Angie good-bye as Bill opened the rear door and removed her suitcase. Then Mary scooted over and pulled herself into the chilly night. They hurried up the walk together, taking long quick strides. Their clothes were getting wet, but they didn't run. A bare yellow bulb hung over the door, just under an awning. At least for the moment they were out of the rain.

"Well, I guess this is it. Take care of yourself, Mary," Bill said, extending his hand. Offering a kiss would be inappropriate. He'd already caused enough trouble. Besides, he could see his daughter's face pressed to the car's rain-streaked window. He would not betray her trust again.

"I will, I promise. Thank you, Bill, for everything." They stood a moment in awkward silence. Then Mary reached past Bill's hand and put her arms around his neck pulling him in to kiss his cheek. She held on for a heartbeat, and then let go, stooping to pick up her suitcase and walk the few remaining steps. "Good-bye, Bill," she said, pausing for a last look over her shoulder as she reached for the door.

"Good-bye, Mary." There wasn't anything left to say. Bill left the protection of the awning, ducked, and trotted down the sidewalk with his boots slapping water. By the time he reached the car and slid inside—Mary was gone.

TWENTY-EIGHT

P ETER STOOD under a light at the corner of the building, rubbing the goosebumps on his arms. He was anxious to find Laurie. She should have answered her door, but he had to be practical. Cutting across the lawn would take him a fraction of the time it would take Ruth to go around. She had to go down the hall, across the lobby, and then work her way back up the other side. And she moved slower than he did. He'd be left standing outside breathing the damp night air until she arrived. He looked at his watch. It was after midnight. There wasn't much chance he'd bump into someone at this late hour. He turned and went back inside to wait where it was warm. As he leaned against the wall, slipping his hands into his pockets, his fingers wrapped around the envelope Ruth had given him. He pulled it out and examined the scuffed and soiled paper. He flipped it over, but didn't see a name or address on either side. He flicked back the unsealed flap and removed the pages, unfolding them so he could read. At least they were typed. His eyes caught the salutation: "Dear Mom." Peter turned to the last page, *must be from Eric,* he thought, but the note was unsigned. He skipped back to the start.

Dear Mom:

Where do I begin? I have so many questions about things I need to know, but my time grows short, and I find myself running out of strength.

I keep wondering, what's it like to die, to be here

one minute, and the next be gone? I'm about to be snuffed out like a candle, my life a mere breath, a vapor, leaving nothing behind but darkness. I don't mean to be insensitive. Sometimes I see the pain on your face and I think this must be harder on you, than it is on me, but questions about the meaninglessness of my existence fill my head, and I have no where to turn for answers, except to you.

What am I, Mom? I mean, what am I really? I wonder about this thing called life. What is it? What makes me—*me?* The Bible you so often quote would say I'm made of dust. Science would say I'm made of matter, which, when you get right down to it, is the same thing. But matter (or dust if you will) doesn't think. Even rocks are made of matter. As far as I can determine, my thoughts are what define who I am. Is thought, or intelligence, what you call a soul? Is that the invisible me, the spirit, or is there something else? Right now, I'm very much alive. There are electrical impulses in my brain that tick off thoughts, but in a day or two, my brain will stop and my thoughts will evaporate, and I, as a person, will cease to exist.

So I have to ask: What happens to the real me, the thinking part, the electrical impulse, the energy and creativity? Does everything just stop, or does the essence of life, as you seem to think, go on? I want to believe you, Mom, I do. I want everything you've said to be true, particularly the part about living forever. But it's a little like wishing on a star. It seems too good to be true. And to be honest, you lack credibility. You've told so many lies in the past, I don't know what to believe anymore.

I love you, Mom. I have no trouble saying that now, but it wasn't always so easy. Don't forget, I grew up under the old you. I watched your drunken tirades. I felt the cruelty of your tongue. I still remember crying myself to sleep, wanting dad to come home, but you'd chased him off, Mom; you chased my father out of the house. And where were you when I needed you? Passed out under the table, that's where. I had to take care of myself. I think it's wonderful that you've found Jesus. I'm happy to see how much you've changed. I've enjoyed every sober minute we've shared, but forgive me if I say that I still don't trust you—not completely. The scars are too deep. I keep waiting for you to show up drunk. I keep expecting to hear how I'm the cause of all your trouble.

I'm glad it hasn't happened. To be fair, I haven't once smelled the demon alcohol on your breath, nor have I felt the slightest hostility. It makes me want to believe you when you say I can have the same life-changing power. I've always doubted it was possible, but seeing you makes me think it's true.

I know I'm expressing some heavy thoughts, but that's where I'm at right now. I need to get them out, and I doubt I'll have the strength to say all this when I see you tonight. That's why I'm taking such pains to write everything down. And painful it is. I think you'd laugh if you could see how long it takes me to type one silly word. I'm growing weaker by the minute. My time is short, the end of my life is near, and I'm afraid. I can almost feel my atoms beginning to dissolve, but I can't quite bring myself to believe that once I'm pronounced dead, all those thoughts that make me who I am will scatter like so much dust in the wind. There has to be a spirit locked inside me, waiting for release. If, as you promise, Jesus can set this spirit free, then who knows, maybe I'll give your Jesus a try. I've got nothing to lose, and everything to gain. I have to stop writing now, Mom. My eyes are tired, and my fingers ache. I feel like my soul is ebbing away, ashes to ashes, and dust to dust...

Peter stared at the pages in the dim light of the corridor. The words pierced. How many times had he asked those same questions? *Why am I here? What's it all about?* But the answers eluded him. The emptiness of not knowing had taken him to the edge of the cliff several times, but the fear of not knowing had kept him from jumping off. He folded the letter, slipped it into the envelope, and stepped outside. *Burrrrrrrrr.* He rubbed his arms briskly. He would have to give the letter back. Ruth couldn't possibly have meant for him to keep it. But she'd want to know what he thought. How was he supposed to respond? *Explain what you meant about living forever.* She'd love an opening like that. He tucked the letter into his pocket and set off, shuffling across the lawn.

The night was a moonless dark, filled with the smell of musty grass. Peter wrapped his arms across his chest, massaging his goosebumps, his senses heightened by his anxiety. Where was Ruth? As he approached, he kept looking at the apartment, expecting to see a light to come on. She should be unlocking the door by now. What was keeping her? The world seemed quiet. Even the dogs were still. The only sound was the pounding of his heart as he stood there, waiting. His head snapped up when he saw something move. The drapes began to rustle, and he heard a deadbolt click. Then Ruth's face appeared at the door.

"Peter," she whispered, "are you there?"

Peter stepped forward and swept the drapes aside. The fabric flopped loosely in the breeze, coiling around his legs as he entered. Ruth closed the door and pulled the drapes even. "She's not here," she said. "I already checked."

"Can we turn on a light?"

"Not unless you want everyone knowing we're here."

Peter felt his way into the bedroom. He had to see for himself. By sweeping his hand across the blanket he could tell the bed was still made, but the covers were mussed and the pillow had a shallow indentation.

"I told you," Peter said.

"I didn't say I doubted you, but I don't think there's cause for concern. She'll probably be back any minute. You want to sit and wait?"

Peter bit his lip. *Fear! Fear, fear, fear, fear, fear.* He didn't want his fear controlling him. He wanted to sit down with Ruth, continue their talk, shoot the breeze, and not be so paranoid, but he couldn't because something was really bugging him, an unsettled feeling in his gut that wouldn't give quarter to the idea that Laurie was all right. Where was she? The place was too small to get lost in. "You didn't see her on your way over?" he asked. "What am I saying, of course not. It's just not like her. Where does the doctor live?"

Ruth balked at the question. Her white-gloved hands went floating to her hat to make an unnecessary adjustment. She moved the red beret to the side and reinserted her pearl-drop hatpin. "Probably in town somewhere," she answered. "To tell the truth, I haven't the foggiest. Why?"

"So he doesn't have an apartment here? He doesn't stay in that building over there?" Peter was pointing in the direction he'd seen Dr. VanEtter earlier but in the dark it was hard to tell.

Ruth fidgeted with her fingertips, twisting her gloves until she could feel the soft fabric under her fingernails, then pulled them tight again. "No. No one lives out there. That's just our medical facility, and the physical therapy center. There's also a pool with a changing room, and the laundry and"—she suddenly realized the implication of what she was about to say—"the room none of us wants to think about, but there's no reason they would have Annie in there. They don't know she's one of us. They think she's a customer."

"I saw the doctor over there, and it's after midnight."

"Uhmmm. Okay, I know it seems odd, but he does have an office in that building. He's probably working late."

Peter's stomach felt queasy. "Where's Laurie?" he said.

Ruth wished she could provide an assuring word. She was wringing her hands so hard her glove nearly slipped off. Peter's suspicions were beginning to hit home, no point in pretending otherwise. "I don't know. Maybe she couldn't sleep and went for a walk. I'll bet she's at the vending machine getting a snack. That always helps me sleep. Perhaps we should go looking."

"We? Both of us together? You think it's okay?"

"I don't know. I suppose so. I can't see why not. I just came through the lobby and didn't see anyone, but that's not unusual this time of night. Besides, you're supposed to be Edith's nephew. There's no law that says you can't look around."

BILL WAS pumping adrenaline. He couldn't have explained it for the life of him, but the minute the door closed on Mary, an uneasiness set in that he couldn't seem to shake. His hands held the steering wheel in a white-knuckle grip. He had to keep checking his speed. If he wasn't careful, he'd get a ticket. He wished he could understand what he was feeling. He brought his thumb to his mouth and bit a hangnail, then pulled it back. Was he nuts? He hadn't done that in years. He shook his head. He couldn't say it was her voice he heard, not her real voice, but it was like she was calling him from across the miles. Maybe it was some kind of prayer. No, he couldn't explain it. He went over their conversation one more time. She hadn't said anything to suggest she needed his help. She'd probably kill him for butting in, implying she couldn't take care of herself. That's if he could find a way to approach her without blowing her cover. The whole thing was crazy, but he couldn't turn back. His gut was telling him something was wrong. Maybe someday they'd look back at all this and have a good laugh—*uh huh, think again*. He looked over at Angie. Her eyes were open and staring straight ahead. They looked eerie in the faint glow of the light from the dashboard. She too, was troubled. He wondered what was going on in her head. She must think he was losing it, but there was no point in trying to explain what he himself didn't understand. He backed off the accelerator: pushing ninety—*again*.

PETER FOLLOWED Ruth as they sauntered down the hall toward the lobby. Off to their right, the community center was quiet. Ruth veered over to take a closer look. The lights were out, but as her eyes adjusted to the dimness, she could make out an indistinct form sitting alone in the dark. It was Jack Rosen.

The little colonel stared out across the expanse of the room, eyes locked onto an invisible television, the program playing in his mind.

FORTY THOUSAND men, women and children were marched out of Buchenwald. They walked mile after never-ending mile, walking nonstop for days, their footsteps muffled by the rags wrapped around their feet, their toes frozen blue, without food, or warm clothes, or shelter, or even a place to lie down at night. Their guards were mere boys, seventeen and eighteen years old. Men with fighting experience had been sent to the front to try and stop the allied advance. Their young escorts weren't able to manage such a large group. Over a period of days, the line had stretched and broken apart. Jack found himself in a company of about five hundred walking skeletons guarded by a dozen swastika clad juveniles. Their group was the one furthest back, and they were falling a little further behind every day.

The young soldiers had to know the war was over. They were marching toward Berlin in retreat. It was just a matter of time. They had standing orders to shoot anyone that stopped, or tried to flee, but after days of senseless walking, they had lost the will to kill. Fortunately for them, most of their prisoners had also lost the will to escape. Jack could have run away. He could identify only one senior officer, a frustrated man trying to maintain command of a dozen defeated boys. It wasn't enough to prevent him from taking off. If he stole some clothes and headed south, sooner or later he'd meet up with Patton's Third Army.

Jack stayed behind for one reason, and one reason only. His interpreter had contracted pneumonia and was burning with fever. In his weakened state, he could not have escaped, and Jack refused to leave him behind. One day, as they were dragging themselves down the road, the man began coughing. It was a deep-throated, lung-exploding hack that went on for miles, until he finally stopped walking and bowed over clutching his chest. Jack put an arm over the man's shoulder and tried to ease him forward, but the man wouldn't take another step. As Jack encouraged him on, the man buckled and collapsed, right in the middle of the road. Jack reached out to pull him up, but was pushed aside by the throng that was stepping over and around the fallen body. A young blonde soldier with frayed cuffs on his uniform ran up and thrust his rifle into the man's chest, shouting in German. He looked like he was about to pull the trigger when Jack, who couldn't think of anything else to say, screamed: "WATCH YOUR FLANK!" Not understanding English, the young soldier turned. He thought Jack had yelled "AMERIKANISCH TANK," so he spun around, off balance, thinking an American tank was bearing down on him. Jack instinctively grabbed the rifle and pushed the boy, who stumbled backward, toppling over the man he was about to shoot. The senior officer, who had stopped to see what the commotion was about, suddenly found a rifle pointed at his face. Immediately his hands went into the air, and, just as quickly, other guns were leveled at Jack. The officer, fearing he would be killed when his troops opened fire, barked an order and the dozen boys under his command laid down their weapons. Jack single-handedly captured thirteen enemy soldiers, liberated almost five hundred men, and was subsequently decorated for bravery. And for all that, as he sat in this dark room, he realized he was helpless when it came to freeing the prisoners of Emerald Valley.

RUTH APPROACHED. "We're looking for Annie," she said, making sure her hat was properly seated on her head. "Have you seen her?"

Jack woke from his thoughts, shot a wary glance at Peter, and challenged: "Who's he?"

"Sorry." Ruth's hands began fluttering around her face like little white doves. "Jack, this is Peter," she said, touching Peter's arm. "He's Edith's nephew. I'm showing him around. Peter, this is Jack."

"That new girl? Haven't seen her," Jack finally said. "Hasn't been around all evening."

"You're absolutely sure? You haven't seen anyone?"

"Course I'm sure. Everyone's in bed, just like I'd be if it weren't for my rheumatism. No one's been around except you. I saw you go by a few minutes ago. And before that Dr. VanEtter, but that's only because someone took sick."

"Someone? Who? Who got sick, Jack?"

"Don't know, some blonde woman. Never saw her before. But the doctor went rolling right by the door there, with the lady strapped to a gurney. Couldn't have been more than a half hour ago."

Ruth placed a cotton hand on his shoulder and straightened herself holding onto her hat. Her black currant eyes found Peter. "Okay, all right, it appears you were right. There is cause for concern." With both hands she tipped her hat back and adjusted it for comfort, readying herself. She didn't like even thinking what she was about to say. "If they have her over there, it can only be for one reason. Peter, we have to go after her."

Peter leveled his eyes at Ruth, the strain evidenced by the tiny red fissures around his pupils. "Go after her?"

"Go after who?" Jack piped up.

"I haven't got time to explain, Jack, but I think the woman you saw was Annie."

"No it wasn't. I could see her plain as day, young lady, pretty too, but definitely not Annie."

"Jack! Annie's not Annie! She's a newspaper reporter wearing a disguise. She was looking into the claims made by Joe and I. If they've got her over there, they must have found out who she really is. This can't be good. Peter, we have to go."

"Annie's not Annie? Well I'll be. I was just beginning to take a shine to that one. Yes sir." The little colonel pounded his fist into his hand. "Well, let's go. If they're looking for a fight, we'll give 'em one. They're messin' with the wrong bunch. Colonel Rosen at your service," he said, saluting Ruth. "Permission to assemble the troops."

The statement was so matter of fact, Peter wondered if the little man was delusional. They didn't have any troops. All they had were themselves. Three frail people did not an army make. What made this miniature man and this tiny little woman so brave? Testosterone? Could an old lady even have testosterone? And what made the diminutive man believe he was a soldier? He was ready to fight, ready to defend, ready to put his own life on the line for the sake of another. What provided such courage?

"We have to hurry. If Annie is over there, she could be dead already," Ruth said. "Sorry Jack, we don't have time to assemble the others. Every passing minute means there's less chance of finding her alive. We'll have to go with just the three of us, at least until we see what we're up against. If we don't find anything, we'll disband, no harm done, but if she is over there, and she's being held against her will, well...I guess we'll have to cross that bridge when we come to it."

They turned to go, Ruth and Jack and Peter, a tiny swarm of flies against a mighty Philistine army. Ruth would have argued that God was on their side, but Peter wasn't so sure. He could only hope that the God Ruth was so adamant about would come to their rescue. *A legion of angels would be nice about now.* The trio turned and began hurrying down the hall, with Peter dragging his untied shoelace, trying to keep up the pace set by Jack and Ruth.

I didn't know what had gotten into my dad. He was trying to act like nothing was wrong, but his eyes looked wild, and he was driving like there was no tomorrow. I was excited at first. I thought maybe he'd heard something about T.J., but that was just wishful thinking. He hadn't mentioned my cat since we'd left Milwaukee. I had no reason to jump to that conclusion, but I couldn't think of any other reason he'd wake us up in the middle of the night. I was wrong. I tried not to let my disappointment show. You'd think I'd at least be glad to get rid of Mary, but I wasn't, and I think my dad knew. I felt awful. He was doing it for Mom. He was concerned about her; he sensed she needed him, but all I could think about was my cat. Why were we in such a hurry? Couldn't this have waited until morning? It felt like my dad was trying to keep something from me. He looked pale, and I saw a bead of sweat rolling down the side of his face. My neck started to twitch, and then it hit me: my mother was gone. I was never going to see her again...

"OUCH!" Laurie's eyes popped open. She tried to wince, but her arm was strapped down. She tried to scream but her mouth had a strip of duct tape across it. Her cry came out in a muted muffle. *"Muuuouch!"* The doctor was standing over her pushing a needle into her arm. Her body was fixed in place, but she raised her head, shaking it violently, her eyes bulging. They were going to kill her, *"NooouuuuNooff."*

Dr. VanEtter ignored the interruption. He moved across the room, wheeling a cart with two plastic bags of fluid dangling from hooks, and a rack with a small monitor that looked like a tiny TV with wavy green lines. The rack bumped up against the table. The doctor pulled the tube forward and connected the needle he'd injected into Laurie's arm to an IV of saline solution.

George was slumped in the corner. He sat in a chair wiping his nose with a handkerchief. He refused to look at his victim. His skin looked seasick green. He brought the handkerchief to his mouth, hiccuped, and reached into his pocket for another antacid.

Laurie couldn't believe it was actually happening. She was in the Peaceful Slumber Room, a place designed for comfort and tranquillity, with couches and pillows and overstuffed chairs and pastoral pictures on the walls, but she wasn't feeling comfort, she was feeling terror. This was where they'd killed Henry and Leonard and...how many others??? But she wasn't supposed to be there. She rocked back and forth rolling her shoulders trying to twist out of her restraints but it was useless. She was going to die. *"Muuufftnoooooo."*

Stuart reached over and deftly flicked a switch that drew electrical current from somewhere. The monitor began tracking Laurie's vital signs. He took the hypodermic syringe and pushed the plunger up until he saw lethal liquid spilling from the tip of the needle. His hands were shaking, making it difficult to drive the point of the needle into the rubber shield of the IV lock, but he managed. His thumb bore down on the plunger, keeping the pressure on until the full dose had left the cylinder.

"Nuuuuuooofff!" Laurie screamed, her head raised, her eyes still bugging from her face. This was not happening, not happening, it was a dream, another dream, another dream. No, this was real. Her head was beginning to spin, a cyclone of fury enveloped her brain, *fight it, fight it, don't give in.* She was about to die. Oh God, no! What to say? "Forgive me Father for I have sinned," she said it over and over because she didn't know what else to do: *forgive me Father for I have sinned, forgive me Father for I have sinned, forgive me Father for I have sinned.* Somewhere in her background she remembered that faith was required for peace with God and she realized, if she was about to meet him face to face, they had better be at peace. *I believe, I believe, oh God, help me believe!* And she knew she *did* believe. She

had to believe. How could she ask God for anything, if he wasn't there to ask? *Oh sweet Jesus, Son of God—forgive me!* She forced her eyes to stay open but for some reason her vision clouded, leaving her in the dark. *No, I don't want to die. I'm not ready. I...I need to see Angie...Bill, help me. Please God, I'll do whatever you want.* Her head fell back, too heavy to hold up any longer. The swirling was making her dizzy, a blizzard in her brain, a vicious storm dragging her into blackness. *If I should die before I wake, I pray the Lord my soul to take.* Now, more than anything, she wanted to follow the light, but the blackness continued to drag her down into a long tunnel, *down, down, downnnnnn,* until she realized she had stopped feeling. Her senses were muted by a wad of cotton, and her brain was numb, and thoughts stopped coming, and finally even the imaginary lights inside her mind faded to black.

A long monotonous tone droned from the monitor. Dr. VanEtter looked up. "Okay it's done. We have to burn her tonight. We don't want anything left but ashes. You still have the key?"

George didn't answer but gave a grim nod. The skin of his face seemed to be sucked in and wrapped around his skull. His head looked shrunken and stuck to the pole of his neck like a witch-doctor's juju.

"Snap out of it. We still have to dispose of the body. Go get the car and bring it around. I'll meet you at the door."

RUTH, Peter, and Colonel Jack stood in the hall just outside the Peaceful Slumber Room. This was where they would start their search. If this room was empty, they could take their time inspecting the rest of the building. To their surprise, the door opened. Mr. Bergen's head appeared, a pale sickly glob, and his eyes, empty and white, met theirs. For a moment he stood there blinking, like he didn't believe what his eyes were seeing, then his eyes opened wide and he stepped back closing the door.

The colonel was closest. He reached out to grab the handle but the door slammed shut. He found the knob and gave it a twist but it was locked. Ruth stepped forward and inserted her key. The colonel pushed the door ajar. George stood on the other side, looking like the terrified victim of a voodoo hex. A handkerchief protected his nose and his eyes were hollow and veined. Ruth marched in, followed by the colonel and Peter. They saw what was happening. Laurie was strapped to a table with her eyes frozen open. Her skin was tight as paper and slightly blue. Her arm was attached to tubes and monitors and...suddenly, Peter began shrieking: "TURN IT OFF! TURN IT OFF!"

Dr. VanEtter's jaw began to tremble. He heard Peter screaming, "TURN IT OFF!" He whirled around, "TURN IT OFF!" and stood in front of Peter with his hands raised to keep him back. "George get the car," he said. "Go George. Come on, snap out of it!"

George made a half-hearted attempt to squeeze by but the little colonel stood in his way, challenging him. He tried to step to the side and skirt around, but Jack went with him, blocking his way. George looked pleadingly at Stuart who started toward the colonel. Peter moved to intercept him but when he tried lifting his foot, he found he was standing on his untied shoelace, which threw him off balance. As he stumbled forward, Stuart reached out and pulled him to the ground.

Once again Dr. VanEtter turned toward Jack, but Peter wasn't through. He crawled up on all fours and with all his strength, tackled the doctor around the shins and began to lift. Jack saw his opportunity and shouted, "WATCH YOUR FLANK!" Then he gave Stewart a push that sent the doctor toppling over backward. Peter held onto the man's feet and raised him off the ground. The doctor careened backward with his feet in the air and his hands groping for Jack, until his head hit the tiles. Peter jumped up pumping his fists like a boxer, spoiling for a fight, but Dr. VanEtter was already out cold.

TWENTY-NINE

AS ONE LIFE is taken, another is born. All animals, birds, fish and insects have cycles to fill, a rebirth of their respective populations, a process through which the world is ever replenished. Life is brief, it is but a vapor, it comes and it goes on the wind. That which was created from dust goes back again, sifting itself into the seventeen basic elements of matter. Only that which is realized while life exists has value. Once life expires nothing can be accomplished. But the good that is done while life continues...that can last forever.

PETER RUSHED to the machine, frantic to save his friend, but there was nothing he could do. The needle had been pulled from Laurie's arm and was dangling from a tube where it had fallen when they'd interrupted Dr. VanEtter. The constant drip of saline solution formed a small puddle on the floor. Peter balled his hand into a fist and put it to his mouth, biting his finger. The lights seemed to flicker. He felt dizzy, like the room around him was spinning. And that sound, what was making that horrible sound?

Colonel Jack glared at George, daring him to run. George resigned himself and went back to his chair where he collapsed in a heap like a pile of limp laundry, wiping his nose on his handkerchief. Jack turned and poked the body of Dr. VanEtter with his toe. The man was unconscious. Ruth flew to the counter where she used the phone to call the police.

Peter's hand grew wet in his mouth. How was this possible? Laurie had been alive...now she was...how was it possible? Her eyes were open but they were vacant, staring at nothing. This wasn't Laurie. It couldn't be. The real Laurie had to be somewhere else. The questions voiced by Eric filled his head: was the body just a vessel containing a spirit, which in reality was the essence of life? When a person took that final breath, and their spirit departed, where did it go? It had to go somewhere—*heaven?*—*hell?*—and what part did Jesus play in the grand scheme of things? Peter reached out and took Laurie's wrist to feel for a pulse, but there was none. He knew there wouldn't be. The line on the monitor was flat. A steady peal rose from the machine—*that awful sound!* He turned and slammed his fist down, *again, again,* and *again,* until the face of the monitor was broken and his hand was bleeding, and the noise had stopped. Ruth ran to his side and threw her arms around his waist. "Let it go Peter. We can't bring her back. Let it go." Peter put his hand to his mouth, tasting blood. *It isn't fair!* Then his shoulders started jerking and he broke into sobs.

THE SUN had been up for several hours when Bill finally pulled into the parking lot of Emerald Valley. It took a second for him to grasp what was happening. His head swiveled back and forth, taking in the scene. He glanced over at Angie. She was wide awake, had been the entire trip, but she'd been unusually still. She'd sat staring straight ahead, her eyes glassy, without making so much as a peep. Bill wondered what she was thinking. Over the miles his foreboding had increased with his daughter's quiet, and now he understood why.

The parking lot was filled with activity. There were a half dozen police cars parked at odd angles, an ambulance, several news vans and a bustle of people hustling in and out of the building. The weight he'd been carrying came crashing down around his head. He felt drops of perspiration prickling his forehead as he turned the vehicle into a parking space. His heart was pumping overtime. Maybe Laurie had released the story. That would explain the commotion. Maybe he'd find her inside, surrounded by a cadre of microphones and cameras. *"Please God, let it be that,"* but in his heart, he was prepared for the worst. He set the parking brake and pulled himself out. He wouldn't bother with Angie's wheelchair. It would take too much time. He would carry her in his arms.

RUTH WALKED beside Peter. The place was a mayhem of traffic. Counselors, investigators and emergency medical personnel co-mingled with the entire management, staff and resident population of Emerald Valley. Policemen were everywhere, trying to gather and hold everyone for questioning. The media show would have made Laurie proud. There were television cameras, radio journalists, even a writer from Laurie's own newspaper. Laurie had become the story, but it would have to be written by someone else. Ruth vowed to make sure it got told right.

Cash and Louis were back, somewhere, lost in all the commotion. They had arrived from the hospital in a squad car with lights flashing and were escorted inside by uniformed officers, giving them an air of importance. They were on record as among those who filed the original complaint. Their testimony was essential. The four, Edith, Ruth, Louis and Cash, and to a lesser degree even Peter, had already told their story a hundred times to a hundred different people. They had achieved celebrity status. It was a status Ruth did not want.

The young president, Carl Shiffer, and his crew were in a meeting all morning trying to contain the damage. They had their own version of truth they wanted presented to the press. Alfred Porter, Charlotte McKidry, and a host of others had been fed the party line about what they could, and could not, say. Notably absent from the meeting was Barbara Marks, who elected not to play along, even if it cost her her job. It wasn't much of a job anyway, and once the story got out, selling suites at Emerald Valley would be impossible, in spite of the promised changes.

Ruth wore her standard red outfit, a red wool skirt with a white cotton blouse and red blazer. As she walked, her white-gloved hand stroked her red plume like a bird adding twigs to its nest. "Well, I guess this is it," she said. "You'll probably be moving on. Can't say as I blame you. I wish your visit could have turned out better."

Peter nodded. "Terrible about Laurie," he said. His voice was still soft, but he held his head high, and his shoulders were back. He was trying to lose the effeminate swish. He was trying to walk the way he thought John Wayne would have walked.

"She's in God's hands, and those are good hands to be in. It's not for us to question. We just have to leave it with him. I'm more concerned about what will become of you. Have you given it any thought?"

Peter shrugged. The world was changing, and he along with it. Already his skin felt thicker, and his pretty face, tempered by the strain of battle, looked more profound. He had learned something about himself. He wasn't a coward, nor was he weak, he was...well, he was regular. That's what he was. He had the same fears as anyone else, and the same ability to overcome them, given the right motivation. "Yes," he said, "I've thought about it, but I'm not sure about what to do. It's going to take some time to sort things out. I mean, I think about it a lot, but it's hard, know what I mean? I wish someone could show me how to express myself, I mean, show me how to be a man in a man's world, without making it awkward, but that's asking a lot."

Ruth began nodding her head. Her woodpecker's knot jiggled so hard she had to capture it with her gloved hand to keep it from flying away. "You're more of a man than you think, Peter. We all saw what you did. You jumped in to save Jack, without worrying about yourself. That took guts. You're already a man's man in my eyes, but it wouldn't hurt to talk to God about it. If you're trying to figure it out, he'll show you the way. And you can always count on me to pray. But I'm prattling on. Sometimes I'm just an old fool who doesn't know when to shut up. How are things on the home front? When do you plan to go back to work?"

"I don't know. There was a message from the studio on my answering machine. They were asking the same thing, but I called and told them I wasn't ready. Know what I did? It was crazy. I went back to collect my makeup, but I just stood there looking at all those stupid tubes and bottles. Finally I swept everything into the trash and walked away. Guess I have a number of decisions to make. What about you, what are your plans?"

Ruth's head began bobbing. "I'll be here," she said. "I don't have anywhere else to go, and someone has to stay and make sure this mess gets straightened out. We're forming a resident's council. We're the ones paying the bills. It's high time they started listening to us. Besides, I hear Joe is coming back, and he's going to need my care. I have plenty to keep me busy; don't worry about me."

Peter shook his head. Little Ruthie was one crusty old bird.

They moved through the corridor slowly, oblivious to the noise and distraction of the front-page story unfolding around them. A man hurried by carrying a young girl in his arms. He looked weary, and to Peter's mind, vaguely familiar. Where had he seen him before? The face in a photograph? *Laurie's...? Couldn't be.* The man turned the corner, out of sight. Peter reached into his pocket and removed the envelope, handing it to Ruth, who took it without comment.

"Will I see you at the funeral?"

Ruth bobbed her head. "Of course," she said.

Peter slipped his hands into his pockets. "Mind if I ask you a personal question?"

Ruth nodded.

"Were you really like that? I mean, the way Eric said."

Ruth paused, closing her eyes for a moment and took a deep breath, placing a hand on her breast. Her eyes fluttered as she opened them and then remained at half-mast, looking off into the distance. "I'd like to say no," she finally said, "but the truth is, I probably was. I don't remember much about that period of my life. I must have blocked it from my memory. I do know one thing, though. I didn't drive Eric's father away. He chose to go on his own. I needed help, but so did he, and we were too weak to help each other. That much I remember." She turned and began walking again. "Poor Eric got the worst of it. I guess I took it out on him. They were so much alike, he and his father, I guess I blamed him for what happened. Anyway, I'm a different person now. It's like I said, with the help of God, people can change." She puckered her lips and folded her arms across her chest defensively. She didn't bother explaining the rest of the letter. Peter was a smart boy. He could figure it out.

She bit her lip, struggling to reconcile her emotions, the agony and the ecstasy, mixed feelings of joy and sorrow. Ben, Joe and Annie had paid a tremendous price for the freedom she now felt. Her Bible was full of stories about how God had sent his people into battle against insurmountable odds. He'd handed Israel the victory time after time, but there was always a cost. No mention was made of the mothers whose sons did not come home—mothers who stood off in the cold shadows, covering their heads to weep and pray. There was always a price to be paid when the children of God went up against the hoards of Satan.

It was not for Ruth to understand. She wanted to celebrate; the Lord had given the enemy into her hand, but her mother's heart mourned the loss. She glanced at the envelope, the token of another battle fought and won—but at too great a cost. Still, she had the consolation of seeing good triumph over evil. Vice President of Finance, George Bergen, and his accomplice, Dr. Stuart VanEtter, had been led away in handcuffs, chained like defeated foes. Their day of judgement was coming. A jury of their peers would decide their fate.

They had come to the lobby. From here Peter would be leaving. He slid a finger into the collar of his black knit sweater, suddenly feeling warm. He should get rid of this thing, buy something plaid, something with a button down collar. Ruth's eyes, dark as raisins, were waiting for a parting word. She was so little, and yet so strong. He wanted to hug her, and hug her, and hug her, and not let go. Maybe it wasn't manly, but he couldn't help it. He felt the hot moisture begin swelling in his eyes and his shoulders begin to quake. "I'll miss you," he said.

"You better not. You better come back and visit. And do it often. We old people have nothing better to do than sit around waiting for friends to call."

"Count on it," he said, stooping over to take her in his arms.

THE ASSEMBLY HALL was full to overflowing, whispers and speculations vibrating across the aisles. The residents were seated with their heads forming bright rows of buffed steel wool. It looked like attendance would surpass that of the information meeting held to discuss the disappearance of Louis and Cash. Well, why not? Louis and Cash were back. It was reported they would be giving part of the presentation.

In a small office across the hall, Louis Wiarton sat melting in his chair. Drops of perspiration were dotting his temples and tickling the underside of the curly red locks around his pink ears. "I...I d...d...don't want to answer questions," he spat.

"Oh sure you do," Cash said, slapping his friend's meaty shoulder. "You, Ruth, Edith and I are heroes. A lot of lives were saved because of us. You have to give them a chance to say thanks."

Louis tried looking back over his shoulder but his thick neck wouldn't bend that far. "B...b...but I d...d...didn't do anything."

Edith crossed the floor, wrapped in her shawl. "I'm with you. It's drafty up there. They've got an air-conditioning vent right over the stage. I'll probably catch a death of pneumonia."

But Cash would not be deterred. "Look. We have to tell our story. It's not fair to keep them guessing. They're bound to get it wrong. Besides, we deserve credit for what we've done."

"Leave him alone," Ruth interjected. Her hand floated out with her cotton gloved finger bobbing up and down. "Louis, you don't have to answer anything. Just come up and stand beside us. You too Edith. You won't freeze to death. There will be enough of us up there to say what needs to be said." All this posturing and strutting around the way Cash was doing wasn't right. What was there to brag about? They only did what had to be done. Besides, if anyone deserved recognition it was Ben, Joe and Annie. The way things were going, the ones who gave the most would be given only a footnote saying they were victims. No! That was not going to happen. The only reason Ruth agreed to be part of this falderal, was so she could make sure the story got told right, and that she was determined to do. She would take nothing from the parts Louis, Cash and Edith had played. A few others like Jack and Peter, and perhaps even Barbara Marks deserved mention as well, but she was there to herald the ultimate sacrifice made by Annie, Joe and Ben—*Greater love hath no man than he lay down his life for a friend.*

A current of chatter ran through the assembly hall. Many still hadn't heard the whole story; the rumor mill was out of control. Once again, a chrome stand holding a microphone that trailed a length of snaking black cord stood on a raised platform, but owing to last minute preparation, the sound system was ill equipped to handle the acoustics. The air hissed with static and, when Al Porter took the mike to begin his introduction, the resounding feedback pierced the ears of even the most deaf in the audience. *Screeeeeeeeccch!*

"Oh, ouch, oouwheee, there, that's better," Al said, as he yanked the echoing mike away from the speaker to kill the feedback. He was in his slickest double-breasted suit, dark navy wool with pinstripes, and had his black hair combed back in roaring waves. "First, I want to thank you all for coming. I know you have a lot of questions about what the police are doing here and the events which have occurred of late, and I want to assure you they'll all be answered. We have a very short agenda. We'll start with a brief address from our president, Mr. Carl Shiffer, who will give an overview of the current situation, and a few people you all know, Ruth Wheatly, Edith Woodhouse, Louis Wiarton, and Cash Williams, have been asked to take your questions. For those of you who don't know, these four were involved in solving a problem we were having here at Emerald Valley. In fact, we had a meeting earlier this week to discuss their concerns, and I've been monitoring the situation ever since. I'm pleased to see the issue has now been resolved to everyone's satisfaction. So without taking any more of your time, I'm going to turn the meeting over to our president, Mr. Shiffer. Carl..." Al turned his head keeping his body in front of the microphone to block feedback from the speaker.

Karla sat in the front row next to Big Elmer. She turned to look over her shoulder, eyeing the size of the crowd, and noticed Jack still trying to find a seat. Her bright multicolored sleeve shot into the air and waved him into a chair next to herself.

"Hello Jac...ooops, I'm sorry. I heard what you did last night," she said, leaning in close to his ear. "That was very brave. I guess you deserve to be addressed as Colonel." She swept her polyester, parrot-print skirt aside as he squirmed into the chair.

"I already told you that. And I told you to watch your flank, but you didn't listen about that either. I guess you'll be listening now." His eyes danced in the light the way the sun sparkles on water. He felt rejuvenated. In fact, he felt better than he had in years. A new day was dawning, and it felt good to be alive.

Karla took it in stride. Her eyes were bright, white marbles on her ebony face and her lips, thick and full, were painted glossy red. "You know Colonel, I was just asking Elmer here, if he'd like to go for a walk with me after the meeting. I think we all could use some fresh air. Would you care to join us?"

Jack squinted. He suspected a trap, but when Karla didn't say anything else, he relaxed his trim silver mustache and let his thin lips curl into a smile. "You need an escort do ya? Well, you're talking to the right man. Colonel Rosen at your service. It would be my pleasure to assist the lady and her friend any way I can."

Big Elmer sat on Karla's other side. The sheltie was in his lap. His huge hand stroked the nap of the dog's neck over and over and over, without pause. He still wasn't talking, at least not to people, though sometimes, alone with his dog, he did struggle to vocalize a word or two.

The other dogs had been released. They were being passed around and enjoyed by the group at large. One of the recommended changes was that, under guidelines yet to be established, pets would be allowed. *You gotta like that*, Karla thought. *It's too bad Annie isn't around to see it.*

The exuberant president was in his element, back on top and in control. Losing George was the best thing that could have happened. It resolved the internal power struggle, and it provided a logical explanation for the failure of the company's shares. They had plunged to an all time low, but now at least they had a reason. Through a hastily put together teleconference, a decision was made by the board to request another halt in trading, at least until this mess could be straightened out. Pragmatically speaking, George's involvement in embezzlement and murder couldn't have been discovered at a better time. Try explaining to irate shareholders that the only reason the company's shares were plummeting was that the chairman had lost confidence in the program, had resigned from the board and was selling his position. Now they could say the decline occurred because one man had attempted to divert company funds to his own bank account, but that the situation had been rectified. *Of course the Chairman of the Board resigned, wouldn't you?*

With unanimous board approval the Peaceful Slumber Room was

being dismantled. There was no way this would be allowed to happen again. It was a credible story, bound to solicit shareholder confidence. Some might even see the stock floundering and decide it was a good time to buy back in. Carl was confident the share price was at rock bottom. They had nowhere to go but up. He'd never trusted George. He was only beginning to discover all the additional perks the man had arranged for himself. What a sleaze. Under judicial warrant, police investigators were doggedly tracking down the rest of the money. A totally corrupt individual. Too much greed will bring any man down.

Carl bounced to the front of the stage, slick as a televangelist about to deliver a miracle live and on camera. His smile was crafted and his gait orchestrated and his sandy hair sprayed to look relaxed and windblown, the epitome of a youthful spirit burning with a zest for life. He took the mike from Al and turned to his audience. A sea of spud gray faces with potato eyes stared back at him. He could feel their questions, and see the murmurs on their lips. Most of them had never seen him before. Meeting the president was a novelty—but that was something he was going to change. From now on he was taking a personal interest in the lives of his guests. He forced the smile off his face and replaced it with a somber look. Enthusiasm was inappropriate. People had died. He may have benefited from George's mistake, but this was no time to gloat. It was time to mourn. He took a breath to calm himself.

Carl recognized the man seated with his daughter at the back of the room. They'd met earlier. He looked in bad shape. His eyes were moist and wrinkled. His skin, shadowed by his unshaven cheeks, was drawn. He was an emotional wreck. Carl couldn't help wishing the man hadn't come. He suspected he was after blood. Perhaps he'd be appeased when he heard the peaceful slumber room was being decommissioned. Carl pulled the cord around his feet and raised the mike to his lips.

"I wish I could say good morning," he said, his amplified voice bouncing off the walls, "but the occasion doesn't warrant it. I'm sure you know why we're here..."

Bill sat hugging Angie the way a person clutches something

familiar to give them a sense of reality when everything around them seems unreal. He couldn't think, all he could do was listen and try to make sense of what made no sense at all. Angie squirmed. Bill nuzzled his chin in her hair, and gave her a reassuring squeeze. Ten years ago, when Laurie had refused to join them in Detroit, Angie had been there to see him through the long, dark hours, and thank God, Angie would be there for him again. They didn't need anyone else; they were a team, like two mules on a plow.

THIRTY

BILL BANGED on his notebook, his thick fingers fumbling to stroke the tiny keys, *thump, thump, thump, thump, thump,* but using the little keyboard was slow slugging. His thoughts were moving faster than he could get them on the screen. The boat rolled; he looked out the window in time to see the horizon disappear. He saw the coffee sliding up the side of his mug, then saw the horizon reappear again as the coffee leveled out. The seas were getting rough. Either that, or they had just crossed the wake of another vessel. He picked up the small telephone book and slid it into the drawer. He didn't want the page splashed with coffee. He had debated about whether or not to make the call, but decided against. Maybe someday, perhaps even soon, but not now. He wasn't ready. The boat rose and fell, dipped and swayed, and settled into the calm lumbering of the twin diesel engines. *Must have been another boat.*

He was working in his new office, sitting at the desk in front of his library. With his books surrounding him, he felt he could tap into the great minds of literature. They spoke from the annals of historic prose, whispers from a time when writing was used to communicate moral truth. He would write like that; he was almost there. He could already visualize his characters acting out the plot in his head. All he had to do was bring them to life on paper. Everything was in place. He had the idea, the technology, and the environment. He even had the stimulus of the salty main. He marveled at the classics it had inspired: Homer's "Odyssey," Coleridge's "The Rime of the Ancient Mariner," Melville's "Moby Dick," and Hemingway's "The Old Man and the Sea." He would follow suit. The sun soaked through the window, casting a beam of light on his copper brown arms. Even his tan bespoke welcome change, the good life, everything he'd ever dreamed of, well, almost. He banged out a closing paragraph, paused to take a sip from his mug, and scrolled up to read from the top.

Count this my third and final comment on the events that recently took place at Emerald Valley, the quiet, picturesque retirement home that, for a few unfortunate people, became a death camp. Unless you've been out of the country, you know the story. The continuing investigation has been well documented. We now await the trials of two men, George Bergen and Dr. Stuart VanEtter, who have been arrested and charged with the murders of five innocent people.

No, this was not death with dignity. It was not an attempt to relieve the suffering of a few poor souls who, in seeking comfort, desired to exit this mortal plane. The victims were put down without their consent. In this country, that's called murder.

Death with dignity is supposed to be "merciful." It is meant to be an act of compassion, administered only in the most extreme cases, and only at the request of a terminally ill patient who is in agonizing pain, has no hope of recovery and, in the opinion of two qualified physicians, has less than six months to live. It has come to light that, with respect to the case now going before the court, none of these criteria were observed. Two of the victims, Gus Olson and Blanche Albright, were comatose, and as such, could not have requested the procedure. Two others, Leonard Hobbs and Henry Miller, appeared to be in good health. Friends close to the deceased have stated they had no knowledge of the cancer and lung disease surreptitiously logged into their medical files. Their records appear to have been falsified, as were the forms they each allegedly signed, requesting they be given lethal drugs. Even the supporting witness and physician validations were forged with signatures scanned electronically.

This is old news. The story has been in the headlines for weeks. I needn't belabor the details, but I do think it's time we explore the far-reaching implications of this Pandora's Box we've opened.

I believe that when our Declaration of Independence promised "Life, Liberty and The Pursuit of Happiness," it meant it for all individuals, regardless of race, creed or color. I contend this precept applies to everyone, including the orphaned, the handicapped, the indigent, the infirm, the elderly, those still in the womb, and those outside the womb, whatever shape, size or configuration, all have a right to live. We, as Americans, were promised certain inalienable rights, but they did not include the right to death, whether through murder, suicide, abortion, or euthanasia. Life is what we were promised. Life!

In a series of articles written over a year ago, I predicted we would see an outgrowth of abuse stemming from the legalization of euthanasia. I made no claim to be a prophet. I simply looked at the pattern established by the abortion industry and drew a logical conclusion. You've heard it argued that abortion was designed to help a rape or incest victim, or someone whose life was at risk, terminate an untoward pregnancy. If abortions were limited to these reasons alone, we might, as a society, sanction a few hundred each year, which in and of itself would be tragic, but the staggering reality is that every year we see over a million babies killed through abortion, and not because they are the products of rape, or because the mother's health is at risk, but because they are untimely or inconvenient. Abortion is being used as an alternate form of birth control, but it's not the same thing. Real birth control prevents pregnancy altogether. There is no baby, so there's nothing to terminate. Abortion, on the other hand, assumes an existing pregnancy must be stopped, and the baby, already growing in his mother's womb, must be killed. So we have what amounts to over a million babies being murdered each year, and it's all perfectly legal.

Euthanasia is at the other end of the spectrum, and the "Death with Dignity Act," passed by the state of Oregon, is America's first attempt to see how it works. Once again we're being told it will only be used to put an end to the suffering of people who are in pain. Sound like déjà vu? In the case for its legalization, it was argued that Death with Dignity would be granted only to those who are terminally ill. The question I had to ask at the time was, how long would it be before it became available to anyone wanting to end their life for any reason, or imposed upon those who had no wish to die, but whose lingering life had become a burden on society?

It's likely that, in the not too distant future, we will begin to see as many people euthanized, as babies that are aborted. When an aging mother becomes inconvenient, when her hospital bills start to soar, and her children see that as long as she is allowed to live she depletes the estate, which they soon hope to inherit, someone is bound to consider asking her to drink the hemlock cup. We have to be realistic. Don't think her kids will stand by day after day watching their mother's money be consumed by hospital costs and say, "that's okay mamma, we want you to live as long as you can." She might hang on for another six months. By that time their inheritance could disappear. More than likely they'll speak with a physician who will inform them that their mother's illness is terminal, that there's nothing the doctors can do, and that her quality of life is poor. Then he'll suggest they speak to her about taking advantage of the only other option. Why go on suffering when you can have a painless exit and eternal rest?

I'm sure the loving kids will give the suggestion due consideration. They'll factor in the expense and inconvenience of keeping mom alive, "it's not practical, we can't stay in the hospital with her, she's already half dead anyway, and our inheritance is at stake." Then they'll acquiesce, and proceed to put pressure on dear old mom to do the right thing: "after all, mamma, you've lived a good life, why not go to sleep peacefully and save yourself the indignity of having to use a bedpan?" The day that happens, you who express moral outrage over the abuses at Emerald Valley, will have a hard time explaining to me why mamma's little darlings shouldn't be invited to share a cell with George Bergen and Stuart VanEtter. After all, the kids euthanized mamma to gain control of her money, so what's the difference?

In a worst case scenario, I see a day coming when the deformed, the handicapped, the mentally ill, and all others deemed to have a low quality of life, will be encouraged along similar lines. A few years ago, a Saskatchewan farmer took the life of his handicapped daughter. He was subsequently arrested and convicted, but the jury, in handing down their verdict, recommended a sentence that amounted to little more than a slap on the wrist. They petitioned for leniency because they judged what the man did to be a mercy killing. With this kind of precedence, people with handicaps should be shaking in their boots. Are we as a society now saying a man can kill his disabled child without fear of punishment? And what about those dependent on the state, the mentally and emotionally ill, the indigent and destitute, whose health care comes at the expense of the taxpayer? Will we do everything in our power to help them live long, healthy lives, or will we turn our backs as they are routinely euthanized to save the state money?

Don't be naive and say it can't, or won't, happen. It can, and it will. Open your eyes to what's taken place in the Netherlands. They started as we did, allowing only the terminally ill to end their lives, but over time it's come to where just about anybody can kill themselves for any reason. And growing numbers are being put to sleep without anyone even bothering to ask if it's what they want. It's reported that elderly citizens are refusing hospital treatment for fear of being admitted and never released. What kind of trust can we put in the medical profession when doctors find it more expedient to kill patients, than to keep them alive? It's a whole lot easier to pull the plug on someone who's dying, than it is to keep them comfortable while they slowly ebb away. Why not put them out of their misery?

I'm sorry if I've made you angry, but before you try to set me straight, there are two things you need to know. The first is that I have a handicapped child whose plight is the same as the daughter of that Canadian farmer. I know firsthand the pain a father feels when he sees his child suffer. But I don't think my daughter would be better off dead. I believe she enjoys life. She knows she is loved, and love, not physical condition, is the determining factor for life's quality. Second, the news reported other victims of Emerald Valley, not necessarily those euthanized, but people who saw a great wrong occurring and wanted to make it right. They made a decision to stand up and speak out, and several of them paid a terrible price for their effort. One of those brave souls was Laurie

Best, a newspaper reporter who went undercover to bring the story to the attention of the public. If you've been following the media coverage, you've read, I'm sure, of the sacrifice she made. But what may have escaped you is the little known fact that, besides being a darn fine reporter, Laurie Best was also my wife.

Perhaps now you can understand my emotional involvement. This story is personal; forgive me, but it's hard to keep it from showing. Be that as it may, I've said my piece, and hopefully without undue prejudice. Allow me one final word from a higher authority. The Good Book has an oft quoted passage that reads: "This day I have set before you life and death, blessing and cursing, therefore choose life, that both you and your descendants may live." In light of all we've seen, I suggest we take heed.

Bill hit the save key, and shut down his computer to conserve the battery. It had been almost a month since the arrests were made, a month of questions, and more questions, and darn few good answers. It had been a month of grappling with his conscience. He had put the one he loved in harm's way. His chest felt heavy when he realized how close he and Laurie had come to reconciliation, though it was not to be. They had been so near, and yet so far away. He was prone to moments of despondency, but he was holding on. The past could not be changed, his only hope was for a better tomorrow. As for today, and every day, he had to make the best of it, take each day as it came, one day at a time. He picked himself up and forced a grin. Smile, and the world smiles with you. He was going topside. Sometimes life stinks, but it could be good too...sometimes. He had to put on a happy face. That much, at least, he owed Angie.

Bill wandered through the yacht's mid-section, passing by his daughter's cabin. Her bed was beginning to look like a zoo, a dolphin here, a kangaroo there. Keeping a promise to himself, Bill had made a point of buying another stuffed animal at every new port of call. He ducked outside, imbibing a lung full of salty air. The ocean breeze tossed his hair. They were moving through the waves at a steady clip, breaking whitecaps that foamed in the bleaching sun. He held their speed to be about fifteen knots.

He stood at the stern, over the engine compartment, with the vibration running through his legs. An American flag, caught in the boat's slipstream, was flapping off a pole to his right. He took a deep breath and placed his hands on the rail.

> "When peace like a river, attendeth my way,
> When sorrows like sea billows roll.
> Whatever my lot, Thou hast taught me to say,
> It is well, it is well, with my soul."

Bill blinked several times, trying to hold back. *Just the salt, a little salty air always makes moisture in the eyes.* He wiped his cheek on his sleeve. He fished in his shirt pocket just to make sure the note was still there, and then pulled it out to read it for the hundredth time. It was frayed, and the creases were beginning to come apart. He held it tightly, as it was buffeted by the wind.

Bill.

I know I just spoke with you, but I'm not good on the phone. So much was left unsaid. I struggle even now to share my thoughts, though I'm better at writing them down. Where do I begin?

I have just experienced something I can't explain. Call it a dream, I know I was asleep, or perhaps a vision, because that's how it seemed. I don't know what it was, I just know I was scared. (The truth is, my hands are still shaking.) I'll tell you what it felt like; it felt like a premonition. I hope it wasn't, because I dreamed I was dead. It made me want to do something, but I wasn't sure what I was supposed to do. There's something strange going on inside me, something I can't explain, but somehow, I find myself thinking differently about things like life, death and the hereafter. Up until now I've always defended the philosophy of John Keats. Remember?

Darkling I listen, and for many a time
I have been half in love with easeful death,
Called him soft names in many a mused rhyme,
To take into the air my quiet breath;
Now more than ever it seems rich to die,
And cease upon the midnight with no pain.

Sounds lovely, doesn't it? Death seems noble to the poet, but as I recall, Keats suffered terribly from tuberculosis, yet he never committed suicide, so I guess it wasn't his philosophy after all. Having been involved in a life and death struggle over the past week, I've had to consider the ethics of treating life with such casual disregard. I've come to the conclusion that life is precious. Every minute should be treasured, every moment should be enjoyed. Do I sound like a pro-life fanatic? Heaven help me if I do. Anti-abortionists have been a bone in my throat for years, but I can't help myself. So much has changed.

I was wrong about Angie. God gave her to me (did I say God? Yes God, and that too is part of the mystery) and to reject her was an extreme form of ingratitude. I only hope you and she will somehow allow me to make amends. I'm looking forward to sitting down and visiting with both of you in a few days. We have much to talk about. See you soon.

Love,

Your prodigal and undeserving wife,

Laurie.

Bill folded the paper and slipped it back into his pocket. So near, and yet so far. Who's to say why God allows such things to happen. If he were God, he would have sent angels to help Laurie escape, but then the articles would not have been written, nor would the public outcry have been so great, nor would the state senate be convening a special session to reopen the "right to die" debate. *"And we know that all things work together for good to those who love God, and are called according to his purpose."* Bill took solace in that.

Looking up, he could see the bridge. He grabbed the handrail and hoisted himself up. He preferred taking the stairs. Angie's elevator was too slow. At the top he slid the door back, stepping into the pilothouse.

"How's it going?" he asked the man at the helm, thankful again he'd had the wisdom to hire someone to help pilot the yacht.

"Hey there, Captain. Steady, cruising at about eighteen knots, heading two nine zero on a calm sea. We're almost through the Gulf. That rock behind us there, that's Saltspring Island. We'll see the Straight of Georgia in just a few minutes." The man swiveled in his seat, revealing a calico cat lounging in his lap. He stroked T.J.'s ear, waving off the cat's tail as it flipped up into his beard. The beard was a bone of contention. It was neat and trim and fuller than the one Bill was trying to grow. They were having a contest to see whose beard would come in faster, and so far Peter was winning, something of which he was unabashedly proud. His blue jeans were faded and his plaid shirt, one with a button down collar, had the cuffs rolled back and relaxed on his forearms. But his pride and joy was the "Gone Fishing" baseball cap he wore, a real man's hat, and a gift from his new best friend, Joe Bonner.

Bill nodded, looking out over the helm to the bow. The sun was two o'clock in the sky on a perfect, cloudless day. The boat dipped and rose as they cut a swath through the blue bounty. Below on the polished teakwood deck a gleaming wheelchair sat, its chrome sparkling in the sun, securely fixed in place.

"How's Angie doing?"

"Doing fine captain. She's just sitting there enjoying herself. I figure we ought to bring her in pretty soon, though. Too much sun and she could get a nasty burn."

My mom may very well have been the most beautiful woman on earth. I have a picture she gave me. It was enclosed with the birthday card she sent. It's easy to see why my father loved her, but I'm sure his love went beyond her looks. Beauty fades, but true love is like God's promise, etched on a tablet of stone. It knows no bounds, has no limitation, and transcends all time. I know that's the way my dad loved my mom.

Do I miss her? Of course I do. I can't help wondering what it might have been like if we'd had the chance to meet. There are so many questions she could have answered. When you stop to think about it, I know very little about my mom. But there are three things I do know: she was beautiful, she was brave, and she loved me. Nothing else really matters.

BILL STARED out the glass at his daughter, enjoying her moment in the sun. The way her hair glistened, she looked the spitting image of her mother. He sighed, and then sucked it in. It was hard letting go. After ten years of waiting, he couldn't quite grasp the fact that Laurie was gone permanently. They were ships passing in the night, but that didn't matter. They would be together again someday, in the sweet by and by. In the timelessness of eternity the years would pass like a breath. He would wait for the day when they would see each other anew, face to face. He'd wrap his arms around her, and give her a big ol' bear hug, and all their dark differences would be forgotten. He knew that's how it would be. He didn't know how he knew it—but he knew—and that was enough.